FLUSH

Copyright © 2017 Sky Curtis

Except for the use of short passages for review purposes, no part of this book may be reproduced, in part or in whole, or transmitted in any form or by any means, electronically or mechanically, including photocopying, recording, or any information or storage retrieval system, without prior permission in writing from the publisher or a licence from the Canadian Copyright Collective Agency (Access Copyright).

 Canada Council for the Arts / Conseil des Arts du Canada  ONTARIO ARTS COUNCIL / CONSEIL DES ARTS DE L'ONTARIO  Canadä

We gratefully acknowledge the support of the Canada Council for the Arts and the Ontario Arts Council for our publishing program. We also acknowledge the financial support of the Government of Canada through the Canada Book Fund.

Cover design: Val Fullard

Flush: A Robin MacFarland Mystery is a work of fiction. All the characters portrayed in this book are fictitious and any resemblance to persons living or dead, is purely coincidental.

Library and Archives Canada Cataloguing in Publication

Curtis, Sky, author
        Flush : a Robin MacFarland mystery / Sky Curtis.

(Inanna poetry & fiction series)
Issued in print and electronic formats.
ISBN 978-1-77133-373-3 (softcover).-- ISBN 978-1-77133-374-0 (epub).--
ISBN 978-1-77133-375-7 (Kindle).-- ISBN 978-1-77133-376-4 (pdf)

        I. Title. II. Series: Inanna poetry and fiction series

PS8605.U787F58 2017   C813'.6   C2017-900309-7
                                              C2017-900310-0

Printed and bound in Canada

Inanna Publications and Education Inc.
210 Founders College, York University
4700 Keele Street, Toronto, Ontario, Canada M3J 1P3
Telephone: (416) 736-5356 Fax: (416) 736-5765
Email: inanna.publications@inanna.ca   Website: www.inanna.ca

FLUSH
A ROBIN MACFARLAND MYSTERY

a novel by
Sky Curtis

inanna poetry & fiction series

**INANNA PUBLICATIONS AND EDUCATION INC.
TORONTO, CANADA**

For my family

1.

I LEANED OVER THE BATHROOM SINK to get a better look. The sharp edge of the vanity pressed into my hips as I stood up on tiptoe. But the nearer I got to the mirror, the fuzzier my face became. I put on my glasses and looked again. I squinted. I moved my head back to see more clearly. Didn't help. So, then I cocked it forward. That didn't help either. I moved my head back and forth, back and forth, trying *not* to see what I was seeing. As I stood in front of the bathroom mirror I felt like a demented pigeon pecking at tiny morsels of reality. I saw what I saw.

The evidence was there.

Last night when I'd brushed my teeth I'd had a fleeting awareness of something not quite right with my upper lip. Something was stuck on it, surely that was all. A speck of food, perhaps. I flubbed it off, reassuring myself it was probably a tiny ink mark from chewing my pen at work, or perhaps a random shred of the dental floss I'd used after my dinner of stringy chicken.

But I knew as I slipped into dreamland last night that I had purposefully not seen what was clearly there. And now in the light of early morning, when I bobbed my head closer to the mirror and peered at my mouth, I wrestled with my eyes and confronted the truth. I could clearly see a series of little lines, like small railway tracks marking the journey of my life, emanating from the upper edge of my top lip to somewhere under the downy mustache that I periodically waxed. My mouth was a train wreck.

I, Robin MacFarland, at the age of fifty-five, took a long intake of breath and faced the facts. Fuzzy cheeks. Poor eyesight. And now train tracks.

I was getting old. The proof was everywhere.

I took a step back from the vanity, what a misnomer *that* was, and stood in front of the full-length mirror behind the bathroom door. I gawked at myself in disbelief. How had this happened to me? Inside this mass of flesh I felt exactly the same way as I had when I was twenty. The voice inside my head, yattering away, was the same voice I'd listened to all my life.

I had heard about a book on the subject of aging with a funny title about necks disappearing and now it had happened to me. And no, it wasn't funny. Somewhere in the last decade I had completely lost my neck. I wasn't quite sure where it had gone, but it was no longer connecting my head to my shoulders. In its place was an odd structure that looked like layered folds of meringue. Attached to this sagging mélange were overripe papayas where my upper arms used to be. I twisted my body to look at my back only to discover that splotches of chocolate had been splattered over it willy nilly, a dermatologist's delight.

I had become a parody of an exotic dessert.

Turning back around, my eyes reluctantly travelled from the neck meringue thingy, or whatever it was, downwards. My breasts, those very same breasts that had fascinated my first boyfriend at the age of fourteen for hours, were now like two fried eggs that had slid to the edge of the frying pan and landed somewhere in the middle of my body. My stomach looked like three large scoops of maple walnut ice cream, with the nuts puckering through my skin. Each one of my thighs appeared to be a waffle cone holding up the ice cream, narrowing down to my pudgy knees that were creased with dimples, and giving the effect that they were somehow smiling at me. I was being *mocked* by my knees, because not only was I old, I was fat.

But just how fat? I hadn't weighed myself in years. I nudged the scale with my big toe from the dusty corner of the bathroom into the square of light streaming through the window onto the tiles. I had to use my foot because I had trouble bending over, what with the wobbly jello around my belly getting in the way. That was my first clue that the verdict was going to be very bad indeed. I stared straight ahead as I stood on the scale and didn't look down until all the mechanical whirring had stopped. I wasn't cheered by the length of time this took. But finally the scale was silent and I steeled myself to look at the damage. I tilted my head and forced my eyes to focus on the numbers.

Fuck.

I weighed more than I did when I was nine months pregnant with my fourth child. One hundred and sixty-three pounds and I was only five feet, two inches tall. Holy shit. Maybe if I cut my shoulder length brown hair into a cute pixie I would lose a pound. Maybe if I dyed it blonde I would lose another. Did blonde hair weigh less than brown? It looked like it might. Lighter, somehow. How much did a brain weigh, anyway? Maybe a frontal lobotomy would help this situation. Would I even miss my mind? I already did.

What a mess. What was I doing to myself? This was so awful. I perched my ample bottom on the edge of the tub and rested my head in my sausage fingers. Shaking sighs escaped my lips. A single tear slid down my swollen cheek. And then, finally, deep sobs wracked my body. At last, for the first time in six years, I cried. I didn't get the bag of potato chips from the top shelf of the cupboard. I didn't stuff handfuls of popcorn into my gob. I didn't lick the sticky crumbs off the serving platter that had previously held that delicious carrot cake. I simply cried and cried.

Everything in my life was gone. My husband, the love of my life, well, at least some of the time, had shockingly died in a car accident when I was forty-nine, six years ago, leaving me with four kids, a whopping mortgage with no insurance on it, and six, count 'em, six pets: a hamster, a mouse, a newt, a dog, a bird, and a single fish. Over the years, the sharp stab of acute grief had dulled to a low and constant throb, which seemed to abate only when I was busily moving my hand to my mouth, either with spoonfuls of something sweet during the day, or numerous drinks late at night.

Oh God, the wine. I was a lush. When had the heavy drinking started? Let's not kid ourselves, I knew exactly when. It was when the fish died two days after Trevor's accident. I remembered this specific date because of the irony. The fish died, I drank like a fish.

I gulped for air.

Not only am I old and fat, I'm an alcoholic as well. A new round of fresh sobs shook my dumpling shoulders.

Over the past six years, the children had all graduated from university, amazingly, and moved out, also amazingly, each one having partners, all of the opposite sex, how novel, and all sporting tattoos. Five of the animals were now dead, with only cute little Lucky left, constantly, irritatingly, barking for food.

Like master, like dog?

For the past two years I had rattled around the enormous house all by myself, doing my job for the newspaper, eating, and drinking. Sure, I had lots of friends, but it always came down to the same situation every night: I was old, fat, an alcoholic, and totally alone. There was no one in the house but me.

New wails reverberated in the tiled bathroom as this latest revelation sank in. *I was all alone.*

Even my work at the paper was a disappointment. I had been walking through the rotating doors of the steel and glass building at the foot of Jarvis Street for almost thirty years and where was I? Had I won any distinguished prizes for insightful reporting? Was I an editor? Was I ever on the front page? No. No. And no. Well, to be fair, did I want to be promoted? No.

Well, not really, and I had made that clear: I loved to write, not administrate. Nonetheless, no one had ever offered me a step up. No one. Not even Shirley Payne, my editor and friend, well, a friend as much as a boss could be. Thirty bloody years later and I was doing the exact same job.

Home and Garden reporter. How fucking trite was *that*? So much for being the next poet laureate. Or the winner of the Booker Prize. Or the even a bloody writer-in-residence at some obscure university. I wrote about the mundane details of people's lives. Where they bought their pot holders. Flower shows, for fuck's sake.

I was such a failure. As I sat on the edge of the cold tub I heard the word over and over. *Fail-ure*. Both syllables of the word blew through my brain like the melancholic whistle of a passing train.

I took a deep breath and counted on my five fingers, bending them backwards as I said each word. "Old. Fat. Alcoholic. Alone. Failure." I looked at my open palm. "Good job, Robin. Well done, ol' girl. What a high five."

I had hit rock bottom, the lowest of the low. I shook my head, gritted my teeth, and said "shit" about thirty times as I slapped the side of my thigh. I watched in horrified amazement as it undulated like the waves on a beach. *Shit shit shit* and just *shit*. Something in me snapped.

I was so fucking done with myself I couldn't bear it.

I heaved myself off the tub, swiped some eye shadow across my red rims, and lumbered off to my bedroom. On the way down the hall, I pounded the wall with my fist, muttering like a mad monkey. *Shit, shit, shit*. For good measure I kicked the baseboard. I would Vim off the scuff mark later. When I could bend over. I flung open my drawers and dug through the chaos of clothing until I came across a T-shirt and lycra shorts. I shoehorned myself into them, put on my running shoes, thundered down the stairs, and slammed the front door behind me.

I, Robin MacFarland, was going jogging. I didn't care if I should be heading off to work. I had had *enough*. I was going to rebuild my life. Yes, I was. No more old, fat, alkie, failure, for me. No sirree. I would start today. I was going to lose weight. No more cheesies, no more ice cream, no more chips. Not a nibble. I would drink water and eat sliced grilled chicken breasts on salad. I would run.

Well, sort of.

I clomped along the sidewalk the best I could, dragging my extra fifty pounds literally behind me. What a fat ass I was. I could feel my face burn a hot cherry red against the fresh August morning air. Icy sweat trickled down my back. My feet thudded hard with every step, but on I went, gasping and wobbling. First it felt like the top of my head was going to blow up. Then my arms were going to drop off. My ankles were bending in at an odd angle. But I wasn't going to stop. I'd make it around the block if it killed me. Of course it nearly did, so much so that when I arrived home a whole ten long minutes later, I had to sink panting into a kitchen chair as stars swam across my vision.

But it was a start.

After my shaky shower and small bowl of oatmeal with fresh blueberries and no sugar, which I pretended to enjoy, I sat in front of my computer and fished around on the internet for a dating site. I was going to be proactive, yes I was. The anticipation of a new beginning filled me with euphoria. No more being alone for me! Finally I found a site that promised peace, love, and happiness. *MeetYourMatch.com*. Well, I'd be a believer, and punched in my credit card numbers.

After I was done signing in with my money, I held the credit card in the palm of my hand and tilted it this way and that in a thoughtful daze, watching the little holograph bird flying. That's what I was doing, flying into a new life.

I scrolled through the various pages and filled out information about myself: my politics: socialist; my religion:

Buddhist Unitarian; my ethnic group: white Caucasian; my two hobbies: gardening and reading mysteries; my health: good but allergic to almonds; my children: four. I wouldn't lie about this. Anyone who wasn't scared off by four kids, albeit adults, deserved a test drive. I gaily ticked off boxes that sounded like me, including one that said "mischievous." It was mischievous that I was ticking off the box when I wasn't mischievous, right? I bypassed the box that said "social drinker?" and ticked the one that said I never drank. It wasn't really a lie; I would call my naturopath this afternoon to set up an appointment to get rid of my nightly pesky problem. I was on a roll, baby.

I then wrote a profile in the hope that it would attract a high achieving, well-rounded, happy-go-lucky but successful kinda guy. I needed someone who could keep up to me because, although I was merely a reporter for the Home and Garden section of the *Toronto Daily Express*, I had an active mind. It was as active as a pickled mind could be, that was. *Shut up, Robin, you're smart.* A thrill coursed through me: who would I meet? What kind of job would they have? Office? Classroom? Car?

I didn't care, as long as the fella had a sense of humour, was left of centre in his politics, and was somewhat spiritual. Plus, he couldn't smoke or be a pro-lifer. Those were deal breakers. He had to have nice skin. Most of his hair. Be thinnish. Fairly up on current events. No weird diseases. Nice shoulders. A great conversationalist. Good singer. Excellent table manners. A humanist. Not a golfer. Or worse, a hunter. And no erectile dysfunction.

Piece of cake.

I laughed at myself.

I ticked off all the appropriate boxes and pressed send. Would I have a date over the weekend? No, I'd turn down the hundreds of requests. It was Friday today and I would not look needy. I would take my time. I wouldn't rush into this. I would make thoughtful, mature choices. But now it was up to the ether to respond. Who would it be?

I glanced at my watch. Good heavens, it was nine-thirty. I guess it was a working at home morning.

I called my editor, Shirley Payne, for my next week's assignment. "Hi Shirl, I'm going to work from home for a bit today. Whatcha got for me?" I tried to keep my voice upbeat and in tune with my "new me" attitude.

"Hi Robin, you sound great, really pumped, what's up?"

Shirley, on the other hand, didn't sound great. She sounded like the furnace in an apartment building. Shirley smoked like a chimney. She had been trying to get me to go on a date forever, but had stopped her campaign when I had hissed at her four years ago, "I'm grieving, leave me alone." The truth was much more complicated, but she'd swallowed my line.

"Yeah, you might as well know, I signed up on an internet dating site today."

"Hallelujah! About time! Nine a.m. and you've hit the ground running."

Ha ha ha. More like crawling.

She continued, "You go, girl. But be safe, you hear? Don't give him your phone number, not even your cell so he can reverse look-up your address. You can do that now, even for cells, did you know? Email only. Meet him in a public place. Don't bring him home."

I could picture Shirley's short, hay hair, as everyone in the newsroom called it, bouncing as she rhymed off her safety list, cigarette smoke curling around her head. I laughed, "Whoa, hold your horses, I haven't even gotten an email back yet." As I was saying this, I checked my inbox on the dating site. Nothing. I asked, "What's next week's feature story going to be?"

I checked the site's inbox again. Still nothing. What was *wrong* with men?

Shirley hemmed and hawed and I could hear the click of her mouse as she zipped through websites, "Well, nothing on the

Home and Garden front. There's no new housing developments, no new condo designers to interview, not even a garden show. Nothing really. It's summer. Not much happens in the summer. It's too hot."

I dreaded the summer with its slow pace. It had been quiet like this since the beginning of July. I always ended up with the tedious chore of fishing through the paper's "general" pile of press releases. I resigned myself to doing the job, yet again. "So, you want me to check out the various conventions and events? See if anything sort of related pops?"

Shirley said brightly, "Great idea Robin, I'll email you a batch."

"Thanks a heap," I laughed. We both knew this was not the best way to fill the esoteric, award-winning Home and Garden Section. It was true, I had actually won an award for my reporting one year, but I didn't count it as an achievement. I'd written a scintillating and riveting article on a lily that bloomed only once a year, when the moon was full, for heaven's sake. "I'll go through them here this morning and maybe see you this afternoon."

"Probably not," she rasped. "It's Friday, and I'm going to be leaving early before the traffic builds." Shirley was one of the lucky ones who had her very own cottage. My kids and I shared one with my parents and my older brother's family, and that was another frolicking fun story.

My inbox pinged and I knew the file of bloody press releases had landed. But maybe something interesting and important would show up and I could make a name for myself. Who knew?

Hey! A fabulous thought flashed into my mind, bright, white, and *hot*. Maybe I'd meet someone at a convention. Now that was a good idea. That was a *terrific* idea.

I began flipping through them all, one by one, happily and determinedly. I now had one goal in mind: find me a man. I would pick a convention for men. A guy show. Not a gong show, a dong show. I howled at my joke. How pathetic.

2.

THIS HAD TO BE THE SWANKIEST EVENT I'd ever been to. I hungrily perused the long table adorned with white linen, sterling silver, and bone china. It was a breakfast buffet extravaganza with heaps of fluffy scrambled eggs, mounds of whole wheat toast, tiny pats of butter dotted with dewy chips of ice, pots of homemade jam with tartan labels, and high triangular tiers made of miniature cereal boxes. The smell of salty smoked ham mingled in the air with the sticky sweetness of maple syrup. A shiny retractable lid of a warming tray revealed a hill of buckwheat pancakes. Mmmm, my favourite.

But I didn't throw my face into the feast, mouth wide open like a bottom feeder. Oh no, the new me resisted temptation and daintily poured myself a small glass of a low fat strawberry yogurt smoothie from a fluted pitcher dripping in condensation. I sipped the pink froth slowly, trying to talk myself into savouring the completely unsatisfying drink. I eyed the room over the rim of the glass.

Well, it certainly seemed as if I had picked the perfect conference from the mountain of press releases Shirley had sent me on Friday. I had charged through them with one thought in mind: where would I meet the most men? And *voila!* Here I was, two days later, early Monday morning, and swimming in a sea of testosterone.

The dating site had been dead calm over the weekend, not a

single bite to my tantalizing hook, but I shook off my self-doubt. I knew they would come. I wasn't going to give up because of a slow start. I would get email action soon. But maybe no one wanted to go out with someone who didn't drink like a fish. Shit, I'd forgotten to call the naturopath on Friday. I'd do it later today. And if my profile didn't work, who cared, I didn't need the internet. I was in a roomful of fine, handsome men right now.

On the way downtown to the convention I spotted a bumper sticker that said, "The present is a gift. Open it now." I undid the top button of my blouse.

I wasn't quite sure what the topic of the event was, but a fast glance at the pictures of pipes and pumps in the press release had convinced me it was a guy convention. I had signed up immediately. Nothing like a convention about mechanical engineering stuff to attract the boys. And true to my instinct, here they were, sliding like sharks around the laden buffet table in their grey and black pinstriped suits.

I made sure my laminated media pass was pinned to my jacket lapel. It announced in large letters "PRESS," and I wore it over my left breast in the hope the handsome guys around me would interpret it as a verb, not a noun.

I stood up straight and held my head high. Hopefully, this would smooth out the neck situation and not make me look arrogant and unapproachable. Holding my stomach in was hurting my back, so I gave up on that and casually carried my mammoth purse in front of me, praying I didn't look like a pregnant kangaroo.

This was a great convention. There wouldn't be a room full of this much maleness at any of the other options in the batch of press releases, like say, the cottage show. No, that would be filled with creaking retirees wanting to move north out of the city, or breezy young couples, looking to build their first cottage. I had rejected that press release along with the one on "Interior Designing with the New Fabrics." I knew that would be attended by unavailable gays. Working for the Home and Garden section and living near Toronto's Rainbow Village, I had lots of gay friends, my best friend for one, but now I needed a friend with *benefits*. I was tired of being alone, night after night.

I couldn't do much about being old, but a fat failure and a lonely alkie? That I could work on. I was so done with grieving all my many losses, including the mysterious vanishing act of my belly button.

Sipping my low fat strawberry smoothie and scanning the crowd, eyes barely visible over the lip of my glass, I felt like a famished alligator stalking unsuspecting fish in a slow-moving river. The sense of power quickly evaporated when I could feel the pink liquid settling in the train tracks on my upper lip. I put the glass into a grey bin full of dirty dishes and quickly wiped my mouth with a stiff napkin decorated with coloured balloons. So, the convention was a celebration. I wondered what for.

In the far corner of the room I spied a mop of curly red hair being patted into submission and recognized at once my best friend from the paper, Cynthia, aka Cindy, Dale. What was she doing here? Cindy enthusiastically covered both crime and environmental issues for the front page, which was a far superior beat to my articles about light bulbs and potato peelers. She and I had started working at the *Express* around the same time, long ago, when telephones were shiny black rotary dials. Over the years we had established more than a solid working rapport. We respected each other professionally, most of the time, and were now very good friends, most of the time. Our lives, in a way, had sort of run parallel. Cindy had three children to my four, and she too was a single parent, only she hadn't been widowed. She'd divorced the jerk who had stepped out on her. From that point on, she had announced unabashedly that she was no longer interested in men and was in fact a lesbian. At the time I thought it was a passing phase, but here we were, six years later, and she was singing the same tune.

Cindy and I rarely covered the same news, obviously, but every now and then our paths overlapped. For example, the high-profile symposium on the threat of greenhouse emissions from cow manure when used for vegetable gardens. But really, what was she doing here? I checked the brochure I'd picked up at the entrance for the title of the conference. "Deep Lake Water Cooling System" was splashed over the first page of the program along with the now familiar logo of pipes and pumps. "Valve Opening Ceremony" was the subtitle. Hence the balloons on the napkins. I puzzled over this for a minute or two, trying to figure out what on earth it meant.

My mind wandered. Maybe someone here would like to take a gander at my valves? Maybe even open them.

Get a grip, Robin.

The real question was, what was *I* doing here? This was a far cry from writing stories about using sheep shit to fertilize roses. Whatever. Shortly all would be revealed in the upcoming keynote speaker's address. Good luck tying this subject matter into the Home and Garden section. Maybe there would be an intersection point somewhere to justify to the paper why I was here.

But it made sense that Cindy was at this particular convention. No doubt the "Deep Lake" referred to Lake Ontario and anything to do with Lake Ontario, that beautiful body of water on the south shore of Toronto, was of concern to environmentalists. She was probably watch-dogging it. More to the point, she was probably wondering what on earth I was doing here. Hardly a venue for a doorknob reporter. That was my last lively article. I snagged her eye across the room and gave her a happy wave. Cindy waggled her fingers back, smiling and tapping her watch and then pointing her finger in the air to signify what I assumed to mean "later." Did she mean we should meet up after the valve opening ceremony at ten? Probably. We'd no doubt tussle over who would write up the event. I knew in advance that she would win, but I didn't care. She could have the stupid story. As long as she left the men to me. Which, of course, she would.

I cast my eye around the room, assessing the potential. Most of the men seemed youngish, well, okay, children really, maybe almost old enough to drive, but probably not over the drinking age. Their cheeks were smooth, their eyes were bright, their legs were strong and muscled. I dwelled on this fine observation for a moment and sighed. But clearly, they were not my age.

But wait. Wasn't that Jack England? The writer from my rival paper? The *Toronto Times*? What was *he* doing here? I flipped through my mental Rolodex and came up with a quick bio. Fifty-four, crime writer, although sometimes in the sports section, journalism degree from Carlton, unlike me with my lowly English B.A. from Queens. And if my eyes served me correctly, pretty hot in a pursed mouth "I'm-a-vegetarian" kind of way. His eyes were as dark as coal, matching his black hair. He had the hungry look of a bicycle rider. Or a runner. Not my type? I had no idea. Maybe a thoughtful new age guy would work better for me now. But if Jack went so far as to read self-help books, well, I probably wouldn't stretch to that. But maybe I would. But no Kahil Gibran. I had my boundaries. But maybe if he did read these things it would show he was on an improvement path. Like I was. So, we would have that in common. Wonder what kind of wedding he'd like.

Ha ha ha. Look at me. *Silly bird brain, Robin.* Wait. Did I call myself a bird brain? I had to stop talking to myself that way if I wanted to get some self-esteem. To stop being a *Failure*. It was all about one's state of mind, I told myself. I had to change my attitude about myself. But still, I had been ludicrous. I'd imagined myself engaged to a guy without even knowing him. He was probably a dolt. I untangled my mind from the fantasy and the self-recriminations and focused on the room.

Straight ahead there was some activity on the stage at the front of the auditorium. A couple of guys in blue uniforms were bending over to adjust black and red wires that snaked out of a podium. They plugged them into a large black box that was, in turn, attached to a wall socket. Probably an amplifier, I thought. I knew about amplifiers because my oldest son, Calvin, the illegal street racer, needed amplifiers for the sound system in his car. Sure enough, a minute later, one of the workers tapped the mike on the podium, sending staccato gunshots around the room. No one looked up. And no one dove for cover.

Don't you love Canada? Anywhere else on earth people would be diving under tables.

I watched Jack reach inside his briefcase side pocket and slide out an iPad. So, he was here for a serious reporting, not only because the conference was a guy thing. Maybe he knew Cindy—their paths probably overlapped. Crime. Environment. Sports. Lots of places to connect. But he was mostly a crime reporter. Why was a crime writer *here*? But it was the sports he wrote about that intrigued me more. *Pole* vaulting in particular. *Robin, Robin, you are sex crazy.*

The microphone was tapped again and finally the chatter subsided. Plates were stacked in plastic grey bins and slowly the sea of cute guys swam towards their seats in an ocean of aftershave. The opening address was about to begin. I found a chair at the back of the room, near the exit into the parking lot, just in case. Of what I wasn't sure. I could see that Jack was looking at me from the corner of his eye. Maybe the red light of the exit sign brought out the highlights in my brown hair, which I tossed with what I hoped was abandon. I'd read that tossing hair with abandon was a magnet for men. I tossed it again.

Ditching the sexual thoughts scampering through my woolly brain, I rummaged in a purse large enough to make a Sherpa guide look over-prepared. Where was my digital notepad?

Finally extracting it from the contents of my bag, much like a dentist would extract a wisdom tooth from a recalcitrant jaw, I admired my shiny new piece of technology. The newspaper had finally issued iPads to all its reporters. Given that I had been astonished by the capabilities of a slide rule in Grade Twelve, I absolutely worshipped my new tiny computer. I saw with dismay some smudges on the screen from the contents of my purse. Melted chocolate? Potato chip grease? A smear of lip balm? The choices were numerous. I surreptitiously buffed what I decided was hand cream off the screen with the tail of my jacket. So much for being suave.

The chairs around me were filling up. The air was heavy with the man odour of deodorant, hair gel, and dried sweat. I felt I was breathing in a flood of mosquito repellent. It was giving me a headache and I leaned into the aisle in an effort to grab a breath of fresh air. My jacket stretched at the seams, putting pressure on the stitching. I quickly sat back, not wanting to expose my ripe papayas.

The fellas around me were mere boys, about thirty or so. Not a grey hair in sight, for heaven's sake. I was many things, but pedophile was not on my list. Maybe I should have picked the cottage show. At least those people would be somewhere near my millennium. On the other hand, I knew what a cougar was and I could be a cougar if I had to be. Cougars were not pedophiles. They were adventurous women. I practiced a low growl and then looked around quickly. Had anyone heard me? Oops.

My kids had told me one Sunday night at a family dinner what a cougar was: an older woman who went for younger guys, so I considered myself cool, knowing the current "in" jargon, even though I knew in my heart of hearts that I was, in reality, a middle-aged somewhat bleary dame who happened to be old, fat, an alkie, all alone, and what was the fifth thing? I couldn't remember. God, I hated menopause. Not just my gums had receded; where the hell was my memory? Gone with the tide of my hormones. I dug through the mud of my brain, couldn't find the nugget of gold I was looking for and added "stupid" to my list.

Robin, stop demeaning yourself. You will never move forward if you think you're stupid. You are smart! I didn't believe it. Working on my self-esteem was going to be a trial, I could tell. Old habits died hard. But I would not be a *Fail-ure*.

And then the keynote speaker entered from stage left and blew me away! Tall, dark, and handsome, he looked about six two, and exceedingly muscular. What a hunk. Plus he weighed more than I did. This looked promising.

3.

THE KEYNOTE SPEAKER FOR THE Deep Lake Water Cooling System Convention ambled onto the stage with the bumbling gait of a gentle giant, and stood self-effacingly in front of the expectant crowd, arms at his side. Who was this guy? My eyes were mesmerized by the way his strong, well-manicured fingers tilted the mike towards his, oh my, very soft mouth. But wait, I examined him intently. There was something about his eyes that was slightly off, a glint of steel, a coldness. Or was it evasiveness? I looked again. No, the expression was gone. I had probably imagined it. Maybe it had something to do with the lighting. I brushed the fleeting thought aside.

No wedding ring. Verrry interesting.

I flipped open my program to read his bio. Todd Radcliffe. Hmmm, nice name. Strong, dignified. Fifty-five. My age! Born in Toronto, undergrad engineering at Queen's. Maybe I knew him. I'd gone to Queen's. Post-grad from Harvard. An MBA no less. And the Dean's Award. Sounded important, but was it? I quickly Googled Harvard's site on my spanking new iPad and found out that winners of this award had made a major contribution to society through outstanding acts of leadership. And lo and behold, there was his name. So at least he wasn't a liar. About that. *Robin, you are so cynical.* I read further. He was one of the first recipients in 1997, when the award was established. My, my, pretty impressive, I thought. Not a bad feat for a Canadian on American soil. I did the math. No doubt he was at Queen's while I was, so we had a starting point for a conversation. Even if he had noticed me then, some thirty odd years ago, he certainly wouldn't recognize me now. And I couldn't place him. But if he got the Dean's Award from Harvard in 1997, then he'd taken a break between his degrees. I wondered what he'd done. Probably showed remote African tribes how to dig wells or something sustainable like that.

When he cleared his throat before speaking, I sat up to listen. After his first few sentences I nodded appraisingly to myself. Mr. Todd Radcliffe certainly knew what he was talking about, if his big techno words were anything to go by. Totally boring, but he had a nice voice. Smoky and grainy all at once. Soothing. My attention drifted.

I caught a whiff of the lovely summer morning when a latecomer opened the exit door behind me and unobtrusively snuck in. My mind floated along my various thoughts: harvesting the ripe tomatoes in my garden, getting a new leash for Lucky, my upcoming coffee with Cindy, going to bed with Todd, red or brown shoes, my son's new job, going to bed with Todd, and then bam, Todd Radcliffe laughed. Like a yoyo, my brain boomeranged back to the handsome speaker, with his salt and pepper hair, cleft chin, and now, freshly revealed, fantastic laugh.

This was important. I couldn't imagine myself with a guy who snorted like a rhino. Todd's laugh was perfect, rich and melodic.

This day, according to the delicious Todd, was the day when the valves would be opened, allowing the Deep Lake Water Cooling System to air condition the first few downtown Toronto buildings.

Ah ha! There *was* a reason for me to be here, a connection I could use for the Home and Garden section: a new system of air conditioning for buildings. Shirley would be so pleased. Not exactly a sexy newspaper selling topic, but I didn't mind. I would prop my drooping eyes open with a toothpick because

Todd Radcliffe, the president of Everwave, the company that had stick-handled the project from start to completion in partnership with the City of Toronto, was very sexy indeed.

I wondered if he would like me. Maybe I was too fat. I adjusted my suit jacket to hide the bulge around my waist. Dammit, I thought, I have to get rid of that muffin top. I stifled a laugh. Muffin top? It was more like the whole damn bakery. The guy to my left turned his head and smiled at me, exposing great dental work. Shit. Had I spoken out loud? I reviewed the past three seconds carefully. My memory was totally shot. What had happened to my brain? This had to be more than menopause. Plainly I had to stop drinking. I would call that naturopath as soon as I got back to the office.

Todd fiddled with his blue and gold striped tie and I wondered if he were anxious. So endearing, I thought, imagine being apprehensive with all that education! What a fancy-schmancy business degree. He took a sip of water between sentences, "As I was saying, this one hundred and sixty five million dollar project will turn out to be a most cost efficient use of our energy dollar. Every penny will go towards clean, renewable, reliable energy. The Deep Lake Water Cooling system is blackout proof, reduces carbon dioxide emissions, reduces energy consumption of the main grids, and provides the city with cleaner water through new pipes that are situated deeper in the lake than the old ones. On top of all this, the Deep Lake Water Cooling System is the largest cooling system of its kind in the world. This is Toronto's massive achievement and we should be proud of our accomplishment."

The crowd clapped enthusiastically. People nodded and smiled at each other and a buzz filled the room. Cindy was typing furiously on her notepad. Jack England was tapping furiously on his. But I, Robin MacFarland, was furiously fantasizing about my new sex life. As if magnetized, my eyes were glued to Todd Radcliff. How embarrassing. I was staring at his crotch. What was wrong with me? Now that I had decided to join the dating game, it was as if I'd lost complete control of my libido. I mentally slapped my wrist. *Enough!* I tore my eyes away and began to tap furiously, dredging up a replay of what he had said. See, I could do it.

"The City of Toronto," Todd continued while I tapped, "is free from a total dependence on the grid, which if there is a blackout, can paralyze the city, just as it did exactly one year ago, today. People will no longer swelter in their office work places if the lights go out. The system was ready in July, but the opening of the valves was delayed to this auspicious day in August, the one-year anniversary of the major North American blackout. This will help remind everyone of what can happen and how wonderful this green project is."

Clapping boomed around the auditorium. But Cindy and I caught each other's eyes simultaneously, over the crowd of silly boys. She could do this easily, being almost six feet tall. Me? I had to lift my bum off the chair a few inches to see her. We were journalists and our brains were in gear, assessing what our ears had heard. If the power goes out, so do the computers and elevators. The city would still be paralyzed. Todd's rhetoric was a little over the top and my assessment of him as a great guy went down a reluctant notch.

Jack, the *Times* crime reporter, rubbed under his nose. Maybe he was thinking. Maybe he had allergies. Maybe he had a coke problem.

Todd perhaps knew he was spouting bullshit because he smiled sheepishly. It was such an engaging smile. I touched my nametag, hoping to draw attention to it. He seemed to look my way. But then he really blew it. "The system has 60,000 tons of cooling capacity, which, for the ladies present, means it can cool 100 office towers or 20 million square feet of office space."

I bristled. How demeaning. *For the ladies?* What was this? The Middle Ages? The "ladies" needed more explanations than the men? I saw that Cindy was packing up. One thing about the environmental political types, they were political in every way. Do not feed Cynthia Dale red meat, admit to her you smoke, or sin of sins, undermine her brilliance by calling her a lady.

I wasn't going to leave the convention because of one politically incorrect statement. Cindy could get really edgy sometimes. I had problems with her various rants, but because they were rooted in the desire to improve the world, easily forgivable. But this could be a great story. Although I hadn't been on the ball for a few years, okay twenty, now I was, and now I was smelling some good dirt. There was a story here. I wouldn't leave because some asshole said "ladies."

Jack caught my eye and gave a rueful smile. An apology for all of mankind? Or was he on the make? Maybe he was being a shyster and wanted to know what facts I had on this whole convention. And why was he here, anyway?

I immediately smiled back. It was a programmed reflex. Someone smiles at me, I smile back. Did that make me easy? Desperate? Too interested? I jolted my daffy grin into a neutral blankness.

Todd was blabbing on, "It reduces CO_2 emissions by 40,000 tons, or in other words it will take the equivalent of 8,000 cars off the road. It has the capacity to cool 8,000 homes. For now it is being used to cool the Metro Convention Centre, the Air Canada Centre, and several downtown office towers including the TD Centre. The system only uses the amount of water that is needed to meet the domestic water needs of the city. The coldness of the lake is not taken from the deep water with the resulting warmer water being pumped back into the lake, creating a destructive plume of heat. No, our system does not harm the lake in any way. I'll tell you how it works."

I glanced over at Cindy. Good, she'd settled down again and was making busy notes about the environmental benefits. She'd gotten over herself. This sounded truly good for Toronto and, I had to admit, it was far more Cindy's story than mine. Perhaps we could collaborate. This idea took shape. Maybe the byline would read "with files from Robin MacFarland." I was trying not to be a failure and just maybe this story would get me out of that Home and Garden rut onto the front page. I wondered if she'd go for it. Did I have enough courage to outright ask her?

"The technology has been around since 1980, in several seaside cities, however our newer technology is more environmentally friendly. In Halifax, Vancouver, and Stockholm, for example, sea water has been used to cool buildings, freeing these cities up from using expensive electricity to run air conditioners, but causing plumes of heat in their harbours, unlike our technology. Toronto, like seaside cities, is ideally situated by a large body of water. Lake Ontario is a very deep lake; less than five kilometers off shore there is a depth of 85 metres. Water at that level is right above freezing, at 3.98 degrees centigrade, even in the middle of a heat wave. This is certainly cold enough to air condition one or two buildings!"

Todd laughed, but this time his laugh had a sort of tinny sound and reminded me of the forced soundtracks on sitcoms. I squirmed in my seat. He'd been yakking away for some time and my stomach was growling for lunch. I looked at my watch. Nine-forty-five. Fifteen minutes before the show was over. Perhaps I'd have a muffin with Cindy afterwards. To join the other ones on my hips. They could all be friends.

"It works like this." Todd ran his hand through his wavy hair. And still no ring. "Three parallel intake pipes run from the lake slightly less than five kilometers off shore. This is just over three miles, for those of us who, like me, who grew up before the country became metric. At this point the pipes are 83 metres deep, or 272 feet. The pipes have a circumference of 162.5 centimetres."

I looked around. It seemed that few people in the room were over fifty and would have trouble with the metric measurements: me, Todd, Cindy, and Jack. Jack with the smiling black eyes. Hmmm. Everyone else had never known the meaning of

"Give him an inch and he'll take a mile." I would like to give Todd an inch just to see what he would take.

"The water goes to the filtration plant on Toronto Island and then flows because of gravity through an existing tunnel to the John Street Pumping Station. This station is linked to a cooling plant below the Metro Convention Centre by a closed system energy transfer loop."

My oh my, those were highfalutin words. Did he know what that was? "Closed system energy transfer loop?" Whoa.

"Here the coldness is transferred from the cold lake water to the cooling system and the water is then returned to the John Street Pumping Station for distribution to Toronto residents. In summary, the coldness of the lake water, not the lake water itself, is used to cool the buildings. The final result is cleaner air and cleaner drinking water."

I saw that Cindy was typing cheerfully. She recovered from her moods quickly.

Jack caught my eye. Again. Embarrassing. I allowed my mouth to twitch upwards as I looked downwards. Seemed I could still flirt, after all these years. Was he flirting with me?

"This is a wonderful green project which has terrific benefits for the City of Toronto and its residents. The water used to cool the closed system is cycled into Toronto's drinking water. Because it is both from the bottom of the lake and travels through brand new pipes it is cooler and cleaner. As a spokesperson for the company and the keynote speaker of this conference, I would like to thank you all for coming today, the day we open the valves to the new coolest system around."

I silently groaned in mortification for poor Todd's use of the archaic idiom. Coolest system? What? Were we all back in grade school? But everyone else happily clapped and looked suitably impressed. Maybe the word "cool" had come back in style while I was growing yet another chin. And then I realized I truly was a fool. It was a *joke*.

A split second too late I laughed loudly. Jack looked at me quickly and then away.

When the laughter died down, Todd asked, "Any questions?"

Cindy's hand shot up. "A great deal of energy must be used to run the pumps. Are there truly any energy savings?"

Todd gave her the same look one might give a puppy that had peed on a rug. He sighed as he flipped through his notes. Cindy would be livid. I put him down yet another notch. "City Hall will use three million kilowatt hours," he looked over his reading glasses at Cynthia pointedly, "*less* energy to cool that building alone, or the equivalent of taking 160 cars off the road, just so you understand. Any other questions?"

I tentatively put up my hand, "I understand that the cooling system is a closed system and that it is not running at full capacity. But how will new users be put into the system down the road?" *Good one, Robin.* Clear. Intelligent.

Todd chuckled, "They'll tap into it."

Some men in the crowd groaned in delight.

Geezus. First the car comment and now I was worthy of a pun?

I straightened my shoulders and gave him the same flat stare I had given my naughty teenaged sons for years. "Exactly how?" I asked icily.

Todd straightened up. Maybe he'd had some politically correct counselling from his company's PR division because he had the grace to look embarrassed. "The cooling mechanism is serviced by an underground network of pipes and new users can hook up to these pipes."

I bent my head and tapped on my notepad. Someone else shouted out, "How does the cold water get from the lake bottom to the Island Treatment facility?"

It was Jack. Nice voice. Commanding but not pushy. Soft vowels. Probably north Toronto. A bit growly. Deep. Even Cindy, the hard-wired lesbian, looked up.

Todd answered factually, "There is a massive pumping station far below the lake surface, sucking the water into the pipes."

"Where exactly is this pumping station?"

Jack again. Determined to get answers. What was his interest? What was he sniffing around?

Todd gazed at the man ruefully, spreading his hands apologetically, and looking like a sad-faced Marcel Marceau. "I'm sure you can understand why that information is classified. No one knows the exact location of this pumping station except me as the president of Everwave, the company that created this project, the vice president, Mr. Richard van Horner, and of course, the captain of the vessel that was used to go to the site to install the pumping station, somewhere off shore. The municipal government also has a record of the location. The labourers who laid the pipe had no idea where they were, only that there was water as far as they could see." He raised his arm as if to the heavens, indicating the vastness of the area.

"Why the secrecy? Are you anticipating attacks on Toronto's drinking water? Or maybe theft?" Jack asked the question calmly but pointedly, as if he were enquiring about the recipes for what were obviously pre-packaged appetizers.

But Todd folded his hands behind his back and smiled nicely, scraping Jack's question into the compost bin. Behind that smile, Todd's eyes flashed with that same cold grey glint I had glimpsed earlier. He sidestepped the question by mini-genuflecting with his head towards his vice president, "If Mr. Richard van Horner could do the honours and open up the valves...."

Jack looked down and typed for two seconds at breakneck speed. He was probably writing "No comment."

Mr. van Horner stood up in the middle of the audience and cut a dashing figure as he sprung up the few stairs to the podium. His lithe figure effused energy as he pumped Todd's hand and was introduced to polite clapping from the audience. His clothes hung on him perfectly, as if they'd been tailored by Harry Rosen, and his tail coat flapped jauntily as he strode to a curtain at the back of the stage. I caught a glimpse of his tight little ass under the flap of his jacket. Now here was a guy I'd be interested in. Of course, he hadn't opened his mouth much, okay, not at all, but still, *really* cute bum. The energetic Richard swept open the blue velvet drape behind the podium with a flourish. Behind it was a shiny length of black pipe running up the back wall. Half way up the pipe was a polished stainless steel lever, jutting out at a right angle. With a bow towards the audience and then with a grandiose gesture, Mr. van Horner pulled the lever down, symbolically opening up the valve. The crowd stood on its feet and clapped loudly, with some of the young men catcalling.

Cynthia looked over at me and rolled her eyes. Boys and their toys.

The "pipe" went nowhere.

4.

CINDY AND I MELTED INTO A red leather sofa in a Starbucks a five-minute walk from the ceremony. We had sunk into the cool leather, absolutely wilting from the short stroll. We sipped at a couple of iced coffees in the air-conditioned café to cool down. It was the middle of August and the pleasant early morning had turned into a heat wave that by the afternoon would cover the city with a shimmering, hot blanket of smog.

"Odd to think that lake water could be cooling this café," I said, my tongue licking the foam off my lips, making sure none was left in the newly discovered lines over my mouth, and took a nibble of my oatmeal cranberry muffin. I'd start on my diet right after lunch. "Pretty cute guys, huh?"

"I wouldn't notice, being of the other persuasion. And stop licking that foam off your lips, it's very suggestive."

"Oh stop," I laughed, bopping her one in the shoulder. "I know you're not interested in me. Besides, it wouldn't work with us. Never will, so give it up. I prefer playing *sports* with guys, like catching balls."

"Robin!" Cindy chastised me with her eyebrows raised, trying to look like a school marm. "Language! You know you shouldn't talk dirty around me."

We scrabbled in our bags for our iPads. Now that our usual sexual banter was out of the way, we could compare information. With computers on our laps we shimmied closer to each other so we could see each other's screens.

Then Cindy sat up straight and looked at me, her big green eyes shining with sparks of indignant anger. She was stabbing her screen with her manicured red nail, leaving little fingerprint swirls on the glowing surface. "That guy, what's his name? Todd? That guy Todd is such a sexist pig. Did you hear him say 'ladies' like women were helpless, drivelling fools? I could have smacked him. Ladies, my ass."

I ignored Cindy's rant and read the screen where she'd jabbed. "But more than that," I pointed at the text I was focused on, "Did you catch the bit about the city not being paralyzed in a blackout because of this new system?"

"Yeah, what fucking bullshit. Of course the city would be paralyzed. How will the worker bees get to their desks with no subway system? How will they work with no computers? How will they see with no lights? How will they even get to their offices without elevators. What an asshole."

She was severely pissed about that "ladies" comment.

"You're adorable when you're angry, you know," I replied.

But Cindy was relentless. "No, I mean it. The guy is a stupid talking marionette. A company prong."

"With a dong," I rhymed, gleefully. I caught her look and smartened up. "But, the point I was going to make is that even without all the other stuff—like the computers being down and no lights in the washrooms—is that the buildings still wouldn't be air conditioned. Oh, they might stay cool for a few hours, but the bloody system runs on pumps and pumps need electricity. How does he expect the water to circulate in his closed loop system without being pumped around it?"

Cindy looked at me and nodded, "You're good."

"Aw, shucks." I batted my eyelashes, although secretly I was pleased. I could do this!

"So, are we going to write this together?" Cindy was staring at her screen, moving some words around, trying to appear offhand, but I knew she knew what this meant to me.

What luck! I didn't even have to ask her. It was being offered! My heart lightened at the possibility that this story might lift me off the Home and Garden pages. "I was hoping you'd say that. I need something new to do, and hooking up with another reporter is certainly new."

"You know I would do anything to help you, Robin. I know you're acting like all is well, joking around with me, but your body language is telling a different story than your light-hearted repartee. There's a subtext going on here. Look at you, hugging your iPad to your chest, hiding behind your gargantuan purse." Cindy placed her hand on my arm, and looking closely asked me, "What's up?"

"Oh, nothing much." I took a breath and smiled with all my teeth.

She stroked my arm. "It's okay, Robin, you can tell me. I can see something isn't right with you."

I tightened my lips, trying to stem the tide of tears that was lurking behind my eyelids. "I'm an old, fat, alone, alkie, *Failure* type of gal."

At least I remembered the fifth problem. This time.

Cindy hooted. "You are not. You're great. You're fifty-five, the mother of four. That doesn't make you old and fat, it makes you..." Cindy stopped while she waited for the exact right word to spring to her lips, "*mature*. And you are not alone, you have your children, plus me, your evil twin, and lots of friends to keep you company."

"But I do drink, you know I do." Cindy and I would sometimes get together on a Friday night after work with our mutual friend Diane Chu and polish off a couple of bottles of wine between the three of us. Truth was, sometimes we'd get totally smashed. Then they would stay over, one in my spare bedroom, the other on the couch.

"Of course you drink. You have four children. And your husband was murdered. It's called survival."

"He wasn't murdered, Cindy," I corrected.

"Hit by a drunk driver? That's murder if you ask me."

"You are so political, Cindy," I sighed.

But Cindy was not to be deviated from her path. "And you're not a failure, Robin. You've held a job at the paper through thick and thin. Many people have been let go over the years, that last recession was a killer, but you are a good and solid employee. You are successful in a very difficult business."

"Well, thanks, but reporting on garden shows is hardly Booker Prize winning material."

"First of all, you report on more than garden shows. There was that great piece about that corrupt land developer last year. That was true investigative reporting. But whatever, maybe you're bored with your section, but that doesn't mean you're a failure. Anyway, let's write this story up together, okay? Get it on the front page. That should make you feel better." Cindy was eyeing a tall, striking woman who'd entered the Starbucks. She lowered her voice, "She would make ME feel better."

I rolled my eyes. "What, you think this is a front page story?"

Cindy dragged her leer away from the lovely young Amazon, "Sure it is. This guy thinks he's such a hot shot? Wait 'til he sees what we can do to his little project."

"You think I can write a good piece?"

"Don't be a baby. Of course you can. You can do whatever you want. Besides, you already caught the major flaw in the whole project."

"Well.... There's another one."

"There is?" Cindy looked truly surprised. "What? What did I miss?"

I took one last gulp of my iced cap for fortitude. "You know your question? The one you asked during the conference about whether or not there are any energy savings because of the energy it takes to run the pumps?" I said, wiping my mouth with the back of my hand. Cindy, the woman who was always so politically correct had terrible table manners so I nearly fell off my chair when she handed me a napkin. I dabbed my lips.

"How could I forget? What a jerk he was to put me down. Big mistake."

"Well, it may save some energy once it's up and running, sure, but what about constructing the project? Think about it. Five kilometers of pipe alone, well, actually three huge pipes. How much energy do they take to build? And then to get a boat of some sort to put them down on the lake bottom. Something that took months and months. Not to mention building all the pumps? There's a huge one at the bottom of the lake. Another below the Metro Convention Centre. What sort of energy do *they* take to make and transport?"

"Gee partner, you were really thinking. You've been wasted on tulips and chrysanthemums."

Wait a sec. I *liked* flowers and they deserved attention. But she was giving me a compliment, and not putting down my years of garden reporting, so I motored on. "We should research this, find out what's really going on, and then present the information to the public. Maybe the math will show that it would take thirty years for the energy investment in the project to equal the daily savings."

Cindy was full of admiration and sat back, assessing me. "I can't believe you came up with all this."

Why not? Did she think I was stupid? No, again she meant it as a compliment. I needed to let go of being vigilant for criticism. "Well, you can research the math. I'm not so hot at that and I know you're good at research and figures."

Cindy waved her phone in the air, "Not me, the technology!"

"So, can you think of anything else?"

Cindy looked at her notes. "Well, he keeps referring to the project as being 'green.' One of my jobs is to make sure that word isn't used flippantly, and I am pretty sure 'green' doesn't apply to this project. Maybe the final result is greener than the initial way of air conditioning downtown buildings, but for a project to be truly 'green' it has to meet certain criteria, including using natural products that don't harm the environment among other things. I could take a look at the stability of the plastic used to form the pipes. I could take a look at the type of oil that's used to lubricate the pumping machines. The one that's under the lake could be seeping out toxins on a daily basis."

I offered, "You could also investigate where the pipes were made and how far they had to be transported."

"You got it. Now we're hopping. You are no way near a failure, Robin MacFarland. Between you and me, we'll turn his green project into a bright red stop sign!"

I laughed and held my cup of cap in the air in a toast. Then I put it down and looked somberly at my good friend. "But I do drink and I have to stop."

She knew right away what I meant. "How bad is it? Do you drink every day?"

"I've been drinking every day forever, it seems."

"No, honey, it's not as bad as that. Maybe for five or six years? Since Trevor?"

"I started drinking like a fish after his accident, but I was at it earlier than that. Even while I was married to him I would drink periodically. It wasn't all a bed of roses, our marriage, you know. I mean, the kids think it was great, and I don't want to let them know any differently, but he didn't treat me all that well, you know, and well..." I could feel my voice fading out. How much did I want to give away?

"What do you mean?" Cindy looked horrified. "Why didn't you tell me? He didn't *hit* you, did he?"

"Oh no, nothing at all like that. He just degraded me whenever he could, like telling me what a bad writer I was, and that I only wrote about shit, which was often the truth—cow shit, sheep shit, you know—that I didn't know how to dress, or fix my hair, and other stuff like that. I never said anything because everyone thought that he was such a great guy. Including you, Cindy."

"And so you started drinking." It wasn't a question.

"All journalists drink, don't they?" I tried a laugh but it came out closer to a sob.

"So, you going to go to AA?"

"No, I researched them and frankly, I have my doubts. They have a terrible success rate, in the single digits, and I need to get over this so I can start a new life. I don't have a choice, I have to stop."

"I thought AA worked?"

"AA works? It depends on what you mean by 'works.' Even the success stories aren't successful in my books, Cindy. Most people relapse, as they call it. Plus most people who go to AA pick up another addiction; going to AA meetings. It's so ironic. That organization has a heavy investment in keeping people alcoholics for life, as far as I can see it."

"Not a popular view and pretty radical thinking for an old, fat, alkie."

"Well, I don't want to put down an organization that works well for some people, but me? I'm going to see a naturopath. I think she'll be able to help me stop."

"When are you going? Can we sneak in a night of debauchery before you go?"

"Sure, I'll see her next week. Let's get together on Friday for pizza and wine. I'll ask Diane to come too."

The three of us had been friends for ages. Diane Chu had been a friend of mine for forty years and luckily hit it off with Cindy when I'd introduced them decades ago. Diane was the only Asian kid at what years ago was a very white Harbord Collegiate. Her parents, newly arrived from China, had purchased a green grocer on College Street, and the family lived above the store. Diane was brave against the prejudice she'd encountered and hard working, her diligence shaming me into doing my homework. She was now a successful Crown Attorney with three kids and the only one of us with a steady marriage.

"Don't you mean pizza and whine?" Cindy drew out the word "whine" into three syllables.

I laughed. We often bitched about our work place when we got together. Cindy and I complained about the *Express* while Diane grumbled about the politics in the courthouse. "True, true. But listen, there's one other angle for the story that we haven't talked about."

"Aren't you the whizz kid. What else have you thought of?"

"Well, the pump in the middle of the lake..."

"What about it? It leaks oil into the lake? It took four trillion megawatts of energy to build? It needs 5 billion tonnes of coal to run?"

"No," I waved my hand in the air, dismissing these options with frustration, "No, it's in the middle of the lake. Get it?"

"So? It's not in the way of anyone. No one can see it. It's almost 300 feet below the surface."

I put my face right up close to Cindy's and whispered, "That's my point. The City of Toronto's water supply is miles from anywhere, completely unguarded. It's wide open for sabotage. Terrorism. Did you hear Jack England's questions?"

Cindy nodded thoughtfully, and whispered back, "You're right. Except for one thing."

"What?" I murmured.

"No one knows where it is!" said Cindy triumphantly.

"No, that's not true. Here, look." I leaned back and scrolled down my iPad. "A few people know: Todd Radcliffe, the president of Everwave; Richard van Horner, the vice prez; plus the captain of the vessel that was involved in the installation of the water intake system. And all those guys who laid the pipes. No wait," I read on my screen, "Radcliffe said that the labourers didn't know where they were. All they knew was that they were surrounded by water. So a few people. Plus the government record. But people at city hall can be bought. Also, I don't know about van Horner or the boat captain, but that Todd Radcliffe? There's something about him that's a little off. He's awfully good looking, maybe that's it, hard to trust a Greek God. England might be on to something."

We began to gather up our things. We had to get back to the paper to file the story before the afternoon deadline. I stuffed my iPad, phone, wallet, and calculator back into my purse.

"What do we know about van Horner?" asked Cindy.

"Not much," I grunted as I heaved my purse over my shoulder. "Except that I am van horney for his tight little butt."

"Butt butt butt he's a man," hooted Cindy as she strutted past the beautiful Amazon, winking at her suggestively.

5.

BY AFTERNOON THE PRETTY SUMMER MORNING had disintegrated into a muggy thunderstorm that seemed to boom for hours. I dashed through the downpour up the path to my house from my beat-up Nissan Sentra, purse banging against my thigh and umbrella threatening to blow inside out. I mined through my bag for my house key by balancing the enormous satchel on my raised knee and shaking the contents to one side as if I were panning for gold. I finally found the bright metal key peeking out from the coal black depths and inserted it into the lock. I stepped over the battered wooden door stoop and entered my domain.

Finally, I was home. What a day.

At least the story had been filed on time. No thanks to Cindy. I'd worked like a demon all afternoon with a backdrop of thunder vibrating the triple-pained glass of the building. All Cindy's promises of calculating this and researching that had been usurped by a great story about the mayor of the city being videotaped smoking a joint. I emailed the Everwave article to her right before the three o'clock deadline and she sent it to her editor, probably without even reading it. Despite this, the Everwave story was submitted "with files from Robin MacFarland" under Cindy's byline. Not really fair, I thought, but whatever, at least my name would go on the front page if it were twinned to Cindy's. It was all good.

I kicked off my shoes and bee-lined straight to the fridge,

peeling off my coat as I went. I flung the fridge door open to a clattering of condiments, grabbed the still clanking bottle of wine from the door and poured myself a huge glass of a dry Reisling white into my fake crystal wine glass. A goblet really, almost a small jug if I were honest. I glugged the whole eight or maybe it was twelve ounces back and then heaved a great big "Ah-h-h." I thumped the empty glass on the counter and poured myself another. Then I got down on my haunches to pat Lucky who had bounded down the stairs when he'd heard the front door open.

"What were you doing up there," I crooned into his curly-haired neck, "were you on a bed? You know you're not to go on a bed, you silly thing." I scratched behind his ears and under his chin while he made little Yoda noises, his version of purring. "You want some dinner, sweetie-pie? Me? I'm starving. But first I'm sure you have to go out."

I opened the back door and laughed as Lucky eyed the rain and looked back at me in disbelief. I nudged him out with my foot and watched from the shelter of my doorway as my little dog lifted his leg on my herb garden, soaking the oregano with a thin stream. I'd have to remember to wash *that* before making my next batch of spaghetti. He scrabbled up the stairs and yipped around my feet as I started gathering ingredients from my fridge for dinner while talking to myself. "You have to eat vegetables you fatso, lots of vegetables." I started tossing things onto the counter beside the fridge. "Zucchini. Carrots. Red pepper. And maybe a tiny potato. Some chicken breast, but nothing larger then a deck of cards. I read that somewhere, Lucky. Lots of lettuce. That's what you need. Lettuce. Not you Lucky, me. With, *ta dah,* low fat dressing." I stood up triumphantly with the dressing in hand and plopped it on the counter.

I then shook out some Senior Premium kibble into Lucky's bowl and soon a symphony of his morsel crunching and my chopping and dicing on the wooden breadboard filled the kitchen. I was going to make myself a celebratory feast!

Robin MacFarland and Cynthia Dale's article was going front page! I'd roast vegetables and meat in a large pan all together, drizzled and tossed with healthy, cholesterol-lowering olive oil. I wasn't actually sure about the properties of olive oil, but I knew it was good for something, so why not? I sprinkled basil and thyme liberally over my dish and then slid the colourful panful into the oven.

I sat in the kitchen's comfortable reading chair with my replenished glass of wine in hand and called my naturopath. I was on a winning streak this first day of the first week of my new life, and I was going to take the next big step towards change. I would stop drinking, yes, I would. When the naturopath's answering machine kicked in, I left a short, hopefully not too slurred message, "Hi, it's me, Robin MacFarland. Remember me? The almond allergy? Anyway, I was hoping to make an appointment to see you next Monday or Tuesday, a week from now. You can leave the appointment time on my answering machine, that is if you have any free sessions. Thanks very much." I left my phone number and then hung up.

I stared off into space in the sudden silence of the kitchen. There was only the sound of the clock ticking slowly and Lucky's munching at my feet. The refrigerator began to hum softly. If I listened hard I could hear the rain outside. Yes, stopping drinking was the right thing to do. I should have done it years ago. But there was some truth in what Cindy had said; I had needed to drink to survive. The last five years had been a nightmare. And before that? No picnic, that's for sure. Trevor had been so fucking *critical*. Anger and love swirled in my heart, a confusing chaos of emotions.

Sure, I had loved him with all my heart, but thank God he was dead. Oh, what an awful thing to think. But it was so true. Over the years, since his death, I had begun to feel better, without his constant rage and rejection. His negativity. His *judgment*. Even with my nightly bingeing, I was happier and more relaxed without his sneering at my clothing choices, my haircut, my writing, my cooking. Yes, I missed him daily, and he had been a terrific father, no question about that. He loved the kids. No, all his poison had been directed at me, certainly not the children, who he'd parented like a champ. He hated me and he loved me, maybe, and my spirit had been badly injured by him. But still, I loved him. It was all so confusing. So, I drank. Hard to give a shit when you're pie-eyed.

And I had survived it all. His degradation. His death. My grief. The kids' grief. And being a single parent of four through those ghastly teenage years. I gulped my wine. The two girls hadn't been so bad, once you got over the face piercings and blue hair. Maggie was the hair, Evelyn the piercings. Tattoos, too. I'd survived the girls and they had survived themselves. Dealing with the cleavage everywhere and those raccoon eyes staring at me with angry accusation, God knows what for, were small potatoes compared to the boys.

The boys? It's a wonder they didn't kill themselves or end up in jail. Calvin street-racing at all hours in his souped-up Honda Civic and Bert leaving the house at twelve midnight, dressed in black, a knapsack on his back filled with clinking spray cans of paint. I shuddered to think of them both wrestling the city to the ground every night, one by revving a turbocharged engine, the other by splattering bricks with crazy graffiti. I didn't know which was worse, Calvin careening towards a high-speed car crash or Bert teetering on a ladder, decorating the side of railway cars. If Trevor had been alive he would have blamed me for that. I could just hear him: *"He got the artistic side from you, you know."* It's a wonder I wasn't in a loony bin. The drinking helped, oh yes, it did.

At my last annual physical the doctor had asked me if I had any trouble sleeping. I had laughed, no, no trouble at all, I passed out every night and slept like a lamb, because I drank quite a bit. When the doctor asked my how much alcohol I consumed, they use formal words like that, I replied that I drank as much as I could and laughed again. The doctor didn't think it was funny. So then the doctor asked me if I had a drinking problem. I had said, no, not at all. I drink as much as I can, fall down, go to sleep, no problem. The doctor didn't think that was funny either. On the other hand, the doctor didn't offer any ideas on how to stop this nightly extravaganza. Which is why I had called a naturopath, not my doctor, and don't get me going on the bloody medical system.

Now on my third huge glass of wine, I was letting loose. The amount of alcohol that went in my mouth equaled the rage that seeped out of my pores. Underneath my cool exterior I was angry at everything. Tonight I picked on doctors. Doctors were *assholes*. I shouted into the room, "*Assholes*." Lucky lifted her head up from her paws and looked at me, her head sideways. Admonished by the dog, my diatribe lost steam.

Nothing like the present to end my nightly slurp. All the things that had made me stressed enough to drink heavily were over. The kids were grown and newly responsible, and the husband was dead. And here I was: an old, fat, alcoholic failure. And why couldn't I remember more than four of the things I was at any one time? I sighed, and listened to the sound of the ticking clock echoing in the empty room: *stu-pid stu-pid stu-pid*. The house was so quiet. Oh right. The fifth thing. All alone. I was an old, fat, alcoholic, all alone, *fail-ure*. I knocked back the glass.

And then my anger kicked up again. Some nights were like that, a roller coaster of emotions that usually ended with me passing out. "Not anymore," I yelled as I thwacked what was now my fourth huge glass of wine down beside me on the telephone table. Changes were in order. The drinking simply had to go. I was not going to be a seventy-year-old grandmother completely fit because I had to carry a heavy case of wine from the liquor store to my car every week. No, I would be a fit grandmother because I did yoga and rode a bike.

I roared right out loud at the mental picture of me in leotards. Would my cellulite show through the thin material, puckering the stretched polyester? What would Trevor say about *that*? The same Trevor who thought women shouldn't even wear jeans to the supermarket. Who'd he think I was? June fucking Cleaver? Nonetheless, I had my pride and there would be no downward dog for me! And speaking of dog, the sound of Lucky scratching again at the back door drew me back into the reality of my kitchen, away from hearing Trevor's relentless voice telling me to change my clothes, we were going out to a nice place, didn't I know? And, I looked a right sight wearing that unflattering white blouse, or those cheap ugly earrings, or those old lady shoes. I exhaled as I got up and let Lucky out, leaving the door ajar in case he was in one of his in-and-out moods.

I strode as well as four enormous glasses of wine allowed me to stride into the living room and turned on my computer. Would there be any responses to my newly posted profile? The weekend had been a dead loss, but maybe now that it was Monday, my luck had changed. I signed in and waited for the screen of the *MeetYourMatch.com* dating site to open. YES! Look at that, three, count 'em, three replies in my inbox! My heart leapt as I stared at the messages in blue type.

The hope that I would not be all alone forever surged through my soul like a runaway train. Maybe I wouldn't be lonely for much longer! Maybe I would be kissing some adorable guy, or maybe doing even more than that. My heart somersaulted. No, I wouldn't think about *that*, not yet. Maybe he would think I was … I was … what? I thought for a minute. The cat's meow! That's what. I giggled. Maybe I would be going out for dinner, or lunch, or at least coffee, and then? I boggled at the thought of going to bed with someone other than Trevor. Someone who thought I was the cat's meow.

I clicked on the first message and looked at the photo, head angled on one side and mouth pursed. "Handsome Starfish" turned out to be not so handsome, with his far too black, obviously dyed, greasy hair slicked back off his high forehead, exposing a somewhat rat-like face with a pointed snout and disappearing chin. Not to be daunted by looks alone, I read on. Oh, for heaven's sake. He knew how to give me what I wanted? He was romantic and liked riding on his motorcycle after a day at work? He drank? He smoked, but only lightly? He loved listening to jazz full volume on his Bose speakers?

Wait! No, no, no. I stopped reading. NO Jazz. I couldn't do jazz. I hated jazz with a passion. To me the sound of a jazz ensemble was right up there with fingernails on a blackboard. I pushed my thumb towards the screen and made a buzzing sound. "Handsome Starfish" was eliminated from the running.

I opened the number two message in my inbox. The next fella, "Dancing on the Beach," looked okay, I thought. But where do they get these names? I glanced at his picture and thought with his wavy hair and strong chin, maybe he'd be a nice guy. I scanned his profile. Non-religious. Okay. University degree. Good. Divorced three years ago. Okay. Liked water sports. Good. Played board games. Good. Hmm, he seemed all right. He didn't smoke. Very good. Social drinker. Well, I could live with that. No major health issues. I gazed at his pictures with renewed interest.

"Dancing on the Beach" was a fairly good looking guy with all the right qualities, at least on paper. I studied his smiling face. Nice smile, too. As I stared at it I saw there was something not quite right. Oh my God, his teeth! Yellow, crooked, chipped. I could never kiss *that*. Ugh, ugh, ugh. Never in a million years. Up went my thumb. Off went my buzzer mouth. "Dancing on the Beach" was history.

It would seem that, to me, Robin MacFarland, jazz and bad teeth were deal breakers. I nodded to myself. You learn something every day.

So that left one last option. I clicked on the final message to open it and was surprised to see no picture. What? Did "Mr. Sail Away" have something to hide? I read his profile anyway. He was almost perfect! Tallish at six two, which would be a bit tall for my height of five two, and athletic, which would match what I was going to be, after I lost fifty or so pounds from running. He was spiritual but had no religious affiliation, which was fitting with my somewhat spotty attendance as a Unitarian, and my Buddhist practice of chanting most days. He was an engineer with a graduate degree and he was in the business world. I wasn't too sure about that, thinking he might be an arrogant fat cat. But cats hated water and he'd called himself "Mr. Sail Away." So maybe he was a different sort of business person. And maybe I was the cat's meow. Nothing wrong with my logic, I giggled, sipping my wine.

I read on. Hmm, he worked with sustainable energy. There, see? My instincts were right. A business person with a conscience. A rare bird. A non-drinker! That was great. No temptation for me. Under "Health" he had put that he was allergic to wasp stings. I considered how this would impact my life and decided that it wouldn't. Besides, my profile said I was allergic to almonds. Everybody these days seemed to have an allergy. No biggie. In the personality section he ticked off the box for slow and steady. I liked slow and steady. Especially when doing you know what.

Why not, I thought, why the hell not? He'd read my profile and seemed interested in me, interested enough to send me a sweet icon, a tiny vase of flowers, so why not answer him back? I noticed that he was online right that second. Sweat prickled between my shoulder blades. *Go for it, Robin.* You don't want to be all alone for the rest of your life, do you?

I threw back the last of my fourth huge glass of wine and picked out a funny smiley face to attach to my return email. Should I write something? Or should I let him make the first move at actual communication. With a drunken laugh I said "Who gives a shit" into the air and typed, *Thanks for the connection. Let's get together on Thursday at 8:30 p.m. at the Starbucks at Avenue and Bloor.* I pressed send with fanfare.

"Mr. Sail Away" answered me back in seconds. He must have been hovering over his computer, fingers poised. *Love to meet you. Starbucks at Avenue and Bloor, Thursday at 8:30 pm it is!*

So, I had a date! That was fast. Holy crap. But what did he look like? I had better check out his teeth. I felt a bit like a vet, wanting to examine a horse's mouth for signs of decay, but clearly it was important to me. So, I wrote back: *What do you look like?* I pressed send.

A picture flew back into my inbox immediately. A handsome face with a square chin came into focus. I looked closer and gasped. I knew this guy. Oh my God, *no*. It was Todd Radcliffe! The ceremony guy! That fantastically handsome man. The same fella I had just finished decimating today in the article I wrote on Everwave, the one that would go on the front page because Cindy had agreed to help me by putting her name on it, too. The guy who might have recognized me from my photo as the journalist who had asked questions at the conference.

I was so addled by this information overload that I went into a sort of drunken auto-pilot mode. My mind was whirring and I seemed to lose the ability to focus my eyes. Conflicting emotions churned in my breast and all reasoning flew out the window. It was as if I had taken leave of my senses. But one thing I knew; I couldn't get out of it now. It would be too embarrassing. And then my fingers, almost as if they didn't belong to me, typed *Great* and then pressed send.

I stared at the blank screen as the reality of what had happened sank in. Clearly I would have to stop drinking.

Clearly I would have to get my name off that article before it came out. I'd text Cindy first thing in the morning.

The smell of burnt food drifted into the living room where I was seated at my computer. Well, I didn't want dinner now anyway. I was already stuffed with grapes.

6.

THE TRAFFIC TUESDAY MORNING WAS TERRIBLE with smelly garbage trucks making my usually zippy trip down to the waterfront from my house in Cabbagetown a stop-and-go trial. And I was in a rush. Shirley had left a grim message on my phone while I was in the shower: *See me as soon as you get in. I'm here until ten.* When the traffic was at a standstill I looked around for cops, and seeing none, dialed Cindy. Boy, did I have to talk to her! My name had to come off that article, and how. When she picked up I switched to speaker-phone just as I was passing the cop shop on Church. No hand-held device ticket for me! I could hear honks and the sound of traffic through the speakers. She was on *her* way to work.

She didn't even say hello and launched immediately into one of her tirades. "Your chain-smoking, hard-drinking, newspaper editor of the Home and Garden section, has left a message on *my* cell phone. Don't you think it's *odd* that your editor is calling *me*?"

Odd, maybe it was odd, but why would that piss Cindy off so much? Sometimes she overreacted.

"Yeah, a bit, but she called me, too." What was going on?

"Listen to this."

Shirley's thrumming diesel engine voice filled my car. I could hear that Cindy, for the first time in her life, was being summoned to Shirley's legendary smoky office. Her disembodied gravelly voice commanded, *"Come in and see me as soon as you get in. Right away."*

I had received almost the exact same message.

"Me too," I said. "The same message. I wonder what's up."

"I've never been to her office. Is it as bad as they say?"

"What do you mean?"

"The smoking."

Oh, that's what had bugged her. "Take your oxygen mask,"

Even though there had been a workplace smoking ban for over a decade, Shirley persisted in dragging on butt after butt, imagining she was fooling everyone by blowing her smoke up into the air vent and periodically spraying her office with a deodorizer. Air fresheners were plugged in to every available socket, vying for space with the tangled cords of computers and landlines. Her office smelled like a second-hand clothing store.

Shirley Payne, my editor, was having an affair with Douglas Ascot, Cindy's editor. So why did *my* boss want to see us both? There must be some connection.

I played the message for a third time as I wheeled into a parking spot in the underground lot below the *Daily Express*. Yes, I was to come immediately, as soon as I got in, Shirley had ruled. She would be in the office until late tonight.

Given it was not quite nine in the morning, that was a fairly large window of opportunity. No excuses. I sat in my car for a minute and sent a text to Cindy, telling her I had to have my name off the Everwave article. I quickly pressed send, took a deep breath, and braved the underground lot.

As I shut my car door I saw Cindy clattering on four-inch heels up the ramp from the next floor down. She was at least six feet tall in bare feet and now she looked like an enormous strawberry lollipop with her bright red hair on top of skinny legs. "Hi," she shouted breathlessly. "Wait up!"

When she got closer to me she said, "Did you catch that story about the mayor? Holy shit. Is that going to be big or what?"

"You going to be covering it?" I couldn't bring myself to mention the text. It was all too awful.

"Just the intro until the senior political people can clear their desks. What's this sudden attention from Shirl-Pearl, the Pain? I don't think I've done anything wrong. Maybe Doug whined to Shirley about something or another during pillow talk and she's going to tell me what it was, sort of behind the scenes, so that I can correct the situation and save her bacon."

But if that were the case, then why were we both being summoned? I doubted it had anything to do with pillow talk.

Cindy had doubts too, but for different reasons. She snorted, "That will never happen. Because then I will owe Shirley big time and of course, Shirley, in due course, will ask for a favour of some kind in return. I will have to hop to it and not tell her to fuck off, like I would anyone else. No, my hands will be tied and I won't be able to speak my mind, because of Doug being my boss."

"You're really running with this, aren't you? It's probably nothing," I lied. I knew it was something.

Cindy laughed, "Not really. I'm worried because we both have to go see her. Maybe I've committed a political sin by having your byline on the article about Everwave. Surely you are allowed to foray out of your regular section, if only briefly. I mean, are you forever doomed to Home and Garden?"

We had reached the elevator and she was still jabbering away. Once again Cindy was churned up. "Look, I will do anything to help you get beyond your belief that you are a failure. If Shirley blocks your attempt to feel good about yourself, after all you've been through, I will fight it. You've been a good friend through my divorce and dammit, your name is going to stay on that article."

"Thanks for the support, Cindy. I do appreciate it." Geezus. What was I going to do?

"You deserve it, after all; the main ideas are yours. Plus you researched and wrote it, for heaven's sake. They will have to kill the article before I'll agree to taking your name off it."

I groaned inwardly. This was such a mess. When Cindy was in this hard-ass mood, I always backed down. I hated confrontation.

As we got closer to Shirley's office, I watched Cindy clench her teeth and throw her purse in front of her body. She was girding her loins for a battle. I was grateful my friend was so protective of me, but something inside me was a little irritated. I could fight my own battles, couldn't I? Yes, I was the new me.

By the time we had reached Shirley's office, Cindy was ferocious and rapped on the door with harsh little taps. I could already smell the cigarette smoke and knew that would make Cindy even more livid. It was an abuse of power, and my political friend didn't tolerate that. Deep from behind the steel and glass door came Shirley's characteristic low throaty rumble, "Come in."

I opened the door to a plume of smoke and Cindy made quite a dramatic show of coughing. She then waved the door back and forth several times, in a mocking effort to air the room out. Shirley fake-laughed *ha, ha, ha* and aimed the air deodorizer right in Cindy's direction and sprayed, implying she was the source of the pollution. As if a squirt of freshener could possibly dispel Cindy's fury, not to mention having absolutely no effect on the cloud of smoke that hung over Shirley's files, her phone, her desk, her coat rack.

I was now seeing Shirley's office through fresh eyes, as if for the first time. I saw the cluttered desk, burdened with tilting piles of files and scattered with empty packets of chewing gum, an effort of Shirley's to control her habit. I noticed that the family photo was lying face down today, its gilt frame peeking out from under a buff-coloured file folder. This did not bode well for us. Everyone knew that if Shirl-Pearl had had a tussle with any member of her family, especially one of her teenage sons, down the photograph would be slammed, her mood crashing with it.

Cynthia placed her body directly in front of Shirley's desk, arms rigidly crossed and head held in what I'm sure she'd hoped was a jaunty, confident angle. Her foot gave a few tentative taps, but I saw second thoughts ripple over her face and watched her decide that toe tapping was over the top. Too cartoonesque. She wanted to convey a "don't fuck with this chick" stance. Toe tapping was out.

Me? I tried to shrink into the background. This was not going to be pretty. What was about to go down was one of the main reasons why I had stuck with flowers all my working life. They were conflict free.

Shirley briefly looked up from what she was writing by hand at her desk and, after slowly running her eyes first over me drooped in the corner against a wall, and then over Cindy's stiff body, said, "At ease, Corpulant." She then continued writing as if we weren't there.

Cynthia caught my eye and sniffed.

I supposed it was funny. I supposed it could have been more degrading; Shirley could have called her "Corpuscle." Maybe this attempt at humour meant we weren't in that much trouble at all, maybe it was something else entirely, like wanting us to organize the office party, or bringing in a platter of my famous carrot muffins. Or, maybe Shirley needed to know where Cindy got her fabulous hair done. Without a doubt Shirley needed this information what with that bale of hay perched on top of her head, straw poking out everywhere.

We waited while Shirley kept her head down, focusing on her page. I hated it when people did that. Come in, sure, but don't expect me to acknowledge your existence, not until I'm done. It was so controlling. As if in response to these thoughts, Shirley held her hand up with her thumb tucked in and her fingers spread, four more minutes was the message. She loved this game. I could see that Cindy was seething. Another abuse of power and frankly, downright rude.

"*Bitch*," she mouthed at me.

Finally, with an exaggerated stroke of her pen, Shirley signed her name on whatever document was so important that it couldn't be sent by email, and wheeled around to her computer screen, flicking it to life. She pointed her finger at it. "I have to talk to you both about this article on Everwave that Mr. Ascot kindly forwarded to me. Yes, here it says, 'Written by Cynthia Dale, with files from Robin MacFarland.'"

I could see Cindy was shifting her weight from one foot to another. She seemed to have made the rapid decision not to reveal her cards and kept her mouth shut. To say anything at all would make her vulnerable. She stood up straight and maintained her head at that cheeky angle.

Shirley looked at her and shook her head in mock puzzlement, "Something wrong with your neck, Cynthia? I have a good chiropractor, if you need one."

"No, I'm fine, thanks," muttered Cindy and briefly put her chin down.

"There's no headline for the piece yet, but I'm sure it will be snappy. I want to ask you a few questions."

"Okay, shoot." I was feeling brave.

"Sit down, will you. Both of you seem so uptight. And you Cynthia, take a chill pill. I'm not going to bite your head off."

Cindy hee-hawed self-consciously and pleated her lanky limbs onto a wooden chair in the corner, after she had lifted off an organized pile of files and placed them neatly on the floor. "So," she leaned forward in her chair as she crossed her exceedingly long legs, "what's up?" She sounded relaxed, even cooperative, but I knew she was barely keeping her tone civil.

"It's common practice, when there are two names on an article to be extra careful about the credits. So far they read, 'Written by Cynthia Dale with files from Robin MacFarland.' I guess you wrote that Cynthia, am I correct?"

Where was this going? "Well, yes, I guess." Cindy's anger was corralled behind a barbed wire fence.

"Did you or didn't you?"

"Yes, I did."

"Okay, Robin?" Shirley turned her head towards me, "So where are your files? You always show me all your research and I don't have any files on this. And I have files coming out of my ears, as you can see," Shirley gestured expansively around the room and tapped the top of her computer. "But no files from Robin MacFarland. So, where are the files?" She turned back to Cindy. "Did she send them directly to you, Cynthia?"

"Ah, well, actually, no."

"But it says 'with files from.' Are you telling me now that that's inaccurate?"

Cynthia squirmed, "Yes, there were no files from Robin."

"So, did she write this article with files from *you*? It's important to be accurate, people around here work hard and they deserve credit where credit is due. So, were they your files?"

I felt like we were being interrogated by a prosecutor at the Supreme Court of Canada. What was the big deal?

"No, they weren't my files."

"Okay, so we can eliminate the word 'files' from this byline altogether, right?" Shirley looked at Cindy for confirmation. When there was a slight nod of a now not so jauntily held head, Shirley, her hands poised in a claw-like arch, deleted the words "with files from" with a series of staccato taps on her keyboard. I knew she had done that for effect. Most people would just hold the bloody key down.

"Now," said Shirley, her eyebrows raised like two inch worms arching their backs in a geisha dance, "we are getting somewhere. Now it reads, 'By Cynthia Dale and Robin Mac-Farland.'"

"I am very proud of Robin being on the front page," Cindy gushed, a fountain of bonhomie.

"Are you then?" responded Shirley frostily. "Well, well. You are *proud* of her. I have a few more questions. You see, I know Robin's work very well. Having been her editor for quite a few years. Am I right, Robin?"

"Yes," I mumbled. I had a sense of impending doom.

"Several decades, in fact. Here in the Home and Garden section of the *Toronto Daily Express*. Yes, I know her work very well. Like you, Cynthia, I am proud of her, too. Finally Robin has taken a step to advance herself in the paper. I won't stand in her way, not at all, but I want that way paved with the truth. The truth is the truth and I want the truth. Do you understand what I'm saying here?"

"Oh, don't worry, everything in that article can be backed up. It is the truth."

"I know the article is the truth, silly billy." Shirley flashed some teeth at Cindy in what could pass as a smile, perhaps of a piranha. "Let's try and get to my point another way. Whose idea was it to question the energy efficiency of the project?"

"Robin's. She has quite a critical mind."

Shirley looked at Cindy with false surprise curling the corner of her lip. "Oh, really? Do you think I don't know that? My own reporter for over twenty years? And whose idea was it to mention the vulnerability of the pump in the middle of the lake?"

I had to speak up. "Begging your pardon, but it's not in the middle, it's only five kilometers out and the lake is—"

"I know it's not the *middle*, Robin. That's an idiom. A figure of speech. Besides, I am talking to Cynthia." The lip curled even more and I was beginning to understand something very bad was actually happening here, but I wasn't sure what. Shirley repeated, "Whose idea?"

"Robin's. She's very creative and—"

"Do I need to remind you again, Ms. Dale, that I am aware of Robin's attributes as a reporter?"

So, now it was Ms. Dale. Things had gone from bad to dreadful.

Cindy didn't know when to shut up. "She did such a good job on this article and I don't understand why you—"

"Ah, now we are getting to the truth. '*She* did such a good job.'" Shirley parroted. "Not *you*, not Cynthia Dale, but Robin MacFarland. *She*. Her. Isn't that right? Isn't it the truth that Robin wrote this article? That the ideas behind this article were Robin's? That there were no files from either you or her. That this, in fact, is *her* article?" Shirley's voice was escalating, with every question blasting like a bullet from a rapid-fire machine gun, aimed right at Cindy's integrity. Shirley was leaning forward, her face a bright red. I'd never seen her like this. She flicked a cigarette pack open and shut, open and shut, the soft snaps punctuating the silence.

Cindy sunk into the wooden chair, trying to disappear. It was true. We had believed that with my name linked to Cindy's it would surely get on the front page. Cynthia had only wanted to help me, so that I wouldn't feel like I was a failure. That I would move forward. She was being my friend. But of course Cindy couldn't say any of this. And neither could I.

Instead it looked as if Cindy had tried to steal the article from under the feet of a susceptible underling, someone who'd had such a bad time for the past five years but had finally pulled up her socks and done great work. It looked as if Cindy was a *thief*.

Cindy said, "Well, we are such good friends and I was there, at the ceremony, and I thought—"

"Stop right there before you convince me to have you fired. What you've done is very, very serious. You are a cheat. A liar and a cheat. That's called plagiarism. And we can't have that at the paper. I don't care what you *thought*," Shirley barked, "whatever it was, whatever you were going to say, will only get you in more trouble. Just stop."

"I'm sorry" Cindy moaned. "I won't do it again."

Oh my God, Cynthia could lose her job. There was a zero tolerance policy on plagiarism.

"Of course you won't. You will lose your job and be blackballed from the *Express*. I believe that you were trying to steal her thunder, that you were trying to cover up your own laziness in not writing an article, but I'm not stupid. I know Robin's work. She's smart and talented. You understand? I know you're friends. I'm letting you off scot-free because you're her friend. Some *friend*."

Even though this was so wrong, I squirmed with the unexpected praise. The whole situation was too much for me. I needed a drink and it was only nine fifteen.

"Yes, thank you. I *am* her friend. I was only trying to—"

"Stop. As I said, I don't care what you were trying to do. Don't EVER do that again. I'll probably have to mention it to Doug."

"Okay." Cindy said worriedly.

"So, you know what's going to happen now?"

"My name comes off?"

Shirley stared right at Cindy with a steely grin on her face as she vigorously and repeatedly struck the delete button with her manicured peter pointer.

7.

THE WASHROOM DOOR BANGED AGAINST the wall. We raced into the sanctuary of the restroom, panting from our narrow escape with Shirley. Cindy's phone buzzed and we both jumped. She pawed through her purse. What if it were Human Relations? Had Shirley changed her mind and have Cindy fired? Where the hell was the damn thing? I watched her frantically search her bag and resisted the urge to rip it from her hands and look myself. Finally her frenzied fingers found it hiding in the side pocket. She whipped it out and the ringing blessedly stopped.

"Missed it," she checked the screen, "Oh, just a telemarketer," she said laughing wildly. "But look, here's a text from you." She read it slowly out loud. "My name can't be on the Everwave article. Have a date with Todd Radcliffe. Long story." She regarded me, baffled. "What?"

"Yeah, I have a date with Todd. Now I'm in big shit. Now only my name is on that article. Your name is clearly out, out, out. Oh God, I need my name off."

This was turning into such a bad day.

Cindy leaned her forehead against the flowered yellow wallpaper on the restroom wall and moaned. Then she dragged herself to the small day bed in the corner and flopped onto it. The restroom was divided two rooms, the first one where people could actually lie down and rest. Someone was in the washroom behind the steel door into the second room; I could hear the water running as whoever it was soaped up their hands.

The adrenaline seeped out of Cindy's body as she stared at the ceiling. I sat down at the end of the bed and put my head in my hands. What a mess. Cindy almost got fired. Her name was off the article. My name was on. My date was going to be a disaster. But now was not the time to drown in self-pity. There was no time to waste. This problem needed to be solved.

Cindy propped herself up on an elbow, brushed her curly red hair off her face and grinned wickedly, "So, how did you manage to get a date with Todd Radcliffe?"

The old Cindy was back.

I lifted my head from my hands. "Well, I went on this internet dating site and he sent me a message without his picture and I agreed to see him and then I got his picture and it was too late, we already had a date, so, like, here I am, with a date, with him."

God, I sounded like a Valley Girl. Perhaps I should be twirling my hair. But Cindy wasn't an idiot. She'd know something was a tad off. She set about finding out the truth and said briskly, "He's a jerk. You know that, Robin, right?"

"Of course I do, but maybe he was tense at the conference and said stupid things because of it. He sounded pretty good in the profile, Cindy," I added defensively, "so maybe he isn't as bad as we think. It's worth a shot. He is pretty cute."

"What? He's an arrogant pig. You *saw* that."

I deflated, "Look, I'm trying to make the best of a bad situation. I can't back out. His connections are everywhere. You should read his CV. If I'm going to get ahead, I can't go back on my word. He could damage my reputation. The one I don't have yet, but will. I'll meet him just the once. But my name has to come off that article."

Cindy was shaking her head like a badger throttling a snake. I hadn't given her what she wanted. "But how did the date happen?" she asked me again.

"I was flustered. This dating business is all so new. I haven't had a date in like two or three decades. I wasn't thinking. It literally happened in a bad dream kind of time warp. I sort of had no judgment." I pictured the empty wine bottle on my kitchen counter.

"So-o-o," Cindy drawled. She probably saw the scenario unfold in her mind, the computer keys being pressed drunkenly and the mad search afterwards for the undo button, "You were drinking?"

"I've called the naturopath and I'm going, I'm going. This was the last straw."

The truth was out, yes, I had been blotto, and now Cindy weaseled into the next little crevasse in the day so far, wedging it wider. "Speaking of straw, what are we going to do about Shirley?"

"Yeah, I know. This is a big problem. But I think we're okay. I think she's let us off the hook."

Just then Avril Deepa, the health reporter, emerged from the washroom, smelling of apple and cinnamon soap. She looked at us on the daybed and said, "Rest is good. A short nap is worth hours of sleep," and bustled out the door.

We gaped blankly as the door clicked shut behind her.

And then Cindy spluttered. "I can't believe she figured it out. Smart cookie! She knows your style of writing and she could tell that I hadn't written the article." She paused and sighed. "We made a mistake about the files."

"Oh my God," I lamented, "I know. I didn't submit any files. I always submit my files. It's her policy. It's her quirk. Or one of them. That's how she knew."

"Actually, I think she knew it was your article from how it was written. She knows you. Your incisiveness and clarity. Your analytical ability. Your factual basis. Your lucid arguments."

"Oh fuck off. You're just trying to butter me up because we're in deep shit."

"No, *I'm* in deep shit. You are the golden one. It looks like I used you, that I stole from you."

"I'll correct that Cindy. This was my fault. I was just too ambitious."

"No," she said, leveraging herself off the bed, "I'm to blame. I should have known better. You don't screw around with credits. Listen, we had better get back to our desks."

We both forced ourselves off the daybed and left the washroom together. "What are you working on today? The mayor fiasco?"

"Yup. Unbelievable. I have to polish up an introductory article about him. Rich fat cat. Apparently his secretary has been arrested. Not that I get to write about that. What about you? What are you working on?"

"A snap dragon show. *Whoopdeedo*." I spun a finger in the air.

"Don't worry, Robin." She sat down at her desk as I made my way to mine, next to hers. "Things will only go up from here. The Everwave article is still on the front."

"Oh yes, in all its glory." I sagged into my chair. "I am now the sole author. I can just see the head. 'Todd Radcliffe, Scam Artist, by Robin MacFarland.' My date is so not going to be fun."

"Maybe he won't show," said Cindy, the eternal optimist.

"Yeah, right. And maybe he doesn't read the *Express*. Maybe he's a *Times* reader. Or even the *Herald*." I was stabbing in the dark here.

"Not the *Herald*. No one reads the *Herald*. Not unless you're a pinko commy. They give that rag out for free at car washes."

I laughed, "I think he's an *Express* reader. He strikes me as a liberal. I'm going to be so fucked."

"No, actually Robin, no, you so won't be."

I laughed again and then saw Shirley leaving her office across the newsroom. "Watch out," I whispered to Cindy, "here comes you know who. She's smiling. Ugh. Don't look up."

"Robin," said Shirley expansively, cocking her hip into my desk, "Great article you wrote." Shirley smiled, baring her fluorescently-capped teeth, "Well done." She moved her head closer to mine, so that only the two of us could partake in the conversation. "Cynthia's name is officially off. She didn't have anything to do with that article, did she?"

"Ah," I choked. "Ah, no, not really."

"C'mon." Shirley smirked, "Not at all. Let's be honest here. She didn't write it. *You* did. She was just trying to steal your thunder, right?"

I had to fix this situation. Cindy was in a very precarious position. Shirley was on her way to Doug's office. Cindy's job could be on the line. You just didn't sign your name to things you didn't write. That was plagiarism with a capital "P." And that meant you were gone. That was the paper's policy. No plagiarism. I had to tell the truth. Did I have the guts? I had to, if I was going to be the new me. What was the worst that could happen?

"Actually Shirley, it was the other way around." I whispered bravely. "I was trying to steal hers. I really need to move on now and she and I thought that if her name were on the article I would get front page exposure."

Shirley looked at me skeptically, one eye twitching half shut. "Ah, okay. It has the ring of truth. Generally speaking, Cindy is honest. For a crime reporter. So, you didn't think you'd get there on your own?" Shirley stood up and thrust her massive chest in the direction of Doug's office while trying to slap down her sticks of straw. Her mind was elsewhere.

"Something like that," I said evasively.

Doug came out of his office carrying some papers and raised his eyebrows at Shirley. The corner of his mouth turned up in the beginning of a smile but when he clued in that I was watching him he quickly recomposed his face. Shirley's mouth was open, just the tiniest bit, enough to show her pink tongue playing along the edge of her far too white teeth. She smoothed her blouse over her mountainous cleavage.

"I had better talk to Doug about all this." Shirley smiled at me naughtily, "I'm sure I can make it all *blow* over," she winked. And then she said sternly, "But don't let it happen again. You are a good writer in your own right, Robin. You got there on your own." While Shirley was saying this last sentence she boogied her eyebrows back at Doug and held up a flaming fingernail, indicating one minute.

"Yes, Shirley. I understand," I said quickly. Please God, let this be over now.

Doug turned on his heel and purposefully strode back into his office. Shirley waited a minute and then followed him, tossing over her shoulder, "It's a great article Robin. Well done. Should be on the web by tomorrow."

Wednesday. Great. The day before my date with Todd. Maybe I should just cancel the damn thing. I watched Shirley's bum wriggle down the aisle as she negotiated the desks before reaching the open door of Doug's office. Such a girlie girl. When the door shut and the blinds were louvered down, I dragged my fingers back to typing about snapdragons. Part of my mind was occupied with what Shirley had said. As I inserted the compelling information that snapdragons come in fifty-six different shades of pastel, I didn't know whether I should laugh or cry.

I looked over at Cindy. She was unbelievably upset. Was my hardy friend actually crying? Well, no wonder. I guess the events of the morning were beginning to sink in. She'd almost lost her job. And truth be told, she should have. You simply didn't plagiarize. Not at the *Express*.

What a damn close call.

I tried to catch Cindy's eye by clicking my tongue and clearing my throat but it was no use. She was determinedly focused on the computer screen, minding her own business. So I sent her a text: *Shirley and Doug are in his office. Your job is safe. Shirley knows you're honest. That it was me using you. No worries.* I pressed send and then heard Cindy's phone chime.

Cindy reached into her bag and read the message. She smiled briefly and although she didn't look at me, I could tell the message had hit its mark. Her shoulders dropped down from being around her ears and she twisted her head this way and that, releasing the tension.

Doug's door opened and Shirley sailed back into the newsroom, adjusting her scarf so that it billowed over her erect nipples. As she glided past Cindy's desk she held up her hand in a stop-like gesture, as if she were directing traffic. She said, "Don't do that ever again." Cindy didn't look up to meet her eyes but nodded once. With these parting words Shirley then floated into her own office, leaving a tail of smoky estrogen behind her.

When her office door shut Cindy finally looked up from her computer. She smiled at me and mouthed, *"Thanks."*

I gestured with my head towards the exit and got up. Time to get out of here. Two discrete minutes later Cindy followed me. We met at the elevator door and both of us let out pent up breaths. Cindy repeatedly stabbed the down button.

The elevator doors swooshed open and as soon as they shut I pouted, "The stupid date is on Thursday. Two days. The article will be in print by then. Tomorrow on the web." I pushed the button for the cafeteria floor.

The doors slid shut and it felt as if the elevator floor was falling beneath our feet as it abruptly descended.

My stomach lurched with the elevator, "I hate going down."

Cindy laughed, "Not much risk of that on Thursday."

My stalwart friend had completely recovered.

8.

EARLY WEDNESDAY MORNING MY ARTICLE, now titled "Everwave Never Wave," was bumped a few hours by the sports reporter, Derrick Johnston's breaking news piece about a shocking bus accident that had happened late Tuesday night involving an entire baseball team. Kids from Newmarket. Everyone lived and there were no major injuries, but buses were yet again slammed for not having seatbelts. Statistics were cited and fingers were pointed. Then on Wednesday, around noon, the Everwave article was further sidelined by Avril Deepa's risky exposé that some chemotherapy drugs actually caused cancer. Well, *duh*. And right before midnight on Wednesday and stretching into the early hours of Thursday, a lion escaped from the zoo and terrorized the northeast corner of Toronto for five hours until it was stun-gunned by a marksman on the SWAT squad. All this bad news was good news for me. The Thursday paper, the D-Day paper, D for Date, would be safe—no article until Friday.

So, oh lucky me, I was free and clear for meeting Todd. No awkward explanations needed, no hemming and hawing. Well, at least about my article. Cindy and I were joking about my close call in the fifth floor washroom of the *Toronto Express* building as we checked our makeup in front of the mirror Thursday morning.

"You got lucky," laughed Cindy, giving me a hug and a placing her hand low on the curve of my right bum cheek.

"Not lucky with you, Hornella." I laughed back, removing Cindy's palm off my bum with two fingers. That woman just didn't give up. "Listen, I gotta dash."

"Knock him dead, I mean it! The guy's a jerk-off."

"That's bad karma, Cindy, *tut tut*," I chastised her with my forefinger. "I'm going to have a fabulous time. He's pretty great to look at." I was trying to convince myself.

Cindy rolled her eyes. I raised my palms upwards as if I were helpless. We both knew the date was a waste of time.

At five sharp I rushed home from work, then fed and lugged Lucky around the block, tugging at his leash when he stopped to pee on bushes. I wolfed down a measly salad for dinner hoping to lose fifty pounds in twenty minutes and then had a shower, fluffing up my hair afterwards with my hairdryer. I tried not to look in the mirror at those tell-tale lines around my lips as I put on my eye makeup.

It had been decades since I had been on a date and it was all flooding back to me: the butterflies in the stomach; the trepidation; the self-doubt; the bad hair. Plus, I already knew I didn't like him. So why was I going? I decided it showed how much I wanted a new partner. Besides, it was good practice. I watched myself in the mirror as I puckered my lips in a trial smooch and then ran from the bathroom in horror. I needed Botox *now*.

I sat on the edge of my bed and had a skirmish with my nylons. I hauled the one-size-fits-all over my lumpy thighs, stood up and then yanked the panty hose up to my waist. The lip of cellulite hanging over the top was not a pretty sight and I tried to tuck it under the waistband. It had a mind of its own, however, scoffing me by bouncing back. At first I thought it was funny, but after three tries of manhandling the disobedient flesh I gave up and flipped through the hangers in my closet, finally picking a long flowing jacket that would cover up this unfortunate situation. I threw on what I'd hoped was a flattering black skirt and raced downstairs. I had taken too long.

I felt like throwing up.

I glanced quickly at my watch. Seven-thirty. Half an hour to get from my house in Cabbagetown to Bloor and Avenue Road. Easy peasy. I knocked back a full glass of wine in three big gulps and savoured the warm glow drizzling through my veins. I would be fine! I would be hilarious! I would be attractive!

I would smell like a wino.

While stuffing some gum in my mouth I opened the door. I would be late if I didn't get my skates on.

I arrived at the Starbucks five minutes early after madly dodging through downtown traffic and parking my rattletrap in an actual garage on Yorkville. I pulled open the huge glass door of the coffee shop and searched the throng. Was he here? No. Good. I spied two empty chairs far in the back and battled my way through the crowd, smacking aside patrons with my purse and dodging ahead of a lost Queen Street type sporting tattoos and a lip ring. He or she was heading towards the same two chairs. It was a race.

Being shorter and able to duck under people, I arrived first, planted my self on a chair, and smiled a victory smile. In response, and like so many of that generation, he/she, hard to tell with the dreadlocks and boots, muttered "*Whatever*" and sauntered to another table that had come free. I tucked my purse close to the chair on the floor and did my best to look relaxed. First impressions were so important. So then I put my purse on my lap, trying to hide my state of affairs. This made me feel perched on the chair like a little old lady waiting for a train. So then I stuffed it beside me. Everything was too squished. Okay, okay, back on the floor it went.

I looked through the sea of people and caught the eye of the kid who I had decided was a thugette, not a thug. I had seen a hint of small breasts under the frayed blue jean jacket. The impudent punk was observing me and writing in her notebook. Great, I thought, the next Margaret Atwood is dissecting me. I winked at her. A fleeting smile pulled up the left corner of her lips and disappeared as rapidly as it had come. We understood each other. Misfits.

And suddenly there he was, the handsome Todd. His greying hair was parted on the side and he wore rimless glasses. Seagull blue eyes. He was sporting casual Sperry topsiders, Khaki pants, an aquamarine tie, and a pastel blue oxford cloth shirt, cuffs rolled up. A navy blazer was folded over his arm. No socks. Yikes, I thought, I'm having coffee with an advert for Marcus Neiman.

I glanced over at the journaling kid and got a *what-the-fuck* questioning look. My kids had given me that look many times, like when they thought I was out of touch with reality. I twitched my right shoulder forward in an imperceptible shrug and flared my nostrils while raising my eyebrows, every so slightly. *Whatever.* I knew and the kid knew this was a total screwup. But hey.

Todd's head was tipped quizzically to one side. It was an exaggerated gesture; he recognized me. "Hi. Haven't we met somewhere before? You look familiar." He sat down and draped his jacket over the back of the chair. While scrutinizing me through his glasses, he ran his fingers through his hair, smoothing the flyaway wisps down. He was smiling like a wolf would at a little rabbit.

My polite gene trampled my *he's-an-asshole* thought. I wasn't going to play *this* game. "Sure," I smiled, "I was at your convention, the valve opening ceremony of Everwave."

Sounded slightly pornographic to me.

"That's right," he chortled, "The reporter. You were with the lesbo. But you look like a pretty lady."

Big mistakes. *Lesbo? Lady?* Man oh man. "The *lesbo* is my colleague and good friend. And I am a journalist, not a pretty lady." I leaned forward aggressively.

The kid surreptitiously checked out the exchange and took notes. When she looked up, I gave her a small shrug.

Todd sat back, looking chagrined. "Sorry. I'm kind of out of practice at this dating thing. My wife left me a year ago, for my best friend actually, not to mention with the kids and half the house, and I haven't been in the game for long."

My brain hummed. Didn't we just meet? For the first time? Isn't this third date material? Why is he telling me all this? Why did it sound so pat? But what did I know? Poor guy, imagine the betrayal. The losses. But he called it "the game." What era is this guy from? Cindy would have a fit.

"That's okay," I said. I crossed my legs. It's only practise I said to myself.

Not sensing how deep the hole had been dug, Todd continued, "Nice legs." He smiled at me knowingly and leaned back comfortably in the chair.

Something inside me contracted.

"Are you living permanently in Toronto now? I read that you were educated in the States." And maybe that's where you got the sexist attitude. Fuck you about the legs. Although I had to admit I did like the compliment, considering what I knew was lurking under the panty hose.

"I've got a condo by the waterfront, King Street West, King and Bathurst."

"Oh, I'm over in Riverdale—well, not quite that far—more the central east end. Have you been to Cabbagetown?"

"Been here for a few years now and have settled in. Sailing at the RCYC. Squash at the Granite Club."

His navy blue blazer probably had gold buttons with the Royal Canadian Yacht Club imprint on them. I was supposed to be impressed? I was a socialist. I'd try again. "Pretty close to the Riverdale Farm. Nice place to walk, through the brickworks and all. Do you have a dog? I do. Lucky."

"I enjoy the restaurants along College. Have you eaten there? Maybe we could go for dinner early next week."

Not bloody likely. "Sure, why not?" Maybe he was anxious. I gave up offering information about myself. He wasn't interested. "How long have you been at Everwave?"

"Tuesday, then. About seven? About three years. From its inception. Me and the vice prez. Stick-handled it to the opening of the valves, although I'm going to be at the helm for another few weeks or so."

Perhaps he had ADD. "So, did you want a coffee? Tea?"

Todd jumped up, "How rude of me. I'll get it. What would you like? And what's your name, by the way?"

"Robin, and tea. Mint if they have it, otherwise chamomile. Thanks."

I studied him as he stood in line, biting his lip and shifting his weight from one foot to the other. His fingers were fidgeting in his pocket, looking like he had a trapped rat in there. I could hear the rustling all the way back to where I was sitting. What was he playing with? Cellophane? He was anxious. Now that was heart-warming, despite his stupid comments. Maybe I'd give him another try. He was unbelievably handsome, with his muscular shoulders straining against the material of his shirt, and so tall. A thrill uncoiled in the centre of my being. He seemed to like me. Lumps and all. Yeah, I'd see him again. If only for the eye candy. Marry him. Stop it! *Get real, Robin.* He's a jerk.

Done her coffee, the kid at the corner table was collecting up her stuff into an Aztec sort of bag with a braided handle. As she walked past me her boots clicked on the floor with a definite authority. This was the youth speaking, her stride said. She cocked her head at Todd in the lineup, looked at me and gave him a thumbs down. "Dishonest" she hissed as she sidled by. Just the one word and loud enough for only me to hear.

I wasn't sure I had heard correctly. There were tons of people milling about, creating a low thrum of noise. Dishonest? How can you read that off a guy in five minutes? Nah, he was nervous. I watched the girl's dreadlocks swing back and forth across her back, the little beads braided into her hair clattering as she strode out the door.

Dishonest, huh?

"Here you go. They had mint." Todd placed the paper cup of steaming tea in front of me and then sat down. "Do you always drink herbal teas?"

His curiosity about me was dazzling. First my name, now herbal tea. "No, only after four in the afternoon. Caffeine keeps me up."

"Not me," he smiled as he took a gulp of his foam-covered coffee. "I drink it all day long." He patted his breast pocket as if looking for something. "Whenever I have a coffee, I want a smoke."

"You smoke?" I asked, incredulous. His profile had said he was a non-smoker.

"Doesn't everyone?"

"Well, no. I don't. Your profile said you were a non-smoker."

"Oh, who tells the truth in those things?"

I do. Sort of. I laughed. So he *was* dishonest. Well, to be fair, I had written I was a non-drinker. "You planning on quitting?" I was. So that made it honest. Right?

"Nah, love the things. I chew gum to control the urges." He dropped his arm and tapped the jacket pocket behind him. I could hear cellophane crinkling. "Always carry it in my pocket. I don't smoke much, five or ten a day."

"Is that a lie?" I asked sharply.

Todd jerked back his head, "Why? Is it important to you? How much I smoke?"

No, how much you lie. "I don't think I could get involved with a smoker. My first husband died and I sure wouldn't want to go through that again."

"Sorry to hear that about your husband. What did he die of? Lung cancer?" He was smiling awkwardly.

"No. Car accident. Drunk driver."

"Murdered, then." Todd's blue eyes were sympathetic.

"You think so?"

"I know so. My mother was an alcoholic. That's why I don't drink."

"Your father?"

"The sweetest man you ever could meet. He was loyal too. Never left her, right up until she died. Cirrhosis. I was just eighteen."

Oh God, maybe he's attracted to me because he somehow knows I drink too much and you know what they say: men marry their mother.

"I drink too much." I blurted. It was a warning. "But I'm stopping."

Todd looked at me over his coffee cup. He had a little bit of foam stuck to his upper lip. I watched carefully as he licked it off. "You started after your husband died?"

I dashed to far safer ground. "My kids are grown now and no one lives at home." Free and single, that was me.

"My kids are grown too. But they all live in Toronto."

"All? How many do you have?"

"Just three."

So, finally an answer.

I poked my chest with my thumb. "Four."

"Looks like two to me."

What was with this guy? "Todd. Enough."

He snickered. I relented and gave a half smile back. He said, "So you are mischievous, like you said."

Too personal. "What's your career plan after Everwave?"

"What? Is this an interview or something? Am I going to be in the paper?" His eyes twinkled behind the polished lenses.

If only he knew. "Just curious."

"Well, my specialty is cooling systems, so I'll stick with that. A food company. Ice cream, it looks like. Van Horner and I are partners in the venture."

His eyes darted around the room. What was that about? Lying about a career path? He was lying about *something*.

Abruptly he crumpled up his coffee cup.

"Listen, Robin, everyone lies on those profiles. You drink. I smoke. Let's have dinner next Tuesday and take it from there."

We stood up together. The first meeting was thankfully over. He held the door open for me and we stood somewhat awkwardly in the cooling night air of August. A kiss? No, a handshake. An undeniable current flowed between us. As we were walking away from each other, I turned around to look. So had he. We both gave a shy wave.

"I'll email you with Tuesday's plan," he called.

Go right ahead, I thought. I watched the night closing in around his retreating back. He cut a dapper figure with his blazer tossed over his shoulder, hooked by his thumb. The night had suddenly become very chilly. It felt about fifteen degrees. I did up the buttons on my jacket. His footsteps echoed in the sudden quiet of the street. For downtown Toronto it was remarkably desolate after the crowd in Starbucks. Where was everyone? I shivered and felt the cool night air on my face. Time to get home.

When I turned around, I slammed right into a tall man wearing a grey hoodie. Where had he come from? Why hadn't I heard him? I'd had no idea anyone was that close to me. Panic coursed through my veins. He pinned me against a recessed doorway and when I looked up I saw it was the gaunt face of Jack England, the crime writer from the *Toronto Times*, his coal black eyes burning. I struggled to take a step back with a sharp intake of breath.

"You gave me a start. Jack, right? Jack England from the *Times*?" His eyes were dark and flashing as his hands pressed hard against my shoulders. Fear curdled in my throat. Should I scream? But I knew the guy.

Suddenly he let me go and grabbed my elbow hard, turned me around, and forced me back the way Todd had left, west along Bloor Street, away from the safety of my car behind the church on the corner. I shrugged my arm, trying to shake him off. He was a strong guy considering he was as thin as a spaghetti noodle. His fingers were like steel pincers. "What the hell do you think you're doing? Let me go."

His fingers dug deeper into the flesh on my arm. "I need to know," he growled. "I need to find out what you're up to." He frog-marched me down the street and into a deserted construction site on the north side of Bloor, my feet barely touching the ground. I was terrified.

9.

JACK BACKED ME UP AGAINST a grimy brick wall half way into the construction zone and trapped me between his arms. His breath brushed against my cheek, the garlic from his last meal making me nauseous. The gritty wall scraped against my jacket and a pebble caught under the heel of my shoe as I shifted my feet, trying not to lose my balance. The odour of urine swirled around me. Where exactly was I? I was totally disoriented. What had happened to the safety of staid Yorkville?

"You promise you won't run?" Jack snarled into my ear. I nodded. I wanted to know what was going on. Jack took a step back, letting his arms fall to his sides. He looked at me expectantly, as if waiting for me to dash away.

I brushed off my jacket where he had gripped my elbow. "What the hell do you think you are doing? You could have picked up the phone and called me, like a civilized human being."

"I need to know what you are up to at work."

"Me? *Up* to? I'm up to a snapdragon show. Back off, asshole." I shoved him with the palm of my hand and he staggered backwards underneath some scaffolding. Somewhere a cat meowed. With this small success, I felt empowered and gave him a punctuating shove in the centre of his chest with my forefinger. The back of my mind registered that his pecs felt much more muscular than they appeared.

"I mean it, stay away from me," I said.

He moved forward, leaning his six-foot frame over me and putting his face right next to mine. "Don't fuck with me, Robin. Why are you meeting with Radcliffe?"

"You following me? Stalking me? That's a pretty serious charge, you know. Get away from me." I stabbed him again in the chest with my finger.

He jabbed me right back in the shoulder. "Tell me what you were doing with him." He pushed me again.

I lost my balance and staggered backwards. Someone walked by on the sidewalk and I could see them looking in to the site, watching what was going on. "I'll scream," I warned.

Jack glanced over his shoulder, saw that we had company and took another step back. He held his hands up, palms up, surrendering. "Calm down. I'm sorry I frightened you. But what are you doing seeing that guy? I was following *him*, not you."

"Why are you following him? I think I have a right to know, considering I was out on a date with him."

"A date? You're crazy. Don't be fooled by that guy, Mac-Farland. He's dangerous."

"Yeah, right. In case you didn't notice, he's a Harvard-goody-two-shoes-Ralph-Lauren-clone. Hardly dangerous."

Jack narrowed his eyes. "Just a date, huh? How'd you hook up with him? I saw you at that ceremony. Then?"

I was secretly pleased. England *had* noticed me at the convention.

"You were there too," I said accusingly. "You're a *crime* writer, what were you doing there in the first place?"

"Same thing your friend Cindy was doing."

"Don't be an ass, she covers environment too, not only crime. The lake is environment."

"Maybe I do, too."

"What are you? Six? C'mon, stop the parrot game, why were you following him?"

Jack abruptly turned on his heel and slithered away. When he reached the wire gate to the opening of the construction site he shouted over his shoulder, "Consider yourself warned, Ro-BIN." When he said "BIN" he kicked the side of the dumpster at the entrance to the site.

Nice, I thought, really nice. And mature as well. He really did act like he was six years old. Not to be outdone however, I shouted "Same to you, Jack-OFF" to his retreating back. Wasn't I the clever one?

He turned around and grinned, as if to say, "Good one!" and then took off, bustling west along Bloor Street in the same direction as Todd.

With my heart pounding in my fingertips I walked as coolly as I could away from the scaffolding and piles of gravel. I stood in the street lights on Bloor, saw where I was, and headed east towards the parking garage where I'd left my car. I pulled my jacket tight across my chest and hunched over as I scurried along. A woman in a hurry. My car was right where I'd left it, inside the entrance on the first floor of the garage. I pressed the button on my key fob and the lights came on as the doors unlocked with a reassuring thunk. I dove into the driver's seat and gripped the wheel, breathing hard. That England was a creep.

Good thing I didn't marry him, *ha ha*.

With damp fingers I turned the key in the ignition and pulled out of the lot. The date wasn't that bad, I thought, but then I corrected myself. That kid had warned me about Todd and now Jack had too. What did they sense that I didn't? Is this why I had ended up in a bad, okay abusive, marriage with Trevor? I was blind to cruelty? To danger?

And ultimately, is this why I drank? To keep from seeing the truth? Or, to help me cope with it? And what was that pain in my chest? I placed a hand over my heart as I stopped at a red light. It was beginning to drizzle and the fine drops formed a translucent gauze over my windshield, bending the red light into rivulets of cherry blood. I looked at my hand, seeking an answer. Was it an emotional ache? Was it fear? Of what?

I was fat enough for a heart attack. Maybe I was going to die.

My trip home was a blur interrupted by the steady staccato beat of my wipers. When I finally unlocked my front door, I stood in the hall and caught my breath. In the peaceful silence everything slowed down. I reassured myself that, yes, my world was normal. The thump of Lucky's feet on the hardwood floor above me as he jumped off the bed was followed by the scratching of nails on the smooth surface as he raced down the stairs to the first floor. I absent-mindedly patted him behind the ears while tossing my keys in the tray beside the door. I was on auto-pilot, my mind drumming with the mystery of it all, my body churned up from Jack's confrontation.

I poured myself a large glass of wine. Of course I did. Thank heavens that naturopath hadn't called me back.

I sat down in the wing-back chair in the corner of the kitchen and mulled over the events of the evening. What was going on? Why was Jack following Todd? I glanced at my watch. Shortly after nine-thirty. I picked up the phone and dialed Cindy. When she answered I said without preamble, "Jack England is following Todd Radcliffe around."

"Who?" mumbled Cindy.

I'd woken her up.

"Todd Radcliffe, the guy from Everwave."

"Oh him. How was your date?" She yawned.

"Sorry if I woke you up, but do you have any idea why this is going on?"

"What's going on?"

I clenched my lips together. It had been a mistake to call Cindy. I'd forgotten that she went to bed early so she could go for a run before work. "Why England is following Radcliffe?"

"No idea. Why, what happened?" Cindy was slowly coming to, her journalistic instincts taking over.

But I was fed up with her. "Nothing."

Silence ticked down the line. Cindy was hurt. I guessed it

was justified. I had now snubbed her and she was the one who had been woken up. "Okay-y-y-y."

I relented, but only an inch. "England grabbed me after I met with Todd and shoved me into that construction zone beside the hotel on Bloor, wanting to know what I was *up to*."

Cindy was wide awake now. "He what?"

I enunciated my words as if I were talking to a child. Still ticked off. "Grabbed me, told me to stay away from Todd, that he was dangerous."

More silence. But by now Cindy had been made aware of the error she made in her initial lack of interest. She gave me a peace offering. "That must have been frightening. Being dragged into that dark place." Conciliatory now and trying to connect with me.

My bristles flattened. "Yeah, not fun. But what am I missing here?"

Cindy breathed a sigh of relief. The fight was over as soon as it had begun. "Leave it with me. I'll find out what the buzz is and call you in the morning."

"Thanks." A sharp click as I hung up. Sure she would. She probably wouldn't even remember the call.

I sat and drank some more wine in my so-called reading chair for a few hours, thinking about the situation, and periodically flicking through a mystery novel. Around midnight I began my nighttime routine of shutting down the house. Lucky was let out and in. I checked to see if the doors were locked. Cast a glance at the stove to make sure the burners were off. Turned out a few lights. And then, finally, lurched into the living room to shut down my computer.

Curiosity about Todd got the best of me, so although it was past midnight, I decided to check out his profile again. I got on *MeetYourMatch*, entered my password, and typed "Mr. Sail Away" into its advanced search bar. Immediately his profile came up. I read it twice through, trying to discover something sinister about him, something that had tweaked England's interest, but as far as I was concerned, it looked pretty innocuous and I shut the computer down. I used the banister to pull myself up the stairs to my bedroom. I was sozzled.

Friday morning dawned clear and crisp; autumn was around the corner with only two more weeks to Labour Day weekend. I gobbled a couple of acetaminophen and waited for the day to look brighter before I left for work. Tonight I'd be having pizza and wine with Cindy and Diane. We'd hash this situation out. When I walked through the glass doors into the open concept editorial office floor, my cup of coffee sloshed over my hand. Great start to the day. Shirley's door was closed and the blinds were drawn. Either she wasn't in yet or she was and someone was with her. Doug?

But no, Cindy's editor, Douglas Ascot, was bent over Cindy's desk. So, Shirley wasn't in yet. Cindy and Doug were in deep conversation and checking her iPad. I wondered what they were looking at. Cindy suddenly tapped quickly on her keys and the two of them became riveted to her computer monitor. They had started a search.

I heard my name being bandied about and moved in closer. What the hell was going on now? I stood at my desk, just a few feet away from Cindy's, and could see over Doug's shoulder. If I squinted my eyes I could see the Google search bar. They were Googling Everwave and the pointer was going up and down the various selections.

"I don't know his name," Cindy was defensive.

"Google this one," he said, pointing halfway down the list.

"No, that's not it."

I moved closer. "Maybe I could help."

Cindy turned her head and looked at me over her shoulder, "Hi, what's the name of the vice president of Everwave?"

Doug looked at me doubtfully. How could I possibly know?

"I was at the convention," I said by way of an explanation. I tunneled through my memory banks and found a gold coin: the vice president's compact bum. Horney. Right. Horner. "Van

Horner. Richard? No, Paul. No, Richard. Yeah, Richard van Horner. Why?"

Doug dismissed me, and turned back to the computer, entering this name into the Google search bar. "You're right." He sounded surprised. "We need to talk to him." He was trying to sound casual. His toes were curled in his Birkenstocks.

Who wears Birkenstocks? And what did Shirley see in him?

"About what?" I persisted. As soon as the words were out my bravery faltered. Cindy saw the tiny flicker in my eye.

She put me out of my misery. "Todd Radcliffe."

Now we were getting somewhere. "Oh him." I was nonchalant. I could pretend too. My hand waved in the air, oh so casually. "What do you need to know?"

But now I had gone too far. Cindy knew Doug would not tolerate this unruliness. Standing up for myself was one thing, probing where I shouldn't go was another. Cindy's eyes darkened, giving me a warning. But I disregarded the furrowed brow, the tenseness around my friend's mouth, because I was galloping towards forbidden information with the determination of a fox hunter. Cindy wanted to protect me before I fell off that particular horse. She gave her head a determinedly negative twitch.

Finally I cottoned on to the seriousness of her message and raised an eyebrow. What was this? A warning? Should I back off? It wasn't my business? I took a step back and looked elsewhere, pretending to be no longer interested. Yeah right.

But Doug turned Cindy into a fool and answered me. "Everything. We need to know where he lived. Where he worked before Everwave. Who he was seeing. Where his children go to school. The name of his goldfish."

Relief fueled Cindy's laugh. It was too loud.

I copied the new humourous tone. I could get good at this game of hide and seek, flushing out information as if it were nothing important. "Key info about anyone, the fish angle. Why would you need to know even *that*?"

Doug stood up his full height and cleared his voice. His mouth turned down like a circus clown's. "Because my pretty little Robin bird, the man is dead."

The news severed me from reality. I felt like I was in the third person, watching myself watching Doug, watching me. What had he said? Todd was dead? How could that be? I saw Doug looking at me carefully. I could feel the blood draining from my face and wondered if my freckles were standing out in a blotchy starkness. Robin bird? This struck me as funny and I wrestled with the giddiness that was bubbling in my chest. *Do not laugh, Robin. Do not.* Cindy held her head down, and, in contrast to me who had stopped breathing, her chest rose and fell in a fast rhythm. She was staring at the computer screen. Hiding from me.

I looked at the back of Cindy's head accusingly. My friend kept *this* from me? After my date? After my phone call to her last night? Why hadn't she texted? This was the sort of information that needed to fly through the ether.

Doug saw my pronouncement of Cindy's guilty betrayal and said, "Oh no, Cindy didn't know either. Not until right now. The second I told you. I was saving the news flash. Just to see."

As if on cue, Cindy's eyes raised up to mine, troubled and full of worry, their dark pupils even darker and leading into a cave that I did not know.

"Was he murdered?" I guessed. I wasn't going to capitulate and ask "see what?"

"Why would you ask that? Why would you guess murder and not a heart attack? Or suicide?" Doug was evaluating me.

I was flustered. "He was in good shape. Fit. Active. Didn't drink."

"I've heard the police have no idea. There's no clue. And how do you know all this?" Doug was beginning to have the same dark look as Cindy. What was going on?

"We went out. Just once." Would "just once" get rid of the look in Doug's eye? It was starting to scare me.

"When?" His voice was clipped. This was not a game now. This was cutting to the chase.

"Last night," I whispered.

He turned to Cindy. "You knew this. You knew this and you didn't tell me?"

Cindy swung one leg over her knee, as if crossing them would give her immunity from a lie. "Don't be ridiculous, Doug." He grunted. "I just found out. When you told us. Hardly time to keep something from you, was there? Be reasonable."

"This looks very bad." He had dismissed his accusation and moved on to the next problem.

"Why does it look bad?" I was so naïve.

Doug gazed at me as if I had the IQ of a shag carpet.

"You were the last person to be with him, then." Cindy was prodding me along, trying to get me to see the light.

But no light dawned on me. I smiled, "Yeah, I guess I was. But wait, no, not if he was murdered. That person was the last one to be with him."

Cindy stood up and grabbed her purse. She looked as if she were getting ready to leave. "Robin, I'm going to give you a crime reporter's hot tip. The last person known to be with a murder victim is probably, statistically, the person who murdered the person. So, that would be you."

I absorbed this information, the wheels turning in my head. "But no, the last person with Todd Radcliffe was probably Jack England. Besides, how was his death discovered?"

Doug plugged his nose and blue a raspberry. "A neighbour."

Right then Shirley made a grand entrance in a fog of perfume and a camel pencil skirt that was way too tight. "Hi everyone." She waved her fingers and raised her coffee in a toast, "Good morning. What's going on?" She was wearing fake eyelashes that had been curled so tightly their sharp little points had left black dots of mascara where they had jabbed above her eyes.

Doug was flustered and said to Shirley, "I think we need to call the police before they come here."

"Why? My skirt is criminally tight?" Such a flirt.

"We have a big problem here. Murder. A suspect." His thumb pointed at me.

The bantering good cheer fell from Shirley's face like a stone. She stood in front of Doug and looked at me with the protective glare of a fierce mother bear. "My office. Now."

I followed Shirley as if pulled by an invisible thread. But I had the presence of mind to look over my shoulder and call to Cindy, "Don't go to the crime scene without me." In the corner of my eye I saw her sit down as I was dragged in the wake behind Shirley's expensive perfume.

10.

WHILE SHIRLEY HUSTLED AROUND HER OFFICE getting settled, I stood by the door and stared out the window. She had a wide corner view, looking south and east. The reverse floor plan of Doug's. I could see a large ship at the docks over to the east, probably around Leslie, if not further. Straight ahead the trees on Toronto Island were beginning to lose their bright green summer foliage as shades of brown and orange crept into their leaves. The sky had clouded over and the lake was gunmetal grey, broken by random white caps. Was this an ominous portent of the day to come?

Shirley hung up her coat on a rack in the corner and shoved aside some files on her desk, making room for her coffee. She stuffed her purse in a drawer, flicked on the overhead light, and turned on her computer. She finally sat down and gestured with an impatient shrug of her head for me to sit in one of the hard wooden chairs that had been pushed against the wall by the overnight cleaners.

I shifted the files that were slumping on the chair onto the floor, sat down, and while I waited for Shirley to stop fiddling around with her bits of paper, heard a siren below on Jarvis Street. There was a feel to the day that was making me shudder. What kind of mess was I in? It felt serious. I wished I'd never met the guy. But then I felt uncharitable. He was dead after all. Eerie to think of that. Last night he was living, breathing, drinking, laughing. And okay, lying. Tonight? All that was simply gone. Unbelievable. No one knew how it had happened. I felt a bit sick.

I watched Shirley busily organizing her day. A day planner was consulted. Her phone was checked for texts. She logged into her email. A finger scratched at her scalp, poking through her bird's nest. And then, without a word she asked, no *demanded*, all the details of the sordid story from me, her hand insisting with beckoning fingers: tell me all.

And so I exhaled and began the long, somewhat embarrassing tale. The valve opening ceremony, the dating site, the article, the date, Jack England, and now the death. Sometime throughout the long recitation Shirley had tilted her chair back and was staring at a spot over the door, lost in thought.

"I'd like to cover the story," I said.

The chair came crashing forward. There was a guffaw. "You would, would you?"

"I think it would be a good opportunity for me. Besides, I knew the guy."

"Well, that's sort of the problem, isn't it?"

I sidestepped. "Do you think Doug would let me? It *is* a crime story. Not flowers. Maybe I could team up with Cindy." Did I actually say that? What an idiot.

"Yes, that worked so well in the past."

I had the grace to lower my eyes. What a fiasco. My cheeks were burning.

Shirley relented, "I'll put in a good word for you." She tilted her chair back again and looked up at the ceiling. Thinking. "I am on your side, Robin. I do want to help you. I'll remind him about that great Everwave story you wrote. The one that came out the morning Radcliffe was discovered *dead*."

She slapped these words into the air as if to strike sense into me. The story had come out? Today? I hadn't yet seen a copy of the paper, and what a thing to miss. My first cover story.

"Such great timing," Shirley continued, "I don't see why he would refuse." She laughed and fell forward, looking down and watching her bosom jiggle as her chair hit the floor. The "me" was implied.

Nonetheless, I was grateful. However she got him to acquiesce was fine by me. Giggle all you want, Shirley. My first cover story and now, hopefully, my first crime scene. Even the words sent a bolt of electricity through me. "Thanks, Shirley."

Shirley had her many idiosyncrasies, but getting things done was one of her strengths. She picked up the phone, muttered a few words that I couldn't hear, and tittered a little with her pink tongue poking out the side of her mouth. Obviously they had connected. The request was made and the answer given. It was a go. I could tell by the way Shirley pushed her enormous chest forward. "No problem," she said to me after she'd hung up. She smiled triumphantly and dusted off her hands. "It's your baby, not Cynthia's. But Cynthia is to mentor you."

I couldn't believe my luck. Here I was in a pile of shit and I still had come up smelling like roses. "Thank you so, so much, Shirley. I can't tell you how much I appreciate this opportunity." I made a hasty exit before she could change her mind.

Shirley stopped me at the door with a large "Ahem."

I turned around. "Yes?"

"Don't embarrass the paper. Be very professional. No drinking on the job. And give your statement to the police before you get to the scene."

I was mortified. Did Shirley know about my drinking or was it merely a general statement?

But Shirley continued without a pause. "If they start asking you where you were after your date, say nothing more and tell them you'll be getting a lawyer. The paper will supply one. We have a good lawyer on staff here for this sort of thing. Russell Whetstone. Even though it was a personal date, you met the fellow initially while doing a story for the paper. Right? That came before the internet connection. Right?"

"Yes, Shirley."

"So, there you have it. Russell is good. And work *with* Cindy, do not do all the work. Get her to do some, not like the last time. She is your teacher; ask her for help. Listen to her."

"Yes, Shirley."

"Be safe. A crime was committed. As far as we know. You may be at risk. On the other hand, maybe Todd's death was from natural causes."

"Yes, Shirley."

"Go to the police before they come to you. Before you go to the crime scene. If, indeed, there was a crime. They will want your information. Go give them a statement."

"Yes, Shirley."

"And check out England's story. Why was he following Radcliffe? What does he suspect or know?"

"Yes, Shirley."

"And don't give Jack a thing. Do not support England."

"No worries, Shirley. I am a true Canadian."

Shirley laughed heartily and waved me out of her office. I felt as if I had survived a meeting with the school principal, somewhat giddy that I didn't get a detention or have to write out one hundred times "I will not date again."

I shut the door on Shirley's cigarette smoke-filled office and tried to keep from skipping to my desk. I was less of a failure than yesterday! Still fat—I could feel my legs rubbing together as I trotted smartly along—and definitely alone after my disastrous fling with internet dating, but I had advanced to crime reporter. I sat at my desk and smoothed out the crinkles that bunched at my thighs in my polyester black pants. The stretchy ones that still fit. I went over the conversation in my head. My ears blazed with Shirley's admonishment to be professional and no drinking. Did she know?

Okay, first things first. That drinking had to go. I hadn't heard back yet from my naturopath so I signed into my email account and sent her a short request for an appointment. Next, I had to talk to Cindy, my assigned guru. On the corner of my desk was a small tidy stack of three-inch paper squares that had been cut from scrap paper. I licked a finger and removed one, grabbing a pen out of the I-heart-Mom mug on my desk. On the small scrap of paper I wrote: "CAN. SEE YOU," and then folded the paper into a small fighter jet. I aimed it carefully at Cindy's back.

At that moment the air conditioning kicked in from a vent in the ceiling to my left, creating a sideways draft that carried the paper airplane far further than I had ever intended, so that it landed with a small elegant whoosh on Derrick Johnston's desk. Derrick Johnston was a Ryerson dropout who had somehow burrowed his way onto the sports desk. He was a real yahoo, with *hoo-ha's* coming out of his mouth with every score he reported. He was the kind of guy that turned his hand into a gun and pointed it at you when he saw you, instead of saying "hi." He opened the paper up, raised his eyebrows as he read the message, scribbled on it, folded it back up, and sailed the plane over to me.

I grabbed it out of the air as it soared by and saw that he had added just one letter to my missive. He'd pressed his pen hard into the paper and written a "T." The "CAN'T SEE YOU" taunted me. What an arrogant and assuming jerk. As if. I'd never go out with someone like him. I changed the "A" to a "U" with a firm stroke and crumpled the plane up into a small ball. I got up and nudged Cindy in the ribs while whispering "bathroom" and pranced past Derrick's desk, dropping the wad on his desk. "Oh, hi Derrick, Cindy and I are going to the *can*."

"What was that about?" asked Cindy as I followed her through the glass door.

"Nothing. He's an asshole." I tossed my comment over my shoulder, just loud enough for Derrick to hear. I twisted slightly trying to see Derrick's reaction to my edit. He had turned a bright pink and was staring wide-eyed at his computer. I laughed.

I tucked my arm into Cindy's as we went towards the washroom. "Welcome to the new me. I got the story!"

We settled ourselves on the daybed in the corner and established who was going to cover what. Lines were drawn in the sand. We nestled next to each other, heads almost touching, with Cindy's red hair contrasting sharply with my dark brown. The story, as we currently knew it, was discussed thoroughly and specific tasks were divvied up. After Cindy's failure to follow through with her end of the bargain on the Everwave story, I was careful to reiterate the jobs.

Because Cindy was working on another story—a gang warlord had been gunned down the night before in the west end—she would dig up everything she could about Todd and Everwave on the internet and in the paper's library. She could do this anytime, even in the middle of the night, or between working on her other story and trying not to get shot by a member of the Vipers.

I would be the upfront visible reporter. She would come with me if she could, but ostensibly it would only be me who would talk to Todd's family, his coworkers, and people from his past and present. I would schmooze with the cops at the scene. Cindy figured that because the police didn't know me they would be freer with their tidbits of information. A Home and Garden reporter had little cause to have a relationship of any kind with the police. Beaten to death by a daisy? Not a story.

Cindy, on the other hand, had been a cop pest for years. The police simply wouldn't talk to her now. When the detectives saw her long legs striding through a crowd of onlookers, her fiery red hair alight as she plowed through the uniforms at a crime scene, they clammed up, telling her to wait for the press conference like everyone else.

Cindy took her mentoring job seriously. "One of the things you have to do is determine the cause of death. Was it natural? Accidental? Suicide? Or a homicide?"

"I'll never remember all that."

"Sure you will. It's an acronym: NASH. You will 'nash' your teeth over this story."

"Thanks. That makes it easy."

As the reality of giving the police an official statement sank in, I became more uneasy. "Listen," I said to Cindy, "I'm not sure I can talk to the police. They are kind of aggressive aren't they? Sort of no-nonsense and mean? How do you get information out of them? I don't know how to do this. Give me some clues."

Cindy took my hand, "I know this is a big deal for you Robin, a really big deal, but you'll be fine. You are so ready for this."

"But, I have never talked to a cop before," I said plaintively, "and I have to give a statement."

"Well, that's not quite true." Cindy took a deep breath and forged on. "You have talked to the police before. Who told you about Trevor's death? Remember? That night when the cops came to your door, hats in their hands? They were pretty normal people, weren't they?"

Even though it was six years ago, the memory of the awful night when the news of my husband's death had been given to me crashed into my brain like a truck. But Cindy was right; the cops had been human, mostly, that sweet young blonde girl and her rolly polly partner. I forgot their names, it had been so long ago now. I remembered talking to them, for hours, it seemed.

And then I remembered that at one point I had had the feeling that they were checking *me* out, trying to assess whether I had somehow arranged to have him killed. Outrageous. Even with all the troubles in my marriage, I would never do that. Luckily our mortgage wasn't insured and his life insurance was one that was included as a matter of course in his benefits and wasn't much. This meant the cops had no money motive, although I remembered I thought they were being kind when they had asked their pointed questions about insurance.

"Well, they can seem pretty normal, but they can be cutthroat too. They know how to play games to get information."

"And so do you, my friend, so do you. You are far wiser now than you were then, and you will be able to figure out what they are doing. What exactly are you worried about?"

"When I give my statement I think they'll think I did it."

Cindy threw back her head and laughed out loud.

I bristled. "Don't *scoff* at me. I was the last person to see him alive. It would be natural to suspect me. You told me that."

"The last person who saw him alive was the person who killed him, not you."

"Good plagiarism, Cindy."

She didn't bat an eyelash. "Look, you are completely innocent, you don't even have to act it. Just be yourself. If they start asking you leading questions, then say nothing and get a lawyer. Simple."

"That's exactly what Shirley said."

"Well, she's right. And the paper would probably supply one. What's the guy's name? Russell Whetstone."

"That's what she said, too."

"So, you have no worries. He's extraordinarily good. You should see him all over this mayor business. Nothing escapes him."

"Well, if I am completely innocent, which I am, then why shouldn't I simply answer all their questions? Won't it look as if I am hiding something if I say I want a lawyer?"

"Remember the police are like terrier dogs with rabid imaginations. If they want you to be guilty, if they *like* you for the crime, believe me, they will bend what you say to suit their theory. You must have a lawyer present if you even get the slightest hint they are thinking about you. Plus," Cindy dropped her voice and spoke like an officious police officer, "anything and everything you say can and will be used against you, etcetera etcetera."

I laughed, "Just like on *Law and Order*, right?" Then I turned serious again. "Well, should I mention Jack England and how he nabbed me?"

"Of course you should."

"Won't he get in trouble? I mean, won't that look kind of weird for him? Suspicious?"

"Tough shit. He's a big boy. He has his own paper backing him. He's a very experienced crime investigator. He knows how to handle the police."

"But they'll think *he* did it."

"And maybe he did! Not your problem. Big boy, remember?"

I remembered how he had pushed me against the brick wall at the construction site. Underneath my fear of the potential danger he was posing, there had been a magnetic attraction pulling me towards him. I had felt the heat emanating off him through his jeans and sweatshirt and every sinewy muscle rippling in his body as he pinned me to the wall. He was a big boy, oh yeah.

11.

I LEFT CINDY WORKING ON HER gang research and took the elevator down from the fifth floor to the parking lot below. I tentatively entered into the maze of parked cars. The fluorescent strip lighting cast eerie indigo shadows behind the cement pillars. Underground parking lots gave me the creeps. I stood stock still and listened. There was no tell-tail shuffle of feet as a boogeyman snuck down a ramp. No soft thunk of a car door as a mugger hid in wait inside a vehicle. I heard nothing but the whoosh of an exhaust fan off in the corner.

I scurried to where I thought I'd left my car, head nervously turning left and right, peering warily into the blue shadows behind the cement columns. As I hustled, I put the long car key between two fingers, closing my fist around the fob. If anyone jumped out at me, I would jab them in the throat. Really? Like that would work. At five feet two inches I would hardly be able to reach a tall person's chest, no less their throat. I'd be better off aiming for their balls.

I laughed at myself. Such a brave crime reporter.

Finally I saw my little red car hiding behind a huge black Ford Expedition and beeped the doors open. I hastened towards it and jumped in, locking the doors with a reassuring clunk. I tried not to race towards the exit as if I were being chased by demons, the hairs rising on the back of my neck. The garage door squawked open and I gunned the car out onto the street, finally free from the parking lot ogre. I pulled over to the curb in the soft morning sunshine, and tried to figure out out the best way to get to the crime scene.

Which was exactly where? I, Robin MacFarland, newly promoted crime reporter, had no idea where I was going. Wait. Didn't Todd say he lived at King and Bathurst? In one of those new condo buildings? Perfect. I'd watched crime shows on TV. The place would be surrounded with yellow tape and police cars and maybe a fire truck or two. I'd look for them.

From where I was sitting beside the ramp into the *Express* underground parking, I was about five minutes away. But I was in a rush. I wanted to see the body. From the deep recesses of my memory I drummed up how my older brother had taught me to leave rubber behind. With a wide smile on my face I revved the engine while it was in neutral, thrust the gearshift into drive, and squealed my tires as I blasted off.

I was a *crime reporter*.

I nodded my head appreciatively, *not bad* I thought, as I drove my rattling Sentra along King towards Bathurst. I was so *cool*. Yes! I nodded and nodded, "Yes, this is good. This is so *good*."

At the first light I came to I felt someone looking at me and whipped my head sideways to see. The driver in the car beside me was smiling sympathetically. Dammit, I thought, I must look like someone from another planet, nodding away. I stopped bobbing my head instantly. The light turned green, I revved the engine and leapt forward, burning more rubber. I'd show him!

Way to go, little Sentra! I patted the steering wheel. Maybe I should get a new car. A Mustang. No, a BMW. No, a *Lamborghini*. God knew I needed a new car. The Sentra was at least twelve years old. Maybe fifteen. The damn things lasted forever. Just like people with pacemakers. Those were the kiss of life. Besides, what sort of image did my beater give? Certainly not the one I wanted. But it worked and I was loyal. Besides, it was good in the snow. Maybe I'd keep it until next spring.

As I approached the corner of King and Bathurst I looked left and right. No police cars. No yellow tape. I went to the next block and turned left. Voila! A circus. Red and blue lights pulsated above three grey police cars randomly scattered across the street. A fire engine idled. A crowd was clotted at the base of the building and held at bay by a single uniform outside a taped off area, a young lad with apple cheeks peeking out from under the plastic peak of his cap. I pulled over to the curb.

Skittish nerve endings vibrated all over my body as I sat in the car. My brain seemed to be singing to me, *dead body dead body*, in a Lady Gaga kind of way. I took a deep breath and tried to centre myself with a very quick meditation. Once the sing-song chatter faded, I planned my moves. They would be crucial if I were to get past the cops into Todd's apartment.

With eyes half closed, I scrupulously picked apart the journey from my car to his apartment in my mind. First, I would weave my way through the crowd, take my press card out of my pocket and sort of palm it so I could show it, but not allow the officer enough time to read it before I stuffed it back into the folds of my jacket. I would state my name with authority and then say "Toronto, mumble, mumble, investigations." Hopefully the newbie cop would think I was from a Toronto facility of some kind. Coroner's office or forensic whatever.

Who was I kidding? I had zippo knowledge of crime talk. I knew flower talk. I knew about the CPFDA: the Canadian Professional Floral Designers Association. And I knew construction talk: the WSIB, or, Workplace Safety and Insurance Board. I didn't know crime talk. Right now, the best I could do was come up with an appropriate wreath for the funeral of a builder. Everything else was simply bullshit.

But I had brought up four kids. I could do bullshit. I was not going to be a failure any longer. I was worthy of success. I'd swagger past the cop like I knew where I was going and head for the elevators. Then I would press Todd's floor number and zoom up.

Shit. I didn't know his floor number. Asking the doorman would give my charade away. So, I pulled out my phone and called Doug Ascot, my editor for this story. This *crime* story. It couldn't be helped. I needed the number.

He answered on the first ring, not giving me time to muster up my in-charge, new-me voice. "Ascot," he barked.

"Oh, hi, it's Robin MacFarland, you know, Everwave, and now Todd Radcliffe's death? Well, I'm at his condo and I don't know his apartment number."

"Neither do I. Figure it out." *Click.*

Hmm, that was a good first out-of-the-office exchange with my new editor.

Figure it out, huh? A thought occurred to me and I Googled 411.ca on my phone. There it was! Two entries for Radcliffe. One was probably his wife's. His, obviously, was the one on King Street and, hooray, it included his apartment number. I was in business and resumed my mental play-by-play. After getting to the elevator doors, I would push the up button and go to apartment 1403 where I would use the same trick with the guy guarding Todd's door: walk with authority, a flash of my press card, pocket it, Toronto, mumble mumble, investigations. I'd get in.

I abandoned my banged-up Nissan Sentra under a no parking sign and stood on the sidewalk, gathering all my resources. I only had one chance to get this to work. I took my press card out of my wallet and put it in my pocket. My fingers curled around it as if it were some sort of rosary. One two three, *go go go.*

I shoved through the crowd, using my left elbow to jostle people out of my way. I pulled myself up to my full stature when I got to the rookie, flashed my press card so that it was shadowed by my palm, and, in my deepest voice, said "Robin MacFarland, Toronto, mumble, mumble, investigations," deliberately throwing the words away as I tucked my ID back into my jacket pocket.

I could feel the cop hesitate for a second. Perhaps he was considering what would happen to him if he road-blocked the Coroner of Ontario, or the Director of the Crime Scene Investigators, or whoever I was. I met his gaze with a challenging look. Coming to a decision, he swung his arm expansively, smiled at me with a nod of recognition, silly boy, and let me pass.

Trying to look powerful and self-assured, I thrust open the eight-foot tall glass doors to the condominium building and floated on my thankfully quiet shoes through the propped open lobby door. I waltzed through the vestibule, past the security desk, and finally to the shiny polished steel doors of the elevator. So far, so good. Suddenly the elevator doors slid open and two official looking guys stepped out, a handsome bear with a cop haircut and a woodchuck with a scraggily pony tail. Both of them had dark bags hanging below their eyes, blue suits, and briefcases. I quickly skittered around them into the elevator with my head down.

I stabbed the door close button repeatedly, like a crazed chimpanzee. Get me outta here! Finally the doors shut. I allowed myself a small smile as my heart slowed. I was doing it! A sultry woman's voice called out the floor numbers as I ascended. Finally: the fourteenth floor.

I stepped out onto lush forest-green carpet that was bordered with gold curlicues. It had a French provincial look to it. The walls were papered with white linen that had been seamlessly applied. Directly in front of me stood a satin-sheened mahogany table with antiqued brass handles on its centre drawer. A large off-white vase holding green ferns and gold autumnal flowers stood in the centre of the table, perfectly placed in front of a gold-framed mirror. This guy had been *rich!*

At the end of the hallway a door stood open. A low hum of muted conversation drifted down the corridor to me. My heart began to thud as I took a deep breath. Was I too old for this? I felt for the press pass in my pocket. Something funny was going on with my eyes. The edges of my vision seemed slightly grey. Glaucoma whizzed through my thoughts. No, it was nerves. Focus on the breath. Focus on the breath. I rehearsed what I needed to say at the door: *I'm Robin MacFarland, Toronto, mumble mumble, investigations.*

I purposefully strode to the open apartment door, planting my feet with deliberation in the soft green carpet. I was important. I was smart. I had *authority*. I would get by the cop guarding the door. With every step, I bolstered my ego. By the time I got there, old, fat, stupid, failure, Robin MacFarland was nowhere to be seen.

And neither was a guard.

What? No guard? All crime scenes had guards, didn't they? At least they did on *Hawaii Five 0*. On *Law and Order*. On *The Mentalist*. Why no guard? Did I have the wrong door? Was this just a regular door that had been left open by an absent-minded millionaire who had come home with his shopping, hands too full of Louis Vuitton to shut it?

I stepped to the right and jiggled the door with my foot so I could see the number on the other side. 1403. In brass electroplate. Yes, this was the place. What now? I stepped over the threshold, waiting for someone to stop me with a shout, but not a peep.

Todd Radcliffe's foyer was floored in tiles of polished white marble. A shiny steel table stood against a crisp, white wall. On it was a potted white orchid, probably fake I thought. The arms of his rimless glasses were open, as if they had been tossed off in a hurry. His car keys lay close to the far metal edge of the table, as if they had been thrown down and slid across the smooth surface. I recognized the glasses from our sort-of date.

Suddenly I remembered his light blue eyes and long tanned fingers. I couldn't believe he was dead. It seemed impossible. How was it that a human being who had lived and breathed just a few hours earlier, who had been so alive, so full of, well, in his case, so full of himself, now be dead? Even though I had a deep belief that the energy of life could not be extinguished, and remained forever in the universe, death still seemed so final.

I pinched the orchid flower to see if it was fabric. My thumbnail left a translucent half moon scar on the delicate petal. Oops. Real. My bad. And then I remembered. I had better keep my hands to myself. I didn't want to leave fingerprints or, what did they call it? *Trace*. Trace evidence. Right. I pulled off the petal and put it in my pocket. Was that overkill?

Kill kill kill looped around in my head. *Steady, Robin.* It was only a dead body.

The door to his front hall closet was slightly ajar and I jostled it open with my elbow. It was virtually empty. Did he actually live here? Inside there was only one item of clothing: a navy blue blazer sitting tidily on a wooden hanger. The expensive kind of hanger that had an arch in it to protect the fall of the fabric. The rest of the hangers were the metal kind one gets from dry cleaners. They twanged together gently in the breeze created by me moving the door.

I inspected the blazer without touching it. This certainly appeared to be the jacket that had been slung over Todd's chair when he had that froth on his lips from his coffee. Lips that I had wanted to lick. I stepped inside the closet to get a better look. Yeah, it was the same one. Getting braver, I fingered the material and saw that yes, the blazer did have gold buttons with the Royal Canadian Yacht Club imprint. No surprise there. Of course he was a member, "Mr. Sail Away."

I mentally reconstructed the sequence of events. He had walked into his *la-de-dah* condo after his date with me, maybe elated at the prospect of dinner next Tuesday—not knowing I would have cancelled, maybe—and taken off his glasses, pitched down his keys, hung up his jacket. I was solving a crime! How great was that! I had to call Cindy. I dug out my phone and whispered hoarsely, "I'm IN!" as soon as she picked up. I knocked into the empty hangers in my excitement, causing them to rattle loudly and quickly tried to hush them with my hand.

"Who is this?" asked Cindy impatiently, as if I were a telemarketer. I knew she had caller ID.

"*Me*. I got into the crime scene. No trouble at all."

"Who's the cop in charge?"

"Don't know yet. I'm still in Todd's foyer. Well, in the front hall closet."

"That's not *in*. In is when you can see the body. Get out of the closet." And this coming from Cindy.

"You get out of the closet."

"I am out, stupid. Go find Todd."

The body. Shit, I'd have to look at a dead body. I heard footsteps. "Gotta go."

What if the person opened the closet door and saw me there, *hiding*? Wouldn't look good. So I poked my head into the foyer and bent over, as if examining something on the floor. Who ever it was went into the kitchen area, off to the left. Close call.

I walked into the living room and stopped, dumbstruck. Holy smokes. What a place! Every time I saw a home like this I was bowled over. How could people live like this? It was too perfect. Floor to ceiling windows exposed a view of Lake Ontario. Everything was white: white walls, white leather sectional couch, a white shag rug, white orchids everywhere, white built-in book shelves, and white and grey art on the walls. I felt like a time warp machine had swooped me up and dropped me into the arctic. But where was Todd? Not here, stinking up this flawless room. Probably in the bedroom, which was likely through that doorway to the left. I looked around the room. Maybe it was the door to the right. A fifty-fifty chance of getting it right.

I walked towards the door on the left. Wrong. It was a den. In it stood two men dressed exactly the same as the ones I had seen earlier getting off the elevator; dark blue suits, white shirts, black shoes. Their scuffed briefcases stood on the carpet. They seemed engrossed in their conversation and paid zilch attention to me in the doorway. I scuttled backwards like a frenzied lobster into the living room.

I bolted through the door to the right. It would have to go to the bedroom. Two more cops, or I assumed they were cops, were coming out as I was going in. I slunk into the ensuite bathroom off to the left to let them by, closing the door slightly in front of me with the back of my hand. No prints. I could see through the crack that one was a female with blonde hair and a handsome square face on a solid body, and the other a pudgy balding fellow with yellowed teeth and a bulbous nose. They were talking about the best place to get sushi for dinner. Flirting? Maybe a couple? Blondie was playing with the buttons of her jacket as she walked by.

While I was in the bathroom, I quietly snooped. The vanity's marble top was polished to a reflective shine. I would have to be very careful about fingerprints. Grabbing a couple of tissues from a box on the back of the toilet and placing them over my hand, I began poking around in earnest. There was nothing interesting in his medicine chest: some painkillers, a tube of toothpaste, a bottle of over the counter sleeping medication. The very barest of essentials. I opened and shut the drawers in his vanity. They were almost empty. Towels, a shaving brush still in its packaging. Gel. On the ceiling I spotted a disgusting bug crawling upside down. Was it a cockroach? Here? Couldn't be. I took out my phone and snapped a picture.

The bedroom was the opposite of the living area. Almost black. The walls were painted a deep burgundy red, the floor was dark stained oak, and the chests of drawers, all three of them, were black lacquered bureaus, each one with carved pearl inlays of bonsai trees and geisha girls wearing red kimonos. A black satin bedspread covered the bed and on it lay Todd. He was on his back, fully dressed, looking almost like a holy man, his black hair tumbling around his head like a mass of tangled seaweed. His right hand was curled beside his throat and his light blue eyes stared opaquely at the ceiling. Had he strangled himself? How bizarre.

The reality of what I was looking at—a very dead body—sank in and I swallowed the bile that was rising in my throat. I started mouth breathing so I wouldn't smell the dead mouse smell that was hanging in the air. I knew that smell from when the kids were young. Several times mice had escaped their cages only to get trapped and die inside the vent system of the house. I felt myself begin to panic as a wave of heat washed over me. A remnant from menopause. A bead of sweat was rolling down my back. How hot was it inside this room anyway?

I found the thermostat on the wall by the door and took a photo with my phone. It was set at thirty-five degrees Celsius. It wasn't me; the room *was* hot. And I'd read Agatha Christie. I knew the murderer had probably turned up the heat to skew the time of death prediction. Didn't fool me an iota.

He was dead all right. I stared at him for a minute with macabre curiosity. I'd never seen a real live dead person. A real live corpse. *Ha ha ha.* I could feel laughter tugging at the corners of my mouth, bubbling inside my chest. I would NOT laugh. I hammered the giddiness back down my throat and focused on what I was looking at.

What on earth had killed him? There was no blood anywhere. Not a drop. I leaned over and examined the bedspread carefully. Nothing. And that hand business sure was weird. What did Cindy say were the four causes of death? Oh right. NASH: natural, accident, suicide, or homicide. *Okay, Robin, think.* Had he died of natural causes, say a heart attack, and the hand was undoing his tie so he could get more air? Was it an accident? Had he banged his head and was raising his hand to feel the lump and then died from a brain bleed? Had he killed himself with sleeping pills and was desperately reaching for life? Had he been murdered and was fighting off his attacker? I had no fucking idea.

I could hear muted voices. People were heading towards the bedroom. I tiptoed back beside the door just as the two guys who had been standing in the corner of the den walked into the bedroom.

Busted.

12.

THE TWO SUITS STRODE PAST ME into Todd's dark bedroom, discussing the case in low tones. I could barely hear what they were muttering and perked up my ears. The tall one said, "It doesn't add up. No forced entry. If someone knocked him off, he let them in. He knew the person." The other was bobbing his head in agreement, clearly the underling sidekick. "And I doubt it was a burglary gone wrong," the tall guy continued. "It doesn't look like anything's out of place. If it was a murder, it probably had to do with the lake water."

They had walked right by where I was standing to the far left of the door by the thermostat. What luck. They hadn't seen me. Could I skulk out behind them? Did I want to? I might miss key information. The younger guy was nodding like one of those dogs glued to a car dashboard and stated the obvious. "Yes, the TV is still there." In the corner was a huge honking flat screen.

I could easily creep out while their backs were turned, but on the other hand, if I made any noise at all, I would be caught. I decided to make my presence known and cleared my throat. Not loudly, just a little, as if it was a natural thing to do. They both turned.

The boss took a step towards me and held out his hand, "Ralph Creston, I'm in charge of the case. And you are...?"

I looked up, way, way up into the guy's flat grey eyes. He must have been six and a half feet. And his eyes were a dull metal as they looked at me. This man could not be fooled. In fact, he probably had a bullshit meter running right now. But I tried to stall. Although I didn't know why I felt I had to. What would it accomplish? Information. Right. That was my goal.

"How do you do?" I lowered my eyes and looked down at my hand as it was swallowed up in his gigantic paw. He had an unexpectedly gentle grasp for his size and I liked the feel of his warm, soft skin. No sparks, it was not a flash and burn handshake, but a slow tingle crept up my arm. When I raised my eyes back up to his I detected a slight shift behind the cold steel, a small movement that revealed a very tiny opening, a reluctant crack, where some warmth shone through. Then I extricated my hand and turned to the underling, "Sorry, I didn't catch your name."

The younger man smiled goofily, revealing a gap in his front teeth. I noticed that he had missed a few whiskers shaving that morning. He had a nail brush growing under his nose. "Larry Stokes."

I looked back and forth at each man, putting on a puzzled look. "I don't recognize either of you from around," I fabricated. "You guys must be from a different division." A wild stab in the dark. Anything to get some information for my article.

"And we're in charge, so don't forget it." This from Larry, the smug little bug.

Creston tried to smooth over the younger man's steam-rolling bad manners. "We're happy to collaborate with you guys, but all information has to eventually reach me. I'm sure you're aware that we've been monitoring Everwave for the past year, as we do anyone who has access to Lake Ontario water. You know, international theft of water is no small crime. We're thinking Todd Radcliffe could be the victim of a crime ring, but so far it doesn't look like murder. No evidence has surfaced. But there are lots of ways to torture someone without leaving evidence. Or maybe he had a heart attack. There is no apparent cause of death."

I nodded sagely as he talked. This was going way better than I thought. They thought I was a plain-clothes police officer from the division that usually covered this part of Toronto. Whichever one it was. How lucky that they were from another cop shop. "And your information is invaluable to me." I felt quite saucy. "What do you think happened here? No blood. The hand. No forced entry. But the temperature's turned up." I put my hands on my hips, hoping I looked as if I knew what I was talking about.

"Hard to say," grumbled Ralph Creston, "forensics have been through the scene. They dusted for fingerprints, nothing, wiped clean. But this place is pretty sterile. Maybe his cleaning person came in today. Everything possible has been examined. Samples were even taken from the soles of his shoes. His hand? Yes, it's interesting, no doubt about it. It might be in a defensive position, so they scraped under his nails, you know, in case he fought off his attacker. Maybe he was strangled. Frankly, I have no idea. Yet."

What did I think about this Creston person? He'd said "cleaning person." Hmmm. He wasn't sexist, then. Respectful. "There are no signs of being strangled. No livid bruises on his neck." I showed off my television expertise in murders, "No petechiae." Look at me go. I mean, I could have said, "Red spots in his eyeballs."

Creston was frustrated. "So far it doesn't look like a murder. More like a suicide. Hard to tell. He could have taken a bunch of pills. But the autopsy will reveal all. I'm requesting a full tox screen."

"When are you guys going to do the autopsy?" I might as well act deferential, giving these cops the sense of power they felt was their due. As if controlling the autopsy time and date gave them *cajones*. In reality I had no clue when autopsies were usually done and I wanted to know.

But Creston was already turning to leave the room, with Larry's rubber-soled shoes peeping like baby birds on the hardwood floor as he followed him. My question dangled loosely in the air. Was this a power play? I decided I had pushed my luck far enough and followed in their footsteps, lifting my feet carefully so my soles made no sound. I'd had enough attention. When the cops veered off to their corner in the very white den I kept silently trucking out the door.

"See you around," I flipped over my shoulder, prancing quickly into the hall.

Creston called out to my receding back, "Nice to meet you. What's your name again?"

But I was already shutting the apartment door and pretended I hadn't heard *his* question. Two could play this game. What a bloody close call. So lucky. As I was shutting the door I heard Creston and Stokes walking towards it, the clue being Stoke's telltale squeaky shoes.

I ran down the hall and punched the elevator button. I had to get off the floor fast! My façade was slipping and wouldn't withstand another verbal questioning from that huge brute of a man. What was his first name again? Ralph. Ralph Creston. Right. No elevator. I spied the exit sign for the stairs and tugged open the fire door. I clattered down the cement stairwell, my right hand holding tightly onto the square metal railing so I wouldn't fall. I felt a hard lump pass by under my fingers. Somebody's chewing gum. Ugh. When I got two floors down I pushed the fire door open, leapt across the hall to the shiny elevator doors, and stabbed the button. Repeatedly. *Jab jab jab*. Where the fuck was it?

The doors opened so suddenly that I jerked back in alarm. My nerves were fried. I pushed L, which I assumed was for Lobby and not Lower because there was also a P, probably for Parking, which would be even lower. My mind was whirring like an egg beater.

The elevator lurched and I thought immediately that I was going to plunge to my death. Panic-stricken, I looked at the numbered lights above the door. How far was I going to fall?

The light flicked off the number eleven. Eleven? What? That made no sense. I was sure I had run down two flights, not three. I knew my math. Fourteen minus two was twelve. Not eleven. Twelve. I was sure of it. And then the twelve button lit up. What was going on? I didn't want to go *up*. I wanted down. Oh my God, I thought, I must have pushed the up button when I was on Todd's floor. This elevator was going up to get me. I felt a soft steadying of the elevator pulley and the doors opened at fourteen, right where I had been. And standing right in front of me were the two cops. Larry Stokes and Ralph Creston. Holy shit.

The ridiculousness of the situation fueled my giddiness. I composed my face. "You going down now?" Oh Geez. Had I said that? I hoped I didn't sound crude. Creston frowned and Larry stifled a snicker.

"Just forgot to look in the kitchen." I edged around them and headed towards the apartment.

Larry called out in his too high voice, "We locked the place up, *tight as a drum*." He laughed again.

The elevator doors were shutting.

"No biggie, I've got a key." I pretended to search in my pocket, in case they could see through steel.

"Let the *body* guys in, then," came the muffled comeback.

I was alone in the hall, worrying about the state of my mind. I had lost a whole floor somewhere along my escape route. Perhaps it was in the same place as my short-term memory.

The drinking had to go.

Damn. Security cameras. They would be hidden in corners and behind heating vents. Very discrete, and also impossible to detect. I eyed the flowering *benjamina fiscus* in the corner with suspicion. Maybe one was buried in the soil, its lens slightly above the edge of the terra cotta pot. I bent over to look closely. Nothing. I looked around and thought I saw some light reflecting off what could be a lens in the far corner of the hall. But maybe the cameras were fake, only meant to spook.

But maybe not. So I pretended to hold a fake key in front of what might be a fake camera. I trotted up to apartment 1403, my arm held out, hand at doorknob height. As I approached closer to the door I saw a series of numbered buttons on a small metal box above the door handle. Keyless entry. Of course it was. Shit.

I had never opened a keyless entry door in my life. The joys of being over fifty. I didn't know what to do to make it look as if something had failed and I couldn't get in. I was struck by what I hoped was a brilliant thought.

Maybe the technology was the same as my car door. Maybe I didn't have to know the combination of the little buttons, I could just press a button on a key fob and the door would open like a vehicle door, remotely. So with an exaggerated gesture I pushed an imaginary button with my thumb on an imaginary fob while my hand was aimed at the lock. I tried the door handle. When it didn't open, surprise surprise, I shook the pretend fob and tried again. When the handle still didn't open, I theatrically blew on the fob. I'd seen my kids blow on bits of technology when they didn't work, like on a keyboard or into a CD player. I tried the fantasy fob again and when it still didn't work, no bombshell there, I shook my head exasperatedly and walked back to the elevator.

When the steel doors opened I stepped in and looked carefully at the floor numbers above my head. *Ah ha*! No number thirteen. I hadn't lost a floor; there was no floor. The builder must have simply avoided the problem of not selling condos on a bad luck thirteenth floor by omitting it all together. Well, that trick sure fooled Todd. He bought a condo on the fourteenth floor, which was really the thirteenth, and look what happened to him.

What *had* happened to him? Had he taken a pile of pills and killed himself? But where was the pill bottle? I hadn't seen one. Oh wait, yes I had, a bottle of sleeping pills in his medicine chest. They were over the counter. Would that be strong enough to kill him? He didn't look murdered. He looked asleep. Except of course for the dead mouse smell. I reviewed what I knew so I could write the article. The cop guy in charge was Ralph Creston. I would have to find out his rank or whatever it was called. And where he was from. The unfortunate sidekick was Larry Stokes. I'd need his rank as well. The deceased had been found lying on his bed. No apparent cause of death. No blood. No signs of a struggle. No finger prints anywhere. No forced entry. Not a burglary. If it was murder then Radcliffe must have known the guy. Motive was a mystery. Creston said something about lake water. My story was taking shape.

Then I laughed at myself. It looked like a suicide, but that wasn't a story. And somehow I didn't believe it. Why would he make a date for next Tuesday if he was planning to off himself? Plus he seemed light-hearted, happy even. I was skeptical of the suicide theory. And someone had turned the heat up to confound the time of death.

The elevator doors opened at the main floor and two guys in crisp brown uniforms were there, waiting with a collapsible gurney on an accordion type of contraption. A folded black bag in plastic wrap was balanced on top. Good luck getting into the apartment guys! And then I saw a uniformed police office behind them with another guy. He was wearing a grey shirt with the name Donald monogrammed in red over his breast pocket. Must be the super. He had a hand full of key fobs.

At least I didn't have to let them in to Todd's apartment. Not that I could. Thank God for bad communication.

I unobtrusively slipped behind them and out into the street. I walked a hurried, stilted, penguin-kind of walk towards my car, gathering speed on stiff legs as I got closer. I called Cindy as I held the phone with my ear to my shoulder, all the while searching in my purse for my car keys.

But all I got was her answering machine, so I left her a short message as I tucked behind my steering wheel. "Okay, good story, I saw the dead body, I got good intel." I tapped the phone to end the call.

Was that the right lingo? *Intel?* That's what they said on *Criminal Minds*, anyway. I whizzed back to the *Express* building and when I saw that Doug wasn't in his office waiting for my return, I knocked excitedly on Shirl's door. I was bursting with all my news and had to tell someone about my achievement. Doug opened Shirley's door, straightening his tie and coughing while Shirley sat demurely behind her desk. Oh, please. Couldn't they stay off of each other for an hour?

Doug sidled around me slightly turning his back, "S'cuse me." He held his jacket over his arm so that it hung over his belt. Right. And then he beetled back to his office, shutting his door.

"What's with him?" I asked Shirley while pointing my thumb at Doug's closed office door, although I knew the real answer. It was a game. A ballgame.

"Oh," Shirley replied breathlessly, checking her lipstick in a small pocket mirror. "Oh, something important came up."

Righto. "So, I got into the apartment and saw him. He looked so, I don't know, kind of like a prophet in a way, just lying there, on his bed. There were no clues at all. He looked like he was sleeping, except his eyes were open."

"What did the police say?"

"There were some cops from a different division. Why would they be there? What does that mean? I think this is bigger than we thought."

"No, what did the police *say*? When you gave your statement? Do you need legal representation?"

Shit. "I haven't given my statement yet." I mumbled.

"You're kidding me, right?" Shirley's eyebrows shot up, moving the stiff yellow straw on her head back an inch.

"No, I went straight to the crime scene. I wanted to get there fast, before they moved the body." Like I knew about these things. "They were coming in with a gurney right when I was leaving."

"Let's get this straight." Shirley was looking mightily pissed off. "You didn't follow my directions. You went straight to the crime scene even though I specifically told you, not once but twice, to immediately give a statement to the police. You didn't follow your editor's instructions."

Well, not quite true, I thought. Shirley Payne was technically my editor, but not on this story. On this story I was to answer to Doug. And Doug had known I was going straight to Radcliffe's apartment because I had called him to ask for the number. I had told him where I was. Maybe my mistake in calling him would save my bacon with Shirley. Suddenly I had an epiphany about where my kids got their deviousness.

"Well, I wasn't sure about the reporting chain and who was my boss." Not a lie so far, not really. "I didn't know the best course of action." Not knowing an apartment number was not knowing where to go, which was a course of action, still not a lie. "Anyway, I called Doug for information from outside Todd's condo building. He didn't know the information, but he knew I was there, and he didn't tell me not to go in."

Shirley sat back, shrewdly assessing my choice of words and the politics of this situation. She hadn't been fooled. While she was thinking, she smiled the kind of smiles mothers have when kids say "wasn't me." But her relationship with Doug eventually won the battle.

"Oh, well," she said, conceding the point I'd won in this inning of saving my ass. "If Doug knew, then I guess it's okay. Hard to know which editor to obey. But I think it would be best to go right now to the police station and give your statement. It would be hard to cover this story if you're a suspect. So get that cleared up right away."

I backed out of the office as graciously as I could. I'd narrowly dodged a bullet.

13.

I PUSHED THROUGH THE SMUDGED GLASS doors of the police station and was yelled at to stop right where I was by a stout guy with a walrus mustache sitting behind the information desk. He boomed at me to wait. Not here, *over there*, on the bench. He flung his massive arm to the right. So I waited. Despite having had four children, two of which were idiot boys doing illegal things, I miraculously had never been inside a police station before. I looked around with curiosity as I sat waiting on a long metal bench like a good little girl.

The first thing I noticed was the colour of the place, or rather, the lack of colour. Everything was washed out, even the lighting was muted. The air vibrated with a faded grey-blue light from all the computers. The walls were coated a pewter grey. The steel desks were enameled with a glossy grey metal paint. This was a far cry from the energetic and vibrant room I had expected.

In front of the computers sat very young men and women, toddlers I thought, who were wearing dark uniforms. Babies really, with unlined faces and shining, optimistic eyes. On their shoulders were the dark badges flecked with white of the Toronto Police Force. It looked to me as if everyone were waiting. The kids, or rather, the force, were all tapping away, keeping themselves occupied, I thought, until something actually happened. They were probably on Facebook.

I pulled out my cell phone and pretended I was texting. I

held it in front of my face and squinted, trying to look as if I was having trouble reading the screen in the bad lighting. I was actually taking a video of my surroundings so I would be able to describe where I was, later. When I was writing my great story. If it was a murder. Slowly I scanned the room. Fluorescent lights. Grubby grey carpet. Glass offices on the perimeter with blinds drawn. Smudged stainless steel coffee percolator in the corner. A stack of cracked mugs. Metal garbage pails. Black chairs. A fly buzzing over some spilled soft drink on the floor. Humming noise from a vending machine. Shouting from behind a door.

My hand froze.

What? Shouting behind a door? What were they shouting about? I strained my ears to hear. I could only make out a vowel here and there. What was the name on the door? Something Stapelton. Staff Sergeant Stapelton? Shit, I needed glasses. With a sudden burst, the door flung open and out stormed of all people, Creston and Stokes. Oh no. What should I do? Here I was sitting on a chipped steel bench, looking like the civilian that I was, clearly waiting for the police. I could not pretend that I was a police officer, not here. Creston's iron hard eyes burned in his reddened face and met mine with a metal clang. He barged towards the bench, his finger pointing at me accusingly. "You were at the crime scene," he roared.

Larry Stokes' soprano voice trilled an annoying echo, "You were at the crime scene."

Their anger was palpable. Surely I hadn't been the cause of it. What was going on? With Ralph Creston almost on top of me and Larry Stokes peering around the massive bulk of his body, I slowly stood up, trying to find some airspace. They were so close to me I could actually feel Ralph's body heat. My mind lingered on that for a second before I registered that I was in deep doo-doo. Their anger had nothing to do with me, I knew that, but still, I was great at feeling guilty and I did. I tried to rise above the crippling feelings because even though my heart was knocking loudly in my rib cage, I knew that in this scenario it would be best if I acted "as if." As if I had full right to be here. As if I knew what I was doing. As if I hadn't been to a crime scene unbidden. As if I had hadn't pretended I was someone else. I needed to be strong and powerful, not weak and ashamed.

I tucked some hair behind my ear and held out my hand, "Robin MacFarland. I believe we met earlier today. Ralph Creston, wasn't it?" I smiled playfully and tried to look impish and brazen at the same time.

"And Larry Stokes," piped up a thin voice from behind Creston, his head appearing from behind Creston's back. With fascination I watched the three bristles over his mouth twitch.

Creston's manners had the best of him. His smile met his eyes as he engulfed my hand for the second time today. Maybe he liked me. "Nice to meet you. Properly. So tell me, who are you and what were you doing at my crime scene?"

As he talked, I could see Radcliffe's apartment unfold behind his eyes. His demeanor changed rapidly and his irises returned to a hard slate. I watched him carefully as his inner film of the memory of our previous interaction played out. "And why were you impersonating a police officer?"

Impersonating a police officer was a very serious accusation. If charged, I could go to jail. With my smile now frozen on my face I continued on playing my "as if" game. I extricated my hand from his huge one and my heart thumped once and then seemed to stop altogether. I had to stop drinking; it was totally messing with my body.

"Ralph, Ralph, Ralph," I said, buying time, and hoping to sound coy, "I never once said I was a police officer, now did I?' I tried to use the tone I used when admonishing Lucky, slightly cajoling yet firm. "You came to your conclusions all on your own. I can't help what assumption you and your staff made." I started enjoying myself. It was sort of fun to be feisty.

Larry Stokes bobbed his head again. A doughy crumb was

embedded in his mustache. My stomach turned. I tried not to look at it.

On the whole, I felt I was doing well, Creston seemed to be listening, so on I prattled, "You know what they say about the word 'assuming'—it makes an ass out of you and me."

I noticed a slight sag of his football player's shoulder as he acquiesced to my logic. He took a deep breath and looked at me, deadpan. "What were you doing there?"

I finally came clean. "I'm a reporter with the *Express* and was assigned the story on Everwave—you know—the opening of the valves ceremony. That was Monday but the story just came out today. Maybe you saw it? When my editor heard this morning that Radcliffe had died, it was natural that I be assigned to the follow up story."

So I'd left out a few details.

Creston took in my story, listening without moving, his unyielding grey eyes locked onto mine. It was like I was standing in front of a Mac truck. I could almost hear the engine turning the machine of his brain, heading towards me.

"How did you get in to my crime scene?"

"It was a snap," I boasted. But when I saw the skin around his eyes tighten I quickly dropped the smug routine. I had to remember, I was in big trouble. I had been caught in a sort-of lie and I had to talk my way out of it.

"I held my press pass in my hand so that it was barely visible and didn't give the cop guarding the scene time to look at it. I stood up straight and said "Toronto, mumble mumble, investigations."

"And just like that you were in."

"Yup."

Creston turned to Stokes and made a writing motion with one hand, the gesture indicating that Stokes should make a note to talk to the rookie who had been so lax in his duties. Stokes fumbled in his pocket, found his phone and started tapping.

"And how did you know which apartment?"

"I Googled the white pages. From my phone. In my car while I was figuring out how to get in."

Creston harrumphed and scrunched up his lower lip while he thought. His eyebrows flattened, defeated, and his head tilted to the right. All made sense, his facial expression said. I took a deep breath and let the butterflies in my stomach settle down.

Cops had been coming and going around us while I was being grilled by Creston. The rhythm of the room had been barely interrupted by the three of us standing by the metal bench near the front door. The two cops had gotten so close to me, that I had backed up and could now feel the cold steel of the bench digging into the backs of my knees. Coffee was being poured and computers were being worked. Suddenly the door that Creston and Stokes had barreled from was opened and a round man with a balding head and sloping shoulders came out, his sleeves rolled up and a piece of paper in his hand. He had an iguana tattoed on his forearm. This was probably Stapleton, the head honcho of this shop.

"Robin MacFarland?"

"Yes, that's me," I said tentatively.

"You given your statement yet?"

"What statement?" asked Creston. His voice escalated. "Reporters don't give statements."

"Statement?" bobbled Stokes.

"No, sir," I answered.

"Come into my office," said Stapelton.

"Reporters don't give statements to the Staff Sergeant, either," exclaimed Stokes.

But I was already hightailing it into Stapleton's office and after a millisecond of hesitation, Creston and Stokes followed, close on my heels. Stapleton acknowledged them with a warning. "No more pissing matches. One a day is my limit. It might be your crime scene but this is *my* witness." He grudgingly let them into his sanctuary.

As Stapleton edged sideways behind his scratched metal desk, the remaining three of us juggled for real estate in the tiny office. The police budget looked a little tight if this was how they treated the boss. Creston settled his firm butt on a bar stool, smack in the centre of the miniature urban sprawl. Sidekick Stokes stuffed his lumpy ass onto the comparative broad field of a leather chair, obviously bequeathed by a demolished hotel lobby. I stood leaning against a bookcase.

I was proud of my location. No one knew better than I did the value of positioning. Location location location. I should have been a real estate agent. I could be putting together mega deals for condo developments along St. Clair or the Distillery District. I would drive a fancy silver car with a built in GPS system and an indoor temperature gauge, like Cindy's. Surround-sound speakers. Bluetooth this and that, whatever Bluetooth was. A Mercedes. But no, the reality was I was such a lonely, old, fat alcoholic who was such a failure that I had even screwed up internet dating. How does one even achieve that? How had pushing "send" end up here? I *had* to stop drinking. Had the naturopath emailed me back? It would be rude to check my phone, here, of all places.

Stapleton pulled out a well-thumbed notebook from his inside breast pocket and poised a pen above it. He was going to *write?* His single bushy eyebrow did a rap dance maneuver as he looked questioningly at me. I shifted back and forth on my feet. "Well?" he said. When I didn't manage to speak, he repeated, "Well?" and tapped his pen on his notebook. "Well?"

I could only think of that old joke about the three holes in the ground; well, well, well. I tried not to laugh and smoothed my hands down my sides. My palms stuck to my pants. What was that material anyway? Polyester? Was I really wearing polyester stretch pants? Geez, I was getting so decrepit. No, I consoled myself, everyone wore polyester these days. Wool pants were out. Unless you were rich and thin and shopped at Holt Renfrew on Bloor Street. Then you wore camel-coloured wool and satin-lined pants with oxblood-coloured boots and a matching bag.

Stapleton cleared his throat. He was becoming impatient.

My brain felt pillaged. "I really don't know where to begin. It's a fairly long story."

"Okay." He exhaled and stood up, his bald head acquiring a row of horizontal lines reflected from the fluorescent tubes above. "Let's go to an interview room, where there's a table and chairs for everyone."

Like meek sheep the three of us followed him out of his office with me sandwiched between Stapleton and Creston. The air between me and Creston felt like thick cotton wool filled with miniscule sparks of electricity. I let myself think "Zowie" for a minute. We paraded down a long hall, past some administration offices, and stopped in front of a room that had a grey metal door and a window filled with high impact glass interwoven with wire. Stapleton pulled out a silver key and thrust it into the lock on the brushed stainless handle. It opened smoothly. He stepped aside and nodded for us to enter ahead of him.

As I walked by the window in the door I flashed back to my long ago—very long ago—days, at Harbord Collegiate. There was a window exactly like this one on the door leading into the cafeteria in the basement. I remembered how one day the quarterback from the football team—what was his name anyway?—lost his temper and smashed his fist into the glass. The shattered window hung together with wires, the star-burst fracture remaining for at least a month before it was replaced. I remembered how the sunlight from the cafeteria refracted through the broken glass, making pretty pastel prisms on the stairs leading into the lunch room.

The screech of a metal chair scraping the tiled floor snapped me back into the present. I skirted around the table to the chair that Stapleton had pulled out for me and was standing behind, waiting patiently for me to sit down. He then sat on the other side of the table and stared at me. I could feel him looking at me looking at the handcuff hook on the table in front of me. It had caught my eye. I had never in my life seen a handcuff hook. Sure, I'd read about them in mysteries, when lawyers go into prisons and their clients are handcuffed to the table, but no, I had never actually seen one. It seemed so flimsy, just a piece of curved metal bolted down. Was it secure? I was dying to give it a shake, to see if it jiggled. It looked like the screws were loose. I tore my mind back into the present. This was serious business.

Stokes was sitting across the table as well, his chair slightly angled towards me. Creston leaned against a wall and when I glanced at him I thought he gave me a look. It had been years, decades, since I had dated anyone, and had no idea what the look meant. If there had been one at all. Was it a come-hither look? Was it a "I want to *you-know-what* to you" look? Or, was it simply a "Don't worry, you're not in trouble" look? Perhaps it was an "I'm hungry and want some donuts" look. I tried not to scrunch up my eyes as I figured out what the look meant. He smiled at me and I tried not to pay attention to the slow burn creeping up inside me.

This was the most sex I'd had in years!

My attention was drawn back to Stapleton by the soft sound of his pen scraping across a page in his notebook. What on earth was he writing? I hadn't even started my story yet. I leaned forward to see the page. He had carefully written "Robin McFarland: Statement" and the date. One of my few talents was the ability to read upside down and I decided not to correct the spelling of my name because then he would know that I could read what he was writing. I might be able to get more info if he was unguarded. The benefit of this ability to read upside down was offset by the mild dyslexia that came with it, but hey, I had survived the fiasco in the elevator.

I glanced at my surroundings. In one corner, the corner opposite to where the ever so handsome Creston was leaning, was a video camera on a tripod. A light underneath the lens was blinking off and on. I hadn't seen Stapleton turn it on and wondered if it were activated when the door was unlocked. Was this station high tech enough for that? Or, had I been daydreaming and simply missed him switching it on? And how did I look? I tossed my head and tried to muss the top of my hair with my fingers. No skunk stripe down my part recorded permanently on film for me.

The table was scarred by cigarette burns and stains. The handcuff hook was worn with the edges gouged. The screws did look a little loose. I briefly calculated the age of the table back to a time long ago time when people were allowed to smoke in public places. Twenty years? Ten? At one end of the table was a black, scruffy tape recorder, again, already turned on. I hadn't noticed that happening either.

Forget the handcuff hook, it was me who had a few screws loose.

This was all very somber. Here I was: a reporter whose most exciting story in the last year was about an unusual shade of turquoise in gerbera's created by a florist in a Dutch greenhouse. How could it be that I was sitting in front of a Staff Sergeant and not one but two recording devices? I resolved to not let my mind wander again anywhere, especially not over Ralph Creston's trim body. When I did that nothing else seemed to compute. Recording machines were turned on and I didn't even know how or when. I looked up into Stapleton's brown eyes. Were they cruel? No, hard to read, but certainly not nasty.

"Okay," said Stapleton, when he saw he had my attention, "tell me about your romantic involvement with Todd Radcliffe." He looked at me with a not unkindly expression on his face, pen poised.

Creston leaned forward.

14.

"WHAT WOULD YOU LIKE TO KNOW? Where should I begin?" I sat back in my chair and tried to look innocent, waiting for Stapleton to ask me a litany of questions. He also sat back in his chair and looked like he was waiting for me to speak. Was this a standoff? Stokes, too, sat back in his chair, a smirk twisting the corners of his mouth. Everyone was sitting back in their chairs and waiting for someone's mouth to open. Except for Creston, who was leaning with his back against the window frame, looking hot.

If this was a psychological game of chicken, I knew I shouldn't be playing. Ultimately I would look stupid because there was no doubt that they would win. Did I truly think I could put one over the Staff Sergeant? In an instant he could get me in a head lock and make my eyes bulge out if he wanted to. They did that on TV. Maybe not in Canada? I could only hope. Were those recorders on? What did flashing lights mean, anyway? On or off? Did I need a lawyer?

"I am not sure where to begin." My fingers were fidgeting. Playing with the damn handcuff hook for heaven's sake. I put my hands in my lap and held them there. But then I remembered a training session on journalistic interviewing techniques. The instructor was vehement: keep your hands visible at all times, otherwise you'll look like you're hiding something. So, I put my hands back on the table, palms flat, hoping they wouldn't leave sweat marks when I moved them.

"Begin at the beginning," chirped Stokes. His breath wafted over the table and smelled like stale coffee and cigarettes.

I addressed the air above Stapleton's head. "I'm a reporter for the Home and Garden section of the *Express* and about two weeks ago, or maybe it was ten days, or perhaps a week…" I faltered here; already this wasn't going well. I am not good with time.

Creston interjected, "We can check, whatever it is you are about to say, so don't worry about being 100 percent accurate."

"Thanks," I gave him a look of relief, "I am not that good with time. And the tape recorder is making me jumpy. Is it on?" No one answered me. I guessed that meant yes. "Anyway, a while ago there were no good flower shows or interior design shows or new condo's or specialty flowers to report on so my editor, or maybe it was me, chose this convention, well, anyway, I ended up going to this conference, well, actually a convention, about deep lake water cooling systems. There's a pump in the middle of the lake, figuratively speaking, not really the middle, closer to shore, that pumps cold water into pipes that cool downtown buildings. There are a few steps in between the lake and the buildings, but that is the general gist of it." I was babbling.

"We know about Everwave's activities and the various stages of the cooling process and building locations." In contrast to my blabber, Stapleton was the voice of reason. He spoke calmly and wasn't sounding impatient, or at least not yet.

Creston shifted on his feet, over by the window. Was he irritated by me? No, he was trying to see what was going on in the street below. I could see chest hair at the neck of his open shirt. I snapped a mental picture to review later. That's enough Robin, put your focus on the here and now.

"They have a pretty good brochure explaining it all. I have one here." I dug deep into my purse, pawing through all my junk for the glossy brochure I had picked up from the convention, hoping I hadn't thrown it out. I knew this wasn't likely, as clearly I hadn't cleaned out my purse in a decade. Finally, after much embarrassing rustling that sounded like a nest of snakes had taken up residence in my bag, I felt the silky surface of the brochure with my fingers. As I put it on the table in front of Stapleton, a small insert of Todd's face looked back at me from the pipe covered first page. He was such a hunk.

I had to get over all my man crazy thoughts. After all, this guy was *dead*.

Stapleton didn't even look at it and tossed me a sympathetic look. "We know you were there. You don't have to prove it. We have the records of everyone in attendance." He flicked the brochure back to me with a neatly trimmed nail. Now he was getting impatient.

"Well, anyway," I shoved the brochure back into my purse. "That's when I first met him."

"You actually met him there?" Stapleton's eyebrows had shot up.

"Well, no, I didn't meet him, *meet him*, I just saw him, so I knew what he looked like. I saw him on the stage."

"Who else did you know at the convention?" This was from Stokes. I wasn't sure if I should answer, he was such a junior minion, but the next few sentences of my statement, the ones about what happened next, were ones I wanted to avoid. These were the sentences about going on an internet dating site while pie-eyed drunk and sending off a contact email. Luckily Stapleton gave me a nod, indicating I should answer Stokes. I had a reprieve for a few moments anyway.

"My best friend Cindy, short for Cynthia, from the paper, was there. She was covering the environmental angle. I was covering the interior space, air conditioning angle." Hmmm. That sounded good.

Stapleton was writing. "Last name?" When he looked up for me to continue, I could see he was thinking "airhead."

For the life of me I couldn't remember Cindy's last name. I'd only known her for a few decades. I probed into the dark and mushy caverns of my brain, desperately looking for this tidbit of information and of course, the more frantic I became, the least likely it would be that I would remember it. I had to get in to see that naturopath. Why hadn't she called back yet? Note to self: call again.

I gushed and laughed, I hoped with childlike innocence, "Do you ever know something inside and out and then, suddenly, you can't remember it at all? Well," I playfully laughed again here, "that seems to be the problem with me right now. I simply can't remember it." My head started humming, bizarrely, that camp song, "*Over hill, over dale, we will hit the something trail...*" and then I blasted out the word "Dale. Her name is Cynthia Dale." I felt so smart.

Stapleton looked up and snarled, "Oh, *her*." He made a note, his pen pushing hard into the paper.

I started to talk faster. "There was also a guy there from a rival paper, the *Toronto Times*. Jack England. He's a crime reporter, sometimes sports. Journalism degree from Carlton. Thin."

"Interesting. He's a crime reporter." Stapleton looked thoughtful.

"Yes, I wondered about that too. It was a valve opening ceremony, not a court case or anything."

Stapleton turned to Creston, "Did you get that? Crime reporter at the *Times*. England. I think we should talk to him." Creston nodded and I could see him absorbing the information.

I rushed in, remembering how he had forced me into a construction zone, "Yeah, well if you do, tell him to not assault women."

Creston stopped leaning against the wall and took a step towards me. "He assaulted you? How?"

Although it would be nice to skim over the drunken stupor bit that was coming up next, and jump right to his question, I knew my messy life bits had to be revealed. I had to tell the story in chronological order. I bantered, "I'm getting to that."

Stapleton interjected, bringing the conversation back, "So you knew Cynthia Dale and Jack England at the convention. Both crime reporters. Then what?"

Then I went home and got drunk and made an internet date with the dead guy, not knowing it was him. Not a pretty story.

"Well," I decided to play what usually worked, the grieving widow card. "My husband died several years ago, drunk driver, not him, the guy who hit him, and I had recently been thinking about dating again." Already I could feel the slow burn of a bright red blush inching up my neck. I couldn't look at Creston. "So, I was flipping through a dating site on the internet and reading profiles of some guys around my age, checking them out, looking at their pictures." I sounded like a porn stalker.

Stokes snickered.

I pushed on. "Anyways, I posted my profile and some of them contacted me. There was this one profile and the guy sounded interesting, sort of my type. So, he wrote me, I emailed him back, I sent him a time and a place, and we made a plan."

"And it was Todd Radcliffe," said Stapleton. Not a question.

"I didn't know it was Todd Radcliffe when I made the plan." I felt defensive. "If I had known, I wouldn't have agreed to meet him."

"Wait a sec," puzzled Stapleton, "two things here: first of all, why didn't you know it was Radcliffe if you'd met him before? Second, why wouldn't you have agreed to see him?"

"His profile had no photo. He was just 'Mr. Sail Away.'" I made finger quotes. "But when I realized I didn't know what the guy I was talking to, I mean emailing, looked like, I asked him for a photo. He sent me one and lo and behold, it was Todd Radcliffe. I nearly died. He had put me off at the convention, sexist, you know, and a bit smarmy, even though he was good looking, but I probably wouldn't have wanted to meet him if I had known it was him. Plus, I had a story coming out, highly critical of the cooling system, and that would make our meeting awkward, to say the least."

"So, let's unpack all this information and get it straight. Let's start with the profile. Was there anything in his profile that jumped out at you. Anything that would explain why someone was after him? Any hints that he had ties with other countries?"

I scrambled through the shipwreck of that night, looking for any flotsam floating around in his profile. "He called himself, 'Mr. Sail Away,'" I said again, oh so helpfully. "But other than that, it was the usual stuff, like number of kids, where he went to school, well, that was in the United States, so there's that foreign connection, if that's what you're looking for, although it was decades ago. Anyway, the profile said that he was easy going, fun loving, what sort of work he did, you know."

"Okay." Stapleton, put his hand up for me to stop while he finished writing what I'd sputtered. "You didn't know what the guy looked like but you agreed to meet him."

"Yes, that's the way it happened, at first."

Stapleton tilted his head and questioned me. "Really?" He didn't believe me.

I wanted to shout "I was pissed outa my gourd," but held my ground. "Yes, really." I sounded demure, I thought, and the worst was almost over. For some reason I didn't want Creston to know I had a drinking problem. "Then I asked him for a photo, he sent it to me, and then I knew that I knew the guy."

'So where did you meet?"

"At the Starbucks at Bloor and Avenue Road. Behind that church on the corner."

"So, even though you knew you didn't actually like Radcliffe, you went anyway. Why?"

"Curiosity," I lied. *Because he turned me on, such a cute ass.* I was trying to keep the story simple.

"What was he wearing?"

"Khaki-coloured pants. Chino's I think you call them. Is

that how you say it? Americans wear them a lot. He went to school in the States. Oh, I said that. Loafers. Docksiders. And no socks. And a blue shirt, sleeves rolled up. A tie. A blazer. Glasses with no rims."

"Sounds like you got a pretty good look."

I blushed again. "I pay attention. It's my job to notice the details. Colours. Shapes. You know…" I drifted off, sounding lame.

Stapleton didn't look up from what he was writing. Why on earth was the Staff Sergeant taking my statement anyway? Surely it was below his pay grade. First the important guys from another division, whatever their ranks were. And now the Staff Sergeant. What on earth was going on?

"And then what happened?"

"He got the coffees, actually I had tea, mint, I don't do the caffeine thing after lunch, too much stimulation."

"You don't say," observed Stapleton wryly. Stokes tittered. Creston frowned. Maybe an ally?

"We talked, and then—"

"Talked about what?" Stapleton interjected.

"About *him*. He was so self-centred. Didn't ask me a single question. Well, not at first. Then he did. Kids, where we lived, he'd said he didn't smoke on his profile, but he did."

"So, he lied to you?" Stapleton looked affronted, as if Radcliffe had personally lied to him.

I rushed to Todd's defense. He was dead, after all. "Everyone lies on those profiles."

"They do?" Stapleton probably was a married guy and had never checked out internet dating sites. "What did *you* lie about?" He bent over his notebook. It looked like his hand was cramping. Maybe he didn't take too many statements.

"I said I didn't drink, but I do, of course, everyone does."

"How much do you drink?"

"I wasn't drunk at the time, if that's what you're asking."

"I'm asking how much do you drink?"

As much as I can. "A little wine with dinner, maybe a glass or two later in the evening."

He looked satisfied. My hands were certainly sweating now. I worried if I moved them they'd squeak on the Formica table top. Just what I needed to preserve my dignity.

"And then?"

"We parted."

"Kiss?"

"Handshake." I tried to sound prim. But then I remembered the electrical current that had passed between us when our hands had touched. How he had turned around to look at me at the exact same time I had turned around. Anyway, what did it matter now, dead was dead.

"So, you parted ways. Did you have a plan to get together in the future?"

Why did he need to know that? Oh, to discount the suicide theory. "Yes, a dinner for next week."

"What night?"

"Tuesday."

"Where?"

"He was going to email me with the plan."

"No input from you?"

"He wasn't that kind of guy." When I said this I saw Creston shift in the corner of my eye. What did that mean? Was he more egalitarian?

"Okay, so you parted with a handshake and then what happened?"

"I was nabbed from behind by Jack England and he forced me into that construction zone beside the hotel. On Bloor."

"Jack England? He was there? Interesting." He looked up at me, "That was probably frightening." Stapleton sounded so factual as he wrote my answer down with his head bent over his notebook, but when he looked up at me again I saw his brown eyes were empathetic.

I remembered how scared I was with the scaffolding and scrap heaps of lumber all around me. "Yes. It was. He pinned me against a brick wall and wanted some information from me."

"Did he have a weapon?"

"No, just his strength."

"He's a big guy?"

Creston butt in. "No, not really, tall, yes, but thin, a bike rider type." I saw him snort with derision and flex his bicep. Guys.

"You know him?" Stapleton asked Creston.

"England? He mostly writes on crime, some international coverage, terrorism. But he's a skinny guy. Wiry. Probably stronger than he looks."

Stapleton looked back at me after acknowledging Creston's summary of England's physical body type. "So, you were scared but not worried he was going to harm you."

"No, nothing like that. I could push him away. And I did." I remembered the feel of his tight chest muscles under my fingers.

"What was the information he wanted to know from you?"

"He said, 'I need to find out what you're up to.' He said those exact words. It's part of my job to memorize what people say. I'm good at it."

"Okay, so he said that. Anything else?" Stapleton was writing rapidly.

"Um." After my saying I had virtually a sound bite memory, I couldn't remember what else England had said. Of course that would happen now. I looked down at the flecks of grey in the Formica tabletop and replayed the scene in my mind. It came back to me. "He also said, 'Don't fuck with me, Robin. Why are you meeting with Radcliffe?'"

"What did you reply?"

"I asked him why he was following me. Then he said he wasn't, that he was following Radcliffe. Then he asked me why I was seeing him, I told him it was only a date. Then he warned me off him, saying he was dangerous and I remember ridiculing the suggestion. I said Todd was a Harvard-type goody two shoes."

"How did it end?"

"I asked him why he was following Radcliffe. Todd."

Both Creston and Stapleton leaned forward, "What did he say?" They asked in unison.

I didn't know who to face, but the answer was simple. "He said nothing. Turned on his heel and left. He warned me off Radcliffe. Kicked a garbage can and said 'Rob-BIN.'"

Stokes chuckled as if making a note of the pun for future reference. Creston rolled his eyes.

"And you said…"

"I think I said something like 'You too, Jack-OFF.'"

Stapleton frowned as he wrote it down. "And then you went where?"

"Home. Of course."

Anybody see you when you got home?"

"My dog." Not much of an alibi.

Stapleton shut his notebook and said, "Okay, I'm going to get this typed up and an officer will bring it to you at work to sign as your statement. If you think of anything else, *yada yada yada*." He slid his card across the table.

"Who should I call, sir? You or Creston?"

Stokes bristled because he'd been left out.

"Me. Creston. Doesn't matter."

Hmm, I thought, Creston. I'd think of something. "Thanks."

Creston handed me his card as well and we all filed out of the stuffy interview room, one after another. In the busy main room of the station Stapleton turned to me and held out his hand. "Thanks for coming in and not yelping for a lawyer. We got the job done quickly and I doubt you had a hand in Radcliffe's death, whatever caused it. Could be a suicide or maybe a murder by an international crime ring for our fresh water. Maybe it was natural causes. We have to investigate all the possibilities. We've been watching him. He had an important job and he knew a main source for our water supply. So it easily could have been an attack on him with some sort of biological agent. Creston's requested full tox."

Stapleton's mind seemed made up, but I doubted his theories. Radcliffe was a happy-go-lucky kind of guy and too.... I didn't know the right adjective. Too clean? Simple? Ralph Lauren? Too something to be involved in terrorism. And theft of water? Nah. Sure, it was a hot issue, Canada having so much of it, but nope, not that guy. Something else was going on.

But thank heavens I was in the free and clear. Such a relief. "Nice to meet you too, Staff Sergeant Stapleton." I laughed to show that there was no harm done and then went out on a limb. "May the force be with you."

He looked at me strangely and then let out a huge bellow. He liked my joke. Then he peeled off from our small group to his office full of purpose, his leather heels snapping on the linoleum, his shiny head reflecting all the lights along his way. Creston guided me through the desks to the exit, his hand igniting the small of my back. We parted on Dundas Street, with Creston and Stokes heading to their five-year-old cop car, a scratched up Ford, and me standing on the corner, cellphone in hand, not wanting them to see my old banger. I would pretend I was checking my mail and wait until they were gone.

In the meantime, who should I call? Cindy? The office? No, the naturopath. This brain wandering thing had to go.

15.

WHAT AN AWFUL INTERVIEW. How embarrassing. How mortifying to admit to those people that I, an investigative crime reporter, well, sort of, went out with someone I hadn't fully researched. No wonder they asked me about the drinking. They probably guessed what was what. The drinking simply had to go. If I couldn't get in touch with the naturopath today, I would find an AA meeting somewhere. Tonight. Even if I didn't agree with their methods and had heard their success rate was pretty low, I would go to a musty church basement and take the first of my twelve steps.

What did Stapleton think was the cause of death? Natural, accident, suicide or homicide? Torture even. He had no idea. It seemed they were banking on the water theft angle as a motivation. And so, it appeared, was Jack England. I gave my head a shake to clear it. If this was a murder to facilitate the theft of our fresh water, whether by an international crime ring or by someone locally, and Radcliffe was involved, I would eat my hat. That Todd Radcliffe was too, too.... I could never find the right adjective. He was too *North Toronto*.

But still, I had to be careful. I was a *murder* suspect, for heaven's sake. Let them think what they wanted to. I knew I was innocent. I couldn't fight what they thought and had to have faith that the law would prevail. *Ha ha ha*. In the meantime, I could deal with my personal issues.

I darted along Dundas towards my car while burrowing in my bag for my keys. Thank heavens I had found a parking space fairly close to the station. I dodged around some dog poo. Wasn't there a fine for that? Then I remembered that I was now keeping my keys accessible, in the side pocket. Where I could find them easily. Too bad my brain wasn't conveniently in a side pocket somewhere. What was wrong with my memory?

Finally, with keys in hand, I held the phone up to my eyes and searched through my contacts for Sally Josper, the naturopath, and tapped her number with my thumb as I walked to my car that was parked across the road from the art gallery. What an idiotic architectural design, Noah's ark envy. She answered first ring.

"Josper." Her melodic voice announced her name with a distinctive underlying force. She even *sounded* healthy.

"Hi, it's Robin MacFarland, I was wondering if I could come in and see you, sometime soon." I fumbled about in my huge bag looking for heaven's knows what. My keys! Oh look! They were in my hand. This was bad. Maybe I had Alzheimer's. Why not add that to the list of things wrong with me?

"Actually Robin, I was just about to call you. I got your messages, and I am sorry that I didn't return them. I've been away on a silent retreat and didn't take my phone or computer. I just got back and now here you are! I've had a cancellation and I could see you in about ten minutes, if you have some free time. Otherwise it would have to be early next week."

Ten minutes? Next week was way better because tonight I was meant to be having pizza and wine with Cindy and my friend Diane Chu. But on the other hand, things were pretty bad with my mind, so, today would be better. Was I ready for this? It was such a big step. I loved my wine. Did I have to stop today? Maybe I wouldn't have to stop, wouldn't be able, and I could keep drinking. But I would tell people that I'd stopped. No, that wasn't the way to get it done. I had to be brutally honest.

I looked at my watch. I had time. The appointment could bleed into my lunch hour. "Sure, I'll be right there. See you shortly."

I waited impatiently in the naturopath's very beige waiting area for her to stick her nose out of her office and announce my name. I flipped through some magazines on eastern this and herbal that, pausing at a page for a second to look at a lotus flower floating on water. I loved it, but did that make me schmaltzy? It was such a common image. Then I started flipping through the pages again. The dangers of vaccinations. GMO foods. Sleeping aids. Organic clothing. So much work to be pure.

Finally the door opened and a woman walked out, sniffling and sneezing, wet with bacteria. I made a note not to touch anything as I heard Sally spraying some sort of aerosol in her office. Finally she stuck out her head. Sally was small, even shorter than I was, about the size of a ten-year-old, with her curly black hair shaved about an inch long.

I dropped my bag at the foot of the chair beside her desk and sat down. "What's that spray you use?"

"You mean after someone is here? It's an air purifying spray. How are you?"

Right to the point, that was Sally. I worried her air purifying spray would make my asthma kick up. "I drink too much."

I could match her point by point.

"Oh?" She didn't sound surprised. "How much do you drink?" She was writing in her file, looking down, fine lines in her light brown skin deepening in concentration as she wrote.

"As much as I can." Although the line was getting old, I kept using it. I thought it was funny.

She smiled and looked up at me. "And how often?"

"As often as I can."

This time she didn't smile. "What do you drink?'

"Anything that has alcohol in it. Wine. Beer, Liquor. Mostly wine."

And now she frowned. "Do you drink during the day?"
"No, only at night. After work."
"Hangovers?"
"No." I fibbed.
"Memory issues?"
"Major." I decided lying wouldn't help. "And yes, I have hangovers."
"Don't worry, your brain cells will regenerate."
Sally was busily taking notes with her petite right hand. That was twice today that people took notes while I talked. I flashed back to Creston leaning his lithe body against the window frame of the interview room.
"How are you feeling in general?"
"Fine, mostly, a little crabby. Distracted. My mind wanders. I'm trying to make some changes."
"Sounds like not drinking would be a place to start."
"I don't know how to stop. Can you help me with this?"
Sally sat back and ran her fingers through her wiry hair. It stood straight up, making her look electrified. "Sure I can. But you are going to have to do a few little things."
"Like stop," I laughed.
Her flashing brown eyes smiled. "Not yet. Every morning when you wake up I want you to think of three things you are grateful for."
"You mean like, 'I'm grateful for my children,' or 'I'm grateful that I'm not hungry?'"
"Absolutely. Be grateful for the details of life, things you don't usually take time to notice."
"My dog's soft fur?"
"Yes, exactly, like that."
"Or, the sound of wind in the trees?"
"Yes, that's exactly what I mean."
I was puzzled. "And the drinking?"
"Oh, don't worry about that." Sally waved her hand dismissively in the air and shut my file.

"But I want to stop drinking." I was completely flummoxed.

"Don't worry, you will." Sally stood up and ushered me to the door. "Come back next week after you've done your homework. Every morning when you wake up. Three things you are grateful for. Make sure you actually feel the gratitude."

I shook my head as I walked past her and out the door. "Okay-y-y-y," I said doubtfully. "Thanks, Sally, see you next week."

I got out to the street and searched for my car. Where had I left it? Oh there, across the road. Brain cells regenerate, do they? Good thing. I had forgotten to pay her. Oh well, I'll catch up next time. Three things. How on earth would that stop me from drinking? I had better hurry back to the office. I stepped over a Tim Horton's coffee cup in the gutter. That was the shortest appointment on earth. I could even get back before lunch and talk to Cindy about my interview.

When I pushed through the glass door of the fifth floor of the *Express* building I could see that almost everyone was at their desks, heads turned towards computers and fingers tapping wildly. What was going on? The next edition wasn't for hours yet. A long fluorescent light flickered in the far corner, promising a migraine to anyone who was light sensitive. Cindy's red hair shone like a flaming beacon in the middle of the room, beside my empty desk. I sauntered over.

Cindy didn't look up as I eased myself into my chair. "So, what's up? Where've you been?" she whispered out of the side of her mouth.

I looked around to see why she was being so secretive and saw that Shirley's door was shut and the blinds were down. But Doug's door was shut too. That was strange.

"What's going on?" I asked.

"There's a new video of the mayor giving a group of kids the finger while stoned and drunk. Unbelievable. It's just been released by the judge. Shirley, Doug, and Sampson are huddled in Shirley's office, watching it. Morrison is in there too. All the poo-bahs." Catherine Sampson was the paper's publisher and Paul Morrison the main legal council, Russell Whetstone's boss. "No idea when Sampson is going to be coming out, but she will be revved and we all want to look like we're on our toes. Story of the decade. Right up there with that video of the police beating up that guy at the G-8."

If the police were right and Todd's death had something to do with the theft of Canada's fresh water, *that* would be the story of the decade. And it would be *my* story. But I didn't think this was the case. He wasn't the type. Not that I knew what the type was. I said, "The finger? Really?"

"I haven't seen it, but if I had to guess, he's probably being a drunken idiot, behaving like a five-year-old." Cindy rolled her eyes. Toronto's mayor had been in the news for weeks. It was getting tedious.

"Gave my statement to the police."

Cindy jerked her head up, her big green eyes full of curiosity, "How did it go?"

I swiveled my hand back and forth from the wrist. "We'll see. I don't think they think I did it, but maybe." I rotated my chair towards my computer and ran my hand over the touch pad. The screen burst into life and I started to type, vigorously, like everyone else in the room.

"That's ridiculous. Of course you didn't do it. Word on the street is that it was an international hit over stealing our water."

"I don't think so, but thanks."

"You don't? Who interviewed you?" Cindy, being a crime reporter, knew most the cops.

"Well, that's what's so weird. Staff Sergeant Stapleton." I kept typing.

Cindy sat still. She was incredulous, her green eyes as round as saucers and her hair bobbing like a red ember in the light, "Wow. Stapleton? He's a big kahuna!"

"I *know*. Plus there were two other guys in the room as well. Creston and Stokes."

"I know those guys. Creston's a good guy, but Stokes?" Cindy smothered a laugh. "But something high level is going on, Robin. They're homicide detectives with an international specialty. Must have been brought in from their home division."

"They have no idea why he's dead. There's no outward clue. All of your NASH things were mentioned. They've ordered high level tox screens."

"They're treating it seriously, that's for sure, and that means there's something more than meets the eye."

"Anyway, I told them all about the convention, the internet site, the date, and even Jack England."

"Jack England? You didn't tell me about him. What's he got to do with anything?"

"Yeah, I did. Last night after my date with Radcliffe. I called you, remember? You were going to check him out for me?" By the look on her face I could tell that she hadn't remembered my call. I didn't think she would.

Cindy was apologetic. "Don't recall a thing about this."

"Well, I had woken you up. You had gone to bed early."

Cindy inclined her head as the memory sort of came alive, "Oh, right. Sorry about that. What he'd do?"

I looked at what I was typing. *The quick brown fox jumps over the lazy dog.* From the depths of my very first typing class in high school had risen the one line everyone had to type, and type quickly, to learn the keyboard. I could see Cindy's nose twitching for a story. I needed to show who was in control. I warned her, "This is off the record, Cindy. He accosted me in the street and wanted to know why I was meeting Radcliffe."

"He *what*?"

"Yeah, he pinned me to a wall and warned me off Radcliffe."

"What did you tell him?"

"To Jack-OFF."

Cindy laughed out loud this time. "You have such a gutter mouth, MacFarland."

So, she had sensed my warning and backed off.

I said, "It wasn't funny at the time." I remembered how my heart had been thumping and my shoulder blades digging into the wall.

"What else did the cops want to know?"

She was gasping for the story. I had to trust her not to scoop me. "They asked me why I agreed to see a guy I had never seen a photograph of."

"Did you tell them that you'd been drinking?"

"Of course not. How did you know?"

"Oh, pulleezze."

I had been reprimanded. "Yeah, they asked me how much I drank. I think they guessed."

"Did you tell them the truth?"

I went on the defense. "Listen, don't bug me about it, okay? I already saw the naturopath and I have begun treatment." I wondered if being grateful for three things in the morning counted as treatment.

Cindy looked impressed and untouched by my rebuke. "So, what do you have to do? Go to AA or something like that? Snap an elastic band that's on your wrist every time you want a drink? Count to fifty before raising a glass?"

I laughed, "No, she's helping me." How she was helping me I didn't want to say. I somehow wanted to keep this journey private. Plus, it sounded weird. Three grateful things?

A cloud crossed Cindy's face and she sucked in her lips. Cindy could handle professional rebukes. Personal rejection was another matter entirely. She knew she had been shut out. The lack of detail was her clue. Would she press the issue or let it go?

"Well, that's great Robin, I'm proud of you." Her bravado barely covered up her hurt feelings. But, she had let it go.

"Well, let's see how I do before we start saying hooray. I'm still allowed to drink, so tonight should be fun." My apology.

"Did you want to go for lunch?" Her acceptance.

"What about those guys in there? Shouldn't we look good

for when they come out?" My fingers had been flying over the keys while I talked to Cindy. I had filled a whole page with the activities of a very fast brown fox.

"Believe me, the mayor's antics aren't going to stop for some time. Those guys are going to be in and out of that office for weeks, trying to report the truth and not get sued."

"You're not on the story?"

"Are you nuts? Wouldn't touch it with a ten-foot pole. I have kids, you know, and I can't risk too much. I actually find it scary that a mayor is chumming up with the wrong kind of people. He's often in the wrong place at the wrong time. People he knows are getting murdered. He drinks like a fish. Besides, I wasn't assigned to it."

The truth was out. "He hasn't been charged with anything yet, right?"

Cindy looked a bit embarrassed. For all her spouting off, she was a firm believer in that old maxim, innocent until proven guilty. "Not yet, but where there's smoke, there's fire, right?"

"Yeah, that's what I'm worried the police will think about me."

Cindy laughed, "You're hot sistah, but not that hot!"

Suddenly Shirley's door opened and I sped up my typing. A herd of dark suited people spilled into the newsroom. It looked like a football scrum that had gone cuckoo, with the players scattering off the field, heads down and charging through the defense in all directions. Cindy and I both were typing like crazy, along with everyone else. Feverish human industry hummed. And then the suits were gone, leaving in their wake a vacuum that filled slowly with silence. A thrum of quiet descended upon the room as everyone stopped their frenetic typing. Faces looked up, questions framed by raised eyebrows.

Shirley bopped out of her office behind the lingering smell of power and sashayed through the rows of desks to what was called The Speaker's Corner. The Speaker's Corner was a raised area of the room towards the back, where the coffee machine perked away on a makeshift kitchen counter over some built in cupboards. She turned slowly, leaned her buttocks against the counter, and faced the room while running her hands over her hips, smoothing the wrinkles out of her tight faux-silk skirt. She was going to make an announcement.

"You will soon find in your inbox a link to a video of the mayor of this fine city, Toronto The Good, ranting away. He is weaving and bobbing up and down a street and gesturing wildly, flipping the bird left, right, and centre, most notably to some kids playing in the street."

Somebody hooted but Shirley seemed saddened by what she had seen. "This video will be shown, I am sure, worldwide, and will discredit the efforts our leaders have made, over the past decade, to put Canada on the international map as a country of some stature, and to demonstrate that we are not simply bimbos in flannel shirts drinking home brewed moonshine while waving chainsaws."

All the men in the room looked down, probably remembering the last time they had been drinking beer and cutting down trees. Shirley acknowledged the embarrassment. "What we do in our private time at the cottage is no one's business." There were some hesitant chuckles and then outright laughs as the tension left the room.

"The mayor of the city defies description, although the word 'asshole' comes to mind. We have assigned our toughest and most senior investigative reporters, Stanley Wong and Karen Marumbo, to this ongoing story, after the initial and comprehensive introductory coverage by Cynthia Dale."

Shirley pushed herself off the counter to launch her shapely form down the long aisle towards her office. Some of the male reporters watched her hips swaying through their eyelashes as they pretended to look at their screens. As she passed my station, her peter pointer tapped my desk and gesticulated towards her office.

I had been summoned. Oh geez, now what?

16.

SHIRLEY'S SIGNAL TO FOLLOW HER into her office set off an alarming series of bangs against my rib cage. I was getting seriously worried about my heart. Adrenalin surged through my body and I felt I was heading for some kind of disaster. What sort of attack would I have? Heart? Or anxiety?

I absurdly gathered up some things off my desk to take to my grilling and stuffed them into my bag like talismans. A gum wrapper, a tube of lipstick, a paper clip, and a six-inch ruler. As if these items would protect me from Shirley's wrath. She could be brutal and she was in a mood. I was certain the picture of her family in her office was face down.

But somewhere in the hamster wheel of my mind blossomed a new concept: I was not worthless. As it caught root and grew, I took a few breaths and came to a fresh resolve. I wasn't going to be a fading bloom in Shirley's office. Standing straight by my desk with the inane objects packed into my bag, I quickly reviewed the facts of my cop interview so I could be rock solid and forthright.

Shirley held her office door open for me and, briefly forgetting my resolution, I crept by her, head down, in shrinking violet fashion. I quickly held it up again. I was a new me, blast it! A lily. A hyacinth.

She shut the door and flounced around to her side of the desk, her eyes mowing me down with impatience. With a ringed hand and long fuchsia nails she gouged the air above one of her file-covered chairs. I was to sit down.

"As you now know," said Shirley, a smile on her face that did not quite reach her eyes, "we are very busy around here with concerns about the leadership of our city. The legal counsel, Paul Morrison is on it, so that we are factually accurate in everything we write and can't be sued by the mayor's office. Every word that goes out about that mayor must have Morrison's approval." As if suddenly remembering that I was in her office, she added, "You don't need to use him, or Russell Whetstone, do you? I mean, how did it go? At the police station?"

Given Shirley's grim mood, I decided to keep my answers upbeat. I pushed back a lock of hair that had fallen in my face. "It went well," I lied. "No problemo."

She gave me a harassed look. "So, you don't need Whetstone?"

"Nope. Everything's okay." I hope. I had better brief him about what was happening, in case I did need him to keep me out of jail, or bail me out. The thought of being in a jail with drug-addicted thieves and petty criminals terrified me. On the other hand, maybe I'd meet the mayor there and get an exclusive interview.

She seemed relieved. "Good. I've briefed him on the situation so at least if you do need him, he won't be surprised."

One less chore for me.

"Great, thanks for your support Shirley. Anything else I need to know? Should I bring Doug up to date?"

Shirley was already at her computer screen, eyes straining at the type. She was absent-mindedly searching for her glasses through the wreckage on her desk. Her fingers joggled goodbye as she was looking at her computer. I took the hint.

Now what? Did I go to Doug's office and report on my police encounter, or did my meeting with Shirley cover all the bases? Oh, what the hell. He was my boss, at least on this article, so I should have gone to him first and not to Shirley at all. I held my hand up at Doug's door and then, summoning all my courage, rapped twice as smartly as I could. My nerves sizzled all over my body.

"Yes," Doug yelled.

I jumped out of my skin. Geez. Why did he have to do that?

"Robin, Robin, Robin," he sang, Mr. Cordiality. "Have a seat. How did it go at the police station? I see you are still a free woman." Doug ran his hand through his thinning hair, fiddling with a few strands to cover his bald spot. He smiled broadly, his new dental caps glowing an eerie mauve, like a neon zipper at a disco.

I laughed, matching his forced camaraderie, "So far still footloose and fancy free. Doug, that's me. It went pretty well, thanks." I was playing with a toggle on my purse. Stop it! Put my hands in my lap.

"Hmmm," he put his hands in front of him on the desk, in a sideways teepee, fingers pointing towards me. "Did they ask you how you initially met Todd Radcliffe?"

So, the third degree. "Yes, I told them that I had been at the valve opening ceremony for the deep lake cooling system and knew him first there."

"Did you actually meet at the convention? And what do you mean 'first'? Was there a 'second?' Bring me up to speed here."

I settled in for the long haul. He was going to get every detail out of me. "In answer to your first question, sir, no, we didn't actually meet at the convention. He was speaking on a podium and I asked him some questions during the question period at the end.

"And what were your impressions of him?"

Did I tell the truth or fudge around? The best bet would be to tell the truth. "He was physically a very attractive male specimen." Was that too clinical? "But I didn't like him much."

"Why not?" Doug leaned forward, interested.

"Well, he was sexist, for one, he was demeaning and dismissive towards Cindy and me, didn't take our questions seriously, and for another..." I paused, wondering how to explain the look in Todd's eye that had spooked me. "His eyes glinted," I said. It sounded so feeble.

Doug didn't laugh. "Glinted," he repeated. "Glinted how, Robin? What was your gut feeling?"

"Something seemed off, like he was dishonest or something. Hiding something. But I put it down to the lighting in the room. Bouncing off his eyes, you know what I mean?"

Doug creaked his chair backwards. "Always trust your first impressions, Robin. It had nothing to do with the light, which was your second thought. Your first hunch that he was dishonest, perhaps a criminal of some kind, is probably the correct thought. You have good instincts, obviously. Follow them."

I was puzzled. I hadn't done a thing to earn this praise. I went out on a limb. "Why do you say that?"

Now Doug laughed, "Well, he's dead, isn't he? He must have been involved in something not kosher. It's your job to find out what."

"Oh." Of course. Why was I so stupid?

Doug continued, his mouth flapping away, while I chastised myself for saying I was stupid. Looked like I was in for a lecture. I settled further down in my chair.

"When you are an investigative reporter you need to find all the facts and then put them into a story that makes sense. You aren't allowed to come to conclusions on paper. No, no, no, Robin, that would get everyone in trouble. But, you have to lead people, ever so subtly, to an idea of what everything means. Juxtapose your facts. For example, this mayor business," Doug pointed a finger at me. "He said he hadn't been drunk for over a year, so we report that. The police, on the other hand, have the video we just saw, time-stamped, showing the mayor dancing a wild jig while flipping the bird at kids playing on the street. So, we report that too. In the very next sentence. We don't say the mayor is a liar, no no. But by juxtaposing the facts, people can draw their own conclusions. See how it works?"

"Yes, sir." I was feeling small. This world was very new to me.

"I'm going to help you with this. You will do well, don't look so worried."

I relaxed my face even though my heart was hopping around in my chest. Again the question: anxiety, or a heart attack?

"Let's look at some of the facts. First of all, what do we know about the deep lake cooling system?"

Because I had written an article about it, I knew my facts. "Well," I took a deep breath as I organized my thoughts into a summary, "a very large pump was put out into the middle of the lake and secured to the bottom and—"

"By whom? Who exactly put out the pump?"

I squirmed. I vaguely remembered something about a captain of a ship. "I don't know."

"Okay, write down the question in your notebook."

I assumed he meant my iPad. I opened a new file and typed in the question.

"Okay, now go on."

I could see this was going to take ages. I was starving. Didn't Doug eat lunch? "This pumps water to a cooling station where the coldness of the water is extracted." I waited for him to interrupt. He didn't disappoint.

"Where is the cooling station and what happens to the water once the coldness is extracted?"

Being too stressed by all this to actually answer all the questions—I did know the answers, or most of them—I made a show of dutifully typing in the questions, then continued my recitation of the facts I knew. "From there, the very cold water is pumped through pipes into some downtown buildings to cool them down. The excess water is diverted to peoples' homes." This was a very condensed version of the operation of the system.

"Which buildings?" He was relentless.

I typed that question into my growing list and continued. I

must have looked impatient. I didn't remember sighing, but perhaps I had.

"Every single fact is important." Doug admonished me, deadly serious. "You know something, Robin. You probably even know who the killer is, if he was killed. The answer to his death lies in the facts that you know." He held his hand up in a stop gesture. Or perhaps it was a blessing. "You must be very careful. Somebody might figure out that you know something. That even if you haven't figured out what that something is, you might."

"I understand," I nodded, trying to sound blasé. I was used to my life being threatened. I had survived four teenagers, hadn't I? "We were told at the convention by Todd Radcliffe that the system was better than the air conditioning systems already in place in the event of a power outage. With this new system, people could continue to work. He said the people of the city would have purer drinking water. We were also told that this new system would save a great deal of energy."

"Hogwash. If there is a power outage, then the pumps won't pump. People can't get up to their offices or have light to see by. The 'people can still work' argument is a non-starter. I'm assuming the old pipes were lead and the new ones are plastic. Is plastic safer than lead? We don't know that. They give off molecules, you know? Baby bottles and all that. Check it out. Plus deconstructing the old system and constructing the new system probably used a great deal of energy. Manufacturing, shipping, gas, etcetera. It will likely take thirty years to recover the savings, and by then, the system will be so old it will need to be replaced. So, no savings."

My opinion of Doug climbed about ten degrees. In two seconds flat he had figured out the flaws in the arguments for the system. But then, maybe he'd read my article and was letting me know he had. "That's what my article was about. The one that was published, but now that Radcliffe is dead there's a better story," I said sadly.

"Nothing is wasted, Robin. You still have the article as background. I read it, by the way. It was very good."

Oh, so he didn't assess the situation all on his own. Back down he went a few ampoules. But then up he clambered again; he'd been interested enough in me to carefully read what I'd written. "Once Radcliffe had done his introductory spiel another guy went on stage to finish up the ceremony and open the valves." I struggled again for the name buried in my brain. Horney. Horner. "Richard van Horner, vice president of Everwave."

"And what did you think of him? First impression."

"Cute ass."

Doug laughed. "What did he seem like to you? In general?"

"He seemed energetic and sort of fun. He clowned around a bit. While he was opening the valves."

"Okay, let's get this straight. Why was the vice president of the company opening the valves, not the president? And how did Radcliffe react to the VP horsing around on stage? Did you notice anything? Like was he impatient or anything like that?"

I looked down, chagrined. "No, I didn't. Maybe Cindy did," I said brightly, "Or Jack England."

"Jack England? What was he doing there? He doesn't usually cover something like this." Doug jerked his head forward, like a Rottweiler guarding his property. "Go find out. Maybe there's an international crime ring component."

I obediently made a note in my iPad, but I sure didn't believe that and I sure didn't want to talk to England.

"So, let's continue with your story. You said it was the first time you had met Radcliffe. Tell me about the second time."

Darn. I had hoped he'd forgotten that "second" mention. My stomach growled. I was *so* hungry. "Well I was doing some internet dating and met him online, independently of the convention. We got together at the Starbucks on Bloor near Avenue Road. That was the night he was killed."

"Anything interesting in his profile? International connections?"

Again, I tried to remember his self-description. Again, nothing jumped out at me as odd. "The cops wanted to know that too. He went to school in the States. Harvard. Other than that everything was pretty regular. Generic. He called himself 'Mr. Sail Away.'"

The pupils in Doug's eyes had sharpened to little pinpoints, maybe because the summer sun had passed over the top edge of the building and was shining through his western-facing window, making his pupils contract, or maybe because he was zeroing in on a serious thought. "Why did you meet with him? I thought you said there was something about him that you didn't like? That he was sexist."

Zeroing in. The truth would be out. "I didn't know it was him before the date was set up."

"How was the date set up? Let's back up here."

"On the internet. We met online."

"Why didn't you know him? Didn't you look at his picture?"

"There was no picture."

Doug was scanning my face for an explanation. I know I didn't look like an alcoholic. No bloodshot eyes, veins in my cheeks, or shaking hands. My nose hadn't swollen up like a bulbous balloon. No aftershave in my back pocket. But somehow I couldn't keep up the façade. "I had been drinking. Not thinking straight." If I could have disappeared, I would have. What an admission. And to a boss. Had I made a terrible mistake?

Doug smiled kindly, "Thank you for your candor. Everyone here drinks too much. It comes with the job." He patted his belly. "Me? I've stopped, but I've taken up eating instead. Ice cream. I crave sweet things. I know where every Baskin and Robbins is in the city."

I was so relieved that I laughed outright. "I do both. Eat and drink. I'm working on it."

"Anyway, so you met with him. How did that go?"

"Terribly and pretty good. On one hand he lied to me about smoking. He said he didn't smoke but he did. And, at times, he seemed evasive. In fact, a hippy earth-type girl walked by and muttered that he was dishonest. I didn't know what to think about that. Anyway, once he relaxed and he stopped being such a sexist pig, I sort of thought he was okay."

"Well, let's go with your first impression. He sounds like he was up to something. And it's my guess that something has to do with our fresh water. Find out if he was killed, maybe tortured, so somebody could get the location of the pump."

"Yes, sir."

"And how did you say goodbye?"

"Just a handshake, nothing more, but we agreed to see each other again." Over my dead body. Actually, his, *ha ha. Don't laugh out loud, Robin.*

"So what else happened? Anything?"

"Afterwards Jack England accosted me, forced me into that construction site west of Avenue Road on Bloor, and wanted to know what I was up to. He pushed me so that I fell backwards into a wall. I pushed back."

"Did you tell the police?" Doug asked sharply.

"Yes, I think they are going to look into it."

"Well, I want *you* to look into it, too. That's twice he's shown up in this account, and there is a reason for that. He's onto something and I want you to get there first. Talk to him under the ruse of being pissed off about him forcibly attacking you."

"No ruse. I am angry."

"Okay, Robin," Doug looked at his hands, his watch, and then met my eyes. I could see his thoughts falling into place. "I think there is a lot more you are not telling me, probably to save time. But I want you to make a note of everything you can remember about Radcliffe and the convention, his profile, and your date.

"Question everything you write down. I mean *everything*. What year was Radcliffe born? Where did Horner come from?

The ship's captain interests me. Where is he now? How much was he paid? Who was on the ship with him? Is he part of this scam? And so forth. Find out everything you can. If you don't know the answers to everything, then go find them out. The answers will lead you to his cause of death. But I think it was either a biological attack by an international crime ring for our fresh water, or a suicide. We'll know more after the autopsy. This is going to take a while, so be patient. It will be worth it."

I was typing down all his questions as quickly as I could. His desk phone rang.

As he picked up the receiver, he kept talking to me. "This is a big story, Robin, so far not as big as the mayor hoopla happening now, but once the mayor steps down, if he does, we will need another great story. I don't want Jack England to get there first. What you're on to here involves taxpayer's money, the environment, the government, people's workplaces, and worldwide concern over fresh water. Pretty sexy. Or at least sexy enough to sell papers."

I stood up to go, "Not to mention a man's death."

"There is that," conceded Doug, already focused on his incoming phone call.

17.

THE VENDING MACHINES WERE CALLING ME. I lumbered down a flight of stairs and bought a cellophane-wrapped egg salad sandwich on what was advertised as whole wheat, but was so pale it was hard to tell. I examined it dubiously. Looked pretty white to me. Whatever it was, it was soggy. I ripped off a corner with my teeth and slogged back up the stairs. I took my first bite and wondered how I was going to swallow a mouthful of wet towel. By the time I got to my desk it had been demolished and sat like a lump in my stomach.

Cindy, on the other hand, was licking the crumbs off the wrapper of a butter tart. She looked at me from under her eyelashes and ran her tongue seductively over the wrapper held up to her mouth. I groaned and rolled my eyes. "Give it a rest." I was in a bad mood. I didn't buy into the international crime ring angle. Todd simply wasn't that kind of guy. And him committing suicide? If pigs could fly. Both the police and Doug were off in la-la land. Yeah, I was cranky.

Cindy put the wrapper down and smiled widely, head tilted, eyebrows raised, and one shoulder up in a shrug. It was her Valley Girl impression. "So, how did it go in there?" She tilted her head towards Shirley's office.

"Oh just fine." I grumbled. "She was crabby because of the mayor so I got in and out quickly."

"And in there?" Cindy tilted her head towards Doug's office.

I could see him looking out his glass window at the skyline. What was he thinking?

"He's pretty good, you know. Asks the right questions, wants to teach me stuff, isn't patronizing. I was surprised. Way better than the police interview."

"He's a smart boss, but don't get on the wrong side of him. He can be fierce."

I'd seen a bit of that aggressiveness when I'd mentioned Jack England's name. Which reminded me, I'd have to find out what he was up to. "Do you have Jack England's phone number? Or email?"

"Why do you want to talk to that lying prickola? He's the competition."

I swung my thumb towards the boss's office. "Doug."

"Oh, you have a directive. Best to obey. He'll want to know what you find out. That guy doesn't miss a beat."

I entered the number she gave me into my phone and debated on calling him right then and there. Might be good to have a witness. "Want to be my witness?" I said to her as I tapped his newly-entered number with my finger.

Cindy had unwrapped another butter tart and answered me with her mouth full, "Sure."

I wanted to snatch it out her hands and inhale it.

I put my phone on speaker. When England answered I could immediately tell he was out and about. The sound of seagulls cawing nearby came through loud and clear. Was he down at the lake? Derrick Johnston, the sports reporter two desks over, looked up at the sound. I turned the volume down.

"Jack England."

He had such a nice voice, sort of deep and rumbly. A little raspy. Cigarettes? Scotch? "Hi Jack, Robin MacFarland here—"

"Yes, I know. I have caller ID."

Well, at least he'd picked up. In the distance I could hear a foghorn. So, he *was* at the waterfront. What was he doing there? "I was wondering if we might get together and talk about a few things." I tried to sound irritated.

"Look," he was shifting the phone to his other hand, "I'm sorry about the other night. I was at the end of my rope and you were sort of in the way."

Cindy was waving at me madly, encouraging me to get him to meet.

"So, where do you want to meet?" Now that was pretty aggressive. Hooray me!

He dug his heels in. "What's this about, anyway?"

"Don't be so suspicious, Jack, I thought you might like to get together. Smooth things over. You know…" I let my voice trail off, trying to sound like I was interested in him. And maybe I was. He took the bait.

His voice lowered a note or two. "How about that same Starbucks you were at with Radcliffe, you know, the night he was killed."

So, England knew Radcliffe was dead and was offering *me* bait. He wanted to know what I knew. I swam by his hook. "Killed? He's dead? But we were going to get together next week. On Tuesday. For dinner. I can't believe this."

"Sorry to bring you bad news." He didn't sound sorry. "Sure, let's get together. How about in half an hour?"

"Half an hour?" Cindy was shaking her head, no, no, no, and mouthing the word "tonight."

Darn. I'd have to cancel the wine and pizza night with the gals. "Impossible. I've got some deadlines right now. Tonight would be better, say around eight-thirty."

Jack scoffed, "Deadlines? Like what? Before the bloom fades off the rose?"

Was he insulting my job? Or me? Fuck him. I had had enough of that sneering and dismissive treatment from Trevor for thirty years. Never again was I going to get involved with a man who got delight from putting me down.

But wait, I wanted something. Information. So, I swallowed

my fit of pique and went along with his petty joke. "Oh, the stress of being the flower show reporter," I said with mock distress. "Anyway, how's eight-thirty tonight for you?"

"Okay. See you then." He clicked off before I said goodbye.

Cindy gave me a thumbs up and said, "Good job. Your first real confrontation as an investigative reporter. You did great. You got what you wanted and he has no idea what it is exactly that you want. Perfect, Robin. Just perfect."

I said ruefully, "Yeah, sure. I have a meeting, but I have no idea what I want. Both the police and Doug think there might be an international crime ring connection. The theft of fresh water."

Cindy tilted her chair back and looked at me intently. "Radcliffe involved in *that*? I don't think so. He's too, just too, too ... *shallow*."

Now that was a pretty good word to describe him. She was right. He didn't have the depth to pull something like that off. Now I had an ally. "I doubt it too, but that's what Doug wants. I don't know what I want."

"Sure you do. You want to find out what England knows about Radcliffe. Why he was following him, if he was. Did he see anything the night he was killed? Where did Radcliffe go after he saw you? That is, if England even followed him."

I thought back to when England had left me on the street. Yes, he had gone off in the same direction as Todd. And at a good clip. Maybe he *had* been following him, like he'd said. But then, he was a journalist, and some journalists were known to lie to get information. "You could be right, Cindy, he probably was following him. He said he was. Not that that means anything. It would be good to know where Radcliffe went after I saw him, if he didn't go home."

Cindy was unwrapping her *third* butter tart.

"How can you eat so many of those things?"

"Easy." She broke it in half and plopped it in her mouth. "I love to hear my fillings sing."

"You'll give yourself diabetes," I said, hoping my jealousy was disguised as concern.

She shrugged and went back to whatever it was she was working on. I snuck a glance at her screen and read the word "heroin." A drug thing, then. Researching. Right now I had bigger concerns. How on earth was I going to unearth the name of the captain of the ship that had taken the pump for the deep water cooling system into the middle of the lake? Doug wanted to know so that meant I did too. My knowledge of ships was a big fat goose egg.

As my eyes travelled over the department to Doug's office for inspiration, I saw standing outside the glass doors of Editorial the same apple-cheeked rookie I had hoodwinked a few hours ago to get into Todd's snow white condo. He tapped on the glass and made a writing motion with his hand on top of a file he was holding. My statement? Must be. I got up and went to the door with a pen in my hand.

"Sorry about this morning." I apologized to the young cop, "I had to get into Radcliffe's apartment. I hope you didn't get into too much trouble."

"No ma'am. Won't happen again, though. Sign here." He pointed to the bottom of a page as he handed the file to me, smiling, sort of.

I leaned against the wall outside the glass doors and took my time reading over what I had said at the police station, flipping the pages slowly while the uniform shifted from foot to foot. I wasn't going to hurry. You never knew when something would come back and bite you in the ass. But Stapleton had accurately recorded what I'd said so I signed it, sending the cop on his way.

When I got back to my desk I Googled everything I could think of to get the captain's name: Everwave boat captain; ship capable of lifting heavy machinery; cranes on boats; vessels, Toronto. That last search gave me information on varicose vein clinics in Toronto, probably a cross-reference with blood vessels.

Not what I was looking for, or not yet. Maybe in a few years.

The futile search did give me an idea. I could simply walk along the waterfront and look around for boats with cranes on them. And then, once I found those ships, I could get the logs and see who was the captain and when. I could find out from Everwave exactly when the pump was installed, and then Bob's your uncle! I could match up the dates with the log and know who the captain was. It sounded like a plan.

Cindy looked over at my Google searches. "What are you trying to find out?"

"The name of the captain of the ship that took the pump out into the middle of the lake. Just a few people know the location. If there's a conspiracy to steal Lake Ontario water, he could be part of it. I'm counting on there being very few boats in the harbour that have cranes. When I find the boat, I'll find the captain. I've Googled everything I can think of, but not a single hit."

"Robin?" She sounded like she was talking to a child.

"Yes?"

"Call Research."

"Research?"

"We have a whole department that finds out that kind of information."

"Research." I said, looking at her dumbly.

Cindy gave me the number. "Call them. You'll have your answer in ten, twenty minutes."

I had never had access to the Research Department before, being a Home and Garden reporter. Being an investigative reporter, if only briefly, certainly had its perks. I dialed the number. A bright young thing answered, "Alison Trent."

She sounded very Lawrence Park and I pictured her in round glasses and a prudish suit from Fairweathers. Long blonde hair parted in the middle and nails polished a demure pink. Her voice sounded somehow familiar, but I couldn't place it. Maybe she was one of my daughter's friends, from high school or something. I introduced myself as a journalist working on the Everwave article.

"I thought that article went out?"

"Yes and no. One went out, today in fact, but now the CEO of Everwave has ended up dead. So now there's a new story. Maybe a crime ring killed him. Maybe for our fresh water. Or maybe it was suicide. Or an accident. Even a natural death."

"So exciting. How can I help you figure out the mystery? What do you need to know?"

She was one of those fast-talking kids, the kind where you have to strain your ears to catch what they are saying. Why did kids today speak so quickly?

I maliciously spoke even slower. "I need to know the name and address of the captain of the ship that ferried out the deep water cooling system pump into the middle of the lake."

"Which lake?"

I certainly hadn't been expecting that question. But it showed that she was on the ball. There were hundreds of lakes in Ontario to choose from, so it was fair enough. "Lake Ontario."

"Oh, okay, and the system? What did you say it was? I caught the first bit, but not the second. Deep lake what?"

I repeated the description, "Deep lake cooling system." I could hear her scratching the information down on a pad. So, although she was up to date on speed-talking, she was still using a notebook. Unusual for a kid. "A boat took out a pump and I need to know the name of the captain of the boat. He is one of just a very few people who knows where the pump was installed. The boat probably had a crane."

"Do you have a time frame for this?"

"I guess not when the lake was frozen." Wasn't I a brainiac?

Alison took a deep breath, "Actually, Ms. MacFarland, Lake Ontario rarely freezes over. In the past almost two hundred years there have been only five recorded complete freezes, well, since 1830, anyway."

"Oh." Silly me. "And call me Robin, Alison."

"Sure, Robin. It's my guess we'd be looking for a ship that went out in June, July, August, or September, no high winds, warmer weather. I'll start my search there."

"Thanks, Alison, I appreciate you helping me."

"No worries. I'll get back to you. What's your cell?"

I gave Alison my number and hung up. So, a Research Department. That would be so helpful.

I got my tablet out of my bag and went over the questions that had arisen in my meeting with Doug. As I scanned through them I saw that there were a few more questions that Alison could help me with. I called her back.

"Alison Trent."

Again her voice sounded familiar. How did I know it? "Hi, Alison. Sorry to be a pest—"

I could hear her sigh. "Listen, let's be clear about this from the start, Ms. MacFarland—"

"Robin."

"Okay, Robin, sorry. It is my job to find out information for the journalists at the paper. I get paid to do it. I like doing it. I might be new at it, only a couple of years in, but I am pretty good at it. So, don't hesitate to call and ask. It's my job. I love information."

So Alison *was* a nerd. I could picture her, pushing her glasses up her nose with an impatient finger. "Thanks, Alison, nice to work with someone so passionate and honest."

"Honesty is important."

"Well, there are a couple more questions I need answering. I need to find out what buildings are being cooled by the system. I also need some background info on a guy named Richard van Horner. He is VP of Everwave. When and where he was born, his address, stuff like that. He knew where the pump was, so maybe he's involved in a plot. I need to know how much the ship's captain was paid, if you can find out. If not I will track him down, once we have a name for him. You know, to see if he's being bribed. Also, is there is any way to find out who was on the ship as well? That would be good to know."

"Easy peasy," said Alison, "I'll get right back to you as soon as I get you some answers. Sounds like an interesting article."

I thanked her and then went more carefully through my list of notes from my meeting with Doug. The questions would lead to discovering a motive for the killing, if, in fact, his death was a murder. I wondered when the autopsy would be done and what it would reveal. The other two things Doug wanted me to do was to go over Todd's profile from the dating site and also to write down everything I could remember from the very brief exchange at Starbucks.

I decided to start with his profile. That seemed easiest as it would be right there in black and white. I signed into the dating site and found, almost to my horror, that five men had sent me smiley faces. FIVE. I moved my chair closer to my computer so no one in the office would see what I was doing, and quickly glanced at their profiles. The first guy, "Mr. Cuddly Bear," had written down as his body type, "Some extra pounds." It was an understatement. The second, "Romantic4U," had oily, straggly, grey hair down to his shoulders. The third profile, "Zoom to the Stars," had pictures of the guy sitting on his Harley. A Hell's Angel? The fourth, "Lovetowalk," had only one picture of him, walking his dog, and then three pictures of his dog. Really? I wanted to go out with his dog? I had my own dog. But the fifth, "Anormalfellow," looked okay. Nice smile, nice thick hair, not thin, not fat, so I read through his profile carefully but came to a full stop when he said he was looking for someone to spend six months of the year in New Zealand with his family. Get real. Six months? My kids would be devastated. Besides, my idea of going Down Under was a little more thrilling than *that*. I deleted them all and looked for Todd's profile.

In one of those momentary lapses in memory that were becoming worryingly frequent, I couldn't remember what he had called himself. Let's see. I had just told Doug. Was it "Dancing Starfish?" No, that was the greasy-haired guy. What was it? I couldn't remember. Didn't Todd's have something to do with sailing? God, I missed my mind. And then I remembered: "Mr. Sail Away."

I plugged "Mr. Sail Away" into the search bar and clicked enter. It didn't come up. I must have remembered incorrectly. So, then I plugged in "Sailaway," then "Sail Away." Still nothing. I was sure I had remembered correctly. But then, maybe not. My memory was pretty shot these days. So I settled down into doing a long search. I typed in what I thought was his age range, the distance from my postal code, and other definers for a search that would lead me to Todd. I pressed enter and saw with dismay that there were thirty-seven matches to my parameters. I went through each and every one, slowly and carefully.

No Todd.

His profile had completely disappeared. It had been deleted. I felt a wave of fear wash over me. It was there last night. I remembered looking at it around midnight. Probably after he was killed. So, who had deleted it? How did they get his password? Why had they deleted it? What was on his profile that had got him killed? Something was off here. An international crime ring wouldn't be interested in a *dating* profile, would they? Well, maybe. Probably not. And I knew it wasn't a suicide. His profile was down and the temperature in his room was up. We'd made a plan for next week, for heaven's sake. He wasn't depressed at all. And, the worst question of all: what had I learned from his profile that put me in danger?

18.

BY FOUR IN THE AFTERNOON I WAS TOAST. What a day. My synthetic lunch was bouncing around in my stomach. A murder scene. The cops. My first alcohol busting treatment. And now I couldn't have have wine and pizza with Cindy and my friend Diane tonight because I had that stupid meeting with Jack-off. I'd have to text Diane. I had been looking forward to spending a night with my gal pals. Cindy had disappeared somewhere, probably following up her gang story. I started to send a text but was sidelined by a message from my daughter Evelyn, Lynnie for short. *Know any cosmetic surgeons?* I groaned. I'd deal with that on Sunday during our family dinner. Every Sunday, like clockwork, my kids were attracted to the family home like iron filings to a magnet.

It was time to write everything down. At least the office was quiet. By late in the day many of the journalists and admin staff had gone home, having started very early in the morning. I stabbed the enter key on my computer and the screen flashed into life. I was typing out all the details I could remember about Todd's profile and my meeting with him in Starbucks when the phone rang. My caller ID said it was the *Express* Research Department.

"Hi, Ms. MacFarland—"

"Robin, Alison, please call me Robin."

She laughed awkwardly, "Hi, Robin, I got most of the info you wanted. Sorry I took so long."

"No, no, that was fast work, Alison. Okay, shoot. I'm ready." I brought up a blank page on my computer screen and put the earphone into my phone so I could type while she talked. Although there weren't many left in the newsroom, I didn't want to disturb the remaining few with my speaker phone. Plus, I didn't want to be scooped.

"Okay. Some of the customers of the deep lake water cooling system are the Toronto-Dominion Centre, the Royal Bank Plaza, RBC Centre, the Metro Toronto Convention Centre, and the Air Canada Centre. So far these are all the downtown customers in the financial district. It isn't a definitive list, and I couldn't find out who the rest of the customers were, but at least there are a few to start with. I got all the rest of the information you needed."

"Thanks Alison, I doubt the customers are that important anyway, I'm not thinking this was a corporate problem. Most likely the murder, if it was murder, was not motivated by an outside business. Those hits are usually done execution style, you know, down on the knees and a quick shot in the back of the head."

Really? Did I say that? Who was I kidding? I had never investigated a murder in my life. My information came from cheap paperback mysteries that I read at night, half cock-eyed with wine.

"Yes, I know what you mean by execution style. TV and all. Anyway, Richard van Horner was born in Holland in 1958 but came to Canada as a baby with his parents in the early sixties."

I did the math. He was almost exactly my age. No wedding ring, but what did that mean these days? Maybe married, maybe not.

Alison continued, "He currently lives in North Toronto, on a street near the end of Mount Pleasant. He bought the house about a year ago." She gave me the address. "Rich guy."

Really rich guy. Those houses by the golf course were valued in the multi-millions. I wondered where all his money had come from. "Are his parents dead? And what did they do?"

Alison clicked her mouse. "Yes, they're dead, but recently, only last year. Both of them at the age of eighty. They ran a small dry cleaning business in the west end. On Ossington. Ummm..." *click click,* "it looks like it was just south of Bloor."

He had probably sold it and then purchased his new home. "That place would be worth a mint. I wonder what he got for it. Any idea what his new house is worth?"

"I can find general estimates by looking on the real estate site. Here, I've got it. Well, there's a property further south on Ossington that's going for two point four, and his house is worth, ummm..." more *clicking,* "there's a house the next street over from his that's for sale for five point six. So about a three million spread."

There was no way he'd be able to support a three million dollar mortgage on his salary, even if he was VP of a major company. He had to have had a windfall of some kind, larger than the sale of his parents' business. So, where did the money come from? Had he been bribed for information about the location of the pump in the lake? I should interview the guy and sniff it out.

"And did you have any luck with the ship's captain?"

"Sure I did," Alison laughed. "I can find anything. That's why I work here. He's Spanish—Agustin Jimenez. Did you know Agustin means 'the exalted one'?"

"No, I did not."

"Well, they call him Jimmy, probably after his last name."

"Did you discover who else was on the ship?"

"Just two guys were on board with him that September: Santiago Martinez and Diego Duarte."

"All Spanish names. Now that's interesting. I wonder if they knew each other from their home country. Anyway, did you get a sense of how much money he was paid while working for Everwave?"

"I looked at his income tax forms for the past five years and there was nothing out of the ordinary that would indicate a huge payment for last year. Year over year he made a fairly consistent amount. I mean, there was no spike in income or anything like that."

"No spike in *claimed* income, that is. He probably wasn't stupid enough to claim a cash payment. Can you find the addresses for Duarte and Martinez for me as well?"

"Already have. Here are the three addresses of the men on the ship."

I typed into my computer the names and addresses she gave me and hit print. That Alison was a real whizz kid. I pictured her hunched over her computer, wearing glasses, her blonde hair tightly pulled back in a ponytail, out of her way. "Alison, how exactly did you find all this information? Especially his income tax. Isn't that protected on a government site?"

She paused, and then laughed. "Let me know if you need anything else, okay?"

So, no answer. I guess as long as I didn't know I was in the clear.

We said goodbye and I looked up to see Cindy looking at me quizzically. She had returned. "I'm back. Sounds interesting. What's up?"

Putting my phone and iPad in my bag and looking for my car keys, I said, "Not sure. Something is up. Todd Radcliffe's profile has disappeared off the dating site. A lot of things need checking out."

"What do you mean, 'disappeared?'" Cindy's chair squeaked when she sat down.

"Gone-zola. *Disparu*. I searched almost the whole site and it didn't come up anywhere."

She frowned. "I don't like the sounds of that. The only person who can take down a profile is the person who wrote it. I mean, there are passwords and everything."

"I know. And I also know that his profile was up and running up past midnight last night. I came home from our date, called you, and then looked at it again, later. Anyway, we can talk about it tonight. No wait, I keep forgetting that our wine and pizza is cancelled tonight because of England. How about Saturday?"

"Sure, Saturday works. Being single and all with nothing to do."

I quickly sent a text to Diane, letting her know about the change of plans. My phone dinged quickly with her reply, a smiley face. I guess that meant that she was good to go on Saturday night, too. At least I got a reply. That woman was so busy sometimes it took days to hear back from her.

Cindy glanced at the car keys in my hand. "Where you going?"

"I'm checking out where van Horner lives. He has a huge house by Rosedale Golf Course. Thought I'd sit on his house for a bit, see what's what. I could maybe talk to him. At least watch him."

"You gotta be kidding me, Robin."

"What?"

"You can't simply sit outside a guy's house in a rust bucket in that neighbourhood." Cindy started pitching her phone and glasses, keys and wallet into her purse. "I'm coming with you and we're going in my Accord. It's not so fancy that it will draw attention, and not too shabby for that neighbourhood."

"Okay, but you'll have to drive me back down here. I'm seeing England, remember, at eight-thirty. Bloor and Avenue Road."

"No problem. Even if van Horner doesn't get home until six or seven, we'll still have lots of time. We can have a hamburger in the car."

As we walked past Doug's office, I could see that he was still staring out the window at the lake, a blank look on his face. What was going on with him? Who had called him and what had been said?

Van Horner lived on a beautiful tree-lined street that had a prettily landscaped boulevard running down the centre. Cindy drove down one side to the dead end at the bottom of the street and then followed the loop around so that we were parked facing the way we had come from. The house was on the driver's side of the car, beyond the boulevard. When I protested that I couldn't see over the central divide, she explained that first, we might need a quick getaway, and second, we needed to have a little protection from being seen.

"I always do this," she said. I shut up and learned, just like Shirley told me to.

We sat outside van Horner's house, a huge Edwardian edifice, eating the hamburgers we had picked up on our way and making a smelly mess of the interior of Cindy's car. Unlike my car, hers was pristine and Cindy frowned at me when I crossed my left leg over my right knee, the sole of my foot barely inches away from touching her glove compartment. I was balancing my French fries in the V formed by my two legs.

"Put your foot down," she snipped.

I removed my foot. "Yes, mum."

We were both quiet for some time, munching away, eyes watching the street for a car, any car. The neighbourhood was dead. The quiet enveloped us as we waited and I fought the carbs slushing through my veins and dragging my eyes shut. I tried to lighten the moment and stay awake.

"A house like this is at least worthy of a proper stake out. I feel badly, giving it only a hamburger out."

Cindy rolled her eyes. It was a dumb joke. We both laughed. The sun sank a little lower in the sky while we waited and watched. Absolutely nothing was happening. A bird flew by. I looked it up on my Peterson app. A jay of some kind. In between van Horner's house and his neighbours', I could see glimpses of the Rosedale Golf Course stretching out behind, with its lovely hills and copses of beautiful trees. Oh, to be rich. I could hear cicadas buzzing in the distance, giving their last mating calls of the hot day. It was a perfect summer evening.

The house was two stories tall, squarish, a formidable pile of a pale yellow stone. Almost beige, but with flecks of gold.

Leaded windows gleamed in the early evening light. The massive door itself must have been custom designed by an artisan in Europe. France, probably. Wrought iron fleur de lies protected a full-length pane of frosted glass.

I was bored. I had no idea that stakeouts were so tedious. I got out my tablet and started taking pictures of the tree-lined street, first one up towards Mount Pleasant and then another down the street towards the golf course. A workman's van was parked at the curb, dirtying up my pretty shot. Then I zoomed in on the house, and took a picture of the lovely door.

Suddenly the garage door groaned open. Cindy and I both instinctively ducked down., "Geezus!" she hissed. "How did that happen?"

"He probably has a long distance remote opener," I whispered back. "Wireless, no doubt." There were advantages to working the Home and Garden section. I knew all the house gadgets. Intimately. We both peeked over the edge of the driver side window.

And sure enough, a shining gold Lexus swooped down the street and slid into the garage. Cindy muttered, "Did you see who was driving? Was it van Horner? I think so. A man for sure, wearing glasses. Did he wear glasses?"

"I can't remember," I said, as I inched the photo lens of my iPad slightly over the dashboard and clicked a picture of the guy getting out of his car as the garage door slowly hummed down. "On the other hand, some people wear glasses just to drive, so that's not a great clue. Now, if I could see his bum, I would know for sure."

"Yes, I remember he had a *gluteus maximus* worth thinking about."

I was surprised my gay friend had even registered his *derriere* and turned to her, settling my iPad on my lap, "You noticed that?"

"Just because I'm gay doesn't mean I don't recognize a great ass on a guy when I see one," she giggled, watching the house.

I pondered this for a minute.

We watched as he headed towards the left side of the garage. "There's probably a door there that goes to a side entrance," I said, confident about my knowledge of floor plans. Once the garage door was completely down we sat back up. Lights came on as he made his way through the residence. "Do you think he senses us watching him?" I asked.

"Nah."

A very pale glow lit up the front bay window on the right. He was probably in the kitchen, behind the front room, which was no doubt the dining room, if his house was a typical centre hall plan. Suddenly a bright light went on in the dining room and then finally the chandelier in the foyer illuminated the frosted glass in the front door. We watched his silhouette bend over, most likely picking up the mail that had been pushed through the slot. He straightened up and we could see the shape of his arms flipping through the letters.

Suddenly there was a deafening bang. Cindy and I jumped a mile and twisted our necks around, looking for the source of the explosion. Down the street, the derelict white van I'd noticed earlier was coughing away from the curb, belching smoke. We laughed hysterically, hands on our hearts. It was a car backfiring! As it passed us I could see its rocker panels were decayed by cancerous rust. When we looked back at the house, van Horner must have gone upstairs because his silhouette was no longer visible in the frosted glass.

"I wonder where he's gone now," mused Cindy.

"Probably going up to his bedroom to change into something more comfortable. A T-shirt with a little alligator on it. Pink."

She laughed a little too loudly, releasing the tension. We dipped our now cold fries in ketchup as we waited for one of the upstairs lights to come on.

"I don't like this," said Cindy, munching.

"What, the fries? A little cold but otherwise, they're perfect," I said, smacking my lips appreciatively. So much for that diet.

"No, that we lost him in the house. I want to know where he is."

"Maybe he's taking a bath."

"Well, I'm curious." She undid her seatbelt and opened the car door. "Coming?"

"What the hell are you doing?"

"I'm going to knock on his front door."

"Are you whacko? What are you going to say?"

"I'm going to say the truth. That I'm the press and I'm doing a follow-up story to the convention."

I threw my napkins in the brown paper bag from the fast food joint, "Good line, yeah, okay, I'm coming." I grabbed my iPad.

We walked up the cobblestone driveway together, Cindy's supermodel legs wobbling slightly in her high heels. I looked this way and that, taking pictures of everything I could see: the trees in the yard, the manicured lawn, the detail in the windows, everything.

"What are you doing?" Cindy asked me, steadying herself on my arm.

"I'm being a reporter for the *Express* Home and Garden section, taking pictures of a nice house. It's a better cover story than yours, I think. Won't make him clam up."

"Oh, right. Good thinking."

Cindy was about to lift the doorknocker, a lion's head, when I noticed a fine filigree of lines fanning out from behind the wrought iron fleur de lies. I grabbed her arm and pulled it back. "Wait," I muttered quietly.

Something was definitely wrong here. My scalp was contracting on the back of my head. Someone was watching us.

"What now?" Cindy scowled at me.

Oh so casually, I made a show of taking a picture of the knocker up close. I nodded imperceptibly towards the frosted glass and said to her through unmoving lips, "Just act normal. Look. See? The glass has been broken. Don't look at it directly, just move your eyes. I think we are being watched."

We both rotated our eyes towards the glass. Slowly but surely a small circular hole in the middle of the lines came into focus.

"Bullet hole," we whispered in unison.

"Okay, now pretend you don't see it. You knock, we'll wait for a second, and then, when it seems like no one is coming, we'll leave, slowly and normally." The hairs on the back of my neck were standing up. I felt so exposed. For sure we were being watched. Would we be shot? I didn't want to die. Not yet. I would stop drinking. What was the name of the firm that cleaned my windows? I would lose weight. I loved my children. Where was my wedding ring? Was the milk out of date?

Amazing what whistles through your mind when you think there's a gun aimed at you.

Cindy lifted the lion's head twice in rapid succession. It clanged emptily through the house. We waited for a minute and she lifted it again. Again it echoed. I raised my shoulders in an exaggerated "what can you do" gesture and we turned and slowly walked down the steps, over the cobblestone driveway and back to her car. We ad-libbed loudly as we went.

"I told you we should have made an appointment." I stated emphatically and loudly for the benefit of anyone watching us, "He's gone into the bathroom, having a shower. You can't just turn up, Mary, you gotta make an appointment."

"How was I to know, Betty? I mean, maybe he wouldn't let us interview him."

Cindy had caught on. Fake names. Mislead whoever was watching.

"Oh well, at least I got a great photo of that lion's head knocker. That will dress up my article on front porches for next Saturday's issue of the *Toronto Times*." I articulated "*Toronto Times*" carefully.

It seemed to take five years to reach Cindy's car. We both opened our doors and got in as slowly as we could.

"I think we threw him off," I said, keeping my head down so my lips didn't show. "Fake names. Different newspaper."

Cindy turned the key in the ignition and rotated the rearview mirror towards her, ostensibly to check her makeup like any self-respecting reporter would do, but she was really examining a wide circle behind us. She exhaled. "That decrepit white van that drove off? It didn't come back. I don't see it anywhere. I'll bet the shooter was in the van."

I didn't think so. For one, from where the van had been parked it would have been an impossible shot. Also, the van had taken off, it was gone, and I *knew* we were still being watched.

The reality was sinking in. I was starting to pant. "We could've been shot, Cindy. We were so lucky."

Cindy pushed the mirror back into position and carefully pulled away from the curb, her knuckles white on the steering wheel. She turned her frightened green eyes towards me and stretched her lips in a fake smile. Without moving a muscle in her face she enunciated through clenched teeth, "Holy Fuck. Holy fuck. Holy fuck."

19.

Cindy turned left onto Mount Pleasant and then turned right on a side street, where there was a set of lights on Yonge to help us cross. We sat at the light puffing as if we'd run a mile, our breath coming fast and furious. She kept checking her rearview mirror.

"No white van. I don't think we're being followed." Her body bounced back and forth with impatience as we waited for the light to change.

As far as I was concerned, the van was long gone. "Somehow it doesn't make sense that the van was even involved in the shooting. It drove by us so innocently. Plus, I mean, Radcliffe and then van Horner? Sounds like pretty high-end crime is going on here, not a rusty van kind of job."

"No such thing as coincidence. Big noise. A gun shot. Pretty coincidental. Nope, the van's related." She made a quick left onto Yonge Street, flinging me against the car door.

"Where the hell are you going? Go straight across. We'll be trapped in the traffic here. We have to get away."

"We have to call the police, Robin, we can't just walk away from this."

I was terrified. I wanted nothing at all to do with any of this. I'd had enough. I shouted, "Of course we can."

"What?" Cindy smiled, calmly. Patronizingly. I hated it. "Wait for the neighbours to discover a bad smell?" Cindy was adamant. "What if he was hit but he isn't dead? What if he's hiding in the house and the reason why we aren't being followed is because the shooter went back, and maybe is going after van Horner right this second? Maybe the shooter only went around the block in that white van and came back. We have to call for help."

"Oh." I wasn't going to argue with Cindy when she was like this. I pulled out my phone to dial 911.

She batted it out of my hand. "Don't use your phone, idiot," yelled Cindy. "You never know what sort of tracing equipment they have. We don't know what we are up against. Two murders? Water? This could be a sophisticated crime ring. We'll go into the food store here." She hung a quick hard right, throwing me against the door again, and then a hard left, that had me thudding against the console. "They have a phone booth outside the back door."

And there it was, it's blue Bell Canada strip across the top. The levered door was folded open and inside we could see the wire from the phone flapping limply. No receiver.

Cindy dashed inside the shop with me schlepping behind her to the customer service desk. "I need to call the police," Cindy announced to the startled store clerk.

I could hear the tinny voice of the 911 operator come out of the phone in Cindy's hand. It was asking calmly if we needed a fire truck, an ambulance, or the police. Cindy's voice was clipped with clear diction, "Gunshot," she snapped. And then spit out the ritzy address. She crashed down the phone and bolted back to her car with me trailing behind her. I turned around and saw the store clerk with her jaw hanging down to her chin.

Within seconds a siren screamed north on Yonge Street. Red and blue strobe lights flashed down the side street where we had parked and then continued north, bathing the boutique-type stores in strobes. "That was fast," I gasped. "Now what?"

In reply, Cindy slammed the car into reverse, spun out of the parking spot, and then threw it into drive. "We go *back*," she whooped as she gunned the car into the roadway, grinning like a maniac.

"You are NUTS!" I screamed.

She turned to me, her eyes dancing with excitement, "Welcome to being a crime reporter, Robin. Having fun yet?"

"Oh, God." I felt ill. The last thing on earth I wanted to do right now was head back to where the sniper had been. It must have been a sniper. But what did I know?

"Do you think it was a sniper?"

"Yup. There was no blood on the door, right?"

"Right."

"So, the shot couldn't have come from inside the house. Van Horner's brains would be all over the door. No blood. The glass was clear, right?"

I was nauseous. But, being a stickler for descriptions of houses, I mumbled, "Frosted."

Cindy shook her head as she drove a few blocks north, squealing a left onto van Horner's street. "You know what I mean, asshole."

"I'm not an asshole. You're the asshole."

We were stressed.

She slowed down and screeched to a stop at the corner of van Horner's street and Mount Pleasant. Looking down the boulevard, I saw immediately that the angles were all wrong for the sniper to be in the van. I could also see that the emergency vehicles had arrived in force. Bathed in rotating red and blue lights were a fire truck, an ambulance, and three darkened cruisers all parked near the house. Cindy snuck down the wrong side of the boulevard, lights off, past the police cordon, did a tight U-turn at the loop, and parked virtually where we had been before. She gave me a thumbs up in the dark: we hadn't been turned back by the police.

We could see shadowy figures moving around the shrubbery. Looked like they were surrounding the house. Suddenly out of nowhere two burly guys ran up the front stairs, taking the steps two at a time, their shoulders hitting the wood surrounding the glass. The door broke open and a square of light filled the almost dark street. We could hear them shouting "Police!" from the interior of the house. And then there was nothing.

Cindy quietly opened her door and didn't shut it all the way. She gestured for me to follow.

I hissed over the roof of the car, "What about the guy? The sniper? The guy with the *gun*?"

"Oh, he's long gone, drove off in that van. He's downtown by now, or on the highway heading for Oshawa. We're perfectly safe."

So why was she being so quiet? Her van guy theory was crap. "If the sniper wasn't the van guy, then what?"

"He's probably over there somewhere," Cindy gestured widely with her hand over the golf course. "He's got tons of acres to lose himself in. But I know it was the van guy," Cindy was unbending. "And he's *gone*."

I wasn't so sure. I had read hundreds of mysteries, and almost every single one was emphatic that the criminal remained at the scene to admire the chaos his handiwork had caused. Was Cindy telling me that this wasn't true? I followed her towards the police activity, just in time to see a person being carried out of the house on a hospital gurney. As I got closer I could see it was van Horner, his face pale and eyes shut. An orange blanket covered his torso and clear liquid snaked into his left arm. His feet stuck forlornly out from under the blanket. I wondered fleetingly what had happened to his shoes. Maybe he took them off when he had entered the house from the garage. For some reason this detail weighed upon my heart. The EMS worker was pressing his latex gloved hand tightly over bright red gauze on Horner's right shoulder. He was pumping out blood. It was dripping down the steel tubing of the gurney, through the mechanism of a wheel, and onto the driveway, leaving oily splats on the cobblestones.

A black SUV zoomed into the driveway, despite a police officer flagging it to stop at the street. The officer jumped aside when it was clear the driver was not going to obey him. A harried woman whipped open the BMW's car door screaming her husband's name. Three wide-eyed children shadowed her, their screams "Daddy, Daddy, Daddy," filling the air. The mother was shouting "Richard," as she clawed her way towards the gurney. A huge policeman grabbed her from behind and held her back. Her face was contorted with fierce determination and I watched in fascination as she lifted her silk stockinged knee and stomped the heel of her Prada pump into the officer's foot. He abruptly let her go and she fell forward, almost on top of her husband.

I nudged Cindy in the ribs, "You gotta admire that."

The wife stroked her husband's face as the EMS workers carried him towards the waiting ambulance. Another officer came up to her and started asking her questions. I strained to hear the exchange.

"Your name, ma'am?"

"Melissa Mowbray," she fired.

"You the sister? Wife? Married to van Horner? First wife? Second? Lover? What's the relationship here?"

When Melissa Mowbray looked up at the cop, she was seething. The look questioned why this *cop*, this lowly rookie, dared insinuate that she was a cheap lover. An interesting reaction, considering her husband was lying on a gurney in front of her, his life-blood seeping through a bandage on his shoulder. Was she more interested in appearances than the life of her husband? Fear presented itself in different ways for different people, I guessed.

"I'm his *wife*, officer, and the mother of his children."

Suddenly she stood up and her eyes bolted around the landscape. Where were her children? The officer, guessing the cause of her current distress, gestured towards her car. Her three children had been rounded up by another police officer and put back into the SUV. I could see their white faces pressed against the windows, their eyes wide with fright as they watched their father's gurney being shoved into an ambulance and the doors shutting with a clang behind him. The oldest one winced and a tear rolled down the little girl's face. The middle child, a boy, was so pale I worried he might faint.

At least their father was still alive, if only barely. The medics were in a huge hurry, so I knew it was touch and go. The ambulance pulled away and charged up the street with the siren yowling eerily in the quiet neighbourhood.

I hugged my body for warmth as the sun slid behind the horizon. Cindy prodded me, "Stage right. Stokes. Creston."

Sure enough, the two guys who had interviewed me earlier that day were striding towards us. I imitated Cindy's flat non-committal mask and activated the recording app on my phone. Maybe I trusted the police, but I sure didn't trust myself to remember everything and I had a story to write.

"So," griped Creston, "If it isn't MacFarland and Dale from the *Express*. Fancy meeting you here. What are you after?"

Stokes, in his usual fashion, parroted, "After?" And then he covered his mouth and suffocated his snicker.

What was with this guy? I looked at Creston who shrugged. "Now that van Horner's been attacked, it's looking more like the two men are victims of an international crime ring focused on the theft of our water. The two crimes are connected somehow. The autopsy on Radcliffe hasn't been completed yet, and all the reports aren't in, so no cause of death so far, but I'm thinking drugs. Probably a truth serum of some sort. So he'd talk about the pump's location. With this attack, I doubt Radcliffe was tortured for the information. His body showed no signs of torture. So they probably used some sort of truth serum. And Van Horner sure wasn't tortured. He never saw that bullet coming."

Cindy ignored all this speculation and answered his question. "We're *after* a follow up story on Everwave and thought we'd come by and interview van Horner. Vice prez. You know, a bit of background on Radcliffe: what he thought of him, what kind of boss he was, you know, plus anything about the company."

Creston pulled out his notebook. "Did you have an appointment?"

Cindy shifted her weight, "No, not really."

"So you were staking out the house, waiting for him to come home?"

"Yes," I owned up. "That's what we were doing. We were sitting in the car, right there, right where we are parked right now." I pointed to Cindy's Accord.

Creston stared at me and said nothing. He was probably waiting for me to become uncomfortable and fill the silence with a confession or something. I had read that cops do that. It was a *game*. Cindy gave her head a small shake. So, don't offer anything, but answer the questions if and when they were asked. I liked it. For a brief second I had a feeling of power as I stared back at Creston.

Creston cast his gaze skywards, as if praying for patience. "Right." We'd won a point. "And what time did you get here?"

Cindy said, "It was about five-thirty."

He wrote it down. "And what, exactly did you see?"

Cindy, being a smart ass, said, "Tall, stone, Edwardian mansion, leaded windows, manicured lawn—"

I thought it was hilarious and added my two bits. "Flagstone steps, European wrought iron filigree…"

Creston's self control was slipping. We had taken our sport too far. "May I remind you, *journalists*," he said, emphasizing the word *journalist* as if he were saying *scum*, "this is a serious situation. A man's life hangs in the balance. A father of three. I don't want to know if there are Pella windows on the house. I want to know if you saw anything that pertains to this investigation. Let's try this again. What did you see?"

I was humbled. "His garage door opened about five-thirty, maybe quarter-to-six, and then a car came down the street—"

"The door opened first? And then the car?"

"Wireless remote opener," I said.

Creston looked at me appraisingly. "Right. What kind of car?" He was taking notes.

"A Lexus. Gold. It pulled into the driveway and went into the garage. Then we saw lights come on in the house as he walked through it."

Creston interjected, "Let's back up a bit. Did you see anything inside the garage when the door was up and when did the garage door shut?" A two-pronged question.

"We couldn't see much inside the garage because of the angle we were parked, and yes, the door slid down, almost immediately, well, a few seconds later, behind the car."

Stokes nudged Creston, "You'd think that would be the time he would have been shot, while he was out in the open."

"Not really. No chance for a head or torso shot with the door coming down." Creston looked at Stokes with his head slightly cocked, as if he were trying to figure out how this guy had made it through the police academy. Then he turned back towards us. "Now tell me about the lights."

Cindy pointed at the double-fronted house. "First there was a dim light in the right-hand window. Then a bright light came on in the same window. And then the light behind the front door came on. It looked like he was leafing through his mail."

Stokes frowned, keeping up. "How did you know that?" he asked, "The glass in the front door is frosted."

I was surprised that he had noticed the detail about the glass. I said, "We could see his silhouette. He bent over, probably to pick up the mail from the floor, and then stood up. His arms were moving, so we thought he was going through it."

Creston asked, "And then what happened?"

"Well, nothing," Cindy nodded in agreement with me.

"What do you mean, nothing?"

"We thought he'd go upstairs and we were waiting for some lights to come on in the second floor. But they never did."

"So what did you do?"

"We got out of the car and were about to knock on his front door when Robin noticed that there was a small hole in the door's *frosted* glass and a spider web of lines radiated out from the hole. It looked like a bullet hole."

"Had you heard a gun being fired?"

I volunteered, "I have never heard a gun shot, so I don't know what one sounds like, but we did hear what sounded like a car backfiring." Cindy looked at me, her eyes widened in contempt. I had given away the story! To the police!

"Where did the noise come from?" asked Creston, suddenly looking interested.

Fuck Cindy. That backfire was not a gunshot. It was merely a coincidental noise. I waved my hand randomly behind me. "The noise came from down the street, but I think the bullet came from over there, across the street from van Horner's house. The junky old van was parked down the street. White." I pointed at right angles down the street.

Cindy had turned her back and crossed her arms. What a baby. A man had nearly been killed and she thought we should keep information from the police?

Creston called out to a couple of officers. He stepped away from us and spoke in low tones to the cops who then took off towards the trees across from van Horner's house. So, he believed me. I thought I recognized the uniforms, but wasn't sure. One had a typical short cop haircut and the other sported a thin pony tail. Where had I seen them before?

Creston then turned to us. "In case the shot came from the van, did you notice anything unusual about it? License plate? Stickers? Dents? Anything distinguishing?"

"No, nothing." Cindy spoke with authority, still angry at me and trying to keep whatever crumbs of information were left to herself.

I offered sweetly, "But the van was covered in pock holes of rust on the sides, near the bottom."

Creston spoke as he wrote, "White van. Rust in rocker panels. Okay, then what?"

Cindy and I glared at each other. I didn't care what she thought. I would be cooperative and I had my little recorder on to prove that I was. I stared at her and twitched my thumb to my chest. It was *my* story. She backed down first and averted her eyes. Okay. She was going to do the right thing. The disagreement was over as soon as it had started. But the trauma of the night was scattering our thoughts. What *had* happened next?

Creston saw our confusion and put us back into the scene. "You were at the front door and you saw what looked like a bullet hole."

"Right," I said, as I remembered the sensation of being watched. "I felt like someone was watching us so I took pictures of the knocker, you know, covering up what we had seen and acting like I was doing a piece on mansions for the paper."

Cindy took over. "Then I banged on the door. We didn't hear a thing, so I knocked again."

"Then we turned and left. I pretended to berate Cindy for not making an appointment. We used fake names and talked about not getting the story for the *Toronto Times,* not our paper, the *Express*. We spoke loudly so whoever was listening would be misled."

Creston flipped through his book and found a clean page. "Then what?"

"We got in the car and left."

"You didn't stay? Check it out? Call?" Stokes was disbelieving.

"Are you kidding?" I said. "And get shot at by him?"

"No way," said Cindy, "I drove to the supermarket just south on Yonge to call. I knew there was a phone behind the store, but it was broken, so we called 911 from the courtesy desk. And now, here we all are."

"Why didn't you call from your cell at the outset?" Creston was writing it all down.

"Because," Cindy pronounced her words slowly, as if she was talking to someone who didn't speak English, "I didn't want the call picked up by someone's tracing equipment."

Creston gave her an appraising eye. "Good thinking," he said. "Did you see any other vehicles around? Other than your own and that van, I mean?"

I spoke up. "No, not one."

"Or her," said Stokes. He was trailing the conversation by about twenty sentences. "A woman could have been the shooter."

I knew it was a "he." There had been a male aura emanating from the stare I felt at the back of my head. Almost sexual and somehow mannish, brutish. It was the feel of animal testosterone. Nothing female.

Creston looked at his right hand man blankly.

The two officers who had gone off in the direction of the trees were heading back. The handsome one was carrying a couple of clear plastic bags in his gloved hand. He held one up, "Some casings." Then he held up the other one. "Blue nylon mesh caught on some bark. Probably from a gym bag or knapsack. I want to canvass the neighbours and ask them if they saw anything."

Creston took the evidence bags and replied, "Yes, and ask them about a white van as well. The shooter may have run from the trees to a getaway vehicle. A white van was seen down the street. Maybe someone noticed a license plate."

Maybe Cindy and I were both right about the shooter.

The cop talking to Creston was fantastically handsome. My mind drifted, imagining how it would feel to be in this fine man's arms at night, being kissed. But I knew this guy from somewhere. Where had my memory gone? I needed to stop drinking. And then I remembered. He had gotten off the elevator at Todd's condo before I had gotten on. What had Creston just said? Oh right, *license plate*.

Wait. I had an idea and pulled out my iPad. I flipped through the photos I had taken while we were waiting for van Horner to come home. "Here, I have a photo of the van." I enlarged the photo and read off the furry numbers of the license plate for Creston. He tried not to look too excited and flipped open his notebook, wrote it down then tore off the sheet and handed it to the other cop with the unfortunate face and ponytail. "Run this," he ordered, turning to the good-looking fella. And then rotating ninety degrees to me, he dictated his cell number, saying, "Send me the photo. In fact, if you don't mind, send me all the photos you took."

I cooperated and heard his phone ding repeatedly as the texts landed.

Creston snapped his notebook shut and Stokes reached into his pocket. I heard a distinct click. So, he'd been taping us on his cell. Maybe he wasn't such a dimwit. I peered at him straight in the eye as I pulled out my phone from my jacket pocket and tapped my recording app. Then I smiled at him, oh so pleasantly. I was catching on.

Creston was holding up the bags and looking through the plastic at the booty. "Good job, guys." He looked towards us and introduced them. "Misener and Melfours. M and M. Two great cops on my team."

Melfours had movie star quality good looks: tall, dark, chiseled jaw, brown sparkling eyes. But way too young for me. Misener looked like a bulldog, his head squashed into his neck as if he'd run into a bar fight. Or a truck. Strands of thin hair were scrapped off his face into a ponytail. He was the one to whom Creston had handed the license plate number. We introduced ourselves to the two cops but knew we had been politely but clearly dismissed.

Cindy turned the keys in the ignition and the dashboard lit up. I saw with a shock it was now five after eight. I had to be all the way downtown to meet England in less than thirty minutes. "I have to be at Bloor and Avenue Road at eight thirty to meet with England. Do you still want to drive me there, after my unfathomable betrayal to the enemy?"

Cindy waved off my sarcasm. "Of course I will." She glanced at her watch, "We're twenty minutes away, max. What did you think of Melfours?"

"Not a match, Cindy. I'd be labelled a bobcat."

"Cougar. You mean cougar."

"Right. Cougar." I couldn't wait to get the meeting with England over with and get home. Good thing it was a dog walker day, otherwise Lucky would be waiting with crossed legs. I sighed. "Just one more thing to do today and then home."

"Unless something happens between you and England." Cindy grinned at me wickedly.

I looked out the window and said, "Gross."

20.

I COULD SEE THE TALL AND SPINDLY REPORTER folded into a leather chair through the grime-covered Starbucks window. Jack England was already drinking something with froth on top and working on his computer. Although he looked pretty innocent, attractive even, the memory of him trapping me against the wall in the construction site made me shiver. I had to confess I was jittery about meeting him on my own. Did I ask Cindy for another favour after our little spat? Yes. Fear won the day.

"I was wondering if you wouldn't mind waiting for me. Then maybe drive me back down to the *Express* so I can get my car?"

Cindy turned her body and leaned back against the car door, the better to see me. "You frightened of *him*?" She jerked her thumb in his direction.

"Yeah, well, something pretty hairy is going on. A guy is dead, another one shot, and England did drag me off the street. The big picture is not as innocent as a skinny guy sitting in a Starbucks with foam on his upper lip."

Cindy nodded slowly, taking it all in, "Sure I'll wait. No problem. Here on Bloor Street, out of view from where he's sitting, with my flashers on. I've got lots of work to do while I wait. And of course I'll drive you down to your rat trap."

"Thanks, you're a good friend, Cindy."

"Don't give it another thought. You're welcome."

As I shut the door I mouthed through the window, "Keep your phone on."

She gave me a thumb's up through the windshield so I'd know she'd understood. As I headed towards the glass door of the Starbucks, I took a last glance at her inside her car. Her red head was bent low over her tablet while cars on Bloor zigzagged around her, punctuating the air with dainty little honks. Canadians are so polite.

When I pulled open the heavy door of the coffee shop a wave of warmish air rolled into the street. Nonetheless, I pulled my light jacket closer around me as I walked towards England's table. It seemed cold inside, or was it just me? Glancing around the Starbucks, I was surprised to see the dreadlocked kid again, writing in her spiral notebook. Our eyes met briefly and a smile played around her lips. I wondered what she was thinking. I was dating tons of guys? I was meeting drug dealers?

As I approached England, I could see that his thinning ebony hair was combed over to hide a bald spot. This was somehow endearing. If I had to describe him, I would say he had boyish good looks: button nose, fair Irish skin framed by raven hair and onyx eyes, and a childlike rosebud mouth all collected in an emaciated face. Not my type. I was already a mother of four, who needed another child? It was hard for me to reconcile his prettiness with the same guy who had threatened me. Well, I thought to myself, straightening up my shoulders, let's see who gets what out of this meeting.

"Hi Jack, thanks for meeting with me." No sense in being antagonistic. "Looks like you've settled in here."

He glanced up from his computer, his obsidian eyes crinkling at the corners as he smiled at me. This was unexpected. So, he was going to play nice and share his toys? His voice had the same low gravelly tone as it did the night before, but it had lost the menacing quality. "I had some free time, so thought I'd wait here until you showed up. Busy day?"

You have no idea. "Oh, this and that. The usual. Deadlines, work work work." I laughed breezily.

"Thanks for telling the police about our little encounter." He was so wry.

I could use a little rye.

"I had to, Jack." I stood in front of him at the table, defending myself. "You were pretty rough. That was an assault. You can't do that. I need you to understand that society doesn't tolerate women being threatened." I was admonishing him as though he were a child.

He had the grace to look down. "I am very sorry. I'm on Prednisone for Crohn's; it makes me a little squirrely. I call it roid rage. I will be more cognizant of its effects and control myself."

So, that's why he was so thin. He was ill. But I didn't acquiesce. "Plus, it's a *murder* investigation." He looked so miserable that I finally relented. "Did you get in big trouble?" I sat down at his table and hung my bag over the back of my chair. I still had my phone in my jacket pocket and felt for it instinctively. With a little touch and feely finger fumbling, I did my best to activate the recording app. Hopefully it and not my newly downloaded calm app went on. My thumb was ready as I listened for the tell tale wind chimes that marked the beginning of a guided meditation. Nothing. I was good to go.

"No." He leaned back and crossed his grasshopper legs at the knee. He was wearing basketball shoes. Geez, how old was he? "I've helped them a lot in the past. Led them towards criminals, you know, that sort of thing. It's a good working relationship."

"So, what did you tell them?"

"Nothing they didn't know already. That Radcliffe was planning to steal lake water from the deep water cooling system, you know, from the pump in the middle of the lake."

"Oh that." I looked at him with what I hoped looked like boredom. But in truth, I felt numb, trying to absorb this astonishing information. Why hadn't the police told *me* this? They'd said virtually the opposite, that he was the victim of a crime ring that was conspiring to steal the water. I guess I wasn't playing the game all that well. But still, you'd think they'd mention that crucial detail at least to Cindy. She'd helped them just as much as England. I knew they dropped tasty morsels in her lap every now and then, in exchange for future gifts. Nothing made sense. Especially not with van Horner's being shot on top of Radcliffe's death. Stealing fresh water? Radcliffe? Not some international group? Hardly seemed likely. Maybe England was making this up to throw me off the scent. But he seemed so plausible.

England was stirring his coffee, watching me carefully as I acted cool, his plastic stir stick hitting the sides with soft little thuds. He seemed mesmerized by the oily pink and purplish streaks in the foamy bubbles of his latte. Suddenly he jumped up. "How rude of me. Would you like some coffee or tea?"

I was jolted out of my thoughts. "Sure, thanks, peppermint tea. No, chamomile. No, peppermint. Peppermint."

"I like a girl who knows her mind," he taunted, acting as if he'd scored a round.

Boys. I smiled into his eyes.

As he departed I dug out my cell phone. Yes! The recording app was on, a miracle. Then I texted Cindy with the information about Radcliffe. She'd be amazed. *Radcliffe was planning on stealing lake water from the pumping station in the middle of the lake. International.*

She responded immediately. *He's throwing you off. Couldn't be.*

My fingers flying, I replied, *Why not?*

Doesn't make sense with van Horner's attack. Maybe somebody else is planning to steal the water, or maybe stealing something else and wants the bosses out of the way.

England thumped the paper cup full of green watery tea in front of me. I put my phone away and smiled my deepest gratitude. So. A liar, liar, pants on fire. I could negotiate this easily. After all, I was the mother of Calvin, the Honda Civic racing maniac. I had nights of practice, sniffing out the truth from the lies. Oh yeah, I knew how to get the facts. The trick to extricating the truth from lies was to get someone comfortable and talking so they'd be on a roll. The truth would slip out between their unsuspecting lips.

I figured there was probably *some* truth in what England had told me. No doubt someone was trying to steal something, just as Cindy said, possibly Lake Ontario's fresh water, but it sure wasn't Radcliffe. I believed his death put that notion to bed. Unless someone wanted him out of the way so they could get it. Now there was a possibility. Maybe. I would have to pry it out of Jack. If he even knew.

"Thanks for the tea, Jack." I put my hands around the paper cup. "It's freezing in here."

"Ironic considering that we're doing a story on air conditioning."

"Oh, is that what it is?" I raised an eyebrow, just one.

"You don't need to get pissy."

"Really? I should forget that you attacked me. For a measly air conditioning story? Is that how you usually communicate?"

England was contrite enough to avert his eyes, "Yes, well, again, I'm sorry. When I get on a story I get carried away."

So, I'd won round two. "On a story about air conditioning?" We were now in the third period of this hokey game. I was still trying to keep him unbalanced.

"Listen, I am sorry. I didn't mean to frighten you. I am sure you felt very threatened. The police have spoken to me and I certainly won't do it again." He took a sip of his coffee, covering his pretty lips with some milky foam. He seemed sincere. I briefly thought about licking the bubbles off his lips.

Round three. But now was the time to be a good team player, get him gushing. "That's okay Jack. I understand. We all get carried away when something is important. It's hard in this business." I passed the ball with a little flattery. "I admire people who are passionate about their work. You were on a mission!"

England's chest puffed out. "Yes, following that guy was a real challenge."

So, he *was* following Radcliffe. Not me. It wasn't a lie. Round four.

"Talk about busy," Jack continued. "For the past few days he's been all over the city. The guy spent more on transportation than I do in rent."

"Yeah, you were kept hopping. I saw you dash along Bloor after him right after you *talked* to me." Good strategy to downplay his attack. Simply wait for the foot in the mouth.

"Man, he was zipping along. By the time I left you Radcliffe was gone. I could only speculate that he had run along Bloor to St. George and was heading to the subway. So that's where I went. Naturally I didn't have the correct change, Murphy's law," Jack complained. "But while I was waiting in line to get through the turnstile I saw him in the crowd ahead of me. I figured he was probably going home, so I caught the next westbound train, got off at Bathurst and took the Bathurst streetcar down to King and then the King car along."

So, Jack knew where he lived. "Did you catch up to him?"

"I did," said England smugly. "He must have dawdled somewhere, because when I arrived at his address he was putting his key in the lobby door."

So, there was the foot in the mouth. A whopper lie. No keys in *that* building, as I well knew. Did I call him on it? Or let him dig himself in deeper. I played along. "Doesn't he live in those new condos, near Liberty Village?"

He nodded. "What a transformation of wasteland."

"I would have thought they'd all have keyless entry."

England's left knee started to pump up and down. "You're right. He was tapping in numbers on a key pad."

"Surely he didn't scan his key fob to open the door?"

Now both knees were bouncing. He was running a stationary

marathon. "Right. I wasn't sure what I saw. But he was there."

Yeah, right. "Did you see anything else? Someone following him, other than you? Like a murderer?" I laughed, offhandedly.

"No, only a few regular pedestrians were around."

"What was he doing by the waterfront earlier today?" A guess, but I was on a winning streak, he was definitely off kilter.

"I don't know." England fudged and then leaned forward, as if he were spreading some juicy gossip, "He was going onto a ship. Probably to get the captain to help him hook up the pump to a diverting pipe to siphon off the fresh water into a tanker." England paused, his black eyes drifting up to the left and his red tongue licking his teeth as if tasting the credibility of his story. Such a card. "Hey?" His piercing tar-black eyes focused on me, "How did you know I was there?"

"When I called you this morning I could hear seagulls." Plus, you told me, stupid.

"Oh. Clever. Anyway, he and van Horner were walking up a gang plank onto one of the boats down there."

"So, because of this you think he was planning on stealing water from the pumping station? That doesn't hold water, *ha ha*. Maybe someone else was planning the theft."

The knee started up again. This man was a terrible liar. Or I was really good at sussing out the "tells."

"Nope. It was his gig. I think he was casing out the boat to see how he could work the theft."

"Hmmm. What was the name of the boat?"

"The Barbara D."

Easy enough to remember. Time for me to head out. I had tons of information and I knew that England had no idea he had given me so much. He probably didn't even know he had so much information. It was clear he didn't know who had killed Radcliffe, that he didn't yet know that van Horner had been shot, or who was trying to steal the water, if anyone.

My head was spinning with the complexity of it all. This was a far cry from sheep shit for award-winning azaleas. I could see out of the corner of my eye the nose of Cindy's car sliding up so she could take a look into the café and then sliding back again. It brought me back to reality. I was dealing with a liar.

"Really, that's the name? Come on England, you've lied like eighty times since we've been here. How many cards do you have to play? What was the name of the boat? The Diane B.? The Catherine F.?"

His boyish face glowered. "Okay, so I tried to mislead you. It's a competitive world out there, Robin. I have to sell papers or I'll lose my job. *The Times* isn't as big as the *Express* and doesn't have the same advertising muscle behind it. I have to resort to any and all means to get information. So, sorry. I was feeding you lines to see what you'd say." He laughed and spread his arms, as if apologizing for my ignorance. "You know nothing," he warbled. "I wanted to beat you to the punch."

He smiled at me innocently, activating those attractive lines around his eyes. All was fair in love and war. Such a darling. But again, not my type. Besides, was he lying now? I thought *The Times* was in pretty good shape. It was a national and we were just a local paper. *The Times* had nice shiny paper and we used plain old newsprint. Their colour photos were crisp and authentic looking. Ours looked like watercolours after a rain. Yeah, it was a lie.

"Look, you are a pathological liar," I said amiably. "From now on everything you tell me is going to be flushed down the toilet. You are busted. I know *The Times* is in good shape, so don't try to weasel out of your behaviour with that lame excuse. I know your *modus operandi*, I had four kids. You think if you feed me bad information I'll either correct it to your face so you'll get something you didn't know, or I'll run with it and be led down the garden path, wasting time."

"Got me," he shrugged. "The boat's name was the Barbara D."

"Yeah, right." I gathered up my purse and put on my jacket. "And Radcliffe was trying to steal water from Lake Ontario.

You know what this gesture means, Jack?" I put my finger in the air and acted out pushing a small lever down.

His lip curled as he watched me.

"It means you're busted, Jack. Every card you played tonight was a lie." I did the pushing the lever gesture again, only this time I blew out a great whooshing sound effect. "This means you are a busted *flush*. It means I know you are only giving me shit, and I am flushing it."

Jack was infuriated, "C'mon Robin, give me a break." This Jack was familiar, his eyes as hard as black ice. But then his mood changed faster than a chameleon's colours and he gave me a wide-eyed blameless look. Great, a psychopath.

I laughed, "See you around, Jack-off."

The young woman with dreadlocks was watching this exchange with interest. When I walked past her slouching in a chair I saw that she had written a full page. She looked up and beamed at me, her hand covering her work. She gestured with her thumb towards England. "Dishonest," she said.

It must have been her go-to word. That was twice she had used it. I nodded in agreement and gave her an exasperated shrug while raising my eyebrows at her hand covering her work. She smiled back at me and extended her other hand in a "what?" gesture, while spreading the other completely over her work.

Looked like everyone had something to hide and no one was embarrassed about it but me. Me? I would wait until I was behind my locked door to pour myself a glass of wine. Okay, a tumbler. But no one would know what I was doing. I would sit there enjoying myself and think about the day. I had it all planned out.

I pulled open Cindy's car door.

She was curious. "So, what did you get from England?" she asked breathlessly.

"Thanks for waiting for me, Cindy." I slammed the door. "I got nothing. He is such a liar."

"All reporters lie; that's why people hate us." She looked over her shoulder and pulled out into the traffic.

"I'm not a liar." I did up my seat belt.

"You will be," she said with conviction, pulling a U-turn and heading east to Yonge Street.

Maybe I would. I *liked* the games.

"He knew nothing about van Horner yet. He says Radcliffe was going to steal fresh water out of the lake, and the name of the boat is the 'Barbara D.' Knowing the way he lies, it's probably the name of a woman with an initial, because his lies usually have some truth in them. I'll get the research department on that. Forget driving me to my car. It's closer to my house anyway. I just want to get home."

"Okay, I need a drink too."

She knew me too well.

"No, I gotta let Lucky out."

"Nice try."

I smiled in the dark. Friends were good.

21.

On Saturday morning I clambered up from the oblivion of sleep. With my eyes still tightly closed, I did a cursory run through of my state of the nation. Arms? Check. Legs? Check. Head? Check. Not bad, all considering. One huge glass of wine had turned into two and then three. Or were there four? How many bottles had I opened? What time did I stop? I couldn't even remember getting into bed. And where was Lucky? I blindly patted the bed around me until I felt his soft head. Okay, at least I didn't leave the dog out all night.

I smacked my lips. After a night of heavy drinking I usually woke up with what felt like cotton balls in my mouth but today I had woken up with a layer of something slimy on my teeth. What was it? Animal fat? Oh joy. Was this the punishment for eating fast food? Why on earth did I sabotage myself? I knew junk food was bad for me. I knew I was fat. I knew I had to lose weight. And yet I still stuffed my face with garbage. I should be eating quinoa and lightly stir-fried kale. Bits of raw fish and rice. Not hamburgers and fries.

I was in such a bad mood.

My duvet was wrapped around my legs and I kicked at it irritably. Already I was hot. The day promised to be a scorcher, yet again. I rolled over in bed, my nightgown straining at my back, constricting my shoulders. I heard a stitch rip. Fuck.

When I opened my eyes sunlight was bashing around the

edges of what was supposed to be a room darkening shade. Another fake guarantee. A lie. Everyone lies. I had read the cellophane packaging. Guaranteed to keep the room dark. Guaranteed to keep a room cool. Guaranteed to insulate. Yeah yeah yeah. Lucky was looking at me expectantly. His head was tilted and his cute little ears were cocked. What the hell did *he* want? I swung my feet over the edge of the bed, felt a pain in my back, groaned, swore, and trudged to the bathroom. It was seven-fifteen.

I climbed back into bed for a few more minutes and felt Lucky snuggle into my chest. I rubbed my tongue over my teeth, trying to scrape off the grease in my mouth. I needed to go organic. Maybe talk to my naturopath about nutrition. Oh wait, the drinking. First things first. What did Sally tell me to do? Yeah, three things. Every morning I was to make a note of three things I was grateful for. And this was day one. Great start. I was in such a bad mood. But okay, I would do the job.

I lay on my back and tried to clear my mind. Years ago I had learned that to calm myself down I should focus on the breath. So I did. Yikes. I should have brushed my teeth. It smelled like a rat had crawled into my mouth and died. My mind wandered. At least I didn't have cigarette breath. Thank heavens I had quit smoking years ago and my asthma had mostly cleared up. I had also grown an inch! It was the oddest thing, given that I was twenty-four at the time. How did that happen? Wait. Concentrate. Three things I am grateful for.

Clear the mind. I lay very still and waited for a sense of gratitude. It was hard to find any sense of thankfulness for the way I felt, frankly, given what an irritable temper I was in. I was such a bitch. For the past few years I had generally been crabby. My bad hair day stretched over a decade. So, it took more than a little effort to try and open my mind to gratitude.

When my mind drifted into any murky canyons, those dark places where my thoughts became trapped, like my marriage, or money stresses, or the kids when they were teenagers, I pushed it back into clarity. After about five minutes of boomeranging back and forth between suffocating dark shadows and bright daylight, my brain finally settled in the light. I felt padlocked doors creaking open and beams of sunshine filtering in. I liked the way it made my head feel, unlocked and somehow wider. Open.

Finding the first thing I was grateful for was now easy. It was right beside me on the covers. Number one: I was grateful for my dog. Granted, I would rather have a man beside me in my bed, well, maybe not, but there was nothing quite like patting the head of a lovely soft pup first thing in the morning. I was right when I told Sally that my dog's soft fur was something I should be grateful for. I reached out and stroked Lucky behind the ears for a minute or two. He was as soft as a velveteen rabbit. He looked at me with his lovely doe-brown eyes and I cooed sweet nothings to him. He rolled over and presented his belly for me to pat. I could feel my heart swell with love for this little creature and the day looked a little brighter.

Okay, on to number two. What was I grateful for? I looked at the sunlight illuminating the edges of the roller blind and knew there was a nice day shaping up outside. I imagined myself doing my job at the *Express*, chasing down leads or whatever crime reporters do, in the pretty sunshine. Oh wait, it was Saturday and I didn't have to go to work! Hooray. I stretched languidly and imagined the sunshine warming my back as I gardened. I sensed my heart lifting. Yes, I was grateful for sunshine and I could feel my thankfulness spreading through my heart.

So, two down, one to go. I was getting a little antsy, lying in bed and doing such a Zen Buddhist thing. Not to be demeaning to those who did Zen Buddhist things. I was a Unitarian and a new Buddhist, hence the meditation app. I needed to calm down my stress levels. Acceptance was key. Non-judgmental approaches. Respect for all. Universal harmony with the divine. World peace through inclusiveness, a goal. But still, I had my problems with Buddhism. I wasn't sure it suited me. All that effort to let go of anger and only feel peace? If you asked me, inner peace wasn't all that it was cracked up to be. It was my opinion that it was fleeting, illusive, and frankly, extremely dull. Anger, on the other hand, was never dull. I'd rather feel a burst of rage, act on it, and move on than spend days trying to sit with it, or ignore it, or clamp it down, only so it could rise up and bite me in the ass later. Anger was a great motivator. Anger created change. Anger was passionate and passion was so *alive*. I wouldn't be lying in bed trying to think of three things if I hadn't got angry at myself for the way I was living. Was I grateful for anger? Seemed a bit contradictory.

On the other hand, maybe my difficulties with Buddhism was why I drank. Did drinking make me feel alive? Did it rev me up so that I felt like I was enjoying a party? Did it drive me? Was it fun? You betcha! I loved it. It was the only time that meek and mild Robin MacFarland could let loose. That letting go of anger business, that just wasn't for me. Not now.

I was out of steam for this gratitude shit. Fuck it. I was done with the stupid exercise. I'd made a good start. And a start was a start. Two things to be grateful for were better than no things. Maybe I would do better tomorrow. I kicked my legs and tried to untangle them from the sheets. I had to get going.

As I put my feet over the edge of the bed I noticed the lovely wood grain in the hardwood flooring. Was it the poet Rumi who said there were a hundred ways to kiss the earth? Yes, Rumi. I felt the souls of my feet touch the wooden floor and thought about the trees that grew out of deep damp earth in lush forests. I could almost smell the muskiness of the moss and ferns as I stood up and stretched forward, working the kink out of my back. My heart felt attached to the universe in a loving way. And there it was, the third thing. Without even trying I had come up with it, the last thing to be grateful for: the earth and all that grew upon it.

The day went by smoothly, with me feeling a little more content with my lot in life. Before the morning really heated up, I puttered in the garden, feeling the sun on my back as I pulled weeds while not caring a jot about dirty fingernails. I took the transit system downtown and picked up my car, completely unmindful of the crowds. Then I did a food shop and wasn't pissed off with the lineup at the checkout. I washed my clothes and didn't mind folding them. I cleaned the kitchen floor without being irritated as I scratched at the dried dog food by Lucky's bowl. I walked the dog without tugging at his leash, telling him to hurry up. I noticed these changes in myself and marvelled at them.

But I still loved to drink. Because we'd had to cancel Friday night, Cindy and Diane came over after dinner for a get together. The three of us made some inroads into a king-sized bottle of wine while watching an old Western on TV. Each week we switched up the genre we picked, searching through Netflix for something that suited us. Tonight we were in a giddy-up, hi ho Silver kind of mood. After the bottle was almost gone we started pouring the ginger ale, wild things that we were. We also scarfed down a whole family-sized bag of potato chips and laughed a lot. At ten we ordered pizza and gobbled it down. We were having fun.

The three of us hashed over our work week. Cindy confessed she was nervous interviewing members of the Vipers. I complained about the lying Jack England and how I couldn't figure out why Radcliffe was dead. And Diane bitched about her current case: a prominent Toronto family member had evaded millions of dollars of taxes and she was trying to put him into jail. Her family had had terrible financial struggles while she was growing up in downtown Toronto above a storefront, and her anger at the arrogance of this fat cat was palpable.

I was grateful that the three of us had such a nice relationship. My friends shoved off around midnight, after several cups of coffee, and we blew kisses at each other across my front patch of grass as they got into their cars. Journalists and lawyers often drank too much, but I knew they'd be okay driving. We'd only had two and a half glasses of wine each over the course of almost five hours. I figured the last thing anyone would do around me was drink and drive, given what had happened to Trevor. I thought about that as I finished off the bottle of wine.

Sunday promised to be muggy and hot. Again. When I cracked open my eyes I went through the same exercise of thinking of three grateful things. I took my time, remembering it wasn't enough to list the three items; I actually had to feel the gratitude permeate into my being. That's what Sally had wanted me to do. This was a mission to change my mind. I was grateful for rain that nourished my garden, grateful for the fresh food in my fridge, and grateful for my children, who were coming for dinner that night with my parents.

After a leisurely breakfast of oatmeal and yogurt, I trundled across town to the Unitarian service. It was always short and sweet, with the constant reminder about the interwebbedness of life. This jived with the Buddhist philosophy as well, and I certainly believed it. But I was glad the service was short, leaving the rest of the day to myself. Periodically throughout the afternoon, while I prepared a vegetarian casserole and chicken stir fry for Sunday dinner, I contemplated the Minister's message: how what affects one person affects all of us, that we are all part of a whole. I wondered how my drinking impacted my family and felt guilty.

That night when everyone was sitting around the table, catching up with each other about their week, I was self-conscious every time I lifted my glass to my mouth for a slug of wine. I felt so guilty about it that I only had one tiny glass while they were in my house. Without the hand to mouth distraction, I found I was able to focus better on what was going on at my table. That was interesting. And perhaps new. I felt guilty about that too.

The dinner didn't start out well. My aging parents were battling to stay in their own home. I listened as my father complained about everything he had to do: mow the grass, clean the windows, wash the floors, take out the garbage, change the tires on the car, fill the oil tank. The endless list was punctuated with him angrily thumping the table, sometimes a little behind the rhythm of his diatribe. He was slowly losing his memory. It was as if one by one post-it notes were falling off his body and scattering at his slippered feet. Around him lay the lost reminders of things to do and I watched as he struggled to pick them up, pissed off at himself. When he was like this, I wasn't about to remind him that they no longer had a car. Every time his hand crashed down on the table my mother cringed. She was bowed over with osteoporosis and her poor back bent even more when he was in one of his moods.

The Zen Buddhist approach to letting anger go was looking more attractive.

None of this affected their appetites however. As I sat at the head of the table, a position I rotated with my kids after Trevor had died, I watched with astonishment as they plowed through heapings of vegetables and chunks of chicken. Had they not eaten properly all week? I didn't dare mention the words "rest home." The last time I brought the topic up my father had shouted at me for two hours, all the while my mother recoiling from his anger, shrinking into her chair, her watery eyes overflowing.

Although the kids were disturbed by their grandparents' slow demise, they sat quietly as my father roared, eating and keeping their heads down. They'd heard it all before. I was so proud of them, watching them blossom and grow into adulthood. Once my father settled down, his anger spent, the kids began speaking, changing the whole tenor of the table.

Maggie, the oldest, was showing off her new boyfriend, Winchester. My mother peered at his chin stud and said, "What a pretty diamond, dear." We all tried not to laugh so that my mom didn't think we were laughing at her, which of course, we were. At least she hadn't commented on the colour of his skin, which was a risk, being from *that* generation and from England.

The answer to the mystery of Evelyn's text earlier in the week was revealed when she asked everyone at the table about laser surgery to erase her tattoos and wanted to know the names of some good cosmetic surgeons. I was grateful she wasn't thinking of altering her body in some way, which I thought was perfect. Calvin, my second oldest, had started a new job and regaled us with hilarious anecdotes about his boss. Bert, the baby of the family, talked about going back to school, which I wondered about; he had always hated school. My older brother Andrew, who was away on a business trip to Israel of all places, would have cheered him on because he'd always felt that Bert was an underachiever. I always replied to his observations about my children that it was none of his damn business and that he had no idea what went on in someone else's family. Andrew and I didn't get along that well. I'd ask Bert about school later, when it was just the two of us. Bertie was sensitive.

Eventually the dinner had turned into a warm and happy evening that ended too soon, with Calvin volunteering to drive my parents home. I was grateful for my family, warts and all. After they left, amid noisy hugs and promises to get together again soon, I sat down in my comfy reading chair in the kitchen and polished off the rest of the bottle of wine, the guilt I felt earlier dissipating with each swig. No doubt about it. I loved to drink. The distress about my parents, the worries about my children, the concerns about the Everwave story, and ultimately the pain in my heart from the holes Trevor had excavated in my self-esteem faded into the distance as I sat in my chair in the kitchen, glugging straight from a bottle of wine, Lucky at my feet.

22.

ON MONDAY MORNING, MERCIFULLY NOT hung over, I dutifully thought of my three things—green leaves, large hunks of granite, my washing machine—and shuffled off to the bathroom. I didn't know if the exercise of feeling grateful would help me stop drinking, but I sure felt a little happier when I woke up. What a crabbola I'd been. For years. I stood under the shower for an extra minute, savouring the soft feel of the cascade. One thing about gratitude, it sure made you feel more present in the here and now.

I hummed as I swiped some eye shadow across my lids and got dressed. I almost danced down the stairs. Yeah, I felt different. I poured myself a small bowl of granola, and then picked out the almonds. Hmmm, this was different. Usually in the morning I got annoyed at my innocent little bowl of granola and ranted at the stupid food companies. Didn't they know tons of people were allergic to nuts? Why didn't they cater to this demographic? It was hardly a niche market. Nut allergies were rampant. Every morning I raged as I picked out the infuriating almonds. But not today. Today I wasn't bothered by the almonds. I put in my spoon and crunched away, enjoying every tidbit as I looked out the window into the back yard. Lucky was barking at a squirrel.

I had had this allergy to almonds since I was little, and thank heavens I had a controllable reaction. Sure, it could be serious, if I didn't get to an inhaler in time, but there was a window of five or ten minutes where if I got to my inhaler I would be as right as rain in about half an hour after a good deep puff. I might have an itchy throat or teary eyes for a bit, but all that would disappear. I was so fortunate, unlike some people whose allergy to peanuts or wasp stings could kill them. Those poor people. Imagine, walking along the road enjoying the sunshine, being stung by a wasp and then BAM, you're grabbing at your throat, unable to breath. The panic must be terrible.

Suddenly my hand stopped its journey to my mouth. Radcliffe had had his hand half way up to his throat. His profile said he was allergic to wasp stings. Was this the cause of his death? He'd been stung by a wasp? Was this what was in his profile that couldn't be seen? Was that why it had been deleted? The murderer didn't want the police to know that he was allergic to wasps? So his death would look like a suicide or an accident? Did the murderer know that I had read the profile? Was I in danger?

Despite sitting in the bright sunlight shining through the kitchen window, my hands turned to ice. I'd had an anxiety attack years ago when Trevor had died, and it had started with freezing cold hands. Eventually they had gone completely numb. I began to pant, terror coursing through my veins. Would I be killed, too? And then I slowed myself down. If I kept up like this I would surely have a full-blown attack. Think, Robin, think. And breathe slowly.

Okay, I *was* in danger if Radcliffe had told the person who wanted to kill him that he was using the internet to find dates. If that person hacked into his profile and read it, they would know Todd had written that he was allergic to wasps. And it followed if that person then read on the messaging feature of the site that Todd and I had connected, then I truly *was* in danger, because I would know about the allergy. That was a lot of "if's" but, nonetheless, my photograph would be on his site because it was part of my profile. All that person had to do was follow Radcliffe to our date at Starbucks, which would have been documented in *meetyourmatch*'s messaging board, and then follow me home to find out where I lived. Had I noticed anyone suspicious that night in the cafe? Seen anything untoward? The coffee shop had been so crowded. It would have been impossible to notice. Besides I was preoccupied. The last thing on my mind while I sipped my herbal tea was looking for a murderer. But a murderer could easily have been there.

Was the murderer England? He had accosted me after I'd left. He had been there, watching us. He'd said he was following Radcliffe, but maybe he was following *me*. Did he start out pretending he was following Radcliffe and then doubled back to follow me? No, it couldn't be. Could it? No, I believed he was following Radcliffe. His narrative sounded real. The details were sort of real. There was that business about the key fob, but then, I truly believed he was creating a web of lies to throw me off.

But had someone followed me home?

My spoon clattered into the bowl. My fingers were now tingling so badly I could barely feel them. My chest was constricting and my vision was fading, the room becoming dark. I was heading for a full-on faint. I shoved my head between my knees and told myself to breathe deeply. I was safe. Nothing bad was going to happen. Slowly I felt the blood returning to my hands and the light-headed feeling dissipated. I carefully sat up and looked at my half eaten bowl of granola. I'd lost my appetite. Although this in itself was a phenomenon, it spoke volumes about how deeply I was rattled. I felt fear burning on my skin.

I had figured out the murder weapon. It must have been a wasp. And I was the only one who knew. It was the one detail from his profile that I didn't remember when I was talking to the police or Doug. The killer had deleted the profile so this bit of knowledge wouldn't be known.

But I knew it. What I didn't know was if the wasp venom was the type that decomposed rapidly in blood, leaving no trace.

According to crime shows on TV there were some poisons that were undetectable. Would the coroner be able to pick up the small bit of venom in Todd's blood? Maybe the coroner could ascertain that Todd had died from a wasp sting. But what the coroner couldn't do was prove that the wasp was used as a murder weapon. She could easily rule it was an accidental death.

I was certain this had been murder. Especially after van Horner's attack. And I would figure it all out, even though my brain cells had taken a beating from my drinking binge last night after Sunday dinner with my kids. What did I know about wasps? I swam through the cloudy waters in my head. Not much, it turned out, but one thing did float to the surface: wasps didn't fly in the dark.

How do you use a wasp as a murder weapon? Think, Robin, think. Someone could have planted a wasp in Todd's room, perhaps in his bed. Right, that was it. Someone snuck in to his condo and put the wasp on the bed, turned out the light, and then left, hoping for the best. Hoping the wasp would stay right where it had been put in the dark. Todd would have lain down in his bed, likely on the wasp, got stung, and then died.

But wait. I shouldn't get ahead of myself. It could have been an accidental death. Maybe a sleepy wasp had been on his clothing when he came in Thursday night. Yeah, one that had landed on him during the day. He had lain down on the bed fully dressed and the wasp, feeling trapped, stung him. So, maybe the whole thing was just an accidental death.

No, neither of these two scenarios could be right. First of all, putting a wasp on a bed was too unreliable. If I were a murderer and wanted someone dead, I would make sure nothing could go wrong. Wasps didn't fly at night, but they *crawled*. There would be no guarantee that a wasp would stay on a bed right where it had been placed. And no guarantee that Todd would lie on it either. Secondly, no normal wasp would be on clothing after dark. As soon as the sun started going down all wasps head home.

No, the wasp hadn't been planted in his bed and it wasn't accidentally on his clothes. Plus, someone went to great effort to delete Radcliffe's profile and why would someone want to do that if it was an accidental death? I was becoming more and more certain that the wasp had been used as a murder weapon.

I kept coming back to the same question: how do you use a wasp as a murder weapon?

Maybe someone had planted a wasp inside his jacket. That would make more sense than putting it on his bed. Or it coming in from outside on his clothing. If I were looking to kill someone with a wasp sting, I would try to maximize the chances of the wasp actually biting the victim. A wasp on a bed could easily scrabble away. A wasp trapped in a piece of clothing that the victim was likely to put on would be a far better bet. A jacket would be perfect. Now I was making some sense.

Planting a wasp in a jacket that a person wasn't wearing would be pretty easy, too. One could sidle up to the jacket if it was draped over the back of a chair, like Todd's had been at Starbucks, for example, and simply slip the wasp into a pocket. But I should consider other options. It could be trapped in a sleeve, or the jacket's lining. I thought about these scenarios. No, the pocket made the most sense. A wasp could escape from a sleeve. And getting one inside a lining would require scissors to cut open a hole and then forcing the wasp into the hole. Too tricky. Right, the most likely scenario was putting the wasp in a pocket and then making sure the pocket flap was folded over the opening to trap it. Perfect. The probability of it biting the victim once the jacket was put on was pretty high. *If* the person put his hands in his pockets. Not everyone did that. But I had seen Todd do just that. While he was standing in line. My bets were on the pocket.

And he certainly had been carrying a jacket, a light-weight summer navy blue blazer. It had been draped over his arm when he walked in, he hung over the back of his chair while we had our hot drinks, and it was slung over his shoulder when he left Starbucks. I could see it clearly in my mind's eye, the jacket jouncing on his back as he sauntered away from me. He'd hooked it over his thumb, like a cool guy in a TV commercial for deodorant.

But how would a murderer transport a wasp? It would have to be in something small, something concealable. Something with a lid. Something it couldn't sting through. I rummaged around in my noggin for various containers. A pill bottle would be perfect. Yes! One could carry a wasp in a pill bottle, say, and then easily shake the wasp out into a pocket, and then pat down the flap, trapping it. I couldn't remember if his blazer pockets had flaps. Probably.

But when was the next time I saw the jacket? At his condo? God I hated my memory. Yes, I think it was hanging up in his condo. Yes it was. Neatly on a wooden hanger in the closet inside the front door. I remembered. It was one of those expensive hangers that have an arch to protect the way the shoulders fell. Right. I remember checking the buttons up close to see if they were RCYC buttons. They were. Had I seen flaps on the pockets? I couldn't remember. I hadn't noticed. I would have to let that question go. Most blazer pockets had flaps and I would have to assume his did too.

But when had he been stung? I guess the question was when had he put the jacket on after leaving the Starbucks? If he hadn't worn it at all, then the jacket was off the hook as the wasp vehicle. How could I find this out? Jack England would know. Jack had followed him, perhaps, from the Starbucks to his condo. If I believed him. That business about the key was pretty questionable. Was Jack actually there? Maybe it *was* Jack who had planted the wasp. Nah, I would have recognized him in the coffee shop. Besides, Jack had been a crime reporter for yonks. He worked with the police. When he felt like it. He wasn't involved in this. Couldn't be. As much as I didn't like him, or maybe I did, I came to the conclusion he was just a rabid reporter, looking for a story. He was not a murderer.

Should I ask Jack about the jacket? Hmm. Jack about the jacket. My mind stalled on this rickety phrase for a minute or two. It sounded like train wheels clattering on rails. I thought about the tracks over my lips. Old. Fat. Alkie. No, no, don't go there, pay attention Robin. Your life is in danger. Focus.

I knew my next moves had to be very careful. I didn't want to get dead. Hell no. Not after feeling so good this morning after my three things. Whatever they were. That feeling of peace and quiet was long gone. Now I felt fright. Actually it was terror singeing the skin off my bones. Doug was right. I knew something that someone didn't want me to know. And that person had murdered one person already and shot at another.

Would these people or that person be trying to get me now? How professional were they? Killing someone with a wasp was pretty creative. And risky. Who exactly was I dealing with? I remembered Cindy slapping my phone out of my hand in case it was tapped so that I wouldn't be associated with witnessing a crime. Who knew how sophisticated these people were. Was someone watching me right now, through my kitchen window? From my garden?

Anger rose in my chest. How dare they! I refused to be intimidated. Never again. Trevor had done enough of that for a lifetime. I flung the back door open with bravado. No one was peering over the fence or hiding behind my forsythia bush. I looked for reflections of lenses in the tree branches and little red target dots on my person. Nothing. I called for Lucky thinking it would justify my looking out the back door, just in case someone *was* watching.

For a second he didn't appear and my heart lurched into my mouth. Had someone killed him? As a warning? Isn't that what pathological serial killers did? Get off on instilling fear in someone before killing them? I'd read about that. Where was that dog? I felt my mouth go dry. And then I heard his tags rattling. Lucky was digging to China in the far corner of the yard. I yelled and he came running towards me, his nose covered with wet clumps of mud. I patted Lucky's soft head and dragged him inside by the collar. Relief bubbled up inside me and erupted into out-of-control giggles. I tamped them down.

And honestly, how would I ask Jack about the jacket without him knowing what I was trying to find out? That the jacket was a vehicle. No, a beehicule. Beehicle vehicle. God, I was funny. Laughter erupted again. Again I shoved it down. I had to pull myself together. I had to call Jack. No, not him. He might be involved in all this. No, he wasn't. But still, I wasn't taking chances. Creston would want to know about the murder weapon. Besides, Creston could keep me safe. Police protection. But could I use my phone? Shit, now I was as paranoid as Cindy. But better to be safe than sorry. I would call Creston, who could keep me safe, and not Jack, who lied.

I put Lucky on his leash, grabbed a measuring cup as camouflage for going to my neighbours. I was out of flour, didn't you know, and my phone, and moseyed next door, all casual. The Blakelys were friendly and I could see their car was still on the street. Someone would be home. They were a young couple who'd bought the house next to mine and were fixing it up. There was a big metal bin in the front now, full of old plaster and dilapidated linoleum. She, Rebecca, was a professor at Ryerson, meaning she could walk to work from Cabbagetown, and he, Brian, was an investment banker and drove downtown. So their car was a clue that someone, at least him, would be home. What a detective I was. I would make a crime reporter yet.

Brian came to the door, his tie undone and hair gelled but not yet combed. "Hi, Robin. You looking for some sugar?"

For a second I thought he was being inappropriate, he was young enough to be my son, but then remembered that I was a panther. No, a cougar. No. It was the measuring cup. "I don't know why I have this in my hand. I left in a hurry." Well, that sounded like I was crazy. "Do you mind if I borrow your phone?"

Brian held the door open wide and let me in. "Sure." He handed me his cell, head slanted to the left a bit. He watched me carefully as I pulled out my phone and scrolled through my contacts. "You out of juice?"

"Juice?" I said stupidly.

"Low battery?" he clarified.

"Ah, yes, no juice. Barely enough to check my contacts."

He nodded as if he were humouring me. He could smell a rat. But I couldn't tell him the truth, could I? Cindy was right. She said I would become a liar if was a crime reporter. Well, I was on that trajectory already. But I decided to come clean and tell the truth.

"Look. I know this looks odd. The measuring cup was a cover for my coming over. I think I'm being watched by a murderer. And I need to borrow your phone because I think mine is tapped."

Brian smiled indulgently. "Don't you lead the exciting life! Is this because of working at the paper?"

"Yes, so here I am, being coy, trying to get the word out about a wasp."

"I see," said Brian, somewhat doubtfully. "I'm a WASP. Is this about racial profiling?" I stared at him blankly. "Listen, I think I'll finish getting ready for work. Rebecca's already gone." He said this with regret. Rebecca was a psych prof, and he probably thought she'd come in handy just about now. "Leave the phone on the counter when you're done."

"Thanks, Brian," I said to his departing back as I looked up Creston's number on my phone and then dialed it on Brian's.

When he answered I burst into tears.

23.

"**W**HOA, BRIAN, IT'S OKAY. You're talking to a police officer and I will help you. How did you get this number?"

Through my tears I was flummoxed. Brian? Who was Brian? Brian was upstairs combing his hair. Oh right, I was using his phone. His name must have come up on caller ID on Creston's phone. I tried to stifle my sobs.

"It's me, Creston. Robin MacFarland," I sobbed, my heart vibrating.

"What are you doing using Brian Blakely's phone? Are you hurt? In trouble? Something happen to your phone? Car accident?" There was genuine concern in Creston's voice. Panic even. What did *that* mean?

A weight pressed down on my chest and I whimpered, "I'm using my neighbour's because I think mine could be tapped." I began to sob again. His kindness tipped me into another wave of upset. I choked out, "It's because of the bee."

"What can't be?"

I sniffled, "No, the wasp. The murder weapon is a wasp."

"Radcliffe was murdered by a WASP? Without any evidence that's racial profiling and we've had pretty good training about that."

This was ridiculous. I had to stop crying. I could hear Brian moving around upstairs. What would he *think*? There was no way I could answer Creston.

"Listen," he said, "Why don't you go home and I'll come over. I have your address. I have to go down to the waterfront now anyway, I'm at Dundas now, so it's sort of on my way. I could swing by. Would you like that?"

I wept, "Yes."

I left Brian's phone on the counter and was soon sitting primly in my living room like a frozen manikin, tears dried, hands clasped in my lap, waiting for Creston. Slowly I began to relax. Help was on its way. While sending a text to Shirley about being a tad late, I heard a car pull up in front of the house. I opened the door and beckoned Creston to come inside quickly. What if someone who shouldn't know I was talking to the police saw that I was? At least Creston's car was unmarked. At least he didn't look like a cop today, in his Sperry topsiders, jeans, and T-shirt. Creston stood in my foyer and I could see that he was looking around without seeming to look around. It was a cop trick. I was trying to see what he saw. The bright colours. The modern art on the walls. Pine wood everywhere. I liked what I liked. No interior designer beiges and blacks for me.

"Thanks for coming over," I said. "I had a bit of a revelation this morning while I was eating my cereal and it scared the pants off me."

Creston looked down at my legs, eyebrows raised.

I smiled at his unspoken joke and moved back from him self-consciously. "Not really, but you know what I mean."

"Tell me," he said.

"Well, I'm allergic to almonds and I have to pick them out of my granola every morning."

"Maybe I should come in."

I winced. Why had I not invited him in for at least a coffee? "Oh, sorry about that, would you like some coffee? Here, come into the kitchen. I'll make you a cup."

He eased himself into one of my kitchen chairs at my pine harvest table and leaned back, his arms dangling over the back of his chair, which pulled his t-shirt tight across his wonderful chest. He looked good in my kitchen, at home and relaxed, one leg over the other. I tried not to stare at the lean line of muscle on his thigh. I got out the mugs and coffee pot, the coffee, and some sugar. The bustling around was good for me. I felt useful and less frightened.

"So, you're allergic to almonds and this frightened you."

"Not quite," I said, my back to him as I was reaching in the fridge for some milk, hoping my muffin top was hidden under my shirt and my bum didn't look too fat. "I had picked the almonds out of my cereal and while I was eating it I was thinking that I was lucky that I don't have really serious reactions to them, unlike some people. Some people are very allergic to nuts and wasps and die terrible deaths, feeling like they're being strangled. Me, my lungs contract and fill up, I mean the allergy *is* serious, but if I get my inhaler in time, I'm okay."

"Yes, I have a niece who is allergic to wasp stings. She carries an EPI pen wherever she goes in the summer."

An EPI pen. Why didn't I think about that? I should have checked his jacket pocket for one.

The kettle boiled and I poured the hot water through the coffee filter. Soon the smell of freshly brewed dark roast filled the air. I carried the pot to the table and poured the coffee into the two mugs.

"Right, well, it's not so bad that I need an EPI pen like she does. Anyway, when I was talking to you about Todd Radcliffe's profile, I had forgotten that he said he was allergic to wasps. It must have been pretty serious if he felt compelled to mention it in his profile, don't you think?"

I put one of the mugs of coffee in front of Creston and sat down. He reached forward for a spoon and the sugar bowl. I inched the milk carton towards him. "Sorry it's not cream, if that's what you like."

"No, this is all fine, Robin. Thank you very much." He gave me a dazzling smile and stirred his coffee with enthusiasm, his spoon clinking on the side of the mug. "Let me get this straight. You're talking about a wasp wasp, not a WASP wasp. Todd's profile mentioned that he was allergic to wasp stings. And now you think a wasp was the murder weapon."

I could tell he thought I was a bit ditzy.

I spoke clearly. I would be taken seriously, yes, I would. "Yes, I am pretty sure that someone used a wasp to kill him."

"Why do you think that? First of all, international thieves don't use wasps to kill. Too unreliable. Secondly, he could have naturally died from a wasp sting. It happens." Creston spread his hands out.

At least he hadn't completely discounted my theory. I gained confidence. "Not at night. Wasps don't fly at night. Besides, why would his profile be down after he was dead?"

Creston looked at me quizzically. The game had changed. "His profile is down?"

"I know," I said triumphantly. "The fact that it's down means something. It came down after he died. I know because I checked it out after I met him in Starbucks and it was still up then. But now it's down. Someone took it down because there was something in the profile that he didn't want anyone to see. And whoever took it down would have to know his password. Or guess it. Or would have had to hack into the site."

"So you think that someone took down Todd's profile after he died because it mentioned he was allergic to wasp stings and he or she was trying to hide that fact so Todd's death would look like an accident or a suicide and not a murder." He wasn't exactly scoffing at me, but he was unconvinced.

Lucky was scratching at the door and I absent-mindedly got up and let him out. "Exactly," I said prissily, sitting back down.

Creston ignored my tone. "Are you sure his profile said he was allergic to wasp stings?"

Did he know how much I had been drinking that night? "One hundred percent positive."

"Well, it's all pretty flimsy, but you never know."

"Plus there was no EPI pen in his condo."

"How do you know that?"

I smiled sheepishly. "I looked around." I remembered how I had rummaged through his bathroom drawers. Had I touched things? Probably. Shit. No, I had put a tissue on my hand. "I didn't touch anything," I said defensively.

Then I remembered the bug on the ceiling. "Wait a sec," I shouted over my shoulder as I ran into the living room. "I have to get my phone." It was on the pine table in the living room, right where I'd left it. As I was walking back into the kitchen I searched through the photos. "Here, look at this." I had found the picture of the insect on the ceiling. When I enlarged it I could see clearly it was a wasp, not a cockroach, not unless cockroaches had wings. "Look, a wasp was on the ceiling of his bathroom. Here's the proof."

Creston looked at the picture with skeptical interest. "Send that to me."

Creston took his last slurp of coffee while I sent him the image. "Well, you seem pretty clear about the wasp and there is evidence that at least a wasp was there." He looked at the picture. "Maybe it was the murder weapon. But it doesn't seem likely. I'm pretty sure Radcliffe was drugged with a truth serum of some kind so he'd be compelled to tell where the pump was located. Van Horner was then shot so the location wouldn't be revealed. Nonetheless, I'll follow up on the wasp and ask Melfours to get that jacket to the lab. Maybe they will find wasp dust or pollen or whatever in the pocket."

Creston tapped on his phone and I guessed he was sending the photo and a text to Melfours. "Misener's at the hospital, waiting for van Horner to come out of surgery. It's pretty dodgy. He lost a lot of blood and he spiked a fever the night he was shot. So, they had to wait for the antibiotics to kick in before they could operate and remove the bullet. It doesn't look good, frankly."

"No, it sounds pretty grim." I was putting the mugs in the sink, thinking about his three darling kids.

"And now we wait for the ballistics report. Misener's put a rush on it." Creston pushed himself up from the table and headed for the front door. "I'd better get going." I admired his broad shoulders under the tight white T-shirt. "Listen," he said over his shoulder as an afterthought, "I'm going down to the waterfront to check out the boat and crew that helped put the pump into the lake. Did you want to tag along?"

Did I? Holy shit, of course I did. "Sure," I said casually, as if I were asked to be part of an investigation every day. "You going to check out their homes first?"

He turned and looked at me vacantly. "Their homes?"

"Yeah, sort of on the way as well. They all live around College and Bathurst."

Creston narrowed his eyes at me. "How do you know that?"

"Great researcher at the paper." I was wiping off the table and putting my uneaten granola in the sink. I'd get to the dishes later.

"So, you'll share the addresses with the cops?" He seemed incredulous. Had I made a *faux pas*? But tit for tat seemed like a good idea. I opened up my briefcase and pulled out the piece of paper with the names and addresses of the captain and crew. I handed it to Creston with a small bow. "Sure, I'll show you mine if you'll show me yours." Then I looked at him straight in the eye. "Who do you really think is planning to steal the water from the lake?"

Creston took the sheet and nodded his head towards the door. "Let's hit the road. Lots to do today."

So, no answer. I locked the back door and sashayed out of the kitchen into the hallway, maneuvering around him in the tight space. I could feel his body heat as I sidled past.

He didn't press the point or me either as he followed me to the front door. I could feel his eyes on my bum. I wondered if it looked like a saggy satchel ass and hoped not. I stuffed my phone into my bag as I opened the front door. Suddenly I remembered Lucky was outside. What if they killed my dog as a warning to me? As I went back into the kitchen Creston called from the porch, "Are you going to get Lucky?"

I wished.

"Yup."

I let Lucky in, locked the back door and caught up with Creston. "Do you think they'll try to kill Lucky?"

"You worried about him?"

"Yeah, a bit."

"Keep him inside. I'll have a cruiser go by your house every half hour. We'll watch your house."

"Thanks, Creston."

"Call me Ralph."

Ralph, huh? Now that was progress. We were both quiet as he pulled out of the parking spot. He cranked the air conditioner up high but the car was still as hot as an oven. He chauffeured me along Carlton for a few blocks in silence. Suddenly he said, "I don't really know."

"Know what?" I asked.

"Know who's trying to steal the water out of the lake. And maybe nobody is. One would think the Americans were doing it, they need water so badly, but we have no evidence that it's the Americans at all. *Nothing*." He looked at me as if to emphasize the point.

"It could easily be someone else. There are lots of really hot countries all over the world who don't have enough drinking water; Africa, Egypt, the whole Middle East."

Creston stated, "None of them seem to be trying to steal the water. Not one. We searched every database last night for a motive for Radcliffe's murder and van Horner's attack and have come up with zilch. Not a single shred of a clue." He clenched his jaw with frustration. I liked a man who didn't pound the steering wheel. I'd had enough of displays of rage from men. Trevor would throw things. Books. Pens. Boxes of cereal.

"Well, maybe if we could find out how the water was going to be stolen, then maybe we would know why." Since when did

I use the royal "we?" Creston, no Ralph, didn't seem to notice.

"Which is why we are going to talk to the crew."

"Well, thanks for your honesty."

"Thanks for letting me know where the crew lives, saves time."

So, tit for tat did have benefits. Maybe if I enjoyed his tat he would like my tit. *Geezus, Robin.* I really had to control myself better. You'd think I was a nympho or something. We drove along in companionable silence for a few more blocks along Carlton.

"You ever been there?" I asked, looking out the window.

Creston glanced at me, his grey eyes soft and enquiring. "Where?"

"Allan Gardens." We'd just driven by the beautiful park. "It's so lovely in the greenhouses, a tropical world of thriving plants. I go there in the winter, when everything is white and grey outside. It lifts my spirits to be around all the coloured blooms on the flowers and the lush shades of green." I wondered if I'd exposed too much of myself. Ralph said nothing and we drove along in silence.

Abruptly he said, "You like gardening?'

"Yeah, I do."

Creston smiled. "Me, too."

The relationship was moving along like a house on fire.

But then, suddenly Ralph was all business. "If Radcliffe was murdered by a wasp, how do you think the killer arranged that? It would be almost impossible to guarantee an outcome."

So, he wanted to bash around my theory. "I've been thinking about that. One would want to be certain that the wasp would sting the victim. He probably planted the wasp in his jacket, maybe in a lining or a pocket, but probably the pocket. When Radcliff put the jacket on, the wasp stung him."

"Pretty risky, and not guaranteed."

"Less risky than putting the wasp on the bed. And not risky if you knew Radcliffe's habits. He put his hands in his pockets all the time. Gum."

"Gum?"

"He was trying to quit smoking and chewed gum constantly. He kept it in his pocket."

"Well, that would be someone who knew him well."

Creston turned and looked at me expectantly as he waited for a traffic jam to open up east of Yonge and College.

"What? Me? C'mon. We only had coffee, a datelet. Plus, there's zippo evidence of my knowing Radcliffe before then. No fingerprints, no items of clothing in his condo, *nothing*." I hoped. He had to check out everyone, I guess. "Anyway, to continue with my theory, I reckon he probably put the jacket on when he left the streetcar and was walking to his condo building."

"Why would you guess that? Why not earlier in the evening?"

"First of all, the guy wasn't wearing socks."

Ralph looked at me, with a mixture of bewilderment and mockery on his face.

I rose to the bait. "A guy who doesn't wear socks probably puts a jacket on as a last resort. It got pretty chilly after the sun went down that night, probably down to about fifteen by nine o'clock. He wasn't wearing it when he left me, but then, he was going down into the subway and then onto a streetcar, so he probably didn't wear it then. But by the time he stepped out of the streetcar, it would have been quite cold, so I'm guessing he put it on then. Makes sense. Secondly, it only takes a few minutes for a person who is dangerously allergic to wasps to actually die. He made it inside the door of his condo, he even hung his coat up. So, he had just been stung."

Creston nodded, "Okay, well, I've already got Melfours on the jacket, just in case you're right. We'll take a look." Then he looked at me appraisingly. "You're pretty smart, for a chickie whose experience is writing about flowers and carpet."

I bristled, "Probably best not to call me *chickie*."

His eyes danced, "Hmmm, the *chicklet* has spunk too."

I punched him on the arm. I didn't care if he was trying to be funny. My fist connected with what felt like steel.

He laughed right out loud and then said in a falsetto voice, "Ouch, that hurts. You're assaulting a police officer. Maybe I should handcuff you."

I wasn't going to dance this dance. "We can confirm the time of the sting with Jack England."

"Oh, him," Creston said derisively.

I felt I had to stand up for him. He was one of us. "He was following Radcliffe that night."

"He was? Now that is very interesting."

What did that mean? "He would know when Radcliffe put the jacket on."

"Yes, or he might lie about it. That's what I like about you, Robin. You don't lie."

"Not much, anyway."

Creston turned right on Bathurst and then did a quick left. "It seems we're here, at…" he glanced at his notes, "Santiago Martinez's place of residence."

"Nice place," I nodded my head with exaggerated appreciation. We were looking at a tall Victorian house with a peeling coat of red paint on the bricks and about twenty bicycles chained to the tilted porch railing. It looked like some had been there for years. Weeds poked through cracks in the poured cement pathway. The sooty windows were covered with tacked up sheets. Obviously a student rooming house.

"Thanks for the address, *chickie*."

"Fuck you."

I thought for a second. Yeah, fuck him. Now that would be fun.

24.

Ralph and I climbed the creaky wooden steps, bleached grey by too many summer suns, and approached the ancient and carved front door. Yellowed varnish was hanging in long strips from the old oak and the leaded door window was covered in years of city grime. The tarnished unicorn door knocker had seen better days, about a hundred years ago. As I got closer, I looked at it in amazement. How had it lasted so long, through so many owners? It was beautiful.

Creston saw me admiring it and said, "You certainly do notice details about houses, don't you?"

"Years of on-the-job training," I laughed as I lifted the heavy brass knocker up and let it clunk down. I could hear it echo in what must have been a meagerly furnished house.

A sparsely bearded young man of about twenty or so answered the door wearing a grey University of Toronto hooded sweatshirt over red plaid flannel pajama bottoms. He had a biology text in his left hand and ear bud wires dangling below his chin. "Hi," he smiled engagingly. "What can I do you for?"

Creston stepped forward and drew himself up to his full height while holding out some official ID. He spoke in his cop voice. "The police are looking for Santiago Martinez. He home?"

The boy's eyes widened. "Santi? What did he do?"

"Nothing, as far as we know. He's a person of interest in a case we're working on."

"Oh phew. Wait here, I'll go get his schedule. It's on the fridge." He turned to leave.

"Schedule?" said Creston.

The boy turned around and looked at us, shoulders up and holding out a hand, palm up. Innocent. "He's a med student and his schedule is pretty harsh. Here, in this house, we're all in sciences. It's crazy trying to keep the place clean and organized, what with labs and lectures and tutorials. So we put everyone's schedules on the fridge to keep track."

The idea of a med student being involved in some sort of water theft didn't seem likely to me. Creston was fiddling with his keys and I guessed he was thinking the same thing. Santiago was probably just doing a summer job when he helped install the pump, not trying to figure out how to suck the lake dry. When the kid came back he handed a grease-stained piece of paper to Creston, who held it gingerly between his fingertips and away from his clothing.

"Looks like he'll be home about three-thirty for a few hours before his evening classes." Creston looked at the young student. "What's your name by the way?"

"Christopher Stanhope, sir."

"Christopher, do you happen to know a, ummm…" Creston unfolded the piece of paper I had given him with the names and addresses of the crew, "Diego Duarte?"

Christopher's face creased in a big smile, "Sure I do. DD and Santi are friends. DD lives around the block, but he's here a lot. You know, dinners and that."

"Hmmm," thought Creston, "What about Agustin Jimenez?"

"Jimmy owns this place. A great landlord. Something breaks, he's on it. He's a sailor or a captain or something. DD and Santi work on his boat in the summer. I could too, if I wanted, but I get too seasick. It's the only small sturdy boat around that has a crane, so they're always working on finicky situations. Great summer job, on the water and everything."

"You wouldn't happen to know DD's schedule, by chance?"

"Yup. It's the same as Santi's. They did that so they could help each other out. You know, if one has to work for Jimmy and miss a class, they can copy the other's notes. Jimmy? My guess is he's down at the waterfront on his boat." Christopher looked at his cheap watch. "Just about now."

"What do you know about the boat?" asked Creston.

"Other than the fact that it has a huge crane folded on top of the cockpit? Oh yeah, it's called the 'Josephine S.' I remember because my sister's name is Josephine."

I inwardly fumed. That Jack England was such a liar. Josephine S. was a far cry from Barbara D. I resolved to never believe anything that came out of his mouth. I was with Creston on this. England was deceitful, period. Kind of cute with an *I-do-yoga*-look about him, but still. A liar. I wouldn't defend him anymore.

"Thanks for all your help," said Ralph. "I imagine we'll see you later today when they're home. "

"I'll be here." Christopher shut the door behind us.

It was such a beautiful morning. Tiny sparrows hopped on the cracked sidewalk, chirping to their heart's content, looking for crumbs. I felt so different. Just yesterday if I'd met a kid like Christopher I would have been highly critical of his plaid flannel jammies and hoodie, thinking he was a lazy no-good for nothing. I would have been judgmental about the ear buds too. Who did he think he was kidding, listening to music while studying? Yeah, right. He was probably stoned, flipping pages randomly while he listened to heavy metal, not a word sinking in from his textbook. And today, here I was enjoying the birdsong and thinking he was such a nice kid, working hard at school and trying to be comfortable while he studied. Was this the result of being grateful for a few minutes these past few mornings?

Meanwhile, Ralph was saying something as he walked down the path to his car. I tuned into his voice, a bit late. "…No point. Let's go straight down to the waterfront."

I dismissed the random thoughts in my head and responded, hoping that I had guessed accurately what conclusion he had come to "Yeah, Diego won't be home and Jimmy is probably down on his boat."

Ralph looked at me over the hood of his weary Ford, head tilted on one side. "And no point in getting coffee either, since we just had some."

Oops.

Better to own up. "Sorry about that. I was off in my own thoughts, thinking about how interesting kids' brains are these days. How they can do five or six things at once and still accomplish stuff. Amazing actually, when you think of it."

"Well, aren't you the positive one. Even after having four kids."

"What about you, Ralph?" I said his name tentatively, wondering how he would react. But he had, after all, told me to call him Ralph. And I had been doing just that, in my head, for some time now. "Any kids?"

Ralph stiffened. "Three. Adults now." His voice was clipped, every syllable articulated.

Better leave that alone for a bit. I picked a safe topic. "Any idea where the Josephine S. is parked?"

Ralph spat, "Berthed."

Anger flared in me. I was not going to be talked to unkindly. "Geez. Excuse me for living." I got into the car and slammed the door.

Ralph settled into his seat and did up his seatbelt. "Sorry. I get upset when I think about my kids." He put on his flicker and pulled out into the road.

But I was tired of being a whipping boy. "You're right, Ralph. I try not to lie. I try to be honest about most things, like how I'm feeling. If I'm angry about something I don't take it out on something or someone *else*. It is important to not kick the dog because someone kicked you."

Ralph took his eyes of the road and looked at me, his eyes

as soft as water running over rocks. "Sorry. I shouldn't have snapped at you." Then he looked straight ahead.

I was bowled over. A man who could take responsibility for his actions and not try and lay blame elsewhere? A man who looked at me with such slow eyes? What was happening? I was speaking up for myself. And the guy had listened! This sort of conversation never went over okay with Trevor.

"So-o-o-o, do you know where the Josephine S., um, *is*?" I avoided the word that had sparked off our first sort-of fight.

There was a long pause. Ralph was probably collecting himself. "Thank you," he said.

I was mystified. "For what?"

"I don't know. Not going on and on about it. Not making a big deal of something that is obviously important to you. Being kind."

"You're welcome. But do you know where the Josephine S. is *berthed*?"

We both laughed.

"No idea. Let's drive around and look for it. It should be obvious, with the crane."

Finally we found the boat, moored at a pier behind a yacht about half a kilometer to the east of the *Express* building. How ironic was that? It had been right under my nose all that time. Ralph pulled his car up onto the sidewalk, which I guessed was okay for a cop to do. The sound of waves and seagulls made me smile. What was with me today? Normally I would be noticing the garbage floating in the water and the smell of diesel from the boats' engines. But no, here I was, enjoying kids, speaking my mind, and waxing poetical about the beauty of the landscape.

The Josephine S. was far smaller than I thought it would be, almost a tugboat in size. It looked a bit like a lobster fishing boat, except for the crane resting on the raised cabin that housed a steering wheel. This was probably what was called the cockpit. Agustin had painted the hull a cherry red and the boat's name was scrolled along the bow in glittering gold letters outlined with a black border.

Ralph cupped his hands over his mouth and shouted in the general direction of the boat, "Agustin? Jimmy?'

For a minute there was no reply, and then a dark head of hair poked up through a hatch. "Yes?" Black eyes crinkled against the sun and the man shaded them with his hand as he looked around for the caller. "Yes?" he called again.

"Over here," Ralph boomed through his hands. "We'd like to talk to Agustin Jimenez, or Jimmy."

"Be right with you." Jimmy scrambled up through the hatch and with sure and practiced steps, fox-trotted down the wooden plank that led from the boat to the shore. He stood in front of us and said, "What's up, amigo? I'd shake your hands but I've been working on the engine. It's running a little rough."

He held out his tanned hands as proof and I could see his fingernails were encrusted in oil. I could also see that he was missing a thumb and a forefinger on his right hand. Jimmy saw me looking at it and smiled good-naturedly, "Caught in a winch when I was eighteen. Won't do that again," he laughed.

Jimmy didn't have a trace of a Spanish accent, although he certainly had a wiry Mediterranean build. He was wearing a pair of cut-offs that had a fringe of frayed white threads that brushed his knobby, olive-skinned knees. Although he looked a bit tattered, the unmistakable scent of fabric softener came off his freshly laundered clothes. He didn't look like a murderer to me, but what did I know?

"You must be left-handed then, seeing what sort of work you do," I observed.

"I am now," he chuckled. "I was born right-handed, but after the winch attacked me I switched over, mostly."

Ralph looked at me candidly. We both knew that there was no way this guy could have handled a tiny wasp or aimed a sniper's rifle. But one never knew what he might know, so maybe it wouldn't be a waste of a trip.

Ralph's phone chimed out Mozart's *Requim*. He looked at the caller ID and excused himself, strolling down to the end of the cement pier and turning his back while he talked. The call was short and when Ralph turned around a black scowl shadowed his features. He strode back to us with firm business-like steps. Gone was the easy-going fella I'd been travelling with.

Creston was now abrupt. "I understand that you were captain of the ship that put the pump in the middle of the lake for a cold water cooling system."

His aggressive tone put Jimmy on the defensive. "I do a lot of crane jobs lifting up stuff for the bigger boats. Refresh my memory." His sparkling brown eyes had flattened.

Creston taunted, "For a company called Everwave? Air conditioning for some large buildings in the city? Ring any bells?"

"Oh right. That was a hundred jobs ago. Last summer. It was a big operation involving welding and deck hands. Yes, I remember it." He looked around, and added, "So what?"

Creston's voice drilled through Jimmy's feigned nonchalance. "Do you know a guy named Radcliffe? Or van Horner?"

Jimmy dropped his adversarial routine and smiled openly at the names. Friends? "Sure I do. Nice guys. In fact, they were here before the weekend, letting me know the system was finally up and running. They thanked me for helping on the project."

Ha. England was so full of crap. He wanted me to believe Radcliffe and van Horner had come down to strong-arm this man into stealing water. I needed a better lie detector.

Jimmy's happy nature prevailed as he thought back to the meeting. "Those guys? Love their jobs. But I think once the system was up and running, they'd be looking for their next project. So, about now. Or soon, anyway."

Creston looked across the water. The news in the phone call was losing impact and he was relaxing. "You mean they were like partners? They worked together on other projects?"

"Yes. I think Radcliffe said something about them starting up an ice cream business. I was even thinking of participating. My wife loves ice cream." Jimmy smiled indulgently. "Anyway, he and van Horner were drawing up the business plan and showed it to me. Proud of it. Why are you asking all these questions about them? Nice hard-working guys. Marriage troubles like most of us, but nothing serious."

Ralph watched him attentively. "Both guys were murdered this week."

Jimmy's eyes opened wide in shock and he took a step back. He gestured wildly with his hands, clearly disturbed by the news. I could tell he wasn't faking his response. This was a terrible surprise to him. "Who would murder them?" he cried. "Are you sure they were murdered? Both of them? But they were nice guys doing regular things."

"That's what I intend to find out."

I looked from one man to the other. Both seemed to be questioning each other. At least I now knew what the call to Ralph had been about. It must have been Misener from the hospital, telling him that van Horner had died. How awful. Those poor kids. No wonder Ralph had become so serious.

Jimmy was peering into Creston's face. "I have to ask you. Am I at risk here? I mean, I was associated with Everwave as well. Is someone going to come gunning for me?"

"I doubt it," Creston bluffed. "I don't think this had anything to do with you. It's an international thing. Tell me about the marriage troubles."

Jimmy looked away, reticent to speak ill of the dead.

Creston spoke kindly to him, "Listen, I need to find their killer or killers. You will be helping these two nice guys by telling me a bit about their problems, not tarnishing their memory."

Jimmy came to a decision. "Well, Radcliffe said he was divorced, but I'm not sure he was. He kept getting calls from this one woman. Anyway, he was always going out on dates. He did that internet dating thing. A new person every week. And I don't think he cared which way he went, if you catch my drift."

I was mortified. I was one in a long list? And some of them were men? Plus, maybe he wasn't divorced? I looked at Ralph. He didn't seem to register the bisexual innuendo.

"And as for van Horner," Jimmy continued, "I think he liked everyone, for a bit of fun, if you know what I mean. But don't get me wrong. He loved his wife and kids. Always talking about his family."

Ralph still hadn't cottoned on to Jimmy's hints. I needed Cindy's take on all this. I knew nothing about the gay scene in Toronto. Not to mention gay men. Except for some interior decorators I had run into over the years. Bisexual men were way beyond my area of expertise.

Ralph seemed to have missed the gay angle completely. "And they were planning an ice cream business together?"

"I know it sounds like small potatoes, but these guys had big plans. Franchises. Did you ever notice how many ice cream joints have sprung up in the city? People are addicted to it. I know my wife loves it. All year long, too. After Friday dinner we pile into the car and get cones to celebrate the end of the week. These guys were going to capitalize on the trend."

"You sound like a businessman yourself, Jimmy," I said.

"I got a degree in marketing from Ryerson," he said proudly, looking at me. "Fat lot of good it did me." He laughed and looked at his blackened hands. "But I'm not doing too badly. I own a couple of houses and run this business here." He gestured at the crane on the boat.

"And you employ Mexicans," said Ralph.

"All legal," Jimmy said righteously.

Creston changed tack. "Not my department. Did either man indicate that they wanted to use your services in the future? Did it sound like they needed your crane, for example? Did they mention anything like that?'

Jimmy scratched his ear. I wondered briefly if he had bed bugs and took a step back. It was a scourge in Toronto. "No. Why would they need a boat for ice cream?"

Creston's phone rang again. He reached into his pocket while saying, "Thanks for your time, Agustin. We'll stay in touch." He pulled out the phone and started sauntering away. I followed, although I wasn't sure I should. Did he need privacy?

"Creston."

I could hear an electronic voice threading through the sound of stays clinking in the wind on some yachts at the pier.

"Thanks for letting me know, Sarah." Sarah Clovelley was the Coroner.

He gawked at me, his eyes stunned, "You were right. Wasp venom."

25.

"REALLY? WASP VENOM? I WAS RIGHT?" We were standing at the end of the pier where Jimmy's boat was docked.

"Seems so, smarty pants. This changes the case." Ralph had recovered his better mood of the earlier morning and was smiling into my eyes with his lovely grey ones.

I was becoming hooked.

"What are you up to now?" I didn't look down at his crotch to check.

He leaned over and brushed a tendril of hair out of my eyes. I caught my breath. "First, I'm going to walk over to that vendor up there and get some street meat. I'm starving. Next, I'm going to observe van Horner's autopsy at the morgue and also speak to Sarah about Radcliffe's death while I'm at it. She might have some solid ideas about when he was stung and where he was stung on his body. She'll probably take another look, now that the toxicology report is in. If I know her, she'll want to get it perfect. If there's a tiny little hole anywhere in his skin, she'll find it. That will help pinpoint where the wasp was located in his clothing, if it was, and from there we might deduce how it got where it was. We could perhaps determine if it was a murder or accidental."

"I know it was murder," I said with certainty. "Tell her to check his right hand. I think the wasp was put in his pocket. It's the only thing that makes sense."

We were heading towards the hot dog cart.

"I'm still not so sure," said Ralph. "I initially thought that the temperature on the thermostat had been adjusted by the murderer to skew the time of death, but Sarah tells me that people who have been stung go first into shock and feel very cold. Todd probably turned that thermostat up himself."

Well, there went that clue. But still, how could it not be murder? Especially now with van Horner's death. Two men who worked together are now both dead? I didn't believe in coincidence.

And I said that to Ralph. "I read somewhere that there's no such thing as coincidence."

"Probably in a Grisham novel," Ralph laughed. "And speaking of coincidence, that old white van you saw outside van Horner's belonged to a gardener. When we interviewed him he said it backfired all the time. That backfiring you heard was just coincidental. The bullet in van Horner's shoulder came from a silenced rifle." He nodded at me and added for clarification, "Ballistics report."

I nodded back, compressing my lips in what I hoped looked like a knowing line, as if I were familiar with ballistic results and silenced rifles. But underneath this lie, I was secretly pleased; my instincts about the van were accurate. Later I would restrain myself from saying "I told you so" to Cindy.

"That was quick." Really? I had no idea how long ballistic reports took. But it sounded good.

"Misener." Ralph bobbed his head, pleased with his guy. "But the van? Not a lead after all. It was great that you had that picture of the license plate; that saved us tons of time. Misener told me all this in that phone call about van Horner's death."

We both were silent for a second or two with only the sound of the water lapping against the hulls of the boats docked on our left as we headed west. "I'm so glad you weren't shot at, Robin, when you were in front of Richard's house."

"Me, too. But do you think I'm in danger now? I know about the wasp allergy."

"Well, now the *media*," he strummed out the word while looking at me, "could possibly print that Radcliffe died of an allergic reaction to a wasp sting. Once that's public knowledge you would be safe. Perhaps the murderer doesn't know that the new testing methods can isolate wasp venom and thinks you are the only risk for the whole concept to be exposed. But if it were common knowledge? I don't think you'll be at any risk."

I looked sideways at him as we rambled together along the lake side of the street. I enjoyed the connection between us as we dallied in a comfortable quietude, with only the sounds of the harbour in the air. I felt at peace listening to distant seagulls cawing and marvelled at them soaring on the light breeze. I wondered how Ralph was feeling about me. I loved the way he had moved that bit of hair off my face. He was gentle and yet so strong. Did he like me? He actually looked a bit uncomfortable. Awkward even.

"You coming with me? To the morgue?"

"Oh, you sweet talker," I laughed to hopefully put him at ease. "What a fun date." He frowned. So that fell flat. "Unfortunately no, I can't make it, I have other plans." I stopped walking. "There are a few things I have to do at work, and I just, *coincidentally*, happen to be at my office." I thumbed at the building over my shoulder. We were standing at the revolving doors of the *Express*. The umbrella on the fast food card was flapping in the breeze off the lake just a few feet away.

"If you say so." Ralph was shuffling his feet and looking down.

What was going on with him? Did he want to kiss me? I took a step closer so if he got his courage up he could do the dastardly deed without too much effort. I watched in amazement as suddenly his arms flapped like a bird's and he enveloped me in an awkward hug while pecking me on the cheek. I gave him a small squeeze back, to let him know I was receptive to the idea of more. Hardly what I would call a passionate embrace.

And then Ralph dashed off without a word, back in the direction of department-issued Ford that he had dumped sideways on the sidewalk. I watched all this with bafflement. Such odd behaviour. Didn't he just say he wanted to get some food?

But I had things to do. I had to talk to Cindy. I pushed through the revolving doors, walked across the glassy marble floor in my squeaky running shoes, and punched the button for the elevator. I felt so *happy*. My morning with Ralph had left me up up up. So far this was one great day.

My euphoric balloon was immediately punctured with Cindy's needlelike stare when I entered the editorial room. "Where have you been?' she hissed accusingly as I sat down beside her and turned on my computer. What a downer to my good mood. "Doug's in a lather."

I looked into Doug's office and saw him staring out at the landscape of buildings to the west. Funny way to show a lather. The guy looked downright depressed. "What about?"

"We've been trying to get hold of you all morning. What's with your phone?'

I checked out my phone. Shit. In the chaotic frenzy of fear in the morning and then all the running around, I hadn't turned the ringer on. I made a show of activating the sound, shrugging my shoulders so she would know what happened. It was a mistake, get over it, the gesture implied. "I guess I had better go talk to him."

"Yes, you better," said Cindy, fuming.

"Look, I have good reasons for forgetting to turn my phone on, and I'll tell you all about it. Come with me?" I hoped she would. Her presence would save me from repeating the story twice.

She pretended to be irritated, but I could tell she was far too curious to let me go into the lion's den alone. Sure, I had been remiss in not getting in touch with her for so long.

"Listen," I said while exhuming my iPad from my purse. "I'm really sorry. I know you've got my back and it's been pretty crazy and a little bit scary lately. Sorry. I'll do better to keep in touch."

She touched my arm as we walked together, "That's okay, Robin, but you look too damn cheerful to be contrite and besides, you're my best friend and I was worried."

"I know," I said, then walked into Doug's office.

Doug turned his chair around from the view. He looked tired to me. I had so little experience in reading men. Who knew what was going on with him? But I didn't want to be the object of his wrath. Not today. I'd had enough emotion for one day already and it was still before lunch. I jumped in with an apology right away, "Sorry I was out of touch for the better part of the morning. I did text Shirley, but I guess you didn't get the message. I didn't turn on my ringer until just now. I didn't realize it was off. A mistake and I won't do it again," I blabbered.

"No, I didn't get the message," he said irately. "Crime reporters can get in trouble, Robin, and I need to know where you are at all times." His head was nodding at the points he was making. "Especially if you're working on a tricky story. If you go AWOL I get very worried. As I said earlier, you know things that others don't want you to know and when this happens, there's danger."

"Yes, sir." If that was the extent of his lecture, I could handle it. Besides, I knew he was right. I just didn't know that the paper was watching out for me. Somehow I was touched. "I'm truly sorry. I didn't understand the seriousness of this job and the potential danger. I really understand that now. I was terrified this morning. Turning on my phone and keeping contact with the paper slipped my mind."

Doug sat up, his face suddenly animated. "You were terrified? This morning? What of?"

"Of exactly what you are talking about. I realized I knew something that someone wouldn't want me to know and I felt in danger."

"What did you do?"

"I called the police."

"From your cell?" Cindy asked sharply.

"No, I was worried about it being tapped so I went to a neighbour's and used his."

Cindy visibly relaxed.

Doug tented his fingers, a now familiar gesture of his that I figured meant he was thinking. "What did you realize you knew?"

"I remembered reading on Radcliff's profile that he was allergic to wasps. That was the one detail I couldn't retrieve from my memory. Well," I coughed discreetly, "the one detail I can remember now that I had forgotten then."

Doug smiled encouragingly. "Why do you think this one detail was an important one?"

"Radcliffe died with his hand half way up to his throat. People who are dying from anaphylactic shock feel like their throat is closing in and they can't get enough air. It's a horrible death." Poor Todd. He might have been a sexist prick, but he sure didn't deserve to die like that.

Doug looked bewildered. His eyebrows were drawn across his forehead in a straight line while he frowned. "Again, why do you think this detail is important? So, his hand was up by his throat. Was he stung? It sounds accidental to me."

And I thought Creston was a hard sell. "I doubt it was accidental. Somebody took down his profile after he was dead. This morning I figured out while I was eating my granola that someone was trying to conceal something on his profile, and given the way he had looked when he died, that one detail, that he was allergic to wasps, was the something."

Doug shook his head. A patronizing look flickered across his face. A bubble of anger got trapped in my gut. "An interesting *hunch*, but Robin, Robin," he sing-songed, "just because someone possibly dies from a possible anaphylactic reaction from a possible wasp sting doesn't mean they were murdered. It could have been a complete accident. Anyway, you were frightened. So you called the police? Not the paper? The police."

Cindy butt in, "She was right to call the police. She could have been in serious danger. One man was dead and the other had been seriously wounded."

I corrected her. "Actually, two men are dead. Van Horner died of his injuries today. He got a blood infection."

Doug jumped on this. "Who else knows about van Horner? When did you find this out?" Doug was paying close attention now, his body tilted forward and his hands flat on his desk.

"I found out just twenty minutes ago, from Creston, when we were at the waterfront."

"Okay, back up the truck. You were at the waterfront. With the police. Why were you there?" Cindy's anger had returned. She had been left out of the action.

"When I called the police, well Ralph actually, I was in quite a state. You know, crying. Anyway, he came over to my house—"

Doug jumped in, "Creston came over to your place? You called him Ralph. What's going on here?"

"He's just a nice guy, okay? That's all."

Doug looked meaningfully at Cindy. She angled her head back at him, just enough that I could catch it. The clock on Doug's desk flipped to the next minute. It was getting close to lunch. And then I got it. Did they think I was going to be a mole for the paper? They could just think again.

"It's not what you think, so forget it."

Doug spread his hands. "And what *were* you doing at the waterfront?"

Cindy nodded. She had really hated not being part of the activities. "I should have gone with you. It's not safe to do things on your own."

They were ganging up on me. "I wasn't on my own, I was with Creston." I looked at their incredulous faces. "He asked me to come with him to interview the captain of the boat that had installed the pump."

Cindy sneered. "So, just a nice guy, huh?" She coughed dismissively, "Right. He *hates* journalists."

I couldn't believe how she was treating me. First she was mad, then supportive, then mad. Ascot too. I was being batted around like a balloon. Hot tears formed behind my eyelids. "Look, believe it or not, he asked me to come with him to the waterfront to talk to the captain of the ship that installed the pump for the cooling system. Somewhere in all this mess is a motive for killing Radcliffe. Creston thinks it has something to do with the international theft of fresh water. The guy was murdered." I held my head up high. I wasn't going to be bullied out of my story.

Doug was looking vacantly over my shoulder. I was tempted to turn my head to see what he was staring at, but held my ground. "You mentioned England yesterday," he said. "That you were going to see him. What does England say about all this?" he demanded. "Did you meet with him last night?"

"Yeah, I did. Cindy came with me." I looked right at her. Did she need brownie points? Is that what was going on with her? Would coming with me to my meeting with Jack count as a brownie point? Why was she being such a bitch? "I was glad she did because he makes me nervous. He is one odd duck."

Cindy was picking at her nail polish. Had I made amends?

"And what did he say?" Doug was visibly reigning in his impatience.

"He said that *Radcliffe* was planning to steal Lake Ontario's fresh water."

Doug hooted. "This is ridiculous. There's no subterfuge. It was an *accidental* death. Cindy?"

Cindy sat on the fence. "I think we need to wait for more evidence to come in."

"There! See Robin? She's a seasoned reporter who doesn't rely on *hunches*." Doug paused for a minute to let his biting words sink in. "And what *else* did you do with Creston?" He was bug-eyed in his zeal to put me down.

I outwardly composed myself but anger was frothing in my chest. "Well, we were going to interview all the people on the boat who were involved in installing the pump."

"That must have been quite a few."

"No, not really, just two others. Two summer students. No one else working on the project laying down the pipe knew exactly where they were."

"So, based on one of your many *hunches*, you think these three killed the two men. With a wasp? Is that what Creston thinks? That it wasn't an accident?"

I decided it wasn't worth the energy to address his stupid hunch comment. "No, I really don't think so. They seem to be upstanding types. You know, busy with other things in their lives. I can't imagine why they would want to kill Everwave executives."

"Let's get back to this wasp *hunch* of yours."

Okay, now I'd had enough of the hunch crap. I didn't care that I had to impress my new boss. I was not going be treated like a bimbo. "Listen, you can be as critical as you like, Doug. Wasps don't fly at night. Radcliffe being stung at ten p.m. was not an accident. His profile *was* taken down. Radcliffe was murdered by a wasp. Wasp venom killed him."

"Right. Is that a fact?" He busied himself with some papers on his desk, dismissing me.

I'd had it. I spat, "The autopsy results came back about half an hour ago. There was wasp venom in his blood." I held the winning hand.

Doug shrugged this off and glanced at Cindy, his tone sarcastic. "Well, that *could* indicate something. Like he was *accidentally* stung."

Since when had the nice new boss turned into such an asshole? I punched back, "I'll bet you any money that the autopsy will show that he was stung in his right hand because a wasp was put in his pocket. The jacket is at the lab now. There will be evidence that a wasp was in that pocket and that it was put there. If you need more evidence, I'll give you more. My *hunch*, as you call it, will be well on its way to being proven. Someone hid a wasp in his pocket, trapping it, and when Radcliffe put his hand in his pocket, the wasp stung him. He was murdered." I stood up. "I will also discover who did it and their motive." I was done here. I didn't care if this was my first assignment and I was the new girl on the block. Besides, I felt like I was going to cry, I was so bloody angry. I would *not* be dismissed. There was a roaring in my ears. "I recall that you, Mr. Ascot, were the one who told me to trust my instincts. Well, I do."

I turned on my heel and stalked out of his office, head held high. Fuck him.

26.

I BOLTED OUT OF DOUG'S OFFICE with my chin up and made a beeline for the washroom at the end of the hall. Dammit. I would go it alone. I went into a cubicle and blew my nose. I would not cry. The door of the washroom swung open and shut. I peered under the stall door: black sandals with a beaded open toe. Cindy.

"So, do you like him? Really?"

"Who?" I said through gritted teeth. "Your asshole boss?"

"No, idiot. Creston."

"What's it to you?"

"I'm your BF. Why are you being so mean to me?"

Cindy was hurt? What was going on? This was such bullshit.

I let loose, my shrill voice echoing off the tiles. "You're the one who didn't support me in Doug's office. Like the two of you were in collusion, thinking of using me to be the paper's spy with the police. You're the one who didn't give me any support for the wasp theory."

"Well, *you* called the police, not *me*. *You* went running to Creston."

Oh. Now I saw. This wasn't about the story. She was jealous of me and Ralph. She was feeling threatened in our relationship. I opened the cubicle door and saw her standing by the porcelain sink, looking utterly dejected and miserable.

"Listen, you are my best friend. By far. BF times two." I swept her into my arms. This was no easy task as she towered a foot taller over me. She leaned down and put her head against my cheek, allowing me to console her. "I called the police because I felt in immediate mortal danger. It was awful. I thought someone was in my yard, watching me. Poisoning Lucky. I could hardly breathe, I was so frightened. I had to get help, right away. So I went to the Blakelys'. Brian was still home, and I borrowed his phone. I even took a measuring cup with me so it would look like I was on a legitimate errand." I said all this into her red hair.

Cindy gave me a squeeze back. "I understand. It sounds horrible. I hate being frightened."

I adjusted my feet as I hugged her more tightly. As I did this, my running shoes dragged on the tiled floor, making a fart noise. Neither of us said a thing in the following silence, just holding each other in the tiled bathroom. And then we both burst out laughing. We were going to be okay.

At that moment the door opened and Hannah Weiner walked in, her swanky suit swishing around her knees, her fancy patent leather purse clutched in her left hand, and her expensive shoes, probably purchased at one of the up-market shoe stores on Bloor Street, completely silent as she walked. Little Miss Perfect. She was a business reporter, always looking up the current financial trends. And always wearing the current fashions.

"Oops, sorry," she said, seeing us laughing together and in an embrace, "didn't mean to intrude on your little *tête-à-tête*. Or should I say, *tit-à-tit*."

Cindy and I hastily parted, "It's not what you think," I laughed.

"I don't *think*," said Hannah archly, her eyebrows raised high on her forehead and her lips spread over her teeth in what could be construed, by some, as a smile, "I read graphs and look at facts. I analyze data. The data in here is very interesting." She swung open a cubicle door and shut it behind her, the latch making a resounding click in the small room. Cindy and I snuck out.

As soon as we were in the hallway we burst out laughing again. What would Hannah *analyze*? Oh, who cared!

"Listen," I said, as we walked down the hallway to the glass doors of the editorial room, "When I was down at the waterfront with Ra-a-a-l-ph," I dragged out his name and joggled my eyebrows, so she would know I was teasing her, "The ship's captain, Jimmy, said that Radcliff swung both ways, not in so many words, but that's what he meant. And he implied that the two Everwave executives were in each other's pockets, you know, really, *really* good friends. So, although he never said it, that they were, um, you know..." I wiggled my wrist. "I think we should get some photos of them, Radcliff and van Horner, and take them up and down Church Street into the gay bars and see what we can find out."

Cindy was dismissive. "Radcliff and van Horner? Gay? With each other? Both were married guys. Not likely."

"And how long were you married?"

Cindy eyeballed me, "Right. I get your point. Okay, let's get ourselves a diffcrent motive than the police have and see if we can wrap this up. I'll go with you."

What a relief. She'd help me. "Where will we get photos? Maybe archives?"

"Yup," said Cindy. "Let's hassle Alison Trent in Research. She'll find some photos of the two of them. They've been in the news for the past year. I'd be surprised if she drew a blank."

We grabbed our bags out of our locked desk drawers and were heading for the elevators when Hannah Weiner strutted up the carpeted hall from the washroom, sliding her forefingers back and forth on each other as if she were sharpening knives. "Tsk tsk," she bared her teeth in her inhuman waxy smile.

The elevator doors opened and we tumbled in. As soon as they whooshed shut, we burst out laughing again. "Must be hard being so perfect," I said.

"Here, push 'L' for 'lower,' Robin. Research is in the basement."

I'd never been in the bowels of the building before. We stepped out of the elevator and walked toward a steel grey door with the word *Research* etched slightly below eye level. The airlock on the door popped when we pushed it open.

I was shocked. What greeted me was the last thing I expected. I couldn't believe my eyes. I had been expecting a nerd; a young woman whose blonde hair was pulled back in a ponytail with thick glasses on her nose. A North Toronto type who had made her parents proud by studying Political Science at McGill and then landing a plumb research job at the country's largest paper. No easy feat when youth unemployment in Toronto was in the double digits.

But sitting behind the chipped Formica topped counter was the very same young woman who I had bumped into not once but twice at the Starbucks on Bloor. It was the same lip ring, beaded dreadlocks, and tattoos. There was no mistaking it. She was the thugette. She looked up at me and smiled, all innocent. This was Alison Trent, as the black embossed nameplate perched on the counter attested.

"You!" I cried, pointing at her.

"Hiya." Alison was unfazed and waved back.

Cindy looked back and forth at us, "You know each other?"

"Have you been spying on me? In Starbucks?" I was flabbergasted. This creature was the furthest image of Alison Trent that I had conjured up as I could imagine.

"No. That was karma." She swung her beads around, spreading an incense smell around the room. "How can I help you?"

I regained my composure. "Well, well," I said, "that guy I was with on Thursday night? The one carrying the blazer over his arm, remember him?"

"You mean Mr. Dishonest? He who wears no socks?"

I chuckled at her description, "Yeah, him."

"What about him?"

"He was murdered."

Cindy interjected, "We think."

"You told me already." Alison was patient and forgiving. Maybe her mother had a mind like a sieve too. "How?"

"Probably a wasp bite."

Alison nodded her head slowly, assessing this information. "Foxy," she said. "Look at the love triangle,"

Cindy asked, "Do you have a picture of him? His name's Todd Radcliff."

"I know." Alison turned and worked some magic on her computer. A printer on a shelf behind her purred into life. She spun her cloth-covered chair around with her heels and scooted over on its plastic casters to the printer, grabbing the piece of paper before it even hit the tray. She pushed her chair back to the counter and handed it to Cindy.

I looked over Cindy's shoulder at the photo. The image wasn't bad, a little grey and grainy, but Todd was certainly recognizable. He was standing in front of a lectern, his finger raised as if making a point. It would do. "Thanks," said Cindy.

"And do you happen to have a picture of Richard van Horner?" I asked. "He was vice president of Everwave. He's been murdered too. Shot. I think he probably spoke as much as Radcliff at various thingies."

"Thingies, huh," said Alison as she was typing at her computer. "Such a helpful description. Let me Google *thingies*." She tapped on her keyboard, "Okay, here we go." The printer did its thing, she did her thing with her chair, and the picture was in my hand. *Presto*.

The image was a little clearer than the one of Radcliffe, but van Horner wasn't alone. On his arm was the beautiful, perfectly coiffed wife that we had seen at his house. I looked closely at her. A teardrop diamond was dripping down her neck onto an ample bosom and a slinky black dress hugged her boyishly thin hips. A perfect figure combination: voluptuously thin. How did she achieve that? A trophy if ever I saw one. I read the caption below the shot. *The couple, Richard van Horner and his wife, Melissa Mowbray, at the*

New Year's Eve Rotary Club charity ball. "How long ago was this taken?" I asked Alison.

She looked up the date in her computer. "Last January, so about six months." Alison stared at the image on her computer. "She looks sort of familiar to me. A typical movie star look, I guess. Do you want me to cut her out and blow him up?"

"I think that's already happened," I said.

"You know what I mean," said Alison, exasperated.

"Sure, it might make it easier for people to recognize him. She's quite a distraction."

In three seconds Alison produced a printed photo of Richard van Horner without his lovely wife.

I inspected it carefully. "Perfect."

Cindy hovered next to me, "Thanks Alison, now we can get to work."

Alison was busy with her printer. "Here's a couple of copies of each." She handed them over.

"Good thinking," nodded Cindy as she took the extras.

"Go and find him," Alison said with a shake of her dreadlocks. "Or her."

"Her," I thought. Stokes had hinted the murderer might be a "her." Now there was a concept. It could easily be a "her." No, that sniper was a "him." I had no doubt. I'd felt that aura.

With pictures in a buff file folder, we drove in Cindy's Accord up Church Street almost to Bloor and found some legitimate parking on a side street. I patted the file folder on my lap. "So, do we split up or do this together?"

Cindy chewed on her lip in thought, "I think we should stick together, Robin. Who ever is behind this is violent. Safety in numbers."

I looked at my very tall friend and thought to myself, yeah, she's an excellent bodyguard. Me, not so much. "Good point."

The bar and grill joints up and down Church were filled with the lunch time crowd from Bloor Street offices and not with a predominately gay clientele at all. Not to be deterred and thinking that Todd and Richard could have come in at anytime, including lunch, after work, or even late at night, I walked up to all the bartenders and showed the grainy images. Cindy's job was to walk around and flash the photos to the patrons. But after about ten shakes of the head from bartenders on the east side of Church and Cindy getting no joy from the patrons, I felt like giving up.

"I'm getting hungrier by the minute. Let's eat," I begged Cindy.

"No, let's keep going." She was in her element, whereas I was a fish out of water.

"I'm hungry," I whined.

"Okay, we'll go up the west side and when we are past Wellesley Street there's a local pub a little further north where we can get a burger."

"Or a salad? I'm turning over a new leaf."

"Very funny." Cindy was already cantering on her long legs into the next place. I waited outside.

I had simply lost my enthusiasm for the task at hand. These guys were way too discrete to go out in public together, that's if, and a mighty big if, they were gay partners at all.

When she came out, I grabbed her arm and started dragging her up the street. "Forget it. I'm starving." I felt like a little kid, grabbing my mommy's hand and tugging. "We can come back and do the next few places after we eat. Let's get some food."

Cindy laughed, "Okay, darling."

I gave her an old fashioned look.

We entered the pub through the bar side and Cindy, knowing her way around, kept walking past the customers to finally push through some wooden double doors. She led me through a restaurant decorated in a cottage theme and out through a fire door to an outdoor patio. She swept her arm towards a table away from Church Street with a view of a delivery entrance to an office building, "Does this suit you, Madam?"

I groaned and shook my head while rolling my eyes. "Sure.

Let's eat." At least we were outside, even if the view was a little too urban for my liking.

A waiter in blue jeans appeared out of nowhere and handed us two menus. The pocket on his black shirt was embroidered with the name "Suzette." Hmmm. I see. My first transgendered person? I quickly glanced at the selection and saw to my relief four different salads. Not an almond in sight. What luck.

"So, Suzette," Cindy was reading the waiter's name off his shirt, "how's business?"

"It's Sam," he grinned, "this is someone else's shirt. Business is pretty good, out here on the patio. Dull inside. I'll be back to take your order in a minute or two."

After he left Cindy looked over the top of the menu. "You getting a burger?"

"Nope. I'm resolved. I want the walnut and blue cheese salad with the raspberry dressing."

"I'm going to try the Caesar. Maybe I'll put some chicken on top. Maybe salmon."

When the waiter returned with some waters we quickly placed our orders. I asked for my salad and Cindy ordered hers.

"Do you want your chicken on top or underneath," he asked Cindy suggestively.

"I'm bisexual, so it really doesn't matter," smiled Cindy, playing along.

"Oh-h-h," he turned like a ballerina on his heel and pranced away. "We'll just see how it *comes*, then."

"Thanks, Suzette, I love a mystery." Cindy watched him shake his bum with amusement in her eyes.

I was having a bit of trouble with the prattle and self-consciously dusted some salt off the top of the table with the palm of my hand. Then I reached into my bag for the photos. I laid them out in front of us and said, "Who would of thought it would be so hard to find someone. It's not like a needle in a gaystack or anything."

Cindy acknowledged my attempt at humour with a sardonic

smile, "Nice one." With the pictures strewn around us, we checked our emails on our phones while we waited for Suzette/Sam to bring us our salads.

I had received one from Creston. My heart gave a little happy jump. When I opened it I read that Sarah Clovelly, the Coroner, had found a small injection site in the back of Todd's right hand. She believed that's where Todd had been bitten. Wow. I was right! The wasp had been put in his pocket, and when he'd put his hand in his pocket, he had been bitten. It would have been easy to slip a wasp into a pocket. Or relatively easy. Just shake one out of a little pill container.

I emailed him back immediately. *Great. Was any wasp evidence found in his jacket pocket?*

The answer flew into my inbox. *No. Probably an accidental wasp bite.*

My ass it was. But that was odd. I'd need some sort of evidence that the wasp had been in his pocket. But, wait, the lab results from the tests on his jacket had yet to come in. Maybe they'd reveal something.

Sam was balancing our huge plates of salads in his hands and had a pepper grinder tucked under his arm. He stood at the side of our table while I gathered up the photos.

"Don't mind my asking, and I'm not being nosey or anything," he shifted on his feet, "but why do you have pictures of Robert and Tim?" I stopped shuffling the papers and looked up at him. His dark brown eyes were curious.

"Robert and Tim? Who are Robert and Tim?"

"Those two guys," Sam gestured with his chin towards the photos, while holding the salads high. "Robert and Tim come in every Wednesday for lunch and sometimes Friday, too." He put the plates down in the cleared spots in front of Cindy and me. "Not that I'm a gossip, but they're a pretty solid item. Little presents and stuff like that. Cards."

"How long have they been coming in?" Cindy hid her excitement well.

"Well, I've been working here for three years, I guess maybe the last two. I mean, they were pretty serious, I think."

Bingo.

27.

AFTER SAM LEFT OUR TABLE, CINDY LEANED towards me. Her head was almost touching mine and I could smell her perfume. It was an old-fashioned one: L'air du Temps. "Do you believe this? You were right, Robin. One of your hunches has paid off. These two were lovers. So, now we have a problem."

She was sawing into the chicken breast on top of her salad and shoving huge hunks into her mouth. I could tell it wasn't that tender as strings were dragging along the edge of her knife. One day I would tell her to chew with her mouth closed, but not today. I needed her help.

I was having trouble following her line of thinking. A problem? What problem? Besides, I was starving and my salad was beckoning. Didn't she ever let up? Take time out from her busy brain? My mouth was full of some kind of dark green leafy mix. It wasn't that good. Why did salads full of vitamins taste like pond scum?

"What's that?"

"This chicken is delicious," she said, chewing hard on a mouthful. Maybe she didn't cook much. She took another huge bite and double forked it in. Cindy wasn't great on table manners. "The problem? Well, to begin with, why are both of them dead? I mean, say if van Horner's wife Melissa did it, then only Radcliffe would be dead, right? Kill off the lover. But, her husband is dead too, so, did she really do it? Why would she kill off *that* meal ticket? With a *gun*? Women don't use guns to kill. They use poison." Cindy sat back and wiped her mouth with her napkin. "God, I was hungry." Her salad had been inhaled. She picked her teeth with her thumbnail, trying to get out one of the strings.

I felt rather proper as I delicately finished my plate. "I disagree," I chewed discretely and swallowed. When I was done I licked my gums, trying to suck off any dark green morsels from my teeth without looking too obvious. "Maybe there was a large insurance policy on him. Or maybe she simply couldn't stand the fact that he had betrayed her. Maybe she hired a hit man?"

"I dunno, Robin. I think there's something else going on. What about the theft of the water? What's that about? We have to think of all the facts, not solely the ones we want to."

"The theft of the water isn't a fact. It's an idea. Maybe England was lying about Radcliffe stealing the water. But let's say he wasn't. Let's not throw cold water on his theory. Let's say he knows something we don't. Besides, Creston said there was no evidence about an international theft, so that's probably a dead end. I think he's a pretty good cop, so he's probably right about this. But he hasn't dismissed the idea and he isn't ready to embrace new theories, but he has his doubts. So, let's not flush Radcliffe as a water thief down the toilet. *Ha ha.* Maybe these two Everwave guys were going to steal water, and someone else wanted it, so they killed them."

"But how would van Horner and Radcliffe pull that off? And who would they sell it to?"

"I don't know. Maybe someone in Boston, from Todd's university days, a water broker or something. The market is huge; everyone needs water, it seems. How they would steal it is another matter." I thought for a moment and tried to imagine a solution to the problem. How on earth does one steal a lot of water? "Maybe England was right. Maybe they were thinking of diverting it from the cold water system pump in the middle of the lake into a tanker. They could siphon off around fifty percent and no one would really notice."

Cindy jumped in, "Or maybe from a pumping station on land, you know, the John Street pumping station, into a big truck, like a milk truck. You know those ones that you see on the highway, all shiny metal? That's a really big container. It could easily go over the border and into the States."

Sam showed up at the table and whisked our plates away. "Tea? Coffee? Me?" He struck a pose. He was so hilarious but I didn't know if I should laugh.

"I'll have a lotta." Cindy on the other hand was right at home.

"Mint tea," I looked away embarrassed and shuffled the photos back into their file.

"Righto." He cha-cha'd away.

"Listen." Cindy had pulled out her compact and was redoing her lips. "Maybe Sam knows more than he thinks he knows about these two. I mean, they came into this place at least once a week, and he probably overheard them talking, you know. He's not an idiot, even though he's being quite silly, performing for us."

"Performing?" I was dumbstruck. I had so much to learn about the gay world.

"Sure he is, you don't think he's really that camp, do you? He's having fun."

"Oh." I had no idea.

"Let's ask him when he brings us our drinks."

"You ask," I said. Cindy had a better repartee with the guy. Sam placed the coffee and tea in front of us.

"I know you don't gossip, or anything like that," Cindy grinned mischievously while slightly widening her green eyes, "but did you ever happen to hear anything Tim and Robert were talking about?"

She was good at this.

"Like what?" Sam said cautiously. "I don't really like to talk about my customers' personal lives."

"Oh nothing like that," she assured him breathlessly. "I dunno, sort of anything interesting in their conversation. Not about them, but you know, businessy kinds of things."

He relaxed. "Oh sure." He wiped away some spilled tea in front of me with a ragged piece of terry cloth that smelled like bleach. "They were entrepreneurs. You know the type, always hustling something new. Like I said, I knew them for a couple of years. At first they talked about a new gadget, a sticker with circuits in it, to track down lost electronic equipment, like computers. An attachable GPS gizmo. They went on about that for a few months but then they gave that up. The technology wasn't advanced enough."

"Always an issue," I contributed, but it seemed from the look Cindy gave me that I should have kept my mouth shut.

"After the GPS gadget doodad they moved onto a solar-powered fountain idea. I think they actually went through with that. They sold these fountains, bird baths, online. I think they did okay. Miniature solar panels, like those lights people use to light up their gardens. It was just a hobby, because they had regular jobs for a company called Everwave. It was in the news recently. Technology that extracts the cold out of lake water for air conditioning."

Cindy played dumb. "So creative. But what about recently?" She was as patient as a cat stalking a mouse.

Sam shut up suddenly and began diligently writing out our bill. Over his shoulder I saw that his manager had come out onto the patio and was surveying his domain. Satisfied with what he saw, all his waiters busy, he blew back into the restaurant.

"Lately?" Sam looked over at the fire door, making sure his boss wasn't coming back. "Well, the most recent idea was an ice cream factory. Ice cream is really taking off in the city. They were having trouble creating an efficient cooling system to freeze the cream. Apparently the energy this takes is the main cost of the ice cream."

"Who knew?" Cindy was looking for her credit card.

I kicked her under the table. She scowled. "What?" As if Sam wasn't there.

"What," I queried pointedly, "was their solution to this problem? Did you hear them talk about it?" I already had my theory.

A light dawned in Sam's eyes. "Oh," he breathed out, "Everwave. Cooling system. Maybe they were going to steal cold lake water to help freeze the ice cream. No, not those guys." He efficiently ran our credit cards through his handheld processor, covering up his discomfiture.

I stood up. It was time to get a move on. Cindy gathered up her stuff. "Thanks Suzette, you've been very helpful." Sam was already clearing off our table. He looked up briefly and waved somewhat guiltily with two fingers as we walked through the patio gate.

"So, what do you think of all that?" There was a buzz in my chest. "We know so much more than we did half an hour ago. Do you think I should tell Creston and Stokes?" We arrived at Cindy's Accord parked around the corner. "I can't make sense of it." She beeped the remote locking system. We got in the over-heated car and Cindy drove south down Church Street. The sun had passed well over to the west now.

I was thinking out loud while holding my hands in front of the air conditioner. "I don't think they were going to steal the water. No. Creston asked Jimmy—"

"Who's Jimmy?" Cindy was squinting in the bright sun that was slashing in between two buildings right into her eyes.

"The captain that installed the pump. As I was saying, Creston asked Jimmy if Radcliff or van Horner had requested any help in the future, you know, with the crane. And Jimmy said no, why would they, they were going into the ice cream business."

"And your point?" The glare was pissing her off.

"They didn't want the water. Maybe they wanted the *technology*. Maybe they were stealing the technology of how to extract cold from water."

Cindy tossed her bag towards me. "Find my sunglasses, will you? I can hardly see." The sun was fracturing into small rainbow fragments through the accumulated street grime on her window.

I rooted in her bag for a pair of sunglasses. When I finally found them I snapped the arms open and passed them to her.

She placed them on her nose. "And it would hardly be *stealing* the technology if they owned the company. Or if they owned the patent."

"But did they own the company? Companies are often owned by many people. There are all sorts of investors who get a slice of the pie. Even the government can have some shares in a company. So it would be interesting to see how much Radcliffe and van Horne actually owned. Maybe they owned nothing and just had salaries. It's possible. So then they would be stealing the technology. We need to find out about the structure of the company. And about the patent. Maybe somebody wanted to stop them from stealing."

"Well aren't you the wealth of information. How did you know all this, smarty pants?"

"I learned a lot when I did that corrupt condo story. Plus my dad always ranted about the companies the government was investing in, about the patents that were great but got no funding."

"I think we should tell Creston, at least, about what we've discovered. Those two were an item. They were planning an ice cream business. I think Ralph's hit a blank wall and is barking up the wrong tree. It's not like he's totally dismissed my idea that Todd was murdered by a wasp. He might be open to this. Van Horner and Radcliffe being together could be a motive. And besides, we are no closer to finding the killer now than we were a few hours ago. It frankly doesn't make sense that the wife did it. From what I could see, when van Horner was shot she acted like she was madly in love with her husband. She seemed truly distressed that he'd been injured. Either that or she's one helluva an actor."

"Yes, she looked like she loved him."

"We're driving right by a police station. I think its Creston's home base. The one on Dundas is where he's been assigned for this case. Shouldn't we go in?"

Cindy vehemently shook her head, tossing her red curls. "Are you kidding? We are about to scoop a great story. The last thing we want to do is go to the police. Next thing you know all the other papers will have the story. They'll pick it up from their moles and scanners. Jack England will be fast on our heels." Cindy drove past the station without a backwards glance. We were going to the office.

Dammit, I had had it up to here with people dismissing me. Maybe it wasn't the best idea to go to the police, but going back to the office? That made no sense at all. That would accomplish nothing. I was itchy to get more information.

"I don't know why we're going to the office. It's not as if we can write anything. We still know nothing. All we have are ideas, not facts. It's a waste of time."

Cindy propped her sunglasses on her head and turned to look at me. Her green eyes were sparking. So, she didn't like to be challenged. Tough shit. "And just where do you think we should be going, oh wise one?"

Geezus. She could be such a bitch. Some friend. Did I want to even be around her? Well, not a lot of choice, given I was sitting in her car. If I were in the driver's seat, where would I be going? Well, back to the police station, for one, stupid idea or not, the police should know about Radcliff and van Horner. But, failing that, Alison might have had a good idea when she said we should look at the love relationships. Yeah, even though van Horner's wife put on a good show, she should still be talked to. Maybe I was wrong about her. Who knew what she knew?

"I think we should be interviewing van Horner's wife. See what she knows." I felt stressed with the effort of swimming against the tidal wave of Cindy's strong will. I waited for her barbed rebuttal. Nothing but silence. Then she yanked the steering wheel hard to the left and the car screeched a U-turn. Back up College Street we went.

"Good idea. Who knows what she knows?"

"My thoughts exactly." I was so relieved that she hadn't fought me on this. I had a strong feeling about where this was going. It couldn't yet put it into words, but I knew something was about to break.

"She'll probably be at home this time of day. Let's go shake up her coiffed hair. She looks like a real estate agent type, what with the highlights and pencil skirt. Google her, why don't you. Melissa van Horner. No, Mowbray. I put my money on her working for a real estate company."

Cindy wasn't great about not being in control and heading north was a big concession. It cost me nothing to acquiesce and be her servant, even though I felt it was irrelevant. I tapped on my phone. Surprise, surprise. Sure enough, she was a number one sales person at a real estate company that catered to the rich crowd. "Yup, you win. Gold-star producer. And that explains the van Horner's big house. *She* made the money. Not him. Their wealth is because of her. See?" I held my phone up for Cindy to glance at.

Cindy took her eyes off the road to look at the picture closely. "Nice teeth." She was jealous. Melissa had perfectly white veneers on her front teeth. Caps certainly weren't covered in a reporter's benefits, unlike Shirley and Doug's.

I mused, "What big teeth you have, Grandma, said Little Red Riding Hood."

Cindy got it right away. "We'll put her through the wringer."

She drove expertly, turning left and right through various side streets until we headed north on Mount Pleasant. When we got to van Horner's street, I saw a section of crime scene tape flapping forlornly against a manicured hedge, out of place in the landscaped neighbourhood. We parked and I tugged at the tape until it was freed. I scrunched it up into a small ball and tucked it into my purse.

Cindy laughed at me, "Always the protector of homes and gardens."

At times she really could be such a know it all. "Fuck you."

Cindy laughed again, "Lighten up," and strode towards the house on her long legs, me scrambling behind her.

When we got to the top of the flagstone steps, I noticed that the frosted glass in the door had already been replaced. Man, what money could buy. It had been repaired over the weekend. Cindy rapped on the glass with her knuckles. The home sounded empty. Then she lifted the brass lion knocker and let it fall. The bang reverberated through the house. Was there nobody home?

Without warning the door opened silently on well-oiled hinges. A lavender scent wafted out and I recognized the brand of the plug-in product. I hated those things. Pollution, if you asked me, but of course, the big wigs who manufactured these things never did. And there stood Melissa Mowbray.

Although she was only in her late thirties, her face had aged a decade or two and looked closer to fifty. Lines sagged around her full lips. Her hair, although highlighted and sprayed into a modern somewhat jagged cut, seemed lifeless and dull. She was dressed in an off-white flowing pant suit, soft and diaphanous. Her eyes were deadened, perhaps with a sedative of some sort. Or maybe she'd been drinking. Maybe both.

This woman was suffering. She had recently lost her husband in a shocking way and she had young children to support. My heart reached out to her and I had to reel it back in. She knew something, I had to remind myself. She was involved in this mess, somehow. I also knew we had to be careful. She thought nothing of smashing her stiletto heel into the top of a policeman's foot. Karate? Kick boxing?

Cindy lowered her voice in an effort to sound sympathetic. "Mrs. van Horner, Mowbray, I mean, I'm sorry to intrude.

I know what you're going through. I am very sorry for your loss." Cindy's hand covered her heart as she said this. I knew exactly what she was trying to do. "We're from the *Express*, the paper that gave your husband a lot of press for Everwave. I was wondering if we could come in and talk to you about what's happened."

A small spark ignited in Melissa's dulled eyes. Everyone hated the press. "You have no idea what I'm going through. Why should I let you in? Leave me alone." Some of her words were slurred. Drinking, then. The door started to swing shut.

"Ms. Mowbray, please." I stopped the door with my foot. "I lost my husband a few years ago. I do know what you're going through. You feel like you can't go on. You are shocked and traumatized. Maybe you would like to talk to someone who's been through the same thing."

"Your husband wasn't *murdered*, stupid. You have no idea how that feels."

Stupid? So, despite the appearance and house, she was from the streets.

"Actually, he *was* murdered. By a drunk driver. Snatched away from my children in an instant. It was devastating." All this was true, even if I left out the bit about my being relieved he was dead. Maybe Melissa Mowbray's life wasn't a bed of roses.

Melissa turned her back and simply walked away, leaving the door swinging open behind her. She staggered on her high heels across the wide expanse of the marble foyer towards double French doors that led out onto a flagstone patio. Cindy and I looked at each other, shrugged soundlessly, and entered the house, stepping around the brown blood stains in the tile grout by the front door.

We weren't stupid; we'd follow her.

28.

MELISSA MOWBRAY METICULOUSLY POSITIONED her tanned and lean body on a plush cushion in a wicker wingback chair until she looked tragic. I was trying not to be cynical about her, but I never did like the really rich. The view over the golf course was stunningly beautiful. Willow trees and stately oaks blew softly in the early September breeze. A tangle of bushes, probably raspberries, seemed weighted down with the burden of ripening fruit. Wasps flew lazily around, their long legs dangling like ill-attached undercarriages on awkward airplanes. Melissa swatted at them absently as her unfocussed eyes drifted about. She had definitely been drinking.

Cindy cleared her throat to get Melissa's attention. It worked. "I'm sorry to be asking questions at this time."

"No you aren't," snorted Melissa. "It's your job and you paps love it."

Paps? What did she mean? Pap test? Oh, I know, *paparazzi*. I was paparazzi? My kids would love that one. Meet my mom, the cougar paparazzi.

Cindy, undaunted, cooed soothingly, "You're right." She smiled innocently, "I'd like to figure out who murdered your husband. We were standing on your doorstep right after it happened."

Melissa jolted up, as if a she were a puppet whose strings had been yanked. She looked directly at me, not at Cindy whom she seemed to dislike, her eyes brightening with a slow burning curiosity. "Is this true? You were there when it happened?"

"Yes, the bullet must have passed directly over us when we were sitting in our car in front of your house." I let the seriousness of what I told her sink in. When it did, Melissa's head jerked up again.

"Oh," she cried, "That must have been horrifying. Did you see the shooter?" She sat perfectly still for a few seconds. I could see the wheels turning in her jumbled brain. "But why were you at our house?"

"We wanted to talk to your husband about Todd Radcliff's death." I watched her carefully. Although she was in a sedated and woozy state I could see she was making an effort to put on a puzzled look. She finally finished arranging her features to her satisfaction.

Melissa squealed, "Todd? He's dead?"

Nice try. I knew she already knew that he was dead. I could tell. Her response was too contrived. Had she been involved? I felt a chill run down my spine and the hair on my arms stood up as if a cold breeze had touched me.

"Yes, he died three nights ago. In his condo."

"Oh," she adjusted her eyes to look sad. "I've been preoccupied with Richard's death and haven't turned on the TV. But that's terrible. How?"

Well, that was interesting. Was she fishing for information? Did she want to know if how Todd had died was public knowledge? I felt compelled to fib. "The coroner has yet to determine the cause. The police think it's suicide. Maybe he had a heart attack. Maybe he took sleeping pills They're doing advanced lab tests to tell." I was steering clear of murder.

I watched Melissa visibly relax, settling her body deep into the cushions of the wicker chair. "Probably suicide. He was depressed lately, you know, always slouching around with his hands in his pockets." She tittered and then covered her mouth. What was she hiding? How well she had known him? Although she was stoned out of her noodle, her neurons were still zapping, making her mouth feed us a pack of lies. Or were they? Maybe there was some truth in what she was saying. She sat forward and abruptly changed the topic.

"But if you were there, you could have helped my Richard. If he had got help sooner, he would not have lost so much blood and he would have lived. The bullet hit an *artery*. He was pumping out blood. Why didn't you help him?" She had started to sob, her thin shoulders shaking. "Why did you leave him there to die?" she bleated with a bit too much protest.

This was going to be tricky. Cindy started manufacturing excuses. "We didn't know he was hit, Mrs. van Horner. Mowbray. We only saw a bullet hole in the glass, and the glass was frosted. It didn't cross our minds that a shot had been aimed at him and that he was lying on the other side of a door, bleeding. The shot's target wasn't visible from where we were standing by the knocker and the glass *was* frosted. We couldn't see in the house. We didn't hear a shot."

Melissa hated Cindy. "Well, you were pretty stupid, weren't you? What do you think a bullet hole meant?" Her mood had flipped; the deeply grieving widow was now spitting mad. I knew this was a precursor to her breaking down all together. Clearly, she loved her husband. And maybe she didn't. I knew what *that* was like. I had to even out her energy with a diversion, and quickly.

"No, no. I know this neighbourhood is very safe. But still, Cindy and I, we aren't used to being in a neighbourhood like this. We had no idea how long the hole had been there. We didn't know how significant a bullet hole was." Why not grovel and make Melissa feel superior? She seemed vain enough that it might calm down her ragged edges. It was the closest I'd come to an apology for why we didn't act to save him sooner. Cindy and I had been in terrible danger and it was only through quick thinking and some acting that we hadn't been shot as well. "We truly did not hear a shot. And we couldn't see through the frosted glass." I changed the topic. "You mentioned that Todd had been depressed lately?" What did she know?

Melissa eyed me shrewdly under her clumped mascara. She dabbed at the streaks of black that had run down her cheeks. "Yes, he had been acting low. I think it was money trouble."

This woman was not to be toyed with. She had moxie. I wanted to investigate that aspect of her personality. "Really?" I said factually, implying I didn't believe her. I didn't. "Do you know any martial arts?"

"What?" Her head flopped suddenly to the side and looked as if it might roll off her neck if lightly touched, she was so startled by the quick change in the conversation. Two could play this game. To cover up her discomfiture, she opened her mouth, letting out a delicate rill of laughter, "You think I killed him with a chop, chop? I was miles away when he died. Looking after my children." Her hand sliced drunkenly through the air in a parody of a karate chop as her girlish twitter tinkled across the patio like a wind chime.

I wasn't fooled. Did she really say that she was miles away when he died? How did she know when he died? She had already admitted she didn't know he was dead. "No, I was just wondering. You look so fit, and toned."

"Yup," she smugly looked at her bicep while flexing it. "I take kick boxing."

"Really? I never would have guessed." I didn't have to guess. The stomp on the cop's foot gave it away. "What gym?"

"Oh, you wouldn't know it. Not one of those namby-pamby joints." She pointed her toes and admired the calf on her leg. "His poor wife."

She caught me off balance as much as I had her. "Whose wife?"

"Todd's. I mean, she really loved him."

What? He had a wife? I was going to leave that alone for the time being. He told me he was divorced. That the wife took everything. What a schmuck.

"You know her?" Cindy asked.

Melissa looked at Cindy with contempt but then decided to reply. "Yes, I know her. The four of us would get together for dinners and stuff. Meet at each other's houses."

He had a wife *and* a house? What about his condo? Oh, that's why there were two listings for Radcliffe at 411.ca. Liar.

"We went to new restaurants together. Last week we tried out one on College near Bathurst. The Elephant. Indian. She and I were the trophy wives, even though we both made more than our husbands. She and I were friends, but I guess now that the guys are..." she paused and didn't say the word. "I guess that's over. Bye bye, Crystal." Melissa's eyelids were drifting down.

She slumped back in her chair and a wasp landed on her arm. She sleepily brushed it away. "If you don't bug them, they won't bite," she drawled without opening her eyes. I could see a long plastic cylinder filled with flying wasps hanging from the branch of a maple tree in her yard. "They don't bother me at all. You have to know how to handle them." Melissa let out a small giggle. I didn't want to know what thoughts were floating about in her pickled brain.

It seemed a good time to get to the nugget of truth about Todd's marriage. "I didn't realize Radcliff was married."

Cindy was restless. She fiddled around with her purse. She wanted to go.

"Yup! But he, you know, he liked guys too." Melissa then covered her mouth with her hand, "Oops."

Cindy was packing up her phone and keys while I kept asking Melissa questions. "He did?" So, she knew that about him. I wondered how much she knew. "Did your husband? I mean, they were good friends, right? How *good*?"

Cindy was ready to go and tapped her watch. She needed to get back to the office. Her Vipers story wasn't finished.

Melissa was off in la-la land. "Oh yes," she let out a bitter bark. And then she suddenly tugged her body up, realizing what she might have given away. Her mouth turned down and she whined, "My poor little Richie. We were so in love and now he's gone. I really don't know how I will get by without him."

Give me a break. Did she love her husband? I thought so. But love could be so complicated. As I well knew. "I'm sorry Ms. Mowbray, I truly am. I know exactly how it feels, but you will survive."

"Oh, I'm a survivor all right." Melissa took a shuddering breath and put her hands on the arms of her chair to push herself up. It seemed to take an enormous amount of will. "Time for you two paps to skedaddle."

"Skedaddle?" Who said that anymore? Where *was* she from? "Just out of curiosity, where did you grow up, Mrs. van Horner?"

"Mowbray," she corrected automatically. She wove her way across the patio, tottering on her three-inch heels, her arm flopping about in the air like a wet spaghetti noodle as she waved it in a generally western direction, "I grew up in downtown Hamilton."

Well, that explained a lot. It was pretty rough by the steel mill.

Cindy was following Melissa to the front door as I rapidly gathered up my belongings. I could hear them chatting, with Cindy making gushing noises, trying to repair the relationship or at least pretend the animosity didn't exist. Then I heard her mention antibiotics and infection. So, she was correcting Melissa about the cause of Richard's death. I wondered how she would take that. Melissa didn't strike me as a woman who would like to be contradicted.

I looked back at the wasp trap and knew it meant something. Melissa Mowbray, successful real estate agent for a top-notch firm, kick boxer extraordinaire, mother of three cuties, was guilty of something sinister. She was not afraid of wasps and had plenty at her disposal. I couldn't wait to leave this house.

Cindy and I drove away at a far more leisurely pace than we had a few nights previously. "She was right, you know. We could have got help to him sooner."

Cindy's knuckles turned the colour of bone as she gripped the steering wheel. She hated being challenged. "No, actually, Robin, no, we couldn't have." She looked at me, her green eyes on fire. "First of all, he died of an *infection*, not a loss of blood. Secondly, if either of us had pulled out a cell phone as soon as we saw that bullet hole, we would have been shot. We saved our lives, Robin, by pretending we hadn't seen it."

I remembered my whispering to her to shift her eyes to look at the hole and not to turn her head. I remembered telling her to act normally and to proceed with knocking on his door as if nothing had happened. I had followed my instincts. "You're right."

"I'm always right." We both laughed, her louder than me.

The conflict was over. But still, Cindy and I weren't exactly getting along today. What was that about? Something to do with my gratitude exercise? I made a mental note to think about that later. With a glass of wine.

Cindy was racing across town. She said, "You know what I can't believe?"

"What's that?"

"That Radcliff had a love nest. A bolt hole. A fancy downtown condo. That he had a house. That he was still married."

I was wondering about the same things. "Yeah, well, I guess I'm a stupid mark."

Cindy went on. "I think Melissa's guilty of something. Did you notice that she didn't bat an eyelash when you mentioned his condo? She *knew* he had a condo. The guy had tons of secrets. With the main one being that he was gay. Or at least bisexual."

"I'm an even stupider mark."

"If your name had been Mark you would have had a better chance with him." Cindy chuckled at her joke.

I was puzzled. "How could I miss that bit about his condo? No wait, I must have been thinking about something else."

Cindy was curious "You think she's hiding something?"

"Yeah, well I think Melissa Mowbray killed Todd. She has wasps. She has a motive. She's feisty."

"Melissa? How did you get that? A motive?"

"She knew that her husband and Todd were having an affair."

Cindy shook her curls. "I must have missed that."

"It was in a small sound bite of a laugh, a short sentence or two, but I was watching her carefully. She was pretty drunk, and I think stoned as well, but not as much as she was letting us believe. I think she was using it as a cover to dig out information from us. But she let that one thing slip."

"I got the part about her not being that drunk, but not the affair. Must be losing my touch."

I gave her an excuse. "You were anxious to leave. And you were probably trying to make amends. Man, did she hate you! What that was that about?"

"Homophobic is my guess."

"Really? She could tell you were gay?"

"Most people can. Whatever, Robin, it is what it is. Call Alison, will ya?"

"Alison? What for?"

Cindy looked at me patiently, "The other wife. Not fair to grill one but not the other. Let's talk to Todd's wife. See what she knows."

When Alison picked up, I asked, "Hi Alison, listen, would you mind finding out the name and address of a software company that's run and owned by Crystal Radcliff? Cindy and I want to interview her about these deaths."

"Hang on for a sec."

I heard her clicking away, her fingers flying over her computer keys. "Okay, here goes." Alison read off from her computer, "Softwareit. All one word. A pun, I guess." She gave me the address of the company.

I whispered the company title a few times until I got it. "Oh, sort of wearing software like clothing. Good name for a woman's firm."

"And her name isn't Crystal Radcliff. It's Crystal Riker."

"How did you find that out?"

Alison laughed, "Need to know anything else?" and clicked off. Such a sassy young thing.

"Okay." I got out my iPad and Google-mapped the address Alison had given me. "We want to go across town to a street north of Lawrence that runs west off Dufferin."

"Right." Cindy did a left onto Yonge from van Horner's street, drove past the grocery store we had called from, and then took a right onto Lawrence. "I'm starving. Those salads were useless. Time for afternoon tea? Want to get some unsubs?"

I laughed. We bought some six inch sandwiches from a Subway on Dufferin and unwrapped them in the parking lot of Softwareit, chomping them while looking at the scraggily weeds growing out of the cracks in the pavement. Still chewing her last mouthful, Cindy opened her car door and said, "Let me do the talking here."

"Only if you don't talk with your mouth full." I muttered to myself. That girl really had to get some manners. I wrapped the remainder of my bun in the waxed paper it had come in, stuffed it back into the Subway bag, and got out of the car.

The steel door of the company had three deadbolt locks and a wired alarm tape running around its perimeter. There was not one but two security cameras, one focused on the door and the other on the parking lot. I guess we'd been watched shovelling our Subways into our gobs. "Pretty good security," I whispered, not moving my lips.

Cindy pushed a yellowed button on the door frame and the discombobulated voice of a receptionist crackled. "Can I help you?"

"Hi, we're from the *Express* and were in the neighbourhood. We're writing a front-page story on female entrepreneurs who have created successful startups. I think Crystal Riker would want to be included in the article."

"Press passes."

Short and to the point. We both reached into our bags and held up our laminated passes to the overhead camera. There was a buzzing noise as the latches electronically unlocked. We were in.

29.

THE STEEL DOOR SILENTLY GLIDED SHUT behind us. Three separate clinks of locks homing into place signalled that it was not only closed, but that we were trapped inside. I felt a quiver of trepidation as I thought about fire. We found ourselves standing on a slate tiled floor in front of a receptionist who was sitting behind a large teak desk. She had wiry grey hair tightly pulled back from her pointy face into a stubby knot on top of her head. A few bristly hairs escaped from a multitude of bobby pins. And I saw, as I got closer, also from her chin. Her sharp nose jabbed towards us aggressively, somewhat like a snake's tongue tasting the air for the smell of prey. Her nameplate on the marble counter in front of her said this was Ms. Nelson. She looked more like a warden than a receptionist. The place was giving me the willies.

Cindy seemed unperturbed. "Hi, we're from the *Express* and we're doing an article on female entrepreneurs."

"So you said." Ms. Nelson was not a friendly sort.

"Is it possible for us to see Crystal Radcliff?"

"*Riker*. Her last name is Riker."

"Right. I knew that. Sorry. Does Ms. Riker have a few minutes to spare?"

Ms. Nelson dropped her piercing gaze and pushed a button on her desk phone with a tight little peck while arranging her headset. "Some press here to see you, seems legit." She waited for a response and then clicked of. "She'll be out in a minute. Have a seat."

Cindy and I sank into buttery soft leather chairs and waited, thumbing through glossy magazines that had been neatly positioned on a glass table. Ten minutes went by, with the only sounds being the rustle of pages turning and the electronic hum of some sort of air filter. When a door to the left of us opened I had to prevent myself from gaping. Crystal Riker was not at all what I expected. Not that I really had any idea at all about what Todd's wife would look like, but the woman who appeared at the doorway leading into a long hall behind her was not what I had envisioned. At all. She was as wide as she was tall.

Her facial features had been buried long ago in folds of flesh and her extended hand was covered in what appeared to be small balls of pastry dough. A wedding ring was barely visible on her left hand that was hanging like a sack of potatoes down her side. She was wearing a bright red muumuu that flowed around her like a boiling pot of spaghetti sauce, jiggling while it bubbled. Todd's wife smiled engagingly, setting off a small tsunami over her jowls. Her voice, when it escaped from the mounds of her chest, was a high squeak, wildly at odds with her bulk. "Welcome," she squeezed out the word. "I'm glad you're interested in Softwareit. I have built up this company from nothing and I'm happy to tell you how I did it. Might be inspiring for young girls."

I stood up and shook her hand, noticing that underneath the squishy skin there was a strong grip. We introduced ourselves and Cindy took the lead. "Thanks for seeing us, Ms. Riker. I know you must be a very busy woman, but this article, as you say, is important in that it will be inspiring to young girls entering the work world. You are a great role model for them"

Crystal beckoned for us to follow her. "Let me give you a quick tour of my little empire." She waved her arms as she lumbered down an aisle through about thirty desks, all occupied by fresh-faced kids wearing jeans and smiling at their boss as she chuffed by. I could see in a flash that they thought the world of her. "This is my think tank area. I employ wonderful young talent from all over the country. My top criteria for working here is creativity. Hard to assess in an interview, but I look at their resumes carefully. I pick young people who have a well-rounded background, not purely scientific expertise. Painters, singers, camp counselors. Most companies would reject them as being misfits. I *want* the misfits. I am personally involved in the hiring. No HR person for me. I know how to find the qualified odd duck in the hundreds of applicants."

Takes one to know one.

Geez. I had to stop being so judgmental. Here I was, being critical of a woman who had given back to society, in spades. And her staff adored her.

At the end of the aisle was her office, the glass door wide open. We settled into her workspace, a modern poured concrete shoebox with a floor to ceiling window that overlooked a small knoll of landscaping, some grass and a few bushes. Not unattractive, but not exactly a green space. She stuffed her rather large bottom into her black desk chair, opened her arms expansively and smiled, "First off, I'd like to apologize for Ms. Nelson. She's very protective of me. Now, what would you like to know?"

Cindy took the bull by the horns. "We're sorry to hear about the loss of your husband, Ms. Riker. It must have come as a terrible shock."

Crystal's eyes narrowed, the top eyelid almost touching the bottom. Her wide mouth flattened into a tight white line. I could hear her breathing come in small shallow breaths. I couldn't read her emotion. Angry, yes. Suspicious? Maybe. Curious? Perhaps a little. I settled on angry. She was probably thinking that we had got into her fortress under false pretenses. But she said nothing. Cindy watched her and seemed frozen in expectancy.

Damn it. Cindy really had to finesse her interviewing technique. I stepped in, figuring that if we were going to get anywhere with this battleship disguised as a comfy grandmother that we would have to send out a few decoys. "So, exactly what sort of projects helped launch your company and what are you working on now?"

Crystal visibly relaxed. "We started with software for schools. Although I never had children, I have always been interested in education, especially for girls. Girls get the short end of the stick in the classroom because boys are always kicking up shit. Teachers spend half their time disciplining the boys and not teaching. Working on computers seems to level this out a bit. The boys are more focused on what they are doing and the girls get the attention they should have. It's win-win."

What? She didn't have children? Todd said he had three! That she got complete custody! This was all so unreal. Plus who says "kicking up shit" in a press interview? So unprofessional. Didn't she have any boundaries? Or was she refreshing? The flower show world was very different than this.

"And now?" I asked.

Crystal looked out the window while fidgeting with a ragged fingernail. She seemed to come to a decision. "I guess it doesn't matter that you know. We're revealing the product in a few days. We're working on technology for the food industry. Software that regulates temperatures for the food industry."

"Well, everyone needs to eat." Some more than others, like me. "Energy costs are going through the roof and if energy use can be made more efficient, the price of food can be stabilized."

Crystal nodded, "So, you understand the importance of the work that we do. The boys kept going on about ice cream, but eventually we'd expand to all frozen foods."

Cindy interjected, "Robin and I wrote a couple of articles on Everwave, your husband's baby, and were quite impressed by the concept of the deep water cooling system. So, yes, we have a bit of background on that."

Crystal again looked at Cindy with dislike. No wonder. Saying "baby" to a woman who hadn't had children could only be a trigger of some kind. Plus it was belittling. Me, I wanted to figure out Crystal's role in the two murders, if she had one. But Crystal's response floored me. I had got it so wrong.

"Yes, Todd had the technology for extracting cold from water for air conditioning, which he used at Everwave. This technology can also be applied to freezers as well. For the past year, Softwareit's been developing it further, so cold can be extracted from regular tap water."

And here I was thinking she was in a plot to steal Everwave's technology. Right out in the open, she was. I took a wild guess. "So, he had rights to the Everwave patent?"

A cloud passed over Crystal's face, "He and the vice president, Richard van Horner, had equal ownership of the patent. Everwave was a totally different company with different investors. The food application would be done under a separate company. We didn't even have a name yet for the new company. It was going to be a three way partnership with them and Softwareit. I don't know what's going to happen now that they're both dead."

Richard had died a few hours ago—how did she know he was dead? I hadn't yet written the story! Was she involved in his death?

"Richard van Horne is dead?" Cindy asked, acting puzzled. So, she had caught on as well.

Crystal's face was an open book of grief. "Yes, it was in the web edition of the *Times* about half an hour ago. Shot. It's all so terrible. We were good friends, the three of us. In fact, the four of us. We went out as couples once a month or so, Todd and I with Richard and his wife, Melissa."

Jack England scooped the story. Damn.

"So you know Melissa?" Despite her heavy hand at times, Cindy could be pretty shrewd at getting out information.

"Oh sure, she and I grew up together in Hamilton. By the

waterfront. Both our dads worked in the mill. Steel town. We're not really good friends, but we have history. And we go to the same kick boxing gym."

That explained the "kicking up shit" comment. She had a blue-collar background, like Melissa. But why hadn't Melissa mentioned that she'd known Crystal as a kid?

"You take kick boxing?" Cindy tried not to sound too disbelieving.

"Oh, I know I'm large. In Hamilton we say 'round.' But that doesn't mean I'm in bad shape. Really, there's such prejudice against overweight people. Kids who are fat are bullied worse than kids who are handicapped in any other way. I kick box with Melissa once or twice a week."

"What gym?" I asked innocently. Melissa hadn't said.

"You wouldn't know it. It's full of unsavoury characters who train hard to be really tough. I like feeling as strong as the guys. West Side Gym."

But Cindy was on the scent of the technology motive. "Melissa wasn't part of the partnership?"

"No, it was a three-way deal. She's busy with her real estate. Highly successful. Makes a ton of money selling houses. She would acquire a third ownership of the patent only if her husband…" Crystal trailed off here and I mentally filled in the blank: died.

Was this the motive? Did she love money more than her husband? And why had Melissa said "Bye bye, Crystal?" No doubt she knew with the two men dead that she and Crystal were going to be partners on the new cooling system. Was she planning to kill Crystal? Was she trying to mislead us? And then a thought struck me. Perhaps the two women were in cahoots together. Maybe they were lovers. No, couldn't be. Melissa was homophobic, that was clear.

"She loved her husband," Crystal said hastily, perhaps sensing all the places we could go with this information. "And I loved mine. Sure, I knew Todd was a bit of a wanderer, both sides of the fence, but he always came home to me at the end of the day. I mean, he loved me and I loved him. I knew that." I watched as if in a spell as her whole body started to shake. Tears spilled from her eyes and slowly rolled down her cheeks. My heart went out to her as she fell apart in front of us. "I can't believe they're thinking that he killed himself. We were so happy together." Her voice cracked. "I don't know what I'm going to do without him. He was all I had," she whispered, her voice tight with emotion.

So the police hadn't told her they were now considering his death accidental or a murder. I watched sadly as this high-powered go-getter wept in front of us. I believed her. This was no show. If she could say that her husband was all she had when she had a highly successful company, tons of money, a roomful of kids who obviously thought the world of her, then that was enough proof of the depth of her love for me. I felt for this woman. She was hard-working, creative, she hired misfits, for heaven's sake. I was now even more determined to discover who had murdered her husband. I knew it wasn't an accident.

Cindy caught my eye indicating that we should quietly slip away, leaving this poor women alone in her grief. Cindy said quietly, "Thanks for your time, Crystal. I know it will all work out." She patted her on her arm as she stood up.

Work out? I thought not. Her husband was dead, for heaven's sake. Plus, with van Horner dead as well, she would have to work with Melissa van Horner on her freezer project. I couldn't imagine the two of them seeing eye to eye, even if they did kick box together.

We hustled out of her office leaving her stooped over her desk. We jostled through the long aisle of desks and finally burst into the waiting room. Ms. Nelson startled up from reading her movie magazine and quickly shoved it in her lap, like a child in school, caught texting. "I'll buzz you out," she coughed and I could hear the electronic unlocking of the door.

"Thanks, we appreciate your help."

We pushed through the steel door and landed on the hot uneven pavement outside. Our steps gathered momentum until we were almost jogging as we hurtled towards Cindy's car. Cindy beeped the locks while we were moving, now at a high velocity. When I reached the passenger door I grabbed the scorched handle and flung it open. A wave of heat tumbled out from the sun-baked interior onto my feet. I toppled into the leather seat, burning the backs of my legs. I turned up the air conditioning as soon as Cindy had the key in the ignition.

Cindy pulled out of the parking spot, warm air blasting from the vents. "I don't think she had anything to do with Todd or Richard dying. Did you see her crying? She was full of grief that her husband had died."

"I can't make sense of this story."

"No, me neither. Let's go through it, bit by bit."

"I think we should tell Creston what we know."

"Are you kidding? He can find his own information. We have a story to write."

Here we go again. Wasn't it *my* story? There was no "we" here. Wasn't she just going along for the ride, in sort of a mentoring role? "*I* have a story to write. And *I* think Creston should know what we've found out." There. I'd spoken up. That was twice in one day. I could get used to this.

Cindy looked suitably chastised. "Right. Sorry, Robin. It is your story, but I am your mentor. It's my job to act in the best interests of the paper. And keeping the facts close to our chest totals a great exclusive story, so no Creston, not yet."

"But what if we are in danger? Two people have *died*."

Cindy was heading south on Dufferin Street towards the lake. We'd be at the office by four-thirty or so. Enough time to report in to Doug.

"We can talk about it with Doug. He's good at assessing stuff like this. In the meantime, do you have the hots for Creston?"

I laughed. Cindy plainly wouldn't give up. Such a nosy parker. "You are jumping to conclusions. Of course not. I have absolutely no interest in him" I was saying these words while remembering the way his eyes had swept over my body and his gentle touch when he brushed my hair off my face.

"It's time for you to meet someone, Robin. Get out there. Enjoy a few guys. Have fun. Do the internet dating thing."

"Yeah, that worked out so well for me. Maybe I should put in my profile: 'Adventurous woman seeks drop dead gorgeous man.'"

"He didn't die because of you, Robin."

"I know that. But still. Kind of puts me off the whole internet dating experience."

We rode downtown in an easy silence. It was nice to be driven around. I looked out the window and let my thoughts swirl in circles. "Thanks for driving, Cindy." I was enjoying feeling gratitude. For a brief moment in time, I felt at peace. That gratitude business was some sort of magic, I decided.

Cindy pulled into the underground parking lot below the office. "So, who do you think did it?"

"I don't know, Cindy. I really don't. There are so many players. Maybe Melissa."

But Cindy was clear. "I place my bets on Melissa. I think she did both murders. Motive. Opportunity. Means."

Despite my periodic reservations about working with Cindy, I was learning from her. First NASH and now *motive, opportunity and means*. MOM. I would have to remember that, the next time I was looking for a murderer. God forbid, not in the near future. "So, you saw the wasp trap?"

"Oh yes. She did it. Absolutely no fear of wasps."

"I know. And even though Todd had made it no secret that he was allergic to wasps, she certainly didn't mention it. But the gunshot? Her own husband?"

"I think she hired a sniper, a hit man, to do her husband. I think both murders were similar in that they were somewhat removed from the murderer."

"Well, that works if it was a hired gun." Listen to me talk, like I knew the jargon. "Do you think she'd be smart enough to take down Todd's dating site? I mean, Crystal on the other hand, she would certainly know."

Cindy countered. "Melissa probably knew him well enough to guess his password. Ask Alison. She gets a bull's eye almost every time. I think Melissa did both murders. She had a hand in the wasp business and she hired a hit man. I feel sure of it. She probably paid someone from that seedy gym she goes to."

"How can we find out?"

"Look at her bank account. If she hired someone she would have to pay them. And snipers don't come cheap. You'd notice some discrepancies in her withdrawals."

"We'll have to go to Creston. No way we'll be able to look in her bank account. You need all kinds of warrants for that kind of stuff. Banks are pretty anal."

Cindy hemmed and hawed. "I don't want to alert Creston. Maybe Alison can find out. Let's talk to Alison first."

30.

OUR STEPS ECHOED EERILY OFF THE concrete walls and pillars in the underground parking lot as we headed toward the basement door. It opened onto the hallway that led to the research department and Alison. Cindy banged the hand-lettered steel door open with her shoulder. Over the edge of the formica counter we saw the top of Alison's head, hunched over her computer.

Cindy barged into the room, "Any way you can find out if Melissa Mowbray paid off a hit man?"

"Um," Alison looked up and then around to see if anyone was listening, "Sure, I could do that," she said nervously. Then she regained her zip. "I think. I could probably find out if she hired a hit *person*."

Kids today were so politically correct.

"Don't do anything illegal," I warned.

"Never," smiled Alison playfully.

Cindy gave Alison a finger wave and pulled me out of the door by the arm. She called over her shoulder, "Thanks, Alison."

When I got to my desk I whipped off a short filler piece on how Todd Radcliff's tox screens had come back revealing that he had been killed by a wasp and the police were so far treating his death as accidental, until more forensic results came in. When this hit the press I would no longer be a target, the only person who knew something that the murderer didn't want anyone to know, that Todd was allergic to wasp stings.

I shot the piece off to Doug, who was listlessly typing on his computer. I heard a ping as my article arrived in his inbox. His movements were slow and deliberate, not at all like the Doug I knew from two days ago. What was going on with him? Maybe an awful edict had come from above. Maybe he was ill.

I swirled my chair around and looked for Shirley. Were we going to be subject to stringent cutbacks? I'd heard a lot of papers were letting staff go. The internet was decimating the printed industry. People read the news on their *phones*. But still, writers created the copy, didn't they? Fear curdled in my stomach. I needed my job. And right when I had finally moved up in the world.

Shirley was standing over by the coffee machine. She looked utterly wretched as she poured herself a cup. She glanced over at Doug's office from under her fake eyelashes, her chest heaving. Then she poured another cup. I snapped my head down as she quietly walked past my desk balancing the coffees and then thumping on the door frame of Doug's office with her elbow. He didn't turn around as he said come in. She shut the door behind her with her foot and I could hear their voices rising and falling. Ah. They were in the middle of a fight. Phew, my job was safe. Hopefully.

I didn't want to look like I was spying and busied myself by tidying up my desk. The clock across the floor ticked slowly towards five and I, for one, wasn't staying late tonight. Cindy seemed to sense all the activity beside her, and started collecting up her various bits and pieces and tossing them into her bag. "I'll give you a ride home," she whispered.

I had completely forgotten that I didn't have my car. Ralph had dropped me off at work this morning after interviewing Jimmy. I mouthed *thanks* and stood up to stretch as the clock hit five.

Cindy looked a little perturbed as we walked past Doug's door. "We should be giving him a rundown of the day, you know."

"Shirley's in there with him. Let's get out of here. I need to get home to Lucky."

As we were standing by the elevator Cindy's cell rang. She looked at the caller ID and said to me, "Alison," and then spoke into the phone. "Cindy speaking." A long pause while she listened. The elevator came.

When we got in Cindy hung up from Alison and said, "Okay. Melissa's business account is fairly erratic because of her work, you know, huge commissions going in and out pretty randomly, but it looks like there were five cash withdrawals of exactly nine thousand dollars each in the past two months. Any cash withdrawal over ten thousand triggers a bank's scrutiny. So she was being careful. Alison thought these withdrawals might be for a hit *person*" Cindy looked at me with the corner of her lip slightly raised in a small smile.

The elevator doors opened to the parking garage. "So," I summarized, "Melissa has motive, opportunity, and means for both murders."

"Yessirrebob." Cindy looked grim.

We scurried quickly towards her car. I thought I saw movement out of the corner of my eye, but it must have been the yellow streamer tied to a vent cover, flapping in the manufactured breeze. Only after getting into Cindy's car and locking the doors did I take a deep breath. I kept an eye on the side mirror as Cindy drove up the ramp to the street.

"You're the nervous one." She saw me looking behind us.

"Yessirrebob." I mimicked her flippancy.

After Cindy dropped me off at home I poured myself an eight-ounce tumbler of cold white wine and took it out to my small back deck. It was one of those lovely summer evenings where the cicadas had quietened down and the crickets were gearing up.

My view was of a somewhat bedraggled garden, much torn up by Lucky, who was now sniffing the perimeter way too intently for my liking. Was someone watching me? Was I paranoid? I would be safe once the story about the wasp venom as cause of death was out this evening on the web.

Despite Cindy's desire to keep our info to ourselves, I felt I should be talking to Creston about all that had been discovered today. I bet he had no idea that Radcliff and van Horner were in a relationship. He'd be floored if he knew that Melissa knew this, wasn't afraid of wasps, had enough money to sink a ship, and had made consistent large withdrawals. Cindy was probably right, that Melissa had done both murders, but I wanted to go over it all in my mind to make sure.

I thought for a bit about Crystal Riker. Was she really exonerated? She had zero financial motivation to kill van Horner. Also, even though she would likely know Todd's password to his internet dating profile, or be able to figure it out, she seemed accepting of his philandering ways. I believed her on this. I wondered if she knew about the condo. She had no motive to kill van Horner either. She had the prizes already; she already owned the technology and her husband would never leave her. No way could I see her hiring a hit. And she loved her husband. She would never kill him.

No, it wasn't Crystal.

Jimmy, the boat captain, was a suspect in that he would be able to help steal fresh water from the lake, if that theory still had legs. A lot of energy had been put into chasing down an international theft scenario, if Creston were to be believed. I believed him over England, who said it was Radcliffe stealing the water. England was a big fat liar. Creston on the other hand, well, he was so *nice*. I loved his soft grey eyes. Well, soft most of the time. Or at least some of the time. Okay, once or twice he looked at me kind of softly. I took a large slug of my wine and forced myself back to Jimmy.

He knew where the pump was and he had the boat. But he had no motive. The risks were huge and his payoff would be minimal. I doubted he would throw away his life in Canada for several thousand dollars, which I guessed would be all he'd be paid to operate his boat under the cover of darkness to divert water from the pump from the lake into a rented tanker. That scenario clearly didn't make sense.

His two crew, those kids, seemed unlikely partners in crime as well. They were med students, for heaven's sake, working hard and going to school. They were new to Canada. Would they risk their futures for doing an illegal job? It wouldn't be worth it.

I had been initially suspicious that van Horner had killed Radcliff. Maybe van Horner wanted more than his fair share and maybe he had bumped off Radcliffe to get it. But that theory went out the window when van Horner himself turned up dead. Besides, if the waiter at the gay bar were to be believed, the two men were lovers. Sure, lovers were certainly known to kill one another, but somehow I didn't buy it. These two guys didn't seem the type to suddenly succumb to domestic violence.

No, all signs pointed to Melissa for both murders. She had motive times three. First of all, she hadn't been part of the deal with Crystal, Richard, and Todd, and she probably wanted in on the massive potential income from the food-freezing technology. Sure, she had tons of money already, but anyone driven the way she was to acquire money the way she did would be motivated by greed. With Richard and Todd dead, she would be made a partner of Crystal's, and the earnings would be split just two ways. Until she killed Crystal. That "Bye bye, Crystal" haunted me. So money was certainly a motive for both murders.

Her second motive was jealousy. I believed that part of her truly loved her husband but there was that old saying that "hell hath no fury like a woman scorned." I doubted she'd be able to cope with the thought that her man was enjoying the company of someone else. Todd was the hated lover and her husband was hated for his betrayal.

The third motive was more complex. She was probably enraged that her husband had taken up with another *man*.

A woman in her position, rich in her own right, and living in a tony Toronto neighbourhood, would never put up with the public humiliation of *that*. Ditched for another *man*? No way. She was a serious homophobe, that was clear in her attitude towards Cindy, and homophobes were certainly known to kill.

Motive was all over her.

Did she have opportunity for both murders? Having Richard shot wouldn't require the accurate timing of a Swiss train. He probably came home from work around the same time every day, and her routine was to round up the kids from various daycares and trot in the door half an hour after him. A shooter would have a wide window of thirty minutes to execute his shot. He could aim at Richard while he was getting out of his car, for example, or through a window as he had done. Easy enough, for a professional.

Planting a wasp on Todd on the other hand, would require her to get up close and personal. I knew she knew that he habitually put his hands in his pockets. But a little more hard evidence would be nice. I wondered if anyone had seen her near Todd that day he died. I wondered if the pocket of his blazer had been tested yet for wasp trace, whatever that might be. The opportunity to kill in both cases allowed her to be far away with an alibi, so the likelihood of her being caught was pretty slim.

Melissa Mowbray also had the means for killing both men. She had lots of money to hire a hit man to kill her husband. The regular withdrawals indicated something suspicious. And she belonged to that shady gym downtown. What was the name of it? West Side Gym. She could probably find a hit man there. Her husband would be shot and she'd be miles away, creating a perfect alibi, as she had with using the wasp. Speaking of which, as far as means for killing Todd, her backyard was filled with wasps. And she wasn't frightened of them. She likely knew about Todd's allergy, considering the relationship the two couples had. It would be a snap capturing a wasp in a pill container and dumping it into the pocket of his jacket.

Yes, Melissa Mowbray certainly had means. She was a perfect MOM.

Sure it was circumstantial, but it was adding up. Creston had the resources to confirm all this with evidence. The jacket was being tested. He could get warrants for her bank accounts and then based on her cash withdrawals, he could get warrants to search her house. He could no doubt get warrants to look at CCTV cameras in the Starbucks and on the subway system. Had she been near Todd on the night he died? I bet my bottom dollar that she had been.

I spent a few minutes thinking about Creston. *Ralph*. I wondered if he liked me, too. His eyes were the colour of lake water and I wanted to dive in. My thoughts wandered lazily about as the wine seeped into my veins. I imagined going out for dinner with him, and then what might happen later.

As if ESP had created a pathway in the ether, my phone rang. I fumbled for it and saw that it was Ralph! Suddenly I was in a tizzy. It was all so confusing. I really liked him. But, there were all these extenuating circumstances. Murder. Well, murders. So inconvenient, getting in the way of my feelings! I giggled a little while the phone rang again. But would I sound a little tipsy? I didn't want him to know that I drank. I eyed the condensation covering the tumbler of wine. Half way down. Hmm. Not too bad. The phone was insistent. I cleared my throat. "Hello?"

He sounded upbeat. "Hi Robin. Did you write that story about wasp venom being the cause of death? I didn't see it in the web edition. I was thinking of you and wondering if you were nervous in your house."

He had been thinking of me, too! My heart jumped. I took a sip of wine, being careful to not clink the glass against my phone. "The story will come out on the web sometime tonight. So, I'm probably safe, although I am still a bit nervous. Lucky is sniffing around the yard."

"I was thinking I'd come over. Have you had dinner yet? I thought I'd bring some Chinese."

Perfect. I could confess all to him. "Hey, that would be great. When can you get here?"

He laughed. "Actually, I'm at the restaurant now, picking it up. That place on Parliament around the corner from you."

"C'mon over. I'll pick out the almonds." Chinese food was notorious for almonds.

"Already done. I remembered."

Just then the doorbell rang, the electronic peel reaching me in the back yard. That was fast. "What? Are you at my door already?" I stood up, holding the phone against my ear and clutching my drink as I walked through the house to let him in.

"No, I'm still in the restaurant. Maybe you shouldn't open it."

His warning was too late. I was already opening the door. Standing on my porch was Melissa Mowbray. She was wearing a white cashmere pullover adorned with a string of pearls. Looming at the curb outside my house was a huge black SUV, a Land Rover. Fear burst through my skin at the sight of her. Thank heavens Ralph was on the phone.

Melissa punched the cell out of my hand and forced me against the wall. I could hear Ralph calling my name through the speaker in the phone on the floor by my feet. Melissa clamped her left hand over my mouth and shoved her right fist against my diaphragm. I had no doubt at all that an upward thrust of that fist could break my ribs. Melissa kicked the door shut behind her and with one quick stomp crushed my phone. I no longer had a connection to Ralph. I prayed he would come quickly.

"So, you figured it out, did you? I saw you looking at the wasps in the trap, putting two and two together. Well, never fear, no one else will know." She took her hand off my mouth but her fist was still jabbing into my stomach.

I babbled to save my life. "The tox screens came back today. I wrote an article about it. Everyone knows wasp venom killed Todd. Not only me. There's proof from the coroner. The game is up Melissa. That was Ralph Creston, the police, on the phone. He'll be here in a few minutes."

She laughed merrily. Was she stoned? Her pupils were large black holes in the center of her blue irises. But how did she know where I lived? Were my instincts right in the garage when I felt Cindy and I were being followed?

"Sure, good story, Robin. I know that wasp venom doesn't show up on tox screens. It decomposes in the blood too quickly. And Ralph Creston's office is miles away, way down Church Street. I'll be able to deal with you long before he gets here."

"The advanced new tests scan for wasp venom. Besides Creston knows. There's no point in harming me. You're going to be caught anyway."

"No I won't, you'll be dead." Melissa took her fist off my belly and opened her hand. She was holding an almond. In the distance I could hear a siren. Ralph.

"You hear that? That's the police coming here." Melissa looked around. "And you can't force me to eat that," I said, clamping my mouth shut. How did she know I was allergic to almonds? Oh right. My profile.

"Wanna bet? I am a good five inches taller than you and stronger than most men." With that she trapped my arms behind my back and rapidly wound some cord around my wrists. She grabbed my locked jaw and squeezed the side of my face hard, clamping her strong fingers on either side. It was the same technique I used on Lucky when I wanted to open his mouth. I felt the almond being pushed through my slightly parted teeth and knew I would be in the throes of a major asthma attack in about five minutes.

I was thinking fast. Melissa probably thought that the almond would kill me. If I pretended to die quickly she would leave and I could get to my inhaler, which was over the sink on a shelf. I purposely made my knees crumple and slumped to the floor, like I was dying. I quietly spat out the almond so it would be hidden under my cheek. As I lay on the floor my lungs were shutting down. I needed air.

Melissa gave me a triumphant kick in the ribs and then ran out the back door. I heard it click shut as if it were a thousand miles away. Lucky was barking frantically in the yard. All I could see were little pinpricks of light shining faintly through a blanket of darkness. My world was turning black.

Suddenly strong arms lifted my head up. Was Melissa back? Had she changed her mind? Air was going slowly in and out of my chest accompanied by a high wheeze. A low voice penetrated my panic.

"Where's your inhaler?" It was Ralph. He smelled like Chinese food.

My throat was so itchy I wanted to scratch it with my nails. I tried to whisper as I looked into his grey-blue eyes, lined with worry. My breath was coming in shallow rasps. "It was Melissa. Sink. Shelf," I gasped as my breath whistled in and out of my chest.

Ralph put his jacket under my head and quickly got the lid off my inhaler, opened the medication with a flick of his wrist, and put the white plastic funnel to my mouth. I took a deep breath of the steroid as he pumped the canister. I felt my lungs open up, almost immediately. I fell back into his arms and waited for the drug to work, which it did, within minutes.

When it soon became apparent that I was going to recover, Ralph got up off the floor, and dug out his phone from his breast pocket. He gave clipped instructions and Melissa's description. I could hear sirens in the distance and knew the neighbourhood was going to be sealed off. Hopefully she hadn't gotten away.

Ralph found a kitchen knife in a drawer and sawed off the cord around my wrists. "She'll be caught, don't worry." He extended a hand to me on the floor and helped me stand up. I felt like a rag doll as he took me into his arms and kissed the top of my head.

Thank heavens he didn't kiss my mouth, I thought. He'd taste the wine!

"Robin?" he said.

I was enjoying being in his warm, strong arms. I could feel his kindness washing over me like warm water nourishing my soul. "Yes?"

"Could you go back to being a flower reporter?"

I snuggled into his arms and said into his chest, "No one tells me what to do."

He laughed, "That's my girl."

I reluctantly broke away from the embrace and nonchalantly started opening up the bags of food and flipping off the container lids. Lucky was sniffing around the table, looking cute and hungry. Although my legs were a little wobbly, my heart had settled down and my breath was flowing in and out without restriction. The spicy smell of Asian cooking filled the kitchen and helped clear my chest.

"So." He perched against the counter. "Why did Melissa try to kill you?"

I was still feeling the effect of his arms around me. So lovely. But I managed to meet his gaze. Why did I feel so shy? "I have so much to tell you." I plunked dishes and silverware on the table, trying to cover up my sudden discomfiture.

"Melissa Mowbray, huh? I never would have guessed her. Well," he said, sitting at the kitchen table and loading up his plate, "it sounds like you solved my crime. Tell me all and I'll take it from here."

I sat down and dug in. Nothing like a death threat to build an appetite.

31.

RALPH AND I SAT AT MY HARVEST TABLE surrounded by half-empty containers of chow mein, chicken balls, and vegetable fried rice. Discarded cellophane packets of plum sauce were scattered here and there. We had hit the bottom of a bottle of white and I didn't think he'd noticed that some had already been missing when we'd started. I was feeling a bit light-headed from the steroids in combination with the drink, but soldiered on through my story about the day.

"So, when Cindy and I were canvassing Church Street for anyone who knew Todd and Richard—"

"Why Church Street?"

"Well, because we had a strong inkling that they were gay."

"How on earth did you come to that conclusion?" Ralph was sitting back in his chair, looking at me in disbelief.

"From what Jimmy said. When we were talking to the boat captain he let a few hints drop about Richard and Todd being more than just friends."

"Hmmm. I didn't catch that." Ralph scratched behind his ear, as if he could fabricate the missing fragment of conversation out of thin air like a magician.

"It was very subtle," I replied. "Plus, you'd received some bad news and were preoccupied."

He flicked away my excuse for him. "So, then..." Ralph gestured with his fingers for me to get on with the story, "you were going up and down Church Street...."

"And we finally ran into someone, a waiter, who knew the two men, had heard them talking about their new ice cream company, but just as importantly, had seen them being cozy together. So, I thought we had a motive for the murders. It was either jealousy or business. Maybe both. Someone wanted to steal the *technology*, not the fresh water at all. They wanted to cool freezers efficiently."

"I remember Jimmy talking about ice cream." He thought for a second. "You didn't like the water theft angle?"

"No, flushed that one," I laughed. "After that, Cindy and I decided to interview the two wives. Melissa Mowbray let it slip out that she knew her husband was having an affair with Todd, and she had thousands of wasps on her back patio to choose from for a murder weapon. So, motive and means. But, she also has tons of money so I was puzzled because she certainly didn't need to steal to make any more. But she knew Todd well, right down to knowing he was one of those guys who always had a hand in his pocket. She and her husband had eaten a lot of dinners with Todd and Crystal, so she probably knew enough to figure out his password. Anyway, I had a sense that she was guilty. She was cut-throat enough, what with her kick boxing lessons and aggression."

"So, Todd and Richard were an item and you think Melissa killed Todd with a wasp, with the motives being greed and jealousy."

"You're right, in a nutshell."

"So, who shot Richard?"

"Melissa. Or rather, Melissa ordered the hit."

"Not Crystal? She had the same motives. Jealousy. Greed."

"No, Melissa. Crystal had no motive to murder at all. She already owned the technology, so she didn't need to kill for the proceeds off it, and she already knew that her husband was having affairs. I believe that she loved him with all her heart and she accepted who he was."

Ralph was dubious. "So why would Melissa kill her own

husband? She had lots of money already. She didn't need the new technology."

"She loves money. People who are really rich can get warped, with odd values. I think Melissa wanted more, more, more." Ralph raised his eyebrows at my vehemence. "Plus, it's my guess that she's so heavily invested in being the successful dame of Toronto's higher society that she could never stomach it being exposed that she had been ditched by her husband for a man. That's my hunch, anyway. She's a homophobe."

"Well, I'll need a little more to go on that that. I can't arrest her because she's rich and you don't like her."

I decided not to take offense. He was probably frustrated by the lack of evidence. "I know, of course you can't. We took a look at Melissa's financials and she made regular withdrawals from her business account of nine thousand dollars. Five of them, so forty-five thousand dollars. I think if you canvass her gym's members you'll find someone who's forty-five thousand dollars richer. If you can get them to talk, you'll get her that way. But I don't need to tell you how to do your job."

"How'd you get access to her accounts?"

"Don't ask."

"Newspapers ... but what about Todd? I need evidence for that murder, too. Lots of people have wasps." He thought for a moment, absentmindedly picking a mushroom out of a container of chow mien and plopping it into his mouth. "Well, I guess I could get CCTV coverage to see if she was there and near his jacket. Maybe of his condo. And maybe the TTC cameras too."

I suddenly had an idea. "You could ask Alison Trent from our paper as well if she noticed her in the Starbucks. Alison was there when Todd and I were." Ralph looked at me, eyes questioning. "Just coincidental," I said firmly. "She might remember. She sort of recognized the picture of Melissa and if you jogged her memory a bit, giving her a context, maybe show her a six-pack, you might have an eye witness if Starbuck's doesn't have a hidden security camera."

Did I say six-pack? I was beginning to sound like I knew police procedure.

Ralph pulled a notebook out from his back pocket. It was curved from the shape of his buttock. I controlled my impulse to touch it. "So, Alison Trent." He wrote her name down and then looked up at me. "What was the name of the waiter at the restaurant on Church Street?"

"Sam/Suzette," I laughed. "His name is Sam, but Suzette is the name on his shirt. He'll probably still be working tonight. Oh yeah, he calls Richard and Todd Robert and Tim. They used pseudonyms."

Ralph wrote this down as well. "Any other brilliant ideas? You're skills are lost on the paper you know. You really work stuff out."

My cheeks reddened at the compliment. "Thanks Ralph. You might look for Todd's EPI pen in Melissa's house or her garbage. And a pill bottle with her fingerprints on it with wasp trace inside would sort of seal the deal," I laughed.

"I agree. It won't be hard getting a warrant for her house now anyway, not after her attack on you."

Ralph stood up and carefully pushed his chair away from the table. "I think I'd better get going on this right now. Sorry about that; I would have preferred to stay. Are you okay to be left alone? I mean, I'm not worried about Melissa coming back. I think she's either long gone or caught by my guys by now."

His phone dinged with a text. "Yup, she's been caught. But are you physically feeling okay?"

"Absolutely," I said. "It isn't that serious of an allergy. I mean, I do need the medication, but once I get it, I'm right as rain." I walked him to the door.

We stood awkwardly in my front foyer, hemming and hawing. Ralph then slowly leaned down and planted his soft lips on mine. He tasted sweet, like plum sauce, and I halfheartedly pulled away, leaving my hand lightly on his chest. I didn't want to frighten him off. "Thanks for coming by and thanks for saving me from some serious distress."

"Just doing my job," he said as he hastily tugged open the front door and raced into the night.

He sure was skittish I thought as I watched his car zoom away. I shut the door behind him and leaned my head against it. My first real kiss in years. My heart felt like it was going to burst. I had a feeling I'd hear from this man again, despite what the issues were that were making him so jumpy.

I gathered myself together and walked back into the kitchen, Lucky at my side. I scraped the leftovers into plastic containers and put them in the fridge, thinking they'd make good lunches for a few days. After washing up our two dishes and cutlery I cracked open another bottle of white and sank into my reading chair in the corner of the kitchen. Lucky curled up at my feet, settling down for the night. What a week.

My mind drifted over all that had happened in the past seven days. I sifted through the chain of events, starting with my date with Todd and ending with Melissa trying to kill me. I ruminated over each incident as I mentally wrote the story in my mind. I knew it wasn't quite finished because of the lack of evidence, but that would soon be rectified, I hoped, once Melissa's huge house had been searched. The story would be over! Excitedly, I slapped my thigh with determination. Yes!

I noticed that my acres of flab didn't jiggle quite as much as a week ago. Had I lost weight? I put down my glass of wine and raced to the bathroom to check, Lucky chasing me up the stairs. Holy smokes. I was down to one hundred and fifty-five from one hundred and sixty-three. Was that seven pounds? No, eight. Eight pounds in eight days. Or was it seven pounds in seven days? Whatever. I'd lost weight!

Back in my kitchen chair with a top up of wine in my glass and Lucky once again at my feet, I reviewed my five things: old, fat, alcoholic, all alone, failure. Okay, I was still old and there was nothing I could do about that. I wasn't quite as fat, having lost a few pounds. I held my glass of wine up to the light and contemplated the prisms reflected in the condensation. Yes, still an alkie, but I had controlled myself at Sunday dinner with the kids. It felt better to be present. Maybe I'd cut back to a mere half a bottle a day. I thought I could do that. I'd try that tomorrow night. I made a note in my phone's calendar to call Sally Josper for my next appointment.

Was I still all alone? Well, yes, I had to admit to myself. I was certainly sitting alone in my kitchen, knocking back a bottle of wine, okay, close to two bottles. Sure, Ralph was a really nice man and I liked him a lot, but I wasn't sure he was emotionally available. He had baggage. On the other hand, so did I. But less baggage than a few years ago when I was married to Trevor.

Trevor. Oh God. I took another sip. It was time to put away my anger at Trevor, to tuck it into a drawer where I kept all my dusty memories. I patted Lucky with my toe. Trevor loved me, I know he did, but he had been resentful of me for some reason. Who knew what? Whatever the reason, I needed to forgive him so I could move on. I shut my eyes and concentrated on opening up my heart. This little action would have been impossible a week ago, but I did it and I deliberately tried to let go of my anger and do my very best to forgive him. I got as far as forgiving him for not being the husband I had hoped he would be. It wasn't perfect, but it was a good start.

I couldn't wait to tell Cindy about what had happened. It hadn't been easy working with her this week. She was such a strong personality and it took effort to speak my mind with her. Well, at least I was doing that. The gratitude exercises were calming me down enough that my true self could emerge. I was growing up!

My phone pinged in the corner of the kitchen, where it had skittered after Melissa's attack. I was amazed that it still worked! A text. I carefully, somewhat drunkenly, got up and held it up to my face. It was hard to read as the face of it had been shattered by Melissa's foot. Speak of the devil. It was Cindy. Oh dear. She'd be furious that I hadn't checked in with her. What a mother hen she was. I guess I should be grateful I had such a good friend. *You okay?* she asked.

I texted back: *Winding down. Melissa tried to kill me, but Ralph came. All is well. The story is almost over. Need evidence that she was the murderer.*

Cindy then texted me. *Holy shit. You hurt?*

I replied, *No, I'm fine.*

She texted, *Okay, see you in the morning. I'm working on the Vipers tonight.*

I sent her some X's and O's to sign off before I tottered off to bed.

The next morning I quickly went through my gratitude routine, had a shower, ate, and dashed out the door, a few minutes late. I was revved up to start working on my new crime story. I would plug in the evidence details as I got them. When I arrived I quickly entered the story that had formulated in my head last night. Cindy's chair was empty. Maybe she was still out on the Vipers. God, what if she'd been shot? I sent her a text and went back to typing feverishly.

Doug came in and looked over my shoulder for a minute, reading what I was doing. "Good work, Robin. Sorry about goading you the other day. I was in a funk. You have great hunches. And I see that you have a natural talent for crime reporting. Maybe Shirley will share you with me."

"Thanks, Doug. Apology accepted. Almost done with this story. I only need to wrap it up with some evidence details. Listen, have you heard from Cindy?"

"Vipers," he said walking away.

Now I knew exactly how she felt when I hadn't checked in with her: worried as all get out. My cell phone rang a few minutes later, just when I was getting back into my Everwave murder story. I looked at the cracked screen. Cindy? No, *Ralph*. My heart flipped onto its side and then righted itself.

"Hello?"

"Robin."

He said my name as if he were caressing my back.

"Hi, Ralph."

He bounced from the soft lover to being a cop. "My team searched Melissa Mowbray's house and found a few things. First of all, there was a pill bottle hidden in her beside table that had wasp feces in it."

"Really?"

"Clearly a wasp had been inside the bottle. Also, the pill bottle had on it," and here he paused for significance, "some gum with fibers stuck in it."

"Gum."

"Yes, gum that matched the brand in Todd's pocket. He was a gum chewer and when he finished a piece he wadded it up and stuck it back into the packaging. So the pill bottle we found in Melissa's recycling had some gum on it with his DNA and fibers that match his blazer."

Gum. Yes, he kept gum in his pocket. He'd told me at Starbucks. "Way better than wasp trace! So now you have your evidence?" I couldn't believe it. She was going to go down.

"That's not all," he crowed. "We also found in her glove compartment his EPI pen. They're prescription, right, so his name was on it. She must have taken it out of his jacket before she dumped the wasp in."

"You can tie her to a wasp *and* him." It was sinking in.

"Not only that," he paused for effect, "your researcher, Alison Trent, positively identified Melissa from Starbucks when you were there with Todd. Apparently Melissa was wearing sunglasses. She stood out because it was night.

"Plus, it was so busy in there; Melissa could easily hide behind others. Todd would certainly recognize her if he saw her. That Alison doesn't miss a trick.

"No joy from the subway cameras, but the CCTV from his condo had you doing an interesting little jig in his hallway."

"Ha." What else could I say as I remembered my key fob pantomime.

"AND," Ralph wasn't finished, "we found the guy she paid off to shoot her husband like you said. He was a member of her gym." Ralph blew out a fast breath, "That's some place. Rough crowd."

"I thought you'd find him there," I said. "So, it looks like you have enough evidence for both murders."

"We picked up Melissa from where she was hiding in the condiment aisle of the No Frills near you and put her in jail. After a night there, we confronted her with all this and she confessed to the two murders."

"She confessed?" I was astounded. I didn't think she was the type who would ever confess to anything.

"Yup. About ten minutes ago. She was so proud of herself. Plus, I think she knew she was cooked anyway and probably wanted to spare her kids a long trial."

"Oh God, her kids. What's going to happen to them?"

"Melissa has absolutely no family and only one or two friends, so I don't know what will happen. Social Services has them right now. We've informed Crystal Riker, Todd's wife, that he hadn't committed suicide, that he'd been murdered by Melissa, and that she'd be going to prison for a long time. With it being a hate crime, among other things, she'll get years and years. I think Crystal's going to make an application to adopt them."

"I hope that works out. She'd make a great mother."

"Did Melissa mention if she'd taken down Todd's dating site?"

"She certainly did. She was furious about it. Funny how the criminal mind works. She was jealous of Todd as her husband's lover, but she was also jealous of Todd's lovers. Doesn't make a whole lot of sense to me."

"She was one weird cookie, that's for sure. How did she guess the password to his dating site?"

"She said that was easy. Todd and her husband often joked about how they were supplying the city with a new source of nice clean water for their toilets and that it would make them very rich. Their gag line was the toilets would flush and they would be flush. She guessed his password was 'flush.'"

"I wonder if she knows that if she hadn't taken down his site, I would never have pursued the wasp as a murder weapon. You might say she had a busted flush."

Jack England crossed my mind. I'd used the busted flush line on him, too. He was so off base about Radcliffe stealing water from the lake. What a great story I had.

Ralph laughed at my joke. "I'd like to thank you personally, Robin. You really helped the police out on this one. We were so wrong about the international slant. You virtually solved the case. I was wondering if I could take you out for a proper dinner on Friday."

Wow. Maybe he'd kiss me again. Maybe not. He sure was one scaredy-cat.

"Sure, I'd love to."

"That's great. I gotta go. I got the whole Vipers gang in here and I have to interview every last one of them."

Vipers? He'd rounded them up? Maybe he knew where Cindy was.

"Maybe I should come down and cover it for the paper." I was so devious.

"Too late. That red-headed Amazon is here already, tormenting us for statements." He laughed again. "She sure is one feisty lady."

Oh good, she was safe. "Journalist. Not *lady*. Journalist."

I could hear him smiling as he said, "See you Friday. Sevenish. I'll pick you up. Lady." A guffaw. And then a click.

I put my phone down on my desk thoughtfully. Shirley had come in at some point during the call from Ralph and was standing behind me, reading the first few paragraphs of my story about the Everwave murders. "This is good, Robin, really good. Front page for sure. I love your description of the guy's house by the golf course."

"Thanks, Shirley. You trained me well."

She waltzed away, her skin-tight skirt creasing below her bum. "Nope, you have talent. You're going to go far as an investigative reporter."

I felt my face blush and lowered my head, quickly inserting all the evidence details before I forgot them. What a week. I was still old and drinking like a fish, but not so fat, and not so alone.

What was the fifth thing? Right: failure. Hell, I could cross that off my list!

Acknowledgements

I would like to thank the people at Inanna Publications for all their editorial and promotional support for this book, with a special thanks going to Editor-in-Chief Luciana Ricciutelli and Publicist/Marketing Manager Renée Knapp.

I am indebted to Shawn Newton at First Unitarian in Toronto and the people at Soka Gakkai International for their ongoing education, inspiration, and encouragement.

Many people love and support me in my life as a writer and I am deeply grateful to my family and friends for their constancy.

Photo: Phil Brennen

Sky Curtis divides her time between Northern Ontario, Nova Scotia, and Toronto. She has worked as an editor, author, software designer, magazine writer, scriptwriter, poet, teacher, and children's writer. Sky has published over a dozen books and is passionate about social justice issues and the environment. Her poetry has appeared in several literary journals, including *The Antigonish Review, Canadian Forum,* and *This Magazine*. Sky is currently writing adult fiction and non-fiction.